IT'S *for* S
YOU

& Other Dark Speculations

For information address Crossroad Press at
141 Brayden Dr., Hertford, NC 27944.

A Macabre Ink Production—Macabre Ink is an imprint of
Crossroad Press.
www.crossroadpress.com

Crossroad Press Trade Edition
2019

IT'S *for* S YOU

& Other Dark Speculations

KEITH MINNION

For my children
Megan & Justin

Introduction

Many people are already familiar with Keith Minnion's work as an illustrator, but those of you who bought this book probably already know one of genre fiction's best-kept secrets: in addition to being a talented artist, Minnion is a storyteller of the highest caliber. This is a career-spanning collection of incredible variety, with something to please every genre fan's taste: from the gritty suspense of "Killer and "Eats," to the science fiction thrills of "Along the River Lethe" and "The Can Man"; from the futuristic swashbuckling fantasy of "Empire State" to the subtle, atmospheric novelette that ends the collection, "Island Funeral."

I first encountered Keith Minnion's artwork in the pages of *Cemetery Dance* magazine, where his beautifully shaded pencil drawings accompanied works by such genre favorites as Douglas Clegg, Ed Gorman, and Bentley Little. Issue 34 of this magazine included a story by Minnion, "It's For You," a dark crime piece that effectively combined police procedural and supernatural elements (this story, besides giving the book its name, also appears in this collection). I remember being impressed by the quick pace of the story, the crisp dialogue, and the careful management of the story's suspense. A few years later, one of my earliest publications appeared in the *Shivers IV* anthology, alongside Minnion's excellent "Up in the Boneyard"—another police procedural, with an inventive premise (not a story about fear of heights, but about fear of a *specific* height...), and the same crisp, effective storytelling style. In all his stories, Minnon's prose manages to be both precise and evocative: he's a writer who knows how to convey exactly the right image or mood.

Here's an example from "The Prince's Birthday." The protagonist watches in horror as his country's six-year-old prince receives a magical and shocking gift during a public celebration: a swarm of mechanical wasps. As Minnion describes the scene, "two things stood out clearly in Andrew's memory":

> The first was of one of Corumn's beasts, grabbing a nobleborn's head with all six of its horned legs, its ebon and orange thorax and abdomen arching out and then down, thrusting and thrusting and thrusting its venomous stinger into the wretch's body while its poisons sprayed the open wounds. The second was of the little Prince himself, standing with legs apart on the low wall of the balcony, waving his sword like a silver baton before some macabre bloody chorus, all the while shrieking in unbridled glee every time a wasp found a new victim on the balcony.

Although obviously a fantasy tale, with its medieval setting and magical elements, this story doesn't shy away from a horrible, precise image as the wasp's stinger repeatedly hits its mark. And the subsequent description of the prince's sadistic reaction is equally horrific—as memorable for readers as it is for the story's main character.

In his fiction Minnion frequently employs an artist's knowing eye for subtle shading, but as the example above demonstrates, he's also ready with a visceral image where necessary. The horror and dark crime stories that comprise roughly 60-70 percent of this collection benefit greatly from Minnion's careful control of image and atmosphere. Consider "A Death in the Forest," where he is able to shift from a light comic tone to a slowly building dread in the closing pages—all the more remarkable a feat in a story that consists mostly of dialogue. Or "Eats," where the main character steps into a *Twilight Zone*-style diner that's more gruesome than anything they'd air during Serling's prime time—even though the story's monster never appears onscreen (a character warns, "if you want to get through this alive, then for God's sake *don't look*"). Or the best example of all, "Island Funeral," a stunning novelette that is simultaneously a poignant meditation on grief, and a disturbing horror story in true classic style; in my judgment, it's a masterpiece.

The science fiction and fantasy stories in this collection highlight another important quality of Minnion's writing: he's always interested in creating imaginative worlds. A fine example of this is "Empire State," originally published in *Asimov's*. It's set in a flooded future and recounts the adventures of a young boy on his first ocean voyage, when he and his crew encounter a band of survivors living in the top (and thus *dry)* floors of New York City skyscrapers. The story works so well because Minnion provides a fully realized depiction of shipboard life, and also gives a full history and culture to the residents of his Empire State Building. Reading "Empire State," I couldn't help but think what a good YA fantasy series it would make—the characters and situations were already so well developed, and the setting offers much opportunity for further adventures.

Worlds of other stories include the futuristic shopping mall of "Along the River Lethe," where memories are sold as precious commodities; the spaceship world of "Bushido," a kind of outer-space comedy of manners with an interesting take on robotics; and "The Can Man," a haunted house-style story with a cybernetic twist, and a delightfully nasty ending. The impression I get from reading such stories is that Minnion has developed a *lot* more of the world than we see on the page, and like the best story writers, he pared the tale down to represent the essential, most memorable episodes.

Obviously this kind of world building is a key skill for a science fiction or fantasy writer to possess, but Minnion takes the same approach to his horror and suspense fiction. For example, there's the visceral inner world of the main character in "Killer," or the nervous inner world of "In the Stacks," whose protagonist feels compelled to count or categorize every detail. My favorite horror stories by any author are those that tend to hint at a more threatening world just beyond the immediate situation, maybe letting some of that darkness take over in the final pages—as Minnion does so effectively with the creeping neighborhood paranoia represented in "Dead End," or in the haunting secrets that lurk beneath the close-knit, isolated culture of "Island Funeral." And "Up in the Boneyard," a fully satisfying story in its own right, contains characters we'd want to spend more time with, and hints at a truly original and frightening monster that genre fans would love to learn more about. Like I said before, it's as if Minnion has imagined much more of the world than he's included in the story—and I could prove my point this time, because there's a novel called *The Bone Worms* that expands this story, and I've been lucky enough to read it, and I hope somebody publishes it soon so everybody *else* can read it.

Keith Minnion is a talented artist, as you'll see with all his illustrations here; he's a talented short story writer, as you'll see by reading any story in this collection. And yeah, trust me, he's a talented novelist, too.

—*Norman Prentiss*
Baltimore, September 2010

Killer

There is a ditch.

In an otherwise empty field of rye.

Below a grey, cold, lowering sky.

Western Iowa. Kansas. Nebraska.

Eastern Wyoming, maybe.

Winter.

The ditch is shallow, its rich, black earth plowed up all along its length by the huge waffle tracks of farm machinery.

A hidden scattering of geometric puddles, down there, frozen solid.

And the remains of bodies.

Fragments of a man. Pieces of a woman.

The woman's dulled, upturned eyes reflect the cold grey of the sky.

Silence, in the ditch. Silence and secrets.

Then an eyelid moves, shifts, bulges, *and a bug crawls out.*

A shiny black and orange sexton beetle.

It clings to the woman's eyebrow, antennae waving.

Then the woman's lips move, and with a tongue as grey as her eyes she whispers—

Cal spasmed under his blanket, his eyes opening on a cold, hard winter morning.

He sat up slowly, grunting with the effort. The air was musty

and sour in the close, cramped bedroom. He pushed the blanket from him and kicked crumpled, empty beer cans aside to find a flat place to put his feet. With his left hand he ran his fingers through his thinning, dishwater grey hair, using his calluses and the nubs of his ravaged yellow fingernails for a comb.

His right hand, thin and white and twisted, lay limp across his thigh. "My sacrifice to the grim reaper," he had told Ernie, the bartender at the Starlight, after the hatchet men in white had finally let him out of the free-clinic in Wheatland. "Gave away a little piece of myself to get a few extra innings, you know?" Small price to pay, I guess, Ernie had said. "You know it, Ernie-my-man. Hell, long as I got one left to wipe my ass and lift a brew, right?"

He shrugged his shoulder, and his dead hand flopped over.

Small price indeed.

A cat rose from the windowsill, stretched stiffly, and meowed.

Cal lurched up, out of the bedroom, shuffled down the short, dark hall to the kitchen, and got a fresh beer from the Frigidaire. He downed it in quick, convulsive swallows, swishing the last mouthful through his cheeks, in and among the canyons and buttes of what remained of his teeth. Then he spit the frothy, phlegmy mess into the sink.

He looked for blood, but this time there wasn't any.

"You ought to go see a doctor about that, Cal."

"What—?" Cal turned, his wife's voice hanging there in the air, in his *ears*, but of course the kitchen was empty. The whole house was, except for the cats. His wife wasn't there. His wife wasn't even—

There is a ditch—

He crumpled the empty can, and then tossed it to the floor to join its comrades, dead soldiers all. A black and orange beetle skittered for cover.

There were three cats, now, arching against his shins. All the inside ones. The ones the outside cats would tear up if ever they got together.

Inside cats and outside cats.

Cal felt like an inside cat, now. Except to go to the Starlight once to drink beer and jaw with Ernie, and to the Pigglie-Wigglie on the interstate to stock up after the pension check came, he hadn't left the house all week. Afraid of what might be out there, waiting to tear him to shreds, if he was stupid enough to let it.

There was no need to go out anyway, not any more. Not since—

The cats meowed louder, riding his sock up his knobby shin in their impatience to be fed.

"Okay," he said, belching as he stooped to scratch each of them in turn, "hold your horses, now, ladies...."

He got the cat food bag and two food bowls from the cupboard and shook a healthy amount into each. Then he doused the cat food with a little warm water and mixed it in with his fingers.

Mixed it in *good*, for the gravy.

The cats meowed together in three-part harmony. Plaintively; no nonsense, now.

"Here we go." Cal gently nudged their heads apart with one of the bowls to get it to the floor. He watched them eat for a few moments, a vague smile curving his lips. Then he returned to the bedroom and wrestled into a sweater and overalls, and a new pair of Altima hightops with velcro straps he had found on display next to the pantyhose at the Pigglie Wigglie. "Thank God for velcro," he had told Ernie when he had shown him those sneakers. "You ever try to tie a shoe with one hand tied behind your back? Huh?" Nope, Ernie had said, can't say as I ever have. "Well it's a pistol, Ernie-my-man, a fuckin' wet pistol, let me tell you."

Outside, the winter rye drove past Cal's property in an endless succession of pale brown waves. The wind coming down from Montana never stopped, out here. He stood shivering in the blue shadows of his side yard with the other bowl of cat food cradled in the crook of his good arm. Above, the cloud cover was solid; it would probably snow before noon. Throw in the wind, it might even blizzard.

Around back he heard the heavy chain rattle and slide, but he ignored it.

> *There is a field.*
> *In the center of the field is a ditch.*
> *In the ditch is a—*

The chain moved again.

Cal turned to the little porch tacked onto the side of the house where the lean-to tool shed met the chimney. He found a mouse and two voles there, laid out neatly, legs in the air, presents—offerings—from his outside cats. The voles were stiff and frozen, but the mouse was a fresh kill, and was still warm and soft. Cal put the cat food bowl down next to them, then turned to the shed, fumbled with the simple latch, and swung its crooked door wide.

"Cal! Don't you forget to feed my baby, now!"

Emily's voice, from around the front of the house.

"I do everything else around here to make ends meet! Lord knows, the least you can do is help me feed him!"

"Yes, dear," he called back, smiling stupidly, for of course Emily wasn't there. She wasn't there *at all*.

He brought out a battered metal bucket, and a sack of Purina Dog Chow. With his good hand he poured the Chow halfway up to the rim of the bucket, then set it on the porch on the other side of the dead rodents.

He fumbled in his coat pocket until his hand closed over the cold brass and steel of the folded bos'n knife there.

His eyes clouded for a moment, and he frowned, clutching the knife in his pocket. Then he grabbed the pail handle, jerked around, and strode purposefully out into the field of dead grass beyond the house. At its center he came upon the ditch, and he went down heavily to his knees in the frozen black earth there, before the carcasses.

He took the bos'n knife from his pocket and pulled the blade free with his teeth.

There wasn't much meat left on them after a week, and all of it was tough, but he sawed off what he could, and ripped off the rest, throwing the pieces into the bucket.

He stood, finally, knocked the dirt from his knees, wiped the knife blade on his thigh, and then snapped it shut.

Back at the house he set the bucket on the side porch, then unzipped his overalls and urinated into the bucket, taking care to soak the meat and Chow thoroughly.

His piss steamed like hot lemon tea. Looked like it, too.

He considered the mouse and the voles for a moment, then scooped them up and added them to the bucket. Then he zipped back up, grabbed the bucket handle, and went around the house to the back where the remains of his garage still tilted—still defied gravity, still taunted that goddamn fuckin' wind from out of goddamn fuckin' Montana—to the place where the dog was chained.

In its two years on earth, the dog, a one hundred and twenty-five pound shit-brindle rottweiler, had worn a near perfect circle of dirt in the grass and weeds by the garage. Right now the dog stood at the perimeter of that circle, its heavy-link forged steel chain pulled absolutely taut and level with the ground. One end of it was securely hooked to a galvanized spike corkscrewed three feet deep in the yard dirt; the other end was shackled to an equally heavy choke chain dug firmly into the dog's muscular, rock-solid neck.

The dog stood silently, impassive, staring at him with flat black eyes. The only signs it gave being hungry were two strings of crystal drool hanging from its jowls, swinging slightly in the wind.

Cal and the dog stared at one another for almost a full minute. Every morning for a week, now, it had gone like this. Every morning he had come upon that fuckin' behemoth of a dog standing like a fuckin' bronze statue at the absolute edge of its circle of dirt, braced at the end of its fuckin' chain, waiting for him.

Seven mornings Cal had gone to the ditch in the field and brought back something for the dog to eat. Every day he had poured Chow in with it; every day he had pissed in it, beer piss, acrid and clear. Or hawked in it, or shat in it. Even *puked* in it, once. Every morning for a fuckin' week, ever since he caught that bastard and Emily—

There is a field.
Wide, long, and private.
In the field is a ditch.
In the ditch is a fucking, bitching slut, and beside her a rutting, whoring, rat bastard.
Or what little is left of them.

The rottweiler would kill him if it could, Cal knew. He had told Ernie that more than once, more than ten times, maybe more than a hundred. But Ernie had only remembered the animal when it had been a puppy shaking and piddling on his bar, all ears and paws, wet nose and pink, licking tongue. Ernie didn't know shit about it now.

Rip his throat out if it could, Cal knew. Lap up his blood, and eat his warm guts whole.

Hatred was a serious thing; in an animal, it was dead serious. Cal knew that too.

He put the bucket down in the weeds just outside the perimeter of dirt. The dog followed the bucket down, and then returned its attention to Cal.

"Come on," Cal said in a husky, broken whisper, "ask for it, you sorry sonofabitch. *Ask* for it." He nudged the bucket with the toe of his sneaker. "Come on, there ain't much left…come on, now."

Every morning; every morning for a fuckin' week.

The dog continued to stare at him with its great, black,

stony eyes.

"You're gonna have to work for this today, doggo." Cal nudged the bucket again. If the dog wanted to, it could just touch the edge of the bucket with its nose. But it didn't. It stared at him instead. At *him*.

"Come on, you sonofabitch dog; come *on!*"

In the end he kicked the bucket, kicked it with everything he had in him, kicked it so hard his dead right arm swung up and the useless meat of his hand slapped him right in the face, poked his eye, and momentarily blinded him.

"Son-of-a-BITCH!" he roared, teetering at the edge of the dirt circle, bringing his good hand up to press against the sting in his eye where the numb finger had poked it. He heard the clink of the dog's chain as a link suddenly straightened, and the perimeter—the killing perimeter, the space where the dog could *get* him—was increased a half-inch....

"Are you teasing that poor dog again, Cal? It's just going to hate you for it. Honestly, why you taunt that poor baby is beyond me! What has he ever done to deserve— Cal? Are you listening to me? Cal?"

Goddamn crazy sonofabitch dog. Every morning. Every morning for a week now.

Every. Goddamn. Morning.

The dog ate the Chow and meat scattered in the dirt with methodical quickness. It smelled the mouse and voles, nudged them with its nose, and then gobbled them, too. Then it raised its massive head, regarded Cal silently for a long moment, then turned and settled itself in the dark hole where the clapboards had separated from the garage's frame.

Dismissed him.

"Cal? You leave that poor baby alone now, you hear me? You leave my baby alone!"

On the wind that drove the grey grass seas, that sang through his head like a spray of hot, fast bullets:

"Cal? Are you listening to me?"

There is a field....

The county police cruiser, a new Ford Crown Victoria painted red and white with black striping, pulled into the yard some time after noon on that seventh day.

Cal heard its door slam, then the sound of boots crunching up the gravel path to his front door. He rolled off the couch, and made it to the door just as three firm knocks shook it in its frame. Cal hesitated, and then opened the door wide.

"Sheriff," he said.

The middle-aged officer, wearing black jack boots, a freshly pressed sky-blue uniform and tall, neatly blocked cream Stetson, smiled tightly. "I left my coat in the cruiser, Mr. Tubbs; you mind if I come in out of the weather?"

Cal scratched his belly, blinking. Then, "Hell no, come on in."

The sheriff shouldered past him deftly, and Cal smelled Old Spice and Needsford Oil and the faint, pungent perfume of cordite. He closed the door, then pointed to the officer's Glock snapped snugly into its holster. "You been firing that thing today, Sheriff?"

"Yeah." The officer's eyes moved, *darted*, all about the room. "They cornered a coyote in the Reedham's barn this morning. Took four slugs before it went down. Blew its head off. *Clean* off."

Cal whistled dutifully. "That's a hundred-fifty clear bounty money, ain't it?"

The sheriff nodded, his gaze ranging swiftly over the scattered beer cans, the crusted plates piled on the coffee table before the TV. And the cats, prowling silently about. "Can't award a bounty to myself though," he said. "That's the bitch right there."

Cal shrugged. "I'd take it. I'd take it in a New York minute."

The sheriff nodded again, moving to the hall doorway, glancing on into the kitchen. Then he turned back. "I take it she's still gone?"

"Like the wind, Sheriff. Like the fuckin' Montana wind. Pardon my French." Cal moved past him to the kitchen. "Can I get you a beer?" He opened the Frigidaire and got one for himself.

Then behind him, so close that Cal almost jumped, the sheriff said, "You living on that stuff now, Mr. Tubbs?"

Cal closed the refrigerator with his knee. "It's getting me through." He popped the can, then took a foamy slurp off the top. "Beats Emily's cooking, anyway."

"The way I hear it, Mr. Tubbs, your wife kept a pretty good table. More than one person commented on that."

Cal took another swallow of beer, his eyes bright. "No accounting for taste, I guess."

"I guess." The officer wandered back into the living room.

Cal followed him. "People been telling you things, then, Sheriff? About me and Emily? You been talking us up?"

"Doing what comes natural, Mr. Tubbs. Just me asking questions, and them answering." The sheriff, looking suddenly taller, tighter, turned and caught Cal's eye, and held fast. "A week is a long time with no word at all, don't you think?"

Cal swallowed a rising burp. "Well—"

"Nothing from your wife's sister in Cheyenne, or her aunt in…where's that aunt, Mr. Tubbs?"

"Cedar City." Cal's voice sounded hollow. "Utah. Nope, nothing from them at all."

The sheriff nodded slowly. "I checked, of course."

"I figured you would."

"And then there's that story Buck Reedham told me this morning, after we bagged that coyote's ass in his barn."

Cal sat down on his couch. Heavily. "Buck Reedham's no friend of mine, Sheriff."

"He mentioned that. He also mentioned a conversation you had at the Starlight down by the interstate the other day, little over a week ago. You frequent the Starlight, don't you, Mr. Tubbs? Run by a man named Ernie Choate?"

"Yeah," Cal heard himself say. Hollow. Dead. Somebody else talking. "I give Ernie some business every now and then. He takes my money; I drink his beer."

"Seems you were talking to this fella Ernie down there about what to do if you caught your wives in bed with another man? Or that's how Mr. Reedham understood it from a couple of stools down the bar. Did you really have a conversation with the bartender on that subject, Mr. Tubbs? About what to do about a cheating wife?"

Cal looked down at his beer. "You could ask Ernie."

"Oh I did. Believe me, I did." Then, softly, calmly: "Do you remember what you told the bartender, Mr. Tubbs?"

"Yeah." So hollow. So dead. "I remember."

The sheriff waited a moment, then he said, "You don't want to tell me what you said, Mr. Tubbs? You got a reason why you don't want to tell me?"

"Hell no!" Cal's eyes blazed defiantly for a moment before they dulled again. "I said…I said I'd probably shoot the bastard, then cut him up into little pieces and feed him to the hogs." He swallowed. "Hogs'd eat anything, I said. Anything at all."

The sheriff lowered himself to one knee; Cal heard the creak in the leather of his holster, in his shiny black jack boots. "You wouldn't happen to keep any hogs on the property, would you, Mr. Tubbs?"

Cal took in a slow, ragged breath, hearing the rattle of the dog's chain in his head, then looked up blearily. "Sounds like you think something *happened*, Sheriff."

"*Happened*." The officer rose. "Oh, yeah. Something *happened*, all right." He placed his hands on his hips. "After a week some people start thinking about a number of things that might have *happened*, Mr. Tubbs." He shifted his gaze to the side window. "After a week maybe I've got to start looking at things a little bit *differently*, if you know what I mean."

Quietly, almost whispering, Cal said, "I don't think you better ask me any more questions, Sheriff."

"You want me to leave, Mr. Tubbs?" The sheriff smiled slightly, revealing a thin slice of white teeth. "You ordering me out of your home?"

Cal stood shakily. "Yeah," he said, "real politely, but yeah. I got that right, haven't I?'"

The sheriff nodded, his smile frozen. Then he turned to the front door, paused, and turned around. "Folks say you've been keeping to yourself this past week. Haven't left the place even once, they say."

"That don't mean nothing," Cal said. "That don't mean nothing at all."

"The bartender at the Starlight says you never miss your Friday night beer. Not for the past couple of years, anyway."

Cal couldn't keep his voice from shaking as he said, "I just *told* you to please *leave*—"

"Unfortunately, Mr. Tubbs, I got some bad news this morning." The sheriff leaned on the door. "Up until this morning, I only had one reported missing person in this entire county." He held up a finger. "Just one."

"Emily," Cal said, stone-faced. "I *know* that."

The sheriff raised a second finger. "Fertilizer salesman named Loman, out of Wheatland. His wife said he hadn't called in a few days, and the company he shills for says he hasn't been around either."

Over his shoulder, through the door glass, Cal saw the rye grass in the field, beckoning. Slowly, carefully, he said, "You saying this guy and my wife...maybe run off together?"

The sheriff shook his head. "That would be too easy, Mr. Tubbs, too pat, don't you think?"

"This farm was my wife's life, Sheriff. This house, the animals...me."

The sheriff nodded again, with just a sliver of a smile. "Nothing but corn cobs to chew on, then, I guess, eh?"

"Corn cobs? What the hell are you talking about?"

"The hogs, Mr. Tubbs." The sheriff opened the door on a stiff, biting wind. "Hogs'll eat anything...isn't that what you said?"

There is a field.
There

Is
A
FIELD.

The blizzard hit with full, howling force by one o'clock, but that was all right. That was just fine. A good, thick blanket of snow to cover things, to *keep* things for a little while longer....

He went out into the middle of it with his Dad's old nickel-plated .45 and killed the dog where it lay in the shelter of the leaning garage. It took four bullets, just like the coyote...just like Emily...but he shot the bastard's head off.

Clean off.

"I brought it home for you, Emily," he said hoarsely, struggling with the words. "I brought that damn dog home for you, you bitch. For YOU!"

Then he shoved the burning metal of the automatic's muzzle into his mouth, closed his eyes on the sudden pain, on the tears that rolled coldly through the ruined stubble of his cheeks—

"Cal! You come in the house, now. It's snowing, for goodness sake! Cal!"

He let the muzzle fall from his lips.

"Cal!"

"Yes, dear." His words were lost in the falling snow. For a moment, he wasn't even certain he had said them aloud.

"Cal?"

"Coming."

He turned, cradling the gun in the crook of his good arm, and went back to the house, the empty house, the house still full of *her*, and waited for the sheriff to return.

On the Midwatch

The words felt good, coming out. Like putting on the new silver-bar collar devices; like the new glowing gold half-stripes on his service-dress blues, sewn next to his tarnished full ensign stripes: you're a Lieutenant Junior Grade, Charlie-boy, he thought. You're fresh from the Pacific Fleet, and tonight you are a Lieutenant (jg) Officer of the Deck underway, just you, only you, your first solo watch since reporting on board without a full lieutenant or lieutenant commander hanging on your elbow, hanging on your every word, on your every move. They're all asleep, now, trusting you, up here. The ship is yours, Charlie-boy, *yours*.

"Attention in the pilot house," were the words, "this is Lieutenant (jg) Lang. I have the deck and the con."

"Aye aye, sir," was the bridge crew's rote chorused reply. Then, "Steady on 350, sir," from the helmsman. And, from the lee helmsman, "All engines ahead standard, sir, zero seven five revolutions indicated for fifteen knots."

"Very well." And those words felt good too. Navy tradition: as OOD he was the only one on the bridge with the authority to say them, the only goddamn one. But hey, let's not let this go to your head, Charlie, he thought. Calm down, boy. This is the midwatch, midnight to four, steaming alone in the middle of the cold, cold North Atlantic, hundreds of miles from any commercial shipping lanes, from any land, from any possible danger. But *still*, you're the OOD, and you have the con; the ship is your total responsibility; the Captain is sawing wood right now, knowing you are up here. Don't get too cocky, please. And for God's sake, *don't screw up.*

He smiled. In the red darkness of the bridge, he could hide the smile in a shadow. Goddammit, he could handle the responsibility. Goddammit, he felt *good.*

He surveyed the bridge:

To the quartermasters on the starboard side, parallel-rulers in their hands, hunched over their charts; to the status-board keeper, crowned with sound-powered headphones, standing ready by his Plexiglas board with his grease-pencil and eraser cloth; to the helmsman, both hands on the huge brass wheel, his eyes locked on the gyro repeater in the panel before him; to the lee-helm, turned to the engineering status board, transcribing a report from main control over his own set of sound-powered phones; to the boatswainsmate-of-the-watch, brewing coffee in the corner, keeping his eye on his messengers; and to Al Douglass, his Junior Officer of the Deck, stooped over the main radar repeater scope, its rubber glare-shield molded to his face.

Then he looked out into the darkness, to where the black star field blended into the deeper, smoother darkness of the midnight sea, miles and miles beyond the ghostly crescent bow.

"How far are we pinging, Al?"

"Fifty thousand yards, sir. I was thinking about bringing it in, though. Keep CIC at fifty?"

"Yeah. Sounds good."

Al pulled his face from the rubber, and green light filtered up, into the overhead. He went over to the 21MC, bent, and talked quietly with the operations crew in the Combat Information Center, the tenders of the heavy electronics and sensors, the only true eyes for the ship in this darkness, in a night this complete. Then he straightened. "CIC Watch Officer says he's got one scope at fifty, and another at eighty. Air-search radar is down again, of course. Sonar is on standby. Fifty and eighty okay?"

Charlie nodded. No harm. No need to have everything done to his exact specifications. He was the newest officer on board, and he knew he had to be flexible. *Bend*, Charlie-boy, *give* a little. It's the mark of a good OOD.

"Sir?"

The Boatswainsmate-of-the-watch emerged from the darkness, carrying a steaming mug of coffee.

"Thanks, Boats." Charlie took the mug, its warmth spreading through his fingers. Both bridge wing hatches were closed and dogged once; outside on the wings both port and starboard lookouts were no doubt freezing their asses off.

A squawk from the 21MC, then. "Bridge, Combat."

Charlie cocked his head in the general direction, and Al took it. "Bridge aye."

"Yes sir, we've got a contact, seventy-eight thousand yards, bearing 342."

"That one will be Alpha," Charlie said, taking a quick gulp of coffee, burning his tongue, then putting the mug down. Take it easy, he told himself. It's thirty-nine miles out, for chrissakes.

"Designate it skunk Alpha, Combat," Al said.

"Combat aye."

"It's probably the *Glover* on local ops." Charlie turned to the status-board keeper. "You get that designation, Willoughby?"

"Yes sir, skunk Alpha."

"I want five minute marks, and a CPA as soon as it tracks."

"Yes sir." Willoughby turned to murmur into his sound-powered phones.

Al already had his binoculars up, looking vainly to port.

"I doubt you'll get her visually, Mr. Douglass; she's over the horizon."

The JOOD grinned. "I guess I'm a little anxious, sir."

Sir. Al was an ensign; the only time ensigns called j.g.s 'sir' was on the bridge. A rare fruit, Charlie savored it. He checked the center-line gyro-repeater. Yes indeed, steady on 350. You should have checked that before, Charlie-boy, when you first took the watch. *Watch* yourself; do it *right*. He leaned on the repeater, staring out into the night, hoping he looked calm, collected, and professional. They're all looking to you, Charlie.

Willoughby spoke up behind him, "Combat's got another skunk, sir."

Charlie straightened. "Where is it?"

"290. Thirty-five thousand yards."

Charlie turned on him. "Did you say thirty-five?"

"Yes sir, thirty-five thousand yards." Willoughby paused, listening to his phones. "They say it just popped up."

Charlie let his breath out slowly. "Okay, designate it skunk Bravo. Three minute marks. Closest point of approach when it tracks." He turned to Al, who was bent over the radar repeater once again. "Got it, Mr. Douglass?"

"Yes sir. It's coming in pretty fast."

"Low flying aircraft, maybe?"

"No, it's not painting right for that." Al took the rubber hood off the radar, and cranked down the gain to a soft green glow. "It's got to be a surface vessel." He made some marks on the glass with a grease pencil. "I can give you a rough CPA on Alpha now, anyway, if you want."

"Yeah."

"It's got a healthy left bearing drift, CPA at about twenty-five thousand at about 270 relative, in about ten minutes if we all maintain our speeds."

Charlie nodded. "Willoughby, check that off Combat's eye. Tell them to put Alpha on watch after it hits CPA."

"Yes sir."

"Bravo's really moving," Al said, making another mark on the radar glass, then connecting the dots with a parallel ruler. "I've got her at constant bearing, decreasing range now."

Charlie's heart jumped. CBDR had another name: collision course. "How far?"

"She's in five thousand already." Al looked up, eyes wide,

rimmed in green. "That's pretty damn fast."

Charlie looked out into the darkness, then crouched by the 21MC. "Combat, Bridge," he said quietly.

"Combat aye."

"What's the story on Bravo?"

A pause, then, "We've got her at CBDR, sir. She's really coming in."

"You got a real-speed on her?"

"...Yes sir." Another pause. "Forty-eight knots, sir."

"*Forty-eight?*"

"We checked it three times, sir. We even got the Senior Chief out of his rack for this one."

"My apologies for the Senior Chief's loss of beauty sleep. Tell him to check it again."

Forty-eight knots. What kind of ship could go that fast?

Apparently following the same thought, Al said, "Surface effect craft, maybe. Maybe a hydrofoil."

"In the middle of the goddamn North Atlantic?" Charlie brought his binoculars up and swept the port side horizon from beam to brow. "Get back on the scope, and let me know when Bravo gets in to twelve thousand. We'll probably come right 20 or 25 degrees to stay clear of it and Alpha."

"Yes, sir."

Charlie turned. "Mark your helm, Barney."

"350 still, sir," the helmsman said, "steady on."

"Very well."

"Alpha's turned to starboard," Al said, from the repeater scope. "I've got her past CPA and opening."

"Good." Go *away*, Charlie thought. I'd rather have these skunks one at a time any day. "Willoughby, tell Combat to put Alpha on watch."

"Aye sir, watch skunk Alpha."

"Bravo, Al?"

"Fifteen thousand and still closing. Dead on collision course still."

Charlie aimed his binoculars in the direction of the contact.

He relaxed his eyes, looking for it at the edges of his lines of sight...*there!* A flash, gone, then back...a yellowish, orangish light...dancing through the waves on the horizon....

He brought his binoculars down. "Boats!"

The Boatswainsmate-of-the-Watch stepped forward. "Sir?"

"Go out and tell the port wing lookout to wake his ass up. I've got this skunk visually in here and I haven't heard a word from him. It's *his* job to sight these damn things first."

"Yes sir."

"Al?"

"Almost twelve thousand, sir. It...wait a minute, just lost it on that sweep."

Charlie swung his binoculars up again. Where was it? It had just been....

"Three sweeps," Al said. "Bravo's gone from my scope."

Charlie focused in and out, looked from side to side. "Keep your ass on that radar, Al. We—"

"Combat just lost skunk Bravo, sir," Willoughby said.

Squawk: "Bridge, Combat."

Charlie stooped, pressed the toggle. "Bridge aye."

"Yes, sir. We're damned if we know what's going on out there."

"Sub, maybe?"

"At forty plus knots, sir?"

Charlie felt his cheeks warm, and was grateful for the darkness. "Bridge aye." He released the toggle, and straightened. "Boats, send someone with a pair of binocs back to the fantail. Get them hooked up on your lookout freek."

"Yes sir."

"Scope's clean, sir," Al said.

Charlie shook his head. "Skunks never acted like this in the Pacific, I can tell you that."

Al grinned briefly. "You'll get used to it. Sargasso is a strange place. Wait till we get up into the northern corridor shipping lanes. Then you'll really pull your hair out."

"Can't wait." Charlie rubbed his eyes. "You'd better—"

The port wing hatch clanged open. "There's something out here," the lookout yelled into the pilothouse. "Jesus Christ there's something *out here!*"

Charlie pushed past him ("Take *care* of this asshole" he mouthed to Al) and stepped out onto the bridge wing.

It was a beam of light under the water, long, straight, rotating like a lighthouse beam, more than one, actually, a succession of beams, like the spokes of some submerged cyclopean *wheel....*

Al came up behind him. "Christ Almighty," he breathed, "that light is *under* the water?"

Yellowed by depth, casting fish-shadows as the impossibly powerful beams swept past....

"What kind of light can penetrate that much ocean and still keep its intensity?"

Charlie suddenly realized his mouth was open. He grabbed the pelorus and took a bearing on where the hub of the light spokes appeared to be.

"290?"

Yeah, 290. Go wake the Captain. This is crazy."

They both re-entered the pilothouse in time to hear the lee-helmsman say shakily, "That ain't no damn bear sub...ain't no damn way that's a bear sub—"

"Quiet on the Bridge," Charlie said, amazed that his own voice was still steady.

Pinnggg. Piinnggg. Piinnggg.

"*What the hell—*"

"Combat put the sonar on line, sir," Willoughby said. "They figured you'd want it on."

Piinnggg. Charlie went to the 21MC and hit the toggle. "Combat. Bridge." Piinnggg.

"Combat aye."

"The next time somebody lights off the sonar without my direct order I'm gonna have someone's ass for breakfast." Piinnggg.

"Yes sir." Piinnggg. "Sorry sir."

"So how's it painting?"

"Huge, sir. Whatever's out there is pretty goddamn huge." Piinnggg. "Senior's on the scope. He—"

One of the quartermasters sang out, "Captain's on the bridge!" A hatch slammed.

"Mr. Lang?" The Captain squinted. "I don't have my night vision yet. What the hell—"

Piinnggg. Piinnggg.

"Tell CIC to turn off the sonar, Willoughby," the Captain said. "We'll wake the whole damn ship with that racket." He went to the forward bridge windows. "Ahah," he said.

"Sir," Charlie began, "it's—"

It had surfaced.

It was a black mountain, rimmed with orange light. There was movement across its surface, *things* scurrying to and fro…there was the sound of horns, of a huge cathedral organ in an all-encompassing ear-blasting discord, vibrating the bridge window glass and everyone's fillings….

"Right full rudder, helmsman," the Captain said, calmly, through the sound. "Steady on 060."

"Right full rudder, steady on 060 aye, sir," Barney said, his voice thick. The bridge was silent, then, the sudden quiet like a thunderclap. The ship turned, heeling slightly, shushing through the water. Then, "My rudder is right full…steadying on 060, sir."

"Very well." The Captain sighed. "Mr. Lang, what are we turning?"

"Zero seven five, sir. Fifteen knots."

"Lee helm," the Captain said, "all engines ahead full; indicate zero nine seven revolutions for twenty knots."

"All engines ahead full, aye sir, indicating zero nine seven revolutions for twenty knots." The engine order telegraph rang up speed brassily. The lee helm said, "Zero nine seven revolutions indicated and answered for, sir, for twenty knots."

The Captain nodded. "Very well." Then, "Mr. Lang, call your relief. Mr. Douglass, you have the deck and the con."

Charlie was astonished. He pointed out the bridge windows to the massive thing in the ocean tracking slowly to port, fading into the night. His mouth was open again, but no sound came out.

"Mr. Lang," the Captain said patiently, his eyes like gray steel, "give the deck and con to Mr. Douglass."

Charlie swallowed. "Attention in the pilothouse, this is Lieutenant (jg) Lang. Ensign Douglass has the deck and the con."

"Aye aye, sir," the bridge team chorused, looking at one another in the red darkness.

"This is Ensign Douglass," Al said then, his voice a trifle high, "I have the deck and the con. Belay your reports."

"Aye aye sir," the chorus repeated.

"Mr. Douglass," the Captain said, "when Mr. Lang's relief comes up you are to give him the deck, but you can keep the con if you feel you're up to it." He looked out the bridge windows, into the darkness to port. "Bring us back to our original course in ten minutes."

"Yes sir." Al glanced helplessly to Charlie. *I'm sorry*, his eyes said.

But Charlie did not notice; he was still astonished, bewildered, still in shock....

"Mr. Lang, I will see you in my sea cabin in five minutes."

"Captain's off the bridge!" Barney sang; the hatch clanged.

Charlie looked to Al. "What...?" he managed.

Al looked out the bridge windows, then to Charlie, then back to the windows. He was clutching his binoculars too tightly, Charlie saw.

"Charlie," he said quietly, "I didn't see anything, understand? I heard about this; Goddammit I *heard* about this...no, I didn't see anything, not a goddamned blessed thing. You're *new*, Charlie, understand? You're *new*."

But Charlie only shook his head, slowly, slowly.

"Call your relief, Charlie," Al said then. "Quickly please. I've never had the deck before. Okay?"

Charlie looked at Willoughby, who turned to his status

board and proceeded to wipe all of the Bravo information off the Plexiglas. Charlie gave the entire pilothouse an all-encompassing look, but no one met his gaze. He turned to the passageway hatch, yanking it open. "Lang is off the bridge," he muttered, and stepped through.

KNOCK THEN ENTER

Charlie knocked, then pushed the door open. The Captain looked up from his desk, from a pad covered with hastily scribbled notes. "Yes, Mr. Lang?"

"You wanted to see me, sir?"

"See you? About what?"

"Well, about what was…about what was out there…what I saw…."

"Saw? What did you see, Mr. Lang?" Something on the midwatch?"

Charlie looked into the Captain's eyes; they were steady, expressionless; he twirled a pencil around in his fingers, around and around and—

"No, sir," he heard himself say.

"Oh?" Around and around and—"You're sure?"

"Yes, sir. I…I didn't see anything."

"Then there's really no need for this discussion, is there?"

"No sir."

"Go hit your rack and get some sleep, then, Mr. Lang."

"Yes sir. Goodnight, sir."

"Mr. Lang."

Charlie paused at the doorway. "Sir?"

"This was your first OOD midwatch?"

"On this ship, yes, sir."

"I see." The Captain began twirling his pencil again. "I think it's fair to say, then, that you've got some things to learn about how we do things around here."

"Sir?"

"Stay clear of the deck log, Mr. Lang. I'll make your entries. Go below and get some midrats if you can't sleep. Goodnight."

Charlie closed the door. Firmly.

Outside, on the main weather deck, leaning on the lifelines, staring into the wind-whipped darkness, he saw...nothing. Nothing but a twenty-knot wake stirring the sea to faint yellow-green phosphorescence. The blackness of the sky and sea was nearly complete.

There's nothing out there, he thought; there's nothing out there at all. Right? Right?

Knowing when to shut up makes a good officer, Charlie-boy. Makes a damn fine officer, you know....

And then, out of the night, he heard the thundering organ discord once more, gentled now with distance...

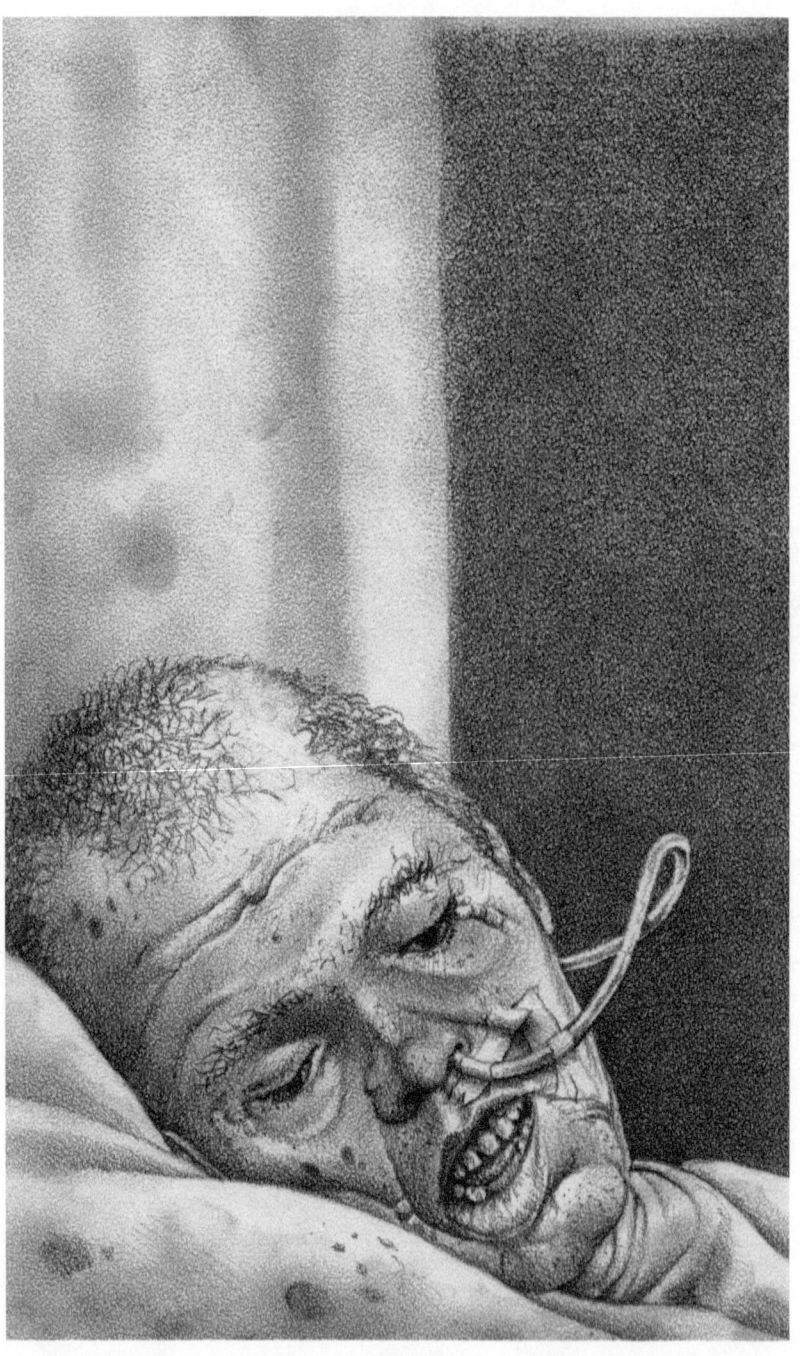

It's for You

The first to die was Detective Sergeant George Small, retired, formerly of the Homicide Unit. At home, said Widow Small; quietly, in his own bed.

John picked up the manila envelope from his desk pile, hefted it, felt the contents shift. "What's this?"

"Flowers for Mrs. Small," Detective Mike Finnean said. "Five buck minimum."

"Jesus." John blinked. "They're dropping like flies these days."

His partner nodded slowly. "They say it always goes down in threes, Johnie."

"Better write your will then, Mike. You don't look so good." John made his contribution, then waved the envelope over his head. "Who's next?"

"Over here." That was Jack Hyde, an old friend and former partner of Small's, as he leaned forward to take a phone call.

John was about to do a Frisbee toss with the envelope when the duty sergeant with the game leg raised his voice over the general clamor of the squad room: "Phone for you too, Detective Graham!"

"Who is it?"

"Your daughter Julie."

John cleared a pile of paper so he could see his phone, depressed the blinking button light, then leaned his considerable bulk into the swivel chair and buried the receiver in his ear. "What's up, sweet pea?"

"You're on your own for dinner, Pops."

John grinned. "What, another date with Donald?"

"Ronald, with an 'R'. Hey, he's buying."

"I hear you. I'll be okay. Tell Donald I said hi."

"*Daad.*"

Snickering, he punched the button light off to break the connection. Across the room, then, he saw that Jack Hyde was still on the phone. "Heads up, Jacky!" He tossed the Small Memorial Fund envelope across the desks and scored a perfect hit in Hyde's 'in' basket.

The other detective didn't move.

"Jack! Hey, buddy, you sleeping?"

The squad room skipped a beat, a moment of odd silence as everyone focused on Hyde. Then the duty sergeant, who had an angle on Hyde's face, uttered a low exclamation, and lurched to his feet.

John met him at Hyde's desk. Together, they crouched to the eye level of the seated detective. Hyde stared back at them with glazed eyes. "He's dead," the sergeant said, incredulous, turning to John. "Ain't he? Dead?"

Hyde held the phone to his ear, his elbow propped between the desk edge and the chair armrest. Afternoon light from the bank of windows over Pine Street reflected in his unblinking gaze. He looked upset to John, like he had just received bad news. But yeah, he was dead all right.

By now, the rest of the dicks and support staff of the Homicide Unit were crowded around. Mike Finnean closed Hyde's eyes, took the phone out of his still warm hand—

"Wait." John reached out, "Don't—"

—And hung it up. "Shit," he said then, "I probably should have checked to see if someone was still on the line."

John frowned up at his partner. "That would have been

smart, Mikey, yeah."

"There wasn't anybody," the duty sergeant said, "his button light was out."

Finnean looked around. "Anybody call the goddamn M.E. yet?"

One of the younger guys said, "I just saw him down the hall," and broke out of the crowd to get him.

"Must have been his heart," someone said.

John rose, feeling his knees crack, conscious, suddenly, of his own heart pounding behind his ribcage. "Of all people: Hyde."

He was Number Two.

An hour later, a shadow crossed John's desk. He looked up. The duty sergeant stood there. "I saw how pissed you were when Detective Finnean hung up Hyde's phone," he said. "So I got a copy of the ISDN log." He laid a computer printout, roughly ripped, in the center of the desk clutter.

John glanced across the room to the dead detective's empty chair, then picked up the sheet and studied it. "This last call is from Fishtown," he said, matching the exchange to one of the older sections of the city, once Italian, then Black, then Asian, now…God-only knew. "Two-hundred American Street." He looked up. "That sound familiar to you?"

"Nope. Might have been a songbird, you know? Hyde had a pretty good network going for the drug snuffs up there."

John nodded. "Did you call it?"

"The number?" The sergeant straightened. "Disconnected, computer voice saying 'the number you have dialed is no longer in service'. Dead end."

"Typical. Hey, thanks anyway." John focused on the number on the printout, memorizing it without even thinking. Then he looked across the room again to the empty chair—two deaths in one day; *Jesus*—and slowly shook his head.

It took another day for Number Three.

Finnean turned onto Broad Street into the clogged traffic

and slapped the steering wheel. "When are they gonna finish fixing this fucking street?"

"I'm in no hurry to get back." John squinted through the windshield at the jam of cars. "The air conditioning was on the fritz when we left, remember? The squad room must be a goddamn oven by now." He leaned forward, put his hand over one of the dashboard vents. "Speaking of which...."

Finnean reached down and twisted a knob; a loud ratcheting sound issued from somewhere under the dash, then the smell of burning rubber.

"That's enough of that!" John turned the knob back to vent fresh, sweltering, monoxide-laced August city air into the car. "So we bake," he said, settling back resignedly.

They crept a block, then Finnean said, "You heard about Kopelman?"

"Augie?" John screwed up his face. "Isn't he living in South Carolina, some golf course retirement set-up?"

"'Living' is no longer the operative word, my friend."

"Oh Christ. Dead?"

"Stroke. Fifteenth Tee."

"Shit." John conjured the old cop's face in his memory. He had been gone for years, but John clearly remembered his loud bark of a laugh, the rancid stink of his cheap cigars.... "It always goes in threes," he said, "remember?"

Finnean chuckled hollowly. "Amen to that."

Another block, then John said, "I worked with him once."

"Who, Augie? At what, age twelve?"

"I was less than a year out, wise guy, same as you, riding shotgun in his prowler one night, covering for his partner Billy Palmer out with the flu or some such shit. Back when they painted the prowlers red, remember? He wouldn't let me drive. We were what, twenty-two?"

"Maybe you were. I had that detour through the Army first, my friend."

John shook his head. "It's still so weird."

"What, Augie Kopelman cashing in his chips on a golf

course? There are worse ways to go."

"Not just him: all of them, all three. It's just too many dying at once. Three in just a couple of days, think about that."

"Augie was in his seventies easy—"

"But Jack Hyde was only a few years older than us, wasn't he?"

Finnean nodded, staring straight ahead. "He was just sixty-three."

John sweated for a long block, then he said, "So how did you find out about Augie?"

"Friend of the Lieutenant's down in Myrtle Beach saw the obit in the paper and made some calls. 'Died with his wedge and his cell phone in his hand,' he said."

"Cell phone? He died on the *phone*?"

"Yeah." Finnean gripped the wheel with both hands, looking for an opportunity to change lanes. "Just like Jack."

The voice on the other end wavered, but had an undercurrent of steel: an old cop's wife, maybe, but a cop's wife, just the same.

"I don't want to disturb your day, Mrs. Small," John said, easing back in his chair, "but I had just a few questions, if you don't mind. About your husband, about…how he died."

"Of course, Detective."

"So you're okay with this?"

"I know the drill." He heard her dentures click. "You just fire away."

John flipped his notebook to a clean page. "Was he asleep when it happened?"

"Well, he was in bed, and it was quite late."

"Were you…I mean, was he…I mean—"

She smiled. "Were we together in bed, do you mean? No. I was in the kitchen. I have this terrible insomnia, you see, and I do the Times crossword in the kitchen, sometimes till two or three in the morning."

"Is that when you discovered your husband, then? At two or

three?"

"Why, no. Actually, it was only a few minutes after the phone rang that I went in to see who George was talking to."

John suddenly felt cold. "There was a phone call?"

"Yes. Your poor wife must be as used to it as I am, all those calls, usually so late."

"Actually, I'm not married at present."

"Divorced? I don't wonder. I'm surprised I lasted as long as I did."

"You said the phone rang...."

"Yes, it rang twice. I assumed that George got it, because it only went two rings."

"And then you went into the bedroom?"

"After a few minutes, yes." She paused. "That was when I found him."

"Do you remember, Mrs. Small, if the phone was hung up or off the hook?"

"That's funny you should ask, Detective."

"Why so?"

"Because now that I remember, the phone was off the hook, lying on the floor next to the bed. It was making that awful beeping they do, you know? So I hung it up just before I called 911." She paused, then said, "I wonder."

"Wonder what, Mrs. Small?"

"George was getting a lot of phone calls from someone lately."

"Someone?"

"I could tell they bothered him, those phone calls, but he wouldn't talk about it."

"He never told you who was making the calls?"

"He didn't, no. But the caller did, the one time I picked up the phone and it was him. 'Tell George it's Jimmy,' he said."

Jimmy. John took a shallow breath. "You've been a big help, Mrs. Small."

"Well I don't see how."

"Really. Thank you." John hung up. He looked at the

phone. Then he shuddered, and pushed it away.

John tented his fingers over a full plate of lasagna. "I have a riddle for you."

His daughter Julie frowned. "I'm no good at riddles. I can never figure them out. Pass the bread, will you?"

"Then you'll hate this one." John handed the basket over. "That's because it doesn't have an answer. Not yet, anyway."

Her frown deepened. "Is this about work?"

"Maybe." John put down his fork. "Now listen: there are these three guys, they each get a phone call, then they die."

"On the phone?"

"Yeah."

"At the same time?"

"No, separate times, separate places."

"Easy. An electrical surge through the phone lines. Phones work on electricity, don't they?"

"They do, but it's not enough to shock you. No, that's not it."

Julie shrugged. "Coincidence, then." She took a bite and chewed slowly; John saw the wheels turning, though. "I need more clues," she said then.

"Okay: the phone that the caller used in one of them?"

"Yeah?"

"It was out of service."

"What about the other two?"

"I'm checking. But one phone call was definitely from a line that was officially disconnected."

"Wow." She blinked. "Spooky. So you think the three calls might be related?"

John nodded.

Julie laughed outright. "That's crazy, right?"

"That's why it's a riddle."

"See that signpost up ahead, Pop?" She laughed again. "You're in the *Twilight Zone!*"

The temp with the tight ass and even tighter jeans dropped the inter-office folder on John's desk, then sashayed out of the squad room with all eyes watching.

"Who the hell does she work for?" someone asked.

"We don't have a 'need to know'," someone else replied.

Less than a minute later John entered the Squad Room from the general direction of the john. He spied the yellow folder immediately, saw who it was from, and grabbed it up even before his ass hit the chair. He undid the string and pulled out a flimsy blue sheet with perforations running down both sides: the phone records for one Detective Sergeant George Small, recently deceased.

There, towards the bottom, just before the outgoing call to 911...an incoming call from the Fishtown exchange, from Two Hundred American Street. He placed the blue flimsy next to the fax he had received an hour before from the Myrtle Beach PD, a copy of a similar blue flimsy of the cell phone account of one August Kopelman, also recently deceased. The last incoming call on the fax was the same: Fishtown exchange, Two Hundred American Street.

John looked at the flimsy and the fax for a long time, trying to believe what his mind was telling him. Three calls from the same address to three cops. Each of them died during the call. Three phone calls, all from Two Hundred American Street. All from a phone number that, as far as the Phone Company was concerned, was not in service.

He got up, finally, and made his way across the squad room to the duty sergeant's desk. The grease-penciled roster was on the wall behind him. According to the roster, Mike Finnean had a court appearance this morning, and his name was written in red. "Red me out, Joe," John said to the sergeant.

The sergeant rose to do the honors. "Where to, Detective?"

"City Hall, Office of Deeds. Then Fishtown."

American Street was a short block of narrow, tired bungalows, with postage-stamp front lawns and sidewalks that were cracked and tilted from trees long-since cut down. Every one of the houses needed paint; three were boarded up; one was burned out. It was a sad, lost little street in a section of the city that had last seen prosperity when people wore 'I Like Ike' buttons and parked Studabakers and Ramblers at the curb, one to a family.

Number Two Hundred, no surprise, was one of the three boarded up houses. White clapboard, low-hipped roof; no second floor to speak of. The little lawn was full of waist-high weeds and rusting and rotting trash. John dismissed the nailed-shut front door and porch windows, and followed the side alley to the rear. There he found a plywood bulkhead door to the basement, its lock rusted shut. He gave the lock a sharp yank, and the entire hasp broke free of the rotted wood and came loose in his hand. Grunting, he pushed the bulkhead door up and over, letting light spill down the concrete steps. Lots of spider webs, with darkness and silence beyond.

John took a step down the stairs, then noticed a neighbor in the next yard, an old woman in a grey housedress, standing in her back door. He pulled out his shield and held it up so the light caught it. "I'm a policeman."

"I know what you are," she shot back. "I'm just watching you; no harm in that, is there?"

"Anybody live here?"

"You mean in that house you're breaking into?"

John waited impassively.

The old woman shook her head finally. "Just those drug addict kids, passing through. Not a real person. Not a family. Not for years."

"Were you around when Jimmy Truewell lived here?"

"Truewell!" She put her hands on her bony hips. "That takes me back. He shot that cop, right here, thirty years ago. Right here. 1963. Thirty-six years ago. He still in prison?"

"Thank you for your time, ma'am." John started again down the basement steps.

The old woman called after him, a sudden anxious note in

her voice: "He didn't get *out*, did he?"

John paused. "No ma'am. He didn't get out."

The first floor looked indeed like a succession of addicts and derelicts had made it a home over the years. But John was only looking for one thing, and he found it in the short hall between the living room and the kitchen: the telephone jack. It was round with three socket holes, made out of porcelain, originally mounted on the baseboard, but now hanging free by just one grimy black wire. There was no phone in sight. He found another broken jack in the first floor front bedroom, but again, no phone, nor any way to successfully plug one in.

In the hall, again, walking from the back bedroom to the front of the house, he heard a sound behind him, a sound he hadn't heard for a decade or so, except in old movies: a rotary phone, dialing.

He whirled around, gun out, finger on the trigger guard, legs automatically braced to squeeze one off....

There in the shadow of the hall, back against the wall, there, for just a moment, just a moment, he thought he saw a young man in a loud short-sleeve shirt, sitting on a chair by a little table, a phone cradled against his shoulder, big shit-eating grin on his acne-scarred face....

Then another sound: a car door slamming, out front, and in a brief moment of distraction John blinked, and the hallway before him was empty once more. Just the dust, the shadows, the broken porcelain phone jack hanging from its wire. "Fuck me," John whispered, easing his stance, raising the gun's muzzle, "Fuck *me*," then slowly re-holstering it.

"John." Mike Finnean stood in the kitchen doorway, dressed in his best suit.

"I thought you were in court," John said, feeling like he'd been caught at something, and knowing he looked it.

Finnean glanced at John's hand still in his coat, still holding the gun-grip, then back up. "Shithead pleaded out. How come you're here?"

"This is where the phone calls came from, Mike, from this house." John gestured to the phone jack hanging from the hole in the wall. "But I don't see how."

His partner was silent, watching him. Then he said, "The call to Jack Hyde, you mean?"

"And to George Small. And Augie Kopelman."

Finnean shook his head slowly. "You've been busy, Johnie."

"I went to City Hall first, checked the deed on this place," John continued. "Right now the bank owns it, but back in 1963 a man named Truewell lived here."

"Jimmy Truewell." Finnean turned his head briefly to hawk into the hall. "That's right. Pimple-faced little cock-sucking piece of shit named Jimmy Truewell."

"Finding that name in all this was a real shot, Mike. Jimmy Truewell. That really jogged my memory, took me back, you know?"

"He killed Augie's partner Billy Palmer that night," Finnean said, looking about. "Right here, in this room. Killed a cop stone cold, and all the state gave him for it was life."

John took in a measured breath. "There was Billy Palmer, yeah, there was Jack Hyde, and George Small, and Augie Kopelman…and *you*, Mike, right? All of you, there that night."

"His drug-addict girlfriend called it in, said he had a gun, said he was threatening her with it. We had two units here in minutes." Finnean pointed down the hall to the front of the house, to the front door. "George was on a beat and showed up just as we were going in. It was dark. Truewell had turned all the goddamn lights off. His girlfriend wasn't even here." Finnean went past John to the living room, looking about. "There was a lot of confusion in here, five of us, one of him, not a lot of room in here, you know? Somehow he got George's piece, then put one into Billy before we could get him down."

"I remember," John said, nodding, "that's how it played out at the trial."

"It could have been any of us, took that slug."

"I know."

"We should have fried the bastard, Johnie. We should have cooked his fucking brains to soup. But no, instead he gets three free squares at Holmesburg every fucking day for the rest of his sorry little cocksucking life."

"Not any more, Mike."

Finnean turned sharply, looked at him, suddenly focused. "He can't be *out*—"

John shook his head. "Correctional Medical Facility at Holmesburg. Coma. From a stroke."

"Who'd you talk to?"

"Grayson, in the Warden's Office. Said Truewell had it in his cell. By the time they got him some attention he was already out of it."

Finnean grabbed his arm. "*When?*"

"The day before George took his phone call." *Before the first of them died*, John wanted to add, but didn't. He searched his partner's face. "Coincidence?"

"Yeah." Finnean let go, turned away. "Coincidence. It must be."

"Somebody sent three good cops to their deaths, Mike."

"That's bullshit, Johnie."

"That somebody? He called them in from *here*." John kicked at the broken phone jack. "From *here*, Mike."

"That's fucking bullshit and you know it."

The questions came out before he could stop them: "Somebody calling in their marker, Mike? Somebody finally getting even?"

Finnean swung about, stepped up into John's face; his voice dropped, low, cold: "What are you saying, partner? You saying something *happened?*"

"You tell me, Mike. You were in here. You were with them."

"You're damn straight I was here! I was dodging bullets with the rest of them! I know what went down!"

"Did he call you from prison too, Mike? Like he called George and Augie and Jack? He called you guys a lot just before that stroke, didn't he?"

"You're a fucking nut case, Johnie. He never—"

"George Small: dead. Jack Hyde: dead. Augie Kopelman: dead. They were all here, and now they're all dead." John wanted to grab his partner's suit lapels and shake him. "What about you, Mike? What about you, now?"

Finnean's eyes followed his voice: cold, dead. "You weren't there, John," he said, now in just a rough whisper, "You weren't there." Then he turned, and disappeared back down the hall to the kitchen. John heard him rattle down the basement stairs. Then, after a moment, his partner's car roared to life in the street, then was gone.

"That went well." John raised his hands, then dropped them to his sides. "Oh yeah, that went *real* well."

The next day Mike Finnean called in sick. Then the day after that, as well. He had it on the books; no one, not even the Lieutenant, raised an eyebrow. And John left him alone, left the folder with the phone records on the corner of his desk, away from the rest of the clutter, unopened, untouched, but there, in plain view.

When he saw the duty sergeant leave his partner's name in red for the third day, however, he decided to make the call. After a few moments, he slammed the receiver down. "Damn!" Then he rose, grabbed his suit coat, and slung it over his shoulder. "Red me out, Joe."

The duty sergeant chuckled. "You got his answering machine too?"

"Yeah."

"So where to?"

"The CMF at Holmesburg."

The duty doctor didn't even offer to accompany him onto the ward. "Truewell, J.? Number Five," he said, hitting the door-lock button. "Left side."

"Thanks." John went for the door handle.

"Detective."

John stopped, turned.

"He's still comatose. He's probably not even going to know you're here."

"I might get lucky. He might come out of it—" John snapped his fingers "—like in the movies, you know?"

"Sure." The doctor nodded sagely. "Right."

John entered the ward: long, painted light blue, windows down the left side, a nurse station on the right. He nodded to the RN behind the counter, who lowered his newspaper and peered at him over black-rimmed glasses. "Yeah?"

"I'm here to see Truewell," John said.

The nurse pointed to the fifth bed with a meaty, hairy fist, then returned to his paper.

John found an old man in Number Five, small, thin to emaciation; his pale, deeply wrinkled skin littered with veins, liver spots, and ancient acne scars. He lay on his back, blanket up to his armpits, hands crossed. On one finger, John saw a small plastic cap with wires attached to a heart/bp monitoring device hanging off the headboard; on the other wrist, a catheter attached to a UV drip bag. John also saw leg restraints attached to the bed frame, going up under the blankets.

His eyes were half-open. That brought John up short for a moment, until he saw that the gaze was unwavering and unfocused; he knew most people died with their eyes open, that you had to close them with your fingers—sometimes more than once—to keep them there. Maybe…? But no, the beeps from the machine beside the bed were regular, and the green spikes on the little screen went by like waves at the beach.

Jimmy Truewell looked out the frosted Plexiglas window, looking into the light, motionless, seeing nothing at all, but alive. His eyes were bloodshot, his mouth open far enough to reveal yellowed, peg-like teeth. A thin thread of drool fell from a corner of his cracked, grey lips to the blue paper pajama top.

John moved a straight back chair next to the bed, and sat down. He looked at Truewell briefly, cleared his throat, and then glanced down the ward to the RN. The nurse never looked up.

Satisfied, John leaned close, and in a whisper, said, "Mr. Truewell, my name is John Graham. I'm a police detective in the Homicide Unit. I don't believe we ever met." He paused, looked down the ward again to the RN, then back to Truewell. "I'm taking a chance that you can somehow hear me." He paused again. This was crazy. Still, he leaned closer and spoke carefully: "I want to talk about Mike Finnean. I want you to know that Mike is a good detective, a good man. I want you to hear that. I want you to know it's true." John looked down at Truewell's hands; they were clenched tightly, pressed up against the blanket and mattress. "Mike doesn't have a family of his own, but his mother is still alive, and he's got a sister and a couple of nieces." John blinked back sudden, surprising tears. "He's in the Knights, you know, and every Thanksgiving he's out all day delivering those food baskets that they make up for the needy. All those turkeys and canned peas and cranberry sauce. I can remember one year when—"

A screeching noise echoed down the ward, freezing John in mid-sentence. The RN, moving his chair on the linoleum. John looked around quickly, but the RN was still bent over his paper. He turned back—

Directly into the cold, steady gaze of Jimmy Truewell.

John jerked back against the chair, blinking rapidly. "*Jesus…!*"

The old man's head had turned, ever so slightly, and his eyes had shifted from looking out the window….

To looking at him.

The body was in coma, face a drawn, leather mask, but the eyes were very much awake. Awake and aware. They stared at him, stared right into him. *I know you now*, they said; *I know* you *now*….

And John realized that by coming here he had made the single, greatest mistake of his life. The ultimate mistake. "Oh my God," he whispered. I told you my name. Oh my God. *I told you my name!*

Halfway up the stairs to the squad room two vice detectives stopped him to offer their awkward condolences. "What do you mean?" John demanded. There was a siren going off in his head, loud, loud. "What the hell are you guys *talking about*?"

The squad room went silent as he burst in, as everyone stopped, for the briefest instant, to glance at him. He turned to the duty sergeant. "Is it true, Joe?" He looked at Finnean's empty desk, then his name, still redded out on the board.

The duty sergeant nodded, his face wracked in tragedy. "Yes, Detective."

"I'm going home," John said. "I don't feel so good. Red me out for the rest of the day, will you?"

"Sure, Detective, sure—"

But John was already gone.

From his living room chair, John stared at the phone as it rang. In the last two hours, it had rung sixteen separate times. He hadn't answered it, of course. Just sat there, hollow-eyed, listening to the rings echo through the empty house.

I told him my name, he thought, over and over. *I told him my name!*

This time, his daughter burst into the kitchen on the fifth ring. "Hey!" she yelled, dropping something on the counter with a thud, "isn't anybody home?"

John stumbled to his feet, "Julie! Don't answer the—!"

But she already had. "Graham residence," he heard her say, always polite, "...Yes? Sure. One second, please, I'll see."

John fell back in his chair, gulping air—

Julie's voice rose. "Dad? Are you home?"

He knows my name.

His heart staccato'd, knife blades, suddenly plunging—

"Dad?"

Staccato'd, *ripped—*

She poked her head around the door. "Hey, there you are. Were you asleep?"

John looked at the receiver in her hand as his heart tried

once, twice....

    "Here." She held the phone out. "It's for you."

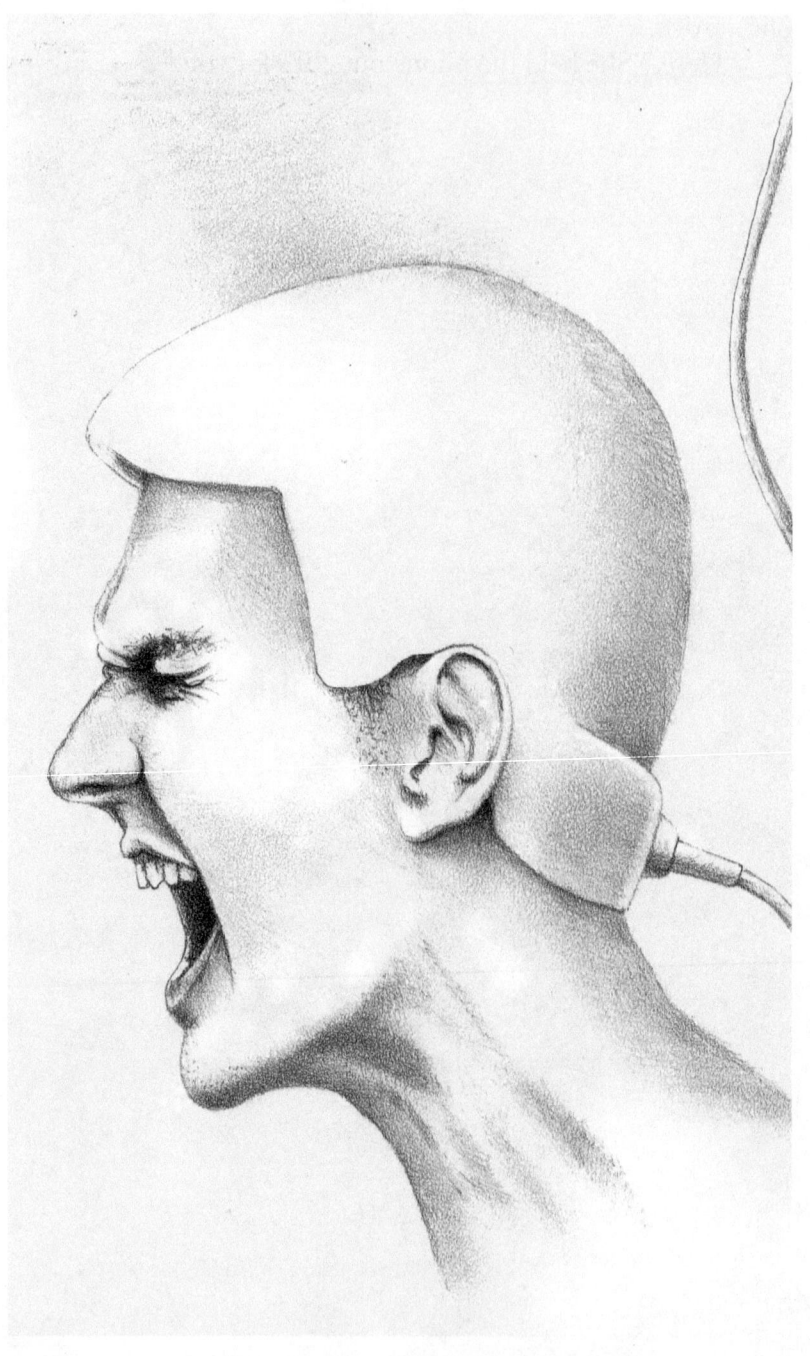

Along the River Lethe

1

Memory houses had lately become such a ubiquitous part of the mall landscape that Harry Swope rarely even gave them a second thought. Not that he ever had to, though. On his salary, with his prospects, he doubted he could afford even a minute's worth of what they had to sell. Maybe not even a second's worth.

But that was okay.

What did he need anyone else's memories for, anyway?

"Hey Harry! You're blocking traffic!"

Harry came out of his reverie, realizing, as he stood like a stalled car in an avenue of mall shoppers, that his friend Sal was right.

"Over here, pal!" Sal waved to him from a bench near an Auntie Anne's Pretzels kiosk. Harry elbowed his way over. As he sat, Sal handed him a wrapped pretzel, still warm and dripping with butter. "You weren't actually thinking of going in there," he said, "were you?"

"Where?" Harry took a bite, "The House of Dreams? Oh, absolutely." He waved his pretzel in the direction of the Raphael's Boutique down the mall. "Then I was gonna go down to

Raphael's to pick out a diamond brooch or two to give to my sainted Aunt Dot."

Sal snorted. "First of all, you probably don't even *have* an Aunt Dot, sainted or otherwise. Second of all, I doubt you've got enough change in your pocket to flush a public pisspot." He paused to watch Harry take another bite. "By the way," he said, "pretzel's on me."

"I'll buy next time." Harry swallowed. "I promise."

Sal snorted again.

A few bites later, Harry said, "I wonder how much people actually get for them."

"Get for what?"

"For their memories." Harry pointed to The House of Dreams with his chin. "In the memory houses. People get paid to share their memories, don't they? I know you have to pay big bucks to experience them, but what about the donors? They don't do it for free, do they? They must get paid, right?"

Sal wiped his mouth with the back of his hand. "I saw a show on the LC where they said you have to sign over all rights and do a non-disclosure thing when you sell. Very legal, very hush-hush."

"You mean they keep the price a secret? About how much they pay you?"

"I mean they keep it secret about the whole thing, not just the money. What the memory *is*, that's the important part." Sal chewed. "Maybe it was the DC. I always get them confused."

Harry looked through the crowd of shoppers to the House of Dreams. He couldn't see what was inside; all the glass was smoky and dark. And the whole time they sat there, finishing their pretzels, sucking their fingers clean, he didn't see one person either go in or come out of the place. It had to be expensive, like he'd heard, like Sal said. Expensive as all hell, probably.

Which meant they probably did pay a lot to get a good memory. And for a really good one, a *unique* one, say…probably a whole lot.

Sal stood. "You finished?"

Harry stood also. "Yeah." He wiped his hands on his pants. "Stick a fork in me, I'm done."

He only had one picture of her that he kept out for others to see. Like a fan. It was a publicity still, 2-D, the kind the official fan web site let you download and print without charging you anything.

Stephanie Sheer, the movie star. Classier than Ho-San, sexier than Zorne, more talented than ten Sheratons. Every movie she had ever made so far had been a blockbuster hit, a huge moneymaker, every single one, and it was all because of her. She had two Oscars and five Golden Globes on her mantle already, and her fan base had to be in the billions. She was America's...no, she was the *world's* sweetheart. The one you took home to meet your parents. And when she took *you* home, the one who screwed your brains out, all night long, and left you sweating in the sheets the next morning, begging for more. Or so those dark, wide, violet eyes promised.

Harry's studio apartment was twelve by twelve by eight (he had measured it once)—one thousand one hundred and fifty two cubic feet—with one window that looked out on an airshaft with a hundred and three other windows (he had counted them once) just like his. For a change of scenery, he could sit on the toilet in his four by six by eight bathroom—add another one hundred and ninety two cubes. He had measured that once, too.

He kept the publicity still in a frame on the wall over the top shelf of his pc cubby. From the saddle he had a perfect view of her. As he stared at the still, he imagined those pouty lips moved, and her familiar voice whispered roughly, "Hey, Harry Bear... what's cookin'?"

Not a whole lot these days, Steph. Not a whole hell of a lot. You did the right thing, dumping me, way back when.

His gaze dropped to the blank monitor screen of the pc where he Hooked In to work, then down to the cubby's top drawer. He touched it open, rummaged under a pile of papers and pulled out a nondescript white envelope. Its corners were fuzzy, and its flap was taped to stop a rip at the fold.

Harry opened the envelope and pulled out the contents. Just a bunch of old 2-D photos from his high school days. Happier times, for sure. Harry and his girlfriend at the lake; at the seashore; a photo-booth strip from Six Flags of Harry and his girlfriend grinning, laughing, doing dumb facial expressions, and kissing in the last shot. The camera had captured instants of memories, single moments, frozen in time. Two characters from another life, another movie. People used to pay for these kinds of memories once, he realized.

Harry sat for a long while, looking at the photos, looking at the two kids having fun, looking at his girlfriend Steph, at her dark, wide, violet eyes....

Beyond the smoky glass door, the young woman seated behind the severe ebony desk said, "I'm sorry, sir, but you will have to make an appointment for that."

Harry said, "I really just wanted to talk to somebody about it, that's all."

The young woman—all scarlet lips and nails and dark chestnut hair pulled back in that Fin style that was so popular these days—hesitated a moment, then touched the console pad before her. She looked at the little screen, then gave Harry a quick wink, and touched the pad again.

A voice said, "Yes, Gage?"

"I have a prospective client here, Mr. Marlowe. He doesn't have an appointment, but he does have a donation question. About Stephanie Sheer."

"Indeed." The voice paused. "Hasn't my nine-thirty postponed?"

"Yes, sir. That's why I thought we might be able to squeeze this gentleman in," and she gave Harry another wink, "if you don't mind."

"By all means," the voice said. "Send him in."

Gage indicated a door to her right. "Go right through there, Mr.—"

"Harold," Harry said, "just Harold. Thanks."

He opened the door and entered another room much like the one he had just left. There were two oxblood leather wing-back chairs flanking a small ebony table. On the table was a crystal vase holding a spray of fresh flowers. Harry was still deciding which chair to sit in when an inner door across the room opened and a tall man in a dark suit emerged. He was bald on top, with a huge dome of a forehead, pale skin, and a weak, damp handshake. "My name is Charles Marlowe," he said in a deep, fluid voice, motioning Harry to sit in the chair on the left. "And you are…?"

Harry sat. "I'm Harold, Harry…I'd rather not use my last name if you don't mind."

"Of course not, Harry. I understand perfectly. Rest assured that we at the House of Dreams take great pains to ensure the confidentiality of all of our clients." Mr. Marlowe took the other chair, settled, and tented his fingers in front of him. "So, then, Harry. Gage said you had a question about donations?"

"Yes." Harry leaned forward. "I was wondering how much a person gets paid to, you know, sell one of their memories."

Mr. Marlowe chuckled. "Well, Harry, it's not quite as simple as you might think. There are a number of aspects to consider. What the memory in fact *is*, of course, is paramount. This can run the gamut from something as simple as involvement in a multiple vehicle accident, say, or a lightning strike, or an important major league home run, to…well…the sky is the limit at the high end. The unique memories, the truly private ones, the *exclusives*." He paused, spreading his hands. "Then of course there are the more mundane aspects: age, duration, viewpoint, re-memory echo clutter. What I am trying to say is that there is no simple price list, Harry. There is no menu, not even for a…who did Gage mention? Not even for a Stephanie Sheer."

Harry looked down at his hands. He unclenched them, then clenched them again. "What if it's a private memory? Just her and me. What if it's an exclusive?"

Mr. Marlowe smiled. "We are always interested in anything

to do with the private experiences of our star celebrities, to be sure. And we already have several Stephanie Sheer exclusives in our portfolio. In fact, I think I can safely say that House of Dreams has more Sheer exclusives than any of our competitors—"

"Nobody has this one," Harry interrupted. "Not unless they got it from Steph herself."

"Indeed." Mr. Marlowe inclined his tall frame, and in a lower, more confidential tone, he asked, "And what, if you wouldn't mind, might this particular memory *be*?"

Harry hesitated for just a moment. Then, gripping the arms of his chair, he leaned past the flowers and whispered into Mr. Marlowe's proffered ear. As he did so, Marlowe's forehead blushed a delicate pink. "Ahh," he murmured. "*Indeed.*"

Harry sat back. "Well?"

"If this can be confirmed, not that I doubt you in the least, but if this can be *verified*...well, Harry...." Mr. Marlowe cleared his throat. "We have been looking for you for a long time, sir, a long time indeed."

"It's worth a lot of money, then?"

"Of course, you must understand that I am not in a position to just simply quote you a price here, now. Not on an instant's notice, so to speak." Mr. Marlowe touched his tiepin. "Gage? Cancel my ten o'clock." Then he rose. "Why don't we go into my private office, Harry?" He helped Harry up, took him by the arm, and steered him toward the inner door. "We can have some coffee, relax a bit, get to know one another a little better." His grip on Harry's elbow tightened the slightest bit. "And then perhaps we can answer that question of yours!"

Sal nearly dropped his cheesesteak into his fries. "They offered you *what*?"

Harry said the figure again. He took one of Sal's fries, but the smell of it, suddenly, made him queasy, so he put it back.

Sal put his cheesesteak down also. "Let me get this straight. You go into a House of Dreams—"

"The same one we passed in the mall the other day."

"Same one, whatever." Hands free, Sal could wave them for emphasis, "So you go in there, you tell them you've got something to sell, and they flat out offer you—"

"I was in there a couple of hours, actually. I spoke with a guy named Marlowe, then he took me to see this other guy, and then they both took me upstairs to meet this *other* guy...and then they made me the offer."

Sal looked at him like he was some incredible stranger all of a sudden, like he was the Man in the Moon. "So...what was it?"

"I told you, Sal, they offered me—"

"*The memory*, anus-brain! What's the memory in that knucklehead of yours that's worth so much money?"

Harry looked down at the remains of his lunch. "I had to tell it to them to get the price, but I never told anybody else, ever. It's private stuff." He looked up. "It's not about you, anyway."

"But I'm your best friend! Hell, I'm your only friend! You gotta spill!"

Harry saw Cheez-Wiz in the corner of Sal's mouth. He pointed to his own mouth. "You've got some shmootz there...."

Sal grabbed a napkin and swiped at his mouth. Harry could see he was starting to get angry. "Listen, Sal," he said, "it was something that happened a long time ago, when I was just a kid in high school. Long before I ever knew you. Like I said: private stuff. Don't get so bent about it."

"Private? It's so private you go to a memory house in a mall and try to *sell* it? Who are you trying to bullshit, Harry? Me? I can bullshit you under the table any day of the week."

Harry could see his point. Why had he gone to the memory house? Why had he really? "I didn't go there to sell it. I just... wanted to see how much it was worth."

"So they offer you an assload of money, and you say *no thanks*?" Sal leaned forward, lowering his voice, "Why, Harry? For God's sake, why?"

Because it's the only thing that's mine, Sal, Harry wanted to say. Because it's all I've got. Because I live in an airshaft studio apartment and I Hook In to a dead end government job and I need my best friend, no, my only friend, to buy me lunch every other day. He opened his mouth, but none of those words came out. Instead, he dropped his hands to the booth table in an empty shrug.

Sal pointed at him with his cheesesteak. "You, my friend, have gotta be crazy not to take that deal. With that much in the bank you could afford an outside apartment with a patio, with a *view* for chrissakes. You could get out of that Hooking government crap job and get a *real* job, you know, work with your hands or something."

Harry shook his head slowly. "I just don't want to give it up, Sal; it's—"

"I know: it's Private Stuff. You are crazy, my friend, you are friggin' certifiable. Back up the Wonder Wagon, boys, break out a Size Medium happy jacket, here's your boy." Sal took a savage bite of his cheesesteak, and Cheez-Wiz squirted.

Now Harry could see that his friend wasn't angry any more. Exasperated and frustrated, maybe, but no longer mad. He picked up another of Sal's fries and ate it this time.

2

Like most people in lower-tier government jobs, Harry worked from his apartment. He Hooked In with his pc. He never knew which federal agency would be using his brain on any given day, but he preferred Agriculture, FEMA or HHS. DOD, State and Treasury always left him with headaches.

His pc cubby was the lowest of the low-end models, third-generation owner, all he could afford. There were no automated house-service amenities, and diapers were messy, so he always made sure to pee, shit, and do a five-minute colon vac before he Hooked In. The one extravagance he allowed himself, however, was a decent drool bib. He picked a fresh one this morning, spread it out over his work tunic, and climbed onto the saddle.

The pc was already on, big black WAITING HARRY letters on a lemon yellow field. He spoke his name and steadied his eyes for the retina scan, then settled back into the head harness as the screen cleared, and the nodes tightened onto his temples and assorted bald spots. His bare feet slid easily into the stirrups as he reached for the handgrips. He knew that this would be pretty much it for the next few hours as a movie he had already seen at least ten times flickered to life on the screen and his consciousness became blurry around the edges.

Sometime later, Harry was jerked from his half-sleep by a loud snapping noise, then static hiss.

What the hell?

As he slowly came to his senses, he realized he was on the floor between the saddle and his couch. Above him, static from the cubby seemed to fill the air of his apartment to bursting.

He blinked away tears, but when he brought his hand up to wipe them, his fingers came away red. Blood? His temples were bleeding, at the points where the head harness nodes made contact. The nodes must have scratched him as he fell.

What the hell?

He got to his knees. As he did so, the pc screen showed a rolling pattern, steadied, then resolved to a uniform grey. The annoying static sound abruptly stopped. Harry slid back onto the saddle, wondering what he should do. Go to the bathroom to tend to his scratches? Just leave the saddle and the pc screen in mid-session? He couldn't remember ever having done that. Never. A drop of blood fell from his eyebrow and landed on his cheek, like a tear. Never been injured on the job either, for that matter.

What do I do? He wondered. What happens *next?*

As if in answer, the grey screen faded to the familiar L-Net logo, with a discreet: "Incoming Call, Harold Swope— Accept/Delay/Deny?" blinking benignly in its little rose-colored box.

"Accept," Harry said, and wiped the blood trickle off his forehead and cheek with his palms.

The logo faded, and resolved again in the face of a nameless

L-Net employee, her head encased in a node harness of the most modern design. No scratches for her. She looked up from something off-screen, and asked for name and pin confirmation.

Harry told her. She had blond hair cut very short, and flat, expressionless green eyes. It took him a moment to realize she was a digital image, a dupe, not a real person.

She said, "An attempt was made to compromise your neural network connection, Mr. Swope."

Harry blinked. "I was *hacked*?"

"L-Net strives to provide completely effective firewall security at all times. The intrusion attempt was foiled without compromise. Rest assured that you were not violated in any way."

Somebody had tried to get into his brain, unauthorized, without his consent? Harry wiped his eyebrow again. But no one was allowed to do that, were they? That was a crime, wasn't it? And anyway, who would want to—?

Above the green eyes of the L-Net dupe, above his cubby's top shelf, Steph's dark violet eyes looked down at him.

The dupe said, "A security report has been filed with the local security net. If you are contacted, feel free to assist them in their inquiry." The dupe paused. "Although we have assessed no neural damage, Mr. Swope, we nevertheless recommend a dispensary visit strictly as a precautionary measure. A hard disconnect is never something to neglect."

Harry refocused on the dupe. "Dispensary. Yeah." He touched his forehead, but the blood seemed to have stopped. "I'll do that, thanks."

"Very well, then. You may Hook back In at any time." The L-Net dupe smiled, then dissolved back to the logo.

Harry looked at Stephanie, then at his handgrips. If they tried it once, they probably would try it again. And next time, maybe they would get what they came for. He twisted in the saddle to look back at his head harness, its front two nodes glistening red with his blood. *Next time....*

Purely on reflex, it seemed, he was out of the saddle, out of the apartment, slamming his vomit-green door behind him, down the endless hall to the lift that dropped him thirty-seven floors to the Level Three street, to the crowds there, the endless, moving mass. He dove in, with no destination in mind, with just the thought that he had to Get Away…and the crowd took him.

As he passed a public link kiosk its light went green and a soft voice said, "Call for you, Mr. Swope," but he ignored it, and went on. At the next kiosk the light was already green, and the door was open. Harry hesitated. It was just a link kiosk, after all. No harnesses, no nodes….

He went in, and let the door close behind him. Outside, the endless crowd went by.

"Hello, Harry." Mr. Marlowe smiled out of the booth monitor.

Harry started at the voice, the face. "How did—" he stammered, "how did you get my number? I never—"

"I thought we might speak again, Harry, in a less private setting, in a more…anonymous one, if you don't mind."

"I've got nothing to say to you."

"Interest has risen considerably since we last spoke, Harry," Marlowe said. "One might say it has…*peaked*."

"I told you, I only wanted to know how much. I'm not interested in selling."

Marlowe's vast white forehead creased the slightest bit. "Perhaps I wasn't clear, Harry. Perhaps I have not indicated just how much, how very much, we desire what it is you have to sell."

"I don't have anything to sell." Harry wiped his mouth, aware that his voice was quavering. "I told you, I'm not interested in selling anyth—"

Mr. Marlowe said another figure.

Harry swallowed.

"I think, Harry," Marlowe said, looking past him to take in the crowd of Level Three citizens streaming by the booth, "that even you would have to admit, this is a very generous offer."

Harry hesitated. In his mind, the picture of Stephanie was looking down at him. He swallowed again. "No."

"*No?*"

"And I mean it." Harry reached forward. "And don't ever call me again."

"Pity. I—"

Harry slapped the pad, sticky with something blue, and the screen went blank. It was House of Dreams who hacked him. It had to be. They had done it. The thought was so completely unnerving he found he couldn't stop shaking. *In my head.* They tried to get *in my head!*

He left the kiosk, battled the crowd back to his apartment building, took the first free lift to his floor, to his vomit-green door, slammed it shut behind him, and retreated to the chair in the corner of his apartment farthest away from the cubby. He stared at the lock mechanisms on his door. Then he was out of his chair, checking the door locks; four steps to the window, testing that. He was thirty-seven floors up, and the concrete walls were sheer. Surely no one could—

He yanked on the window sash again anyway.

"I should call Sal." His voice was flat in the otherwise silent room. He actually made a move toward the cubby before he stopped himself. In order to contact anybody from here he would have to use his pc, open himself up again to invasion. No way, no way.

He went back to the chair in the corner.

An hour later, he checked his door locks again.

An hour later, he did it again; the window, too.

Five more times, overall, before exhaustion finally overcame him, and sleep.

3

They came in the night, just like in the movies. They entered his apartment through the window from above, silently, quickly, and had Harry gas-injected and bound before he could wake. The necessary equipment was wheeled in through the door while the drugs took effect. Just another dream, Harry, just another dream.

It took about five minutes, no longer than any typical snatch and grab. They had to take more than they needed, but that was expected. And anyway, what else was Editing and Post Production for?

Clean up took another five, even down to erasing the foot and wheel prints in the carpet, and then they were gone. And Harry's one thousand one hundred and fifty two cubic feet (plus that extra one hundred ninety-two) of studio apartment space filled up with darkness and silence once more.

4

If Harry Swope sat in just the right spot, the view from his new apartment showed a wonderful slice of the Delaware River and the glittering Camden waterfront. This was where he set up his potter's wheel. On a good day he could throw two or three salad bowls worth firing, and watch the river traffic to boot. Salad bowls were his specialty.

He tried to get most of his work done in the mornings, when the light was best, leaving the afternoons for appointments with clients, and the occasional lark. Like a walk along Penn's Landing, or to go look at the Bell....

He sipped his second cup of coffee of the morning, and went over to his pc to check his schedule before settling in to work at the wheel. The pc was installed in an old, ratty cubby, the only piece of furniture he had kept from his old apartment. It matched nothing else he had purchased since, either in style or price, but for some unaccountable reason it pleased him to have it around, so he had kept it.

He put his coffee cup down beside the console, but he hesitated over the pc pad, a slight frown forming two distinct wrinkles in his forehead. He had a sudden thought of something undone, something he should remember...and he dropped his hand instead to the top cubby drawer. He opened it, rummaged, and pulled out a worn white envelope. There was tape on the flap, fixing a tear. *Something about this envelope. Something....*

He looked inside, turned it upside down, and shook it. Empty. He frowned again. Why was he holding on to an old envelope?

He crumpled it up and threw it in the trash receptacle.

He touched the pc pad for his daily schedule. Lunch with Sal at that new frou-frou South Street bistro. Good; his friend could use some decent food for a change. He stared at the pc screen for a moment longer, eyes unfocused, thinking. Something, *something*.... He'd remember it eventually, he was sure. He touched the pad again, and the pc went dark.

He finished his coffee. Then he scooped a fresh lump of clay from the bin beside his wheel and settled onto the saddle.

Another salad bowl this morning? He smiled. Sure, why not.

Feeling the warm morning sun on his face, Harry wet his hands, centered the clay with practiced ease, and went to work.

Memory houses had become such a ubiquitous part of the mall landscape in the past few years that Harry Swope rarely even gave them a second thought. Not that he ever even meant to. Although he could certainly afford it, experiencing other people's memories held absolutely no appeal for him. He had no desire to partake in even a minute's worth of what those places sold. Not even a second's worth.

After all, what did he need someone else's memories for, anyway?

Dead End

The morning of May 13 dawned overcast with a damp, chilly wind. The TV and radio said the clouds would lift by noon, however, and perhaps clear completely by evening rush hour. But now, as the big hand of the clock on the Occidental Tower inched past five-thirty, the shadows were still long and deep in the dead-end alley off Anchor Street. Trapezoids of window light from the alley's twenty row house kitchens littered the cobbles. The smells of coffee, toast and bacon mingled in the close air with the sounds of silverware on plates, chairs scraping on linoleum, and the murmur of hushed, strained conversations.

Bill Jeeter put his half-empty mug on the windowsill and looked down into the alley. "I wouldn't mind a little rain," he said.

His wife Joanne found places for the previous evening's supper dishes on the drain board, clattering them louder than necessary. "I just wish it was over."

"It will be," Bill said with finality. "Soon enough."

Bill Jr. appeared at the doorway from the hall, his little chin thrust out. "How's it look, Dad?"

Bill almost smiled at his six-year-old's attempt to look tough. He extended his hand, gathering the boy to him. "Never mind how it looks, pal." He ruffled the fuzz of his son's buzzcut as he

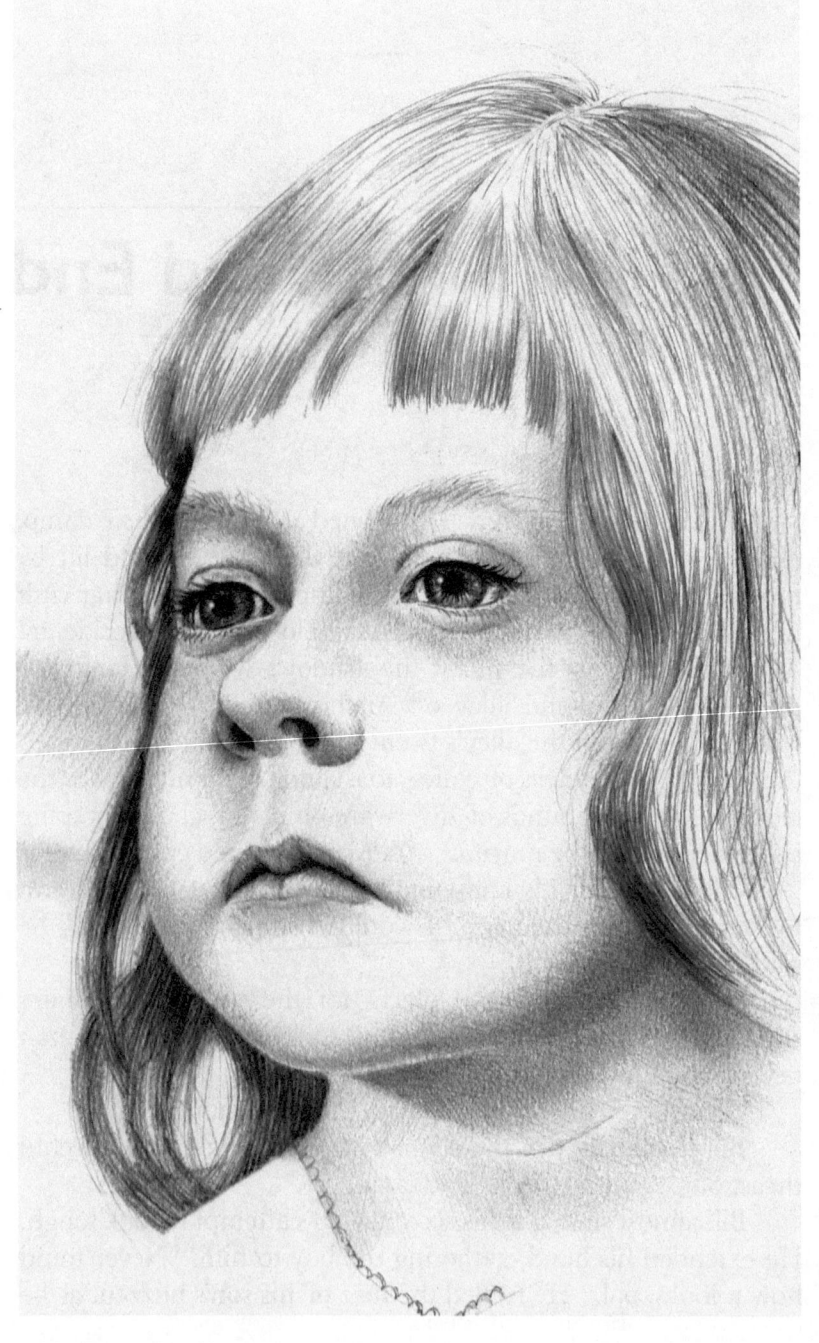

looked across the kitchen to meet his wife's strained gaze. "This isn't our business, anyway."

Bill Jr.'s voice was muffled against his father's shirt, "But Sarah Donofrey told me that—"

"Enough about Sarah Donofrey." Bill nudged the boy with his hip, letting him go. "Get out of those pjs and put some clothes on."

"Long pants," his mother said, wiping her hands on the sink towel. "It's cold out today."

The boy put his hands on his hips and rolled his eyes. "*Mom.*"

Bill feinted a grab, and his son dodged into the hall with a sudden, quick giggle.

"You're going to let him watch," Joanne said, her voice flat.

"Of course I am." Bill took up his coffee again. "We're all going to watch. That's what it's *for.*"

The clock face of the Occidental Tower was like a wide yellow moon against the grey clouds. Its hands read a quarter to six when Sam Pharris came out to conduct the final check. This was only right, since he had done most of the design and construction of the mechanism. He walked around it once, then ran it three times in quick succession. Joanne jerked involuntarily at the sound each time, and her eyes darted about the kitchen like a trapped sparrow's. "Does he have to do it so many times?"

"It has to work," Bill said. He went to the stove and poured himself another cup of coffee. He held the pot up. "There's enough for one more, I think."

His wife shook her head. "I don't think I could hold it down." She took up a position reluctantly, by the window. "We're all looking out our kitchens into this damn alley. All of us." She gestured with her chin. "There are kids hanging out of every second floor bedroom window, too."

Bill joined her. They both found themselves looking at the rear face of the Henry family row house, almost directly across the alley from their own. Bill said, "Which window is Christine

Henry's?"

"The left bedroom. The one with the yellow curtains."

"No kid hanging out of that one."

"My God, Bill." Joanne turned to look at her husband with open dismay. "This isn't funny."

"I know." He took a quick sip of his coffee. "Sorry."

Sam Pharris came out from underneath and dusted off his jeans. Then he looked about, up and down the alley, and gave a short wave. Somewhere, a window came down with a sharp report, but Sam pointedly did not turn to the sound, or acknowledge it in any way. Instead, he dusted his jeans again, and then went back into his house.

"He did a good job," Bill said. "A thing like that's not easy to build, you know?"

Joanne shook her head slowly. "This is crazy."

"Now Jo—" Bill began, but the low, guttural rumble of a truck stopped him. "That must be Danny Stankow."

The rumble raised a notch, stopped, and they both heard air brakes—like a beast exhaling—and then a slow, low beeping as Danny's garbage truck backed off Anchor Street and into the alley.

At the top of the tall brick warehouse wall that formed the alley's dead-end, a family of pigeons flapped into sudden, startled flight.

The truck's massive frame rolled back until it filled the open end of the alley, effectively closing it, sealing it off from the outside world. There was another saurian exhalation of brakes, then the truck grumbled into silence.

"That's it," Bill said, and Joanne shivered again. Then they both looked at the clock over the stove. Six o'clock.

Outside, the Occidental Tower clock slowly struck the hour.

"Time," Bill said, as the last peal faded. Joanne just closed her eyes.

Outside, three basement level doors opened at once, as though on cue, and three men stepped out, wearing work jeans and tee-shirts already sweated up. What set Brad Statler apart from the other two was his large service revolver and black leather holster slung low and loose below his rolling gut. Staring at the gun, Bill said aloud, "I could have been out there."

"Thank God you're not," Joanne rejoined decisively, almost savagely. Then she swallowed, and put her hand to her forehead. "Anyway, they had a vote." She dropped her hand and looked briefly down into the alley. "And those three lost."

Bill Jr.'s voice drifted through the kitchen window from above: "When is it gonna start?"

"Right now, pal." Bill cleared his throat. "Right now."

Brad Statler spoke, loud enough for everyone in the alley to hear. "I'm bringing him out now!"

Joanne left the window, brushed past her husband to the door, then grabbed the jamb and paused. "I've got to go," she said "I can't watch this."

"We all agreed," Bill said without turning, his voice low.

"I just can't watch, Bill," Joanne said. "That's all."

Bill looked at her, then, like she was a stranger, like she wasn't even there at all. "Sure," he said. "I understand." He turned back to the window.

Brad pushed the cuffed and shackled prisoner before him, out his basement door and into the alley. The prisoner wore grey pants, dirty white running shoes, and a faded purple tee shirt with a torn breast pocket and an ample splattering of dried blood. His hair was long and disheveled, dark brown, and oily. During his week of imprisonment in Brad's basement, it was obvious that he hadn't been given the opportunity to wash. Bill could see the gauntness of the prisoner's cheeks beneath his salt and pepper stubble and tight dark gag, proof that he hadn't been fed all that much either.

Bill took a measured sip from his mug, savoring the taste and the warmth of the coffee. Then he put the mug down.

Outside, the two other volunteers helped Brad drag the prisoner up the steps of the platform, forced him to his knees, then used a second pair of hand-cuffs to secure his cuffed wrists to the ankle shackles. The prisoner struggled greatly, but they got it snapped on the first try.

Bill saw the prisoner's neck grow rigid—tendons taut and prominent, Adam's apple working overtime—but the gag effectively muffled his screams.

Brad said something that Bill missed, and the Henry's basement door opened. Roy Henry emerged with his daughter Christine. He was a widower, and little Christine was his only child; the two of them looked very small, walking down the alley.

Christine was wearing a frilly white party dress with a pink sash, white stockings, and shiny white shoes with tiny straps and golden buckles. Her hair, a rich blonde, had been cut in bangs across her forehead. She looked like she was ready to be a flower girl at a wedding, or, short of a veil, to make her first Holy Communion.

Roy Henry led his daughter up to the platform steps, where Brad waited with one hand resting on the butt of his gun. Brad said, "She ready for this?"

"Yeah," Roy replied. "Oh yeah."

Brad knelt. "You feeling all right, little lady?"

Christine nodded, snaking one arm around her father's thigh.

Brad smiled encouragingly. "I need to take you up these steps and ask you one more time, okay?"

Christine looked up to her father and pleaded in a high, squeaking voice: "But I already told them, Daddy. Didn't I tell them enough?"

"Sure you did, honey." Roy met Brad's eye, then gently disengaged his daughter from his leg. "Go up with Mr. Statler, now, like a good girl."

"But Daddy—"

"Mind me, now, Christy. Just a few more minutes and then it will be all over. I promise."

Christine hung her head, and Bill could see that she was fighting back tears. But when she raised her head, finally, her cheeks were dry. She took Brad's hand, and the two of them slowly mounted the steps of the platform.

"Dad," Bill Jr. whispered from his bedroom window, "is she gonna—"

"Shut your mouth, William," Bill shot back, hissing just loud enough for his son to hear. "Just watch."

Brad led the little girl across the raw wood planks to where the prisoner knelt between the two volunteers. The prisoner's bloodshot-rimmed eyes blazed at them as they approached. He struggled with the spit-darkened gag, but Bill could hear only indistinguishable, muffled noise out of him, just a background to the sound of Christine's shiny white patent leather shoes stepping daintily across the green wood.

Brad knelt again. "Okay," he said. "Now. Do you recognize this man?"

Christine's eyes flickered up, briefly. "Yes," she said, in a tiny voice.

"You're sure?"

She nodded, looking down to her feet.

"Okay. Now the big question, Christine. The important one."

"He did it," she said, suddenly, loudly, looking up again. Bill could see she was angry; he could see her hands shaking.

Then she took a big step forward, and before any of the men on the platform could react, she slapped the prisoner hard across his cheek. "You're bad," she shrilled, "really really bad!"

Then Brad had her by the shoulders, pulling her back, giving her to her father, who was at the head of the stairs, and who gathered his daughter to him like she was a fragile balloon that might float out of his reach forever if he didn't hug her tightly, tightly.

Bill swallowed at the lump in his throat. This was the right thing to do. Joanne be damned. This was the right thing.

Roy and his daughter left the platform, and when they were clear of the stairs Brad signaled to the two volunteers. They went over to the scaffold, and together unhitched, then uncoiled the rope. Bill saw the noose clearly for the first time, new and tight and hard, saw Brad take it and slip it over the prisoner's head, and cinch it snugly against his neck, in just the right place to snap his neck cleanly when he dropped. At the scaffolding, the volunteers put the correct amount of slack on the rope, and secured it with the proper knot. Brad checked the cuffs and shackles one last time, then paused in front of the prisoner, and Bill was certain he was going to haul off and cold-cock the sonofabitch. But he didn't. Instead, he followed the other two volunteers down the ladder to the alley cobbles, then helped them pick up the stairs and move it clear.

Now there was only the prisoner, kneeling and noosed, alone on the platform.

Below, Brad offered the locking pin to Roy, but he shook his head. "Let Sam Pharris," Roy said. "He built it."

From his basement screen door down the alley Sam called out, "No way, Roy. Not me."

Bill yelled from his window: "Hell, I'll do it!" just as someone else yelled the same, and in seconds the entire alley was clamoring for the honor. Brad raised his arms, waved them about, tried to yell louder than everyone else, but it took nearly a minute for the noise—the alley's collective release—to taper off finally to silence.

"That was a really stupid thing to do, people," Brad said then, putting one hand on his revolver handle and the other on his hip. "Do we really need to advertise this? Huh?" He turned to the locking pin. "I guess it's me, then."

Bill watched his hand rise from the gun butt, reach out, grasp the metal loop, and then, without ceremony, pull it free.

There was a loud slap of wood striking wood as the portion of the platform under the prisoner swung down on its carriage-door hinges; he dropped; the rope took tension, jerked his body like a tangled marionette as it reached its full length, then left him hanging, spinning slowly, steaming the cobbles below with his urine, suddenly and completely dead.

Christine looked at the trussed and stinking body with wide, empty eyes. "Is he dead, Daddy?"

"Yes, honey," her father whispered roughly. "He's dead."

She nodded, turned, and took her father's hand. "Good," she said, and then looked up to him. "Can we go home now?"

Roy Henry led her away, up the alley to their basement door, opened it, and let her enter first. Then he turned. "Thank you," he said, to Brad, to the volunteers, to the entire alley. "Thank you all." Then he followed his daughter inside.

Brad and the two volunteers waited a full five minutes before they untied the rope, letting the body drop unceremoniously to the cobbles. Then they went about the business of loosening the noose from its deep groove in the purpled, already cooling flesh of the dead man's throat.

It took another five minutes to unfold the canvas tarp, roll the body up in it, and then secure it with wind after wind of duct tape. Like a cocoon, Bill thought, watching them work. Like a goddamn silver mummy.

All three of them manhandled the wrapped body to the open maw of the garbage truck, where Danny Stankow had already gotten it fired up and rumbling, waiting for its first meal of the morning.

They counted to three, then swung the body up into the hopper.

The truck cycled once, whining loudly in the narrow confines of the alley, then flowered back open, and the hopper was empty.

Now it was finally Bill's turn. He and every other man and woman handy with a screwdriver or a hammer left their homes, converged on the platform, and proceeded to take it apart, board by board, until only a pile of nail and screw-prickled lumber was left, piled against Sam Pharris's basement wall.

Somebody used a hose to wash the piss off the cobbles.

Then, with a nod from Brad, Danny Stankow put his garbage truck in gear and eased it out onto Anchor Street, leaving the alley end clear.

Bill saw his son standing in the shadows by the big white ghost of the water heater when he entered the basement. "What the hell are you doing down here?" Then, "Here," he said, holding out his hammer, "put this away for me, will you, pal?"

The boy looked at the tool with moon eyes. "Christy told us last night."

Bill frowned slightly. "Told you what?"

"She said…she said he didn't do it."

Bill's grip on the hammer tightened. "Who did she tell?"

"Me and Sarah." Bill Jr. took a short step back, further into the shadows. "Just me and Sarah, Dad."

Bill stood silently for a long moment, breathing loudly. Then, in a quiet, patient voice, he said, "She was lying to you, pal. It really happened. I know it did. I saw the proof." He dropped to a squat, and laid the hammer on the concrete floor. "It happened."

His son shook his head slowly. "I know it happened; Christy told us. But it wasn't him that did it, the guy you killed. It wasn't him. It was somebody else."

"Who? Who else?"

"I don't know. She wouldn't tell us."

"Come here." Bill held out his arms, and the boy came out of the shadows and let his father gather him in. They hugged for a long while, and Bill could feel his son trembling. "It's okay, pal," he said. "It'll be all right."

"You're the only one I told," his son whispered. "Really, Dad. Just you."

"That's good." Bill hugged him again, hard. "That's real good."

Joanne was in the kitchen when he came up the basement steps. She had a coffee mug before her, with a spoon and a tea bag in it, and water slowly coming to a boil in the teapot on the stove.

He sat down heavily, opposite her. "It's over," he said.

The teapot rumbled.

"Is it?"

Bill looked up, met his wife's eyes. And then she knew. All

along she had suspected, but now she knew.

The teapot began to whistle.

"We just have to pound some nails out of the wood," he said, "that's all."

Joanne got up, went over to the stove, and took the pot off the flame. "Oh," she said. "Of course. You just pound out some nails."

But when she turned, her cheeks were shining with new tears, and the expression in her eyes was broken beyond all repair. "What do we do after that, Bill?" she pleaded, dropping her hands uselessly to her sides. "What happens *next?*"

Up in the Boneyard

October 1985

Most mornings, when the weather wasn't too cold, and almost always by nine, he went down the street from his small walk-up apartment to the fast food restaurant on the corner for a muffin with egg and cheese, and a large coffee, black. Depending on the change in his pocket that day, he picked up the Post as well, and read by the glass window next to the sidewalk until his coffee was gone, or until it was too cold to finish.

The counter people knew him on sight, and they always gave him a smile or a friendly nod, a polite "Good morning, sir," or a "Nice day we're having, hm?" By nine o'clock, most days, the only other customers he had to deal with were old people like himself, who didn't give a tinker's damn about how they looked, and mothers with little children too young yet for school. These were sometimes a problem.

"Look at that old man, mommy!" a chubby boy of four or five exclaimed, and pointed with a finger dripping pancake syrup.

"Shush, honey," the mother whispered, careful *not* to look his way.

The little boy leaned close and imitated her whisper: "But

his face looks *funny*."

His mother put her finger to her lips and frowned elaborately. "I said *be quiet*, Jake. Just eat your pancakes."

But the little boy persisted. "His hands, too. He's got marks and lines and boo-boos all over. I think…I think he was in a fight and got hurt."

"*Jake*."

The old man turned sideways, concentrating on his newspaper.

"Yeah." The little boy nodded. "Musta been in a fight. Hey mister, were you in a fight?"

He raised his paper up, like a curtain, like a wall. The little boy was talking about his scars, of course, the ones that showed above his collar and across his face, and below his jacket cuffs, all the way to his fingertips. After seventy-odd years, they still showed plainly against his pale and wrinkled skin as vivid brown lines, razor-thin, and just as straight.

"Maybe," the little boy suddenly exclaimed, "maybe he's a pirate! Hey mister!"

Enough. His coffee was finished, anyway. The old man shook his paper out, folded it, and tucked it under his arm as he rose.

"I'm *so* sorry," the mother said to him as he passed, "but he's only four…."

A cutting breeze ruffled the end of the newspaper, but the bright sun made him squint, and was warm on his face. He pulled at his jacket cuffs, squinting even more. Little children be damned, he thought, and decided to complete his morning ritual by walking the two blocks to the park.

He passed Mr. Lupe arranging fruit outside his bodega, who smiled and waved as he approached, "Be-u-teeful morning, Mr. Spangler! Be-u-teeful day for the park."

The old man nodded, and smiled back. He paused to pick up a tangerine. "Are these new today, Mr. Lupe?"

"Just in!" The grocer waved him on. "Go, take it, eat it while you watch the boats in the harbor, then come back here and buy a bagful!"

The old man lifted the tangerine in thanks, then crossed the street and went carefully up the stone steps into the park. It was an old city park, with large gnarly beeches, and wandering, rumpled concrete walks. The park followed the edge of one of southern Brooklyn's many low bluffs, and most of the benches had a grand view over endless rows of brownstone tenement roofs that made up the old neighborhoods below. The Verrazano Narrows beyond was a shining blue arc to the Atlantic, framed by the immense suspension bridge to Staten Island that carried its name.

His favorite bench was empty, in full, warm sunlight, and he slid onto it gratefully. He looked to the two blue-grey arches of the Verrazano Bridge, wondering yet again how high they were, and deciding, again, that he should look it up in the library. Surely they were higher than two hundred and fifty feet. His gaze wandered across the borough skyline, such as it was, the tenements, apartment houses, water towers, warehouses and scattering of low office buildings. Nothing as high, nothing high enough, *there*....

He remembered his very first visit to the Woolworth Building after his release from the hospital in the Spring of 1914, avoiding the shiny mahogany and brass elevators, taking the stairs instead, one floor at a time, all the way to the top. My God, he thought, the courage that had taken! And then the Empire State when it opened a decade and a half later, one of a vast crowd of people that first day, again, avoiding the elevators so he could linger on every floor, from the twentieth to the thirtieth stories...but there had been nothing there, in either building.

They had not been there.

He had tried other tall buildings through the years, wherever in the city they sprang up, all with equal failure. No, it had to be *here*, in the southwest neighborhoods of Brooklyn, where the Cow Meadow had once been, *here*, above the tangled and dirty streets now laid out before him....

Then his eyes suddenly darted. Movement, in the jumble of

tenements near the Fort Hamilton recruiting center, just east of the Belt Parkway, something rising...a crane boom, a construction crane, a big one he had not seen before, its spidery tower camouflaged against the hills and suburbs of Staten Island beyond. He counted the streets as anxiousness rose like a bloody bubble from his stomach to his throat. It was there, the exact spot, where this crane now raised its spidery finger, higher and higher, *there*...the site of the old Cow Meadow....

It took him almost a half hour, walking a block, resting, and then walking a few more, to reach the neighborhood of the crane. More than once he stopped, more out of defiance than fear, to turn around and go back to the safety, silence and sanity of his apartment. Oh, the bones in his body ached so!

So what? He argued with himself. So what that they were finally building a new building, and that they were building it *there*. So what? It would probably mean nothing. It would probably mean nothing at all. It probably wouldn't even be *high* enough.

But in the end, even though his joints pulsed with pain, he managed the entire distance from the park on the bluff to the construction site, and he stood across the street from it, using a light pole for support, and slowly regained his breath.

The site was a full city block square, surrounded by a garishly painted plywood sheet wall. The only thing inside that was visible was the yellow and blue crane that soared overhead, its boom swinging slowly against the glare of the morning sky.

The old man dared his legs to move, to take him in for a closer look. Left to themselves, they would have jerked him, danced him away from this place, back up to the safety and sanity of his quiet neighborhood, to the bag of tangerines waiting for him at Mr. Lupe's bodega. But he crossed the street instead and went to the wall, to one of the peephole slots cut into it, and looked through.

On the other side was a vast excavation, even larger than he had feared, filled with shouting men and rumbling construction vehicles and huge, jutting concrete pilings rooted down through the sand and gravel to the bedrock below....

"That's gonna be a big one, all right."

The old man started, then turned. A stout, middle-aged woman in a loud, cheaply cut coat and faded paisley scarf turned from her own peephole and winked at him. "Another thirty story steel and glass refrigerator." She shook her head in disgust. "This is *Brooklyn*, for chrissakes. Since when do we want to look like *Manhattan*, eh?" She looked to the old man for moral support, but he was already speaking. "Thirty?" He was unable to mask the underlying tremble in his voice. "Did you say *thirty* stories?"

The woman jerked a calloused thumb in the general direction of 14th Avenue. "The big sign at the other corner, hotshot, says it's gonna be a thirty, THREE-OH, story condo, with million dollar views of the Narrows and the Bridge." She grunted. "Fat chance you or I will ever have seeing the inside of it when it's done, either. You can bet your cardiac arrest on *that* one, pops."

The old man touched his fingers to his lips. Thirty stories was more than two hundred and fifty feet, wasn't it?

"I remember," the woman continued, "my dad told me this part of town used to be just one big weedy lot, all the way down to the water. Used to have circuses here my dad said. Circuses. Used to call it the Cow Meadow, can you believe that? Cows and circuses in Brooklyn?"

But the old man was no longer listening. Instead, he was looking up, at the crane in the sky over the building site. "Oh my God," he whispered, as the sudden, certain reality of it sank in. The bones within him began aching anew, and he knew why. "Finally," he whispered. "*Finally*...."

May 1913

For a penny a person was led by one of the ground crew through the tall grass of the Cow Meadow to the aeroplane perched like a huge wood and cloth beast in the middle of the open area beyond the carnival tents. No one was allowed near enough to touch the flying machine, of course, but the sight alone of such an exotic device, so close up, was well worth the copper.

An extra penny bought an introduction and handshake with the young aeronaut himself. He was Anthony Spangler, twenty-two years old, tall and spare, with dark eyes and even darker hair. His wide, friendly smile was set in an open, unlined face, and he smelled of castor oil, leather, and healthy sweat. More than one young lady swore they almost fainted, putting their laced and gloved hand in his, warmed by that smile.

"How high will it go, Mr. Spangler?" a brazen voice asked from the crowd.

"High enough to dance with the clouds," the young aeronaut replied at once, grinning.

"Now that," the reporter from the Sun said, "is a quote!" He scribbled for a moment in his notebook, and then regained Spangler's attention. "How long will take you," and he drew a circle in the air with his pencil, "to fly to the Bridge and back in that aeroplane of yours?"

"I only have fuel enough for about twenty minutes," Spangler said, pulling a white linen towel from his jacket and wiping his hands. "I guess I'd better make it back by then, eh?"

"You sound very sure of yourself, sir," the reporter continued, squinting his eyes and pointing his pencil shrewdly. "How much do they pay you to put your life in the hands of a machine like that?"

The aeronaut laughed. "I'm not doing this for the money, sir!"

"For what, then, Mr. Spangler? If not for the money, then for what?"

"Ahh!" Spangler's grin was electric. He leaned close to the reporter. "Have you ever flown in an aeroplane, sir?"

"Not hardly! I get giddy enough on the Broadway train."

"Well let me tell you," and Spangler motioned the reporter

even closer, close enough to growl roughly in his ear, "it's even better than *sex*."

The reporter blushed, just as the chief of Spangler's ground crew interrupted, "We won't have this weather for long, boss." He pointed to the clouds building up in the southwest over Staten Island.

"You're right, Bill." The young aeronaut reached out suddenly and shook the reporter's hand. "For free," he said. "Wish me luck."

"Of course, sir," the reporter said, still blushing. "Luck...."

The aeroplane bounced twice as it raced down the field, then leaped into the air with a roar, all but drowning out the cheers of the crowd as it banked and circled low over the carnival tents.

"He'll need more height to get over the Bridge," the reporter yelled into the ear of the ground crew chief, gesturing to the gothic towers and spider web cables of the Brooklyn Span up the East River.

The chief shook his head. "He's not going to fly over it," he yelled back, "he's going to fly *under* it, like Mr. Lincoln Beachey did. You watch."

They all did, hundreds of faces lifted up, following the slow, stately flight of the fragile biplane as it climbed over the streets and farms of Brooklyn.

The mass of clouds shrouding Staten Island moved across the Narrows more quickly than anyone could have guessed. The aeroplane skirted the edge of them as it circled up, one hundred feet, one hundred fifty, two hundred....

Then the cloudbank engulfed the machine, and the sound of the motor took on a different, almost querulous note. The crowd waited expectantly for the plane to emerge, but the sound of the motor grew faint, tenuous....

Someone cried out, after a moment, "He made a wrong turn!"

"He's headed for Jersey!" yelled another.

The drone of the motor dwindled to nothing.

Moments became a minute.

The crowd was transfixed, then began murmuring.

One minute edged toward two. The reporter sought out the crew chief. "What is happening here?"

Then, abruptly, the aeroplane dropped out of the clouds, silent, gliding down in a tight, dangerous spiral with its motor off. Several people screamed as the crowd surged forward, following the police, the carneys and Spangler's ground crew, all to be near the spot where the machine would surely crash.

They found it in the tidal mud at the edge of the Cow Meadow, a crumpled wreckage of torn linen, looping piano wire and splintered spruce.

The police and carneys kept the spectators at bay as the ground crew threw pieces of the aeroplane aside to pull Spangler clear.

"He's alive!" one of them called out, and a collective sigh ran through the crowd.

Spangler was laid on a blanket spread over the mud to wait for the hospital wagon.

Panting, wiping his forehead with his handkerchief, the reporter found and accosted the crew chief standing over the unconscious aeronaut. "How is he?"

"He's cut up bad, but nothing's broken, I think."

The reporter gestured to the wreckage. "Will it burn? Will it explode?"

The grim-faced man shook his head. "The magneto's off; the fuel tank isn't ruptured; everything's cold; it's safe enough."

The reporter looked from the crash to the crowd of men around the fallen aeronaut. "But what happened? Why was the motor off when he came out of the clouds?" He grabbed the other man's sleeve. "Why did he crash?"

The chief glanced over his shoulder to the aeroplane, then cleared his throat. "There was something in the motor; clogged it; shut it down."

"What do you mean? A broken part? A bird? Did he fly into

a flock of birds, perhaps?"

The chief hesitated. "You're going to put this in that damn paper of yours, aren't you? Anything I say?"

The reporter looked up from his scribbling, pencil poised.

The chief cussed under his breath. "The motor." He gestured behind him, then lowered his voice. "The damn motor's full of bones. Little white bones."

"Bones? So it was birds, then."

The chief shook his head again, violently, this time. "No blood, no feathers, no nothing...*just bones*." He raised his hands, and they were shaking noticeably. "That's all I'm saying." Then he turned away, and went to kneel in the mud by the aeronaut.

The reporter stepped awkwardly through the muck to the craft; the police knew him, and let him pass. He crouched by the hot, oily metal of the motor, pushed a flapping remnant of shellacked linen aside, a piece of splintered strut....

And he saw the bones for himself, just as the ground crew chief had described. Tiny, delicate, pristine in their whiteness, lodged in every slot, every hole, every crevice of the steaming motor.

The clanging of the hospital wagon interrupted his inspection then, and he was hustled out of the way of the horse team. He stayed close enough, however, to see Spangler open his eyes in his bloody face when they lifted him into the wagon; he opened them wildly, like a madman, and everyone in the Cow Meadow heard him scream. *Shrieked*, the reporter wrote in his notebook, *shrieked because he had flown straight into the mouth of hell, shrieked because he was now awake, because he now realized it had been no dream, but a nightmare made real....*

In the umber shadows of a private hospital room that reeked of Witch Hazel, sheet starch and urine, the broken young man in the high, rumpled bed said, "I read what you wrote in that paper of yours." He gestured to a pile of newsprint on the chair beside him. "I never said those things."

At the end of the bed, his hands resting lightly on the

chipped enamel rail, the reporter shrugged. "I thought you came off rather well, Mr. Spangler." He noted the extensive stitching on the young man's face and arms, the oddly straight and regular wounds. "Reaction has been almost entirely positive in your favor."

The young man in the bed was stonily silent.

"You're a hero, Mr. Spangler," the reporter continued, stepping around the bed to stand beside it. My God, he was cut up *every*where. "Even better," he said, "you're a *tragic* hero."

"My tragedy sells your newspapers."

"And builds reputations, sir."

Spangler shifted under the stiff, wrinkled sheet, and a quiet groan escaped him. "Lies sell your papers."

"But what's the lie here? I saw the bones for myself. They clogged your engine and caused your flying machine to crash. Do you deny that?"

Spangler stared at a sliver of light beside the brown window shade. "They stopped the engine," he said, almost whispering, "but they didn't cause me to crash. I could have flown my machine with the motor off; I could have glided it down safely."

"Then why didn't you? Why did you choose to crash?"

Spangler turned from the light. The stitched wounds made him look like a crudely constructed cloth doll. Lord, the reporter thought, he must have a thousand stitches or more, the poor wretch! But what he saw flash in the aeronaut's eyes was what made him shiver, was what made him want to take a sudden step back. "Because," Spangler said, "there was one part of your article that was true."

"What part was that?"

The aeronaut hesitated. "The part about...hell. The part about gazing into the mouth of hell." He raised his head from the pillow, his eyes bright with fever, pleading, almost. "I... *interrupted* them. They...*noticed* me." He strained against the pain, and the contours of his neck stood out in trembling cords. "They looked up from their work, from their evil, secret plans, and they *saw* me...the hatred in their faces, the *madness*...." His head fell back, and he closed his eyes with a silent shudder. "You were right, Mr. Reporter: I gazed into the mouth of hell up there, in that cloud, and it...took away a part of me that I'm not sure I will ever get back." He gathered up the sheet in his clenched fists, shaking, shaking (more wounds, there, on each hand, more stitches), then dropped his head back to the pillow, and looked away. "Until I can return there," he whispered, "I will never get that part of me back."

"But who are these people, these people with so much hatred? How can they be up there, in the sky? What did you really *see* up there?"

Spangler brought his shaking hands up to cover his face.

The reporter pulled something small and white from his waistcoat pocket and held it up. "The bones, then, Mr. Spangler, what do they mean?"

Spangler slowly dropped his hands, focused on the thin, curved bone the reporter held between his fingers, and his already pale face drained of all remaining color. "Where did you get that?" he hissed.

"It was wedged into the engine of your flying machine. There were hundreds of these——"

"*Dear God*," Spangler suddenly cried out, bringing his hands up to hide his face again, "dear God in Heaven get it away from me! Get it OUT!"

The nurse in the hall came around the doorjamb. "That's enough for now," she said flatly.

The reporter turned to her in annoyance, but checked himself when he saw in her expression that she was more than ready to match him.

"At least I'm a sympathetic ear, Mr. Spangler," he said, turning back. "They won't all be, you know."

"Visiting hours end at four o'clock sharp," the nurse said formidably. "It is now four-oh-two."

The reporter reached for his watch fob, but then thought better of it. Instead, he pocketed the bone. "I wouldn't dare to disagree, madam," he said then, and placed his bowler firmly, if not rakishly, on his well-oiled head. "Not for a moment. Not for the *moon*."

The circus, minus its air show, finally packed up and took the rails to Philadelphia. And Anthony Spangler, the next Lincoln Beachey, the next Glenn Curtiss, the next Captain of the Clouds, was never heard from again.

Until 1986, when he made the newspapers one last time.

But for a very different reason.

October 1986

The condominium high-rise had already been finished for a few weeks before the old man named Anthony Spangler summoned enough courage to finally visit it, and to actually go inside.

To go *up*.

To go *back*.

He knew he had to; he had known since that first day a year ago, sitting in the park with his tangerine, when he had discovered it was being built; and then, when he had visited the construction site, when he found out how *high* it would be. And he knew *they* were waiting for him. *They* had always had been there, in the air above that part of Brooklyn, waiting for him, so patient in the hot, acid darkness, whispering their evil secrets, drawing their wicked plans, waiting for him to return. It had only been a matter of time, after all....

Come back, Mr. Spangler, they whispered, *you have something of ours...and we have something of yours, too....*

From the park, throughout the Spring and Summer, he had watched the building go up, a brown steel skeleton slowly skinned over in brick and glass, growing inexorably above the rows of tenements and brownstones that separated *it* from *him*. Slowly, steadily, into the autumn, the building rose to fill the empty air.

On the bureau in the bedroom of his second floor walk-up, neatly arranged, were the newspaper clippings he had collected over those long months, mostly from the Post, because they lived off that sort of thing. *Construction Worker Takes Fatal Leap*, was one, *High Rise Mishap Results in Near Death*, another, and a third, most telling: *Oh Dem Bones, Dem Bones*....

The construction company, according to this last article, had been finding bones, little ones, always picked clean and bleached white, on the floors of the uncompleted upper stories, most on the twenty-eighth floor, but, tellingly for Spangler, none below. Some of the workers on these highest floors had even found the little bones in their lunch boxes, and the contents, the sandwiches and packaged snacks, oddly disturbed. Rats, bats, stray hawks or owls littering with the debris of their kills... *something* had been depositing the bones up there. Beyond that, even the Post had not dared to speculate. Just odd; very odd.

Beside the clippings on the bureau were a wooden crucifix, a vial of blessed water, and a silver-bladed knife with a carved ash handle. He had no way of knowing if any of them would help, or what real purpose they might serve; there had been no one to ask, no book in the library to read, nothing to research.

Every day, during the past year, every day after the day he *knew*, he had felt his body begin to fail him. Sometimes it was just his joints aching, and a few aspirin and a nap had been enough to deal with it. Other times, though, his limbs and fingers actually throbbed with pain. Those times, aspirin and sleep had not been enough, and he had been forced to drink himself into a stupor to dull all feeling. Today, this final day, his legs shook, his feet tapped the floor, his fingers danced, all on their own, his entire body seemed to do a rock-and-roll boogie to some mad, macabre beat. But it did not stop him; it only made his resolve that much more certain. I have to do this, he said to himself. I can't live this way any longer. I have to do this. I have to. Spangler shifted his gaze from the bureau to the bedroom window. It was a good day, warm and clear. A good day to—

He nodded his head. Today. It had to be today. If he waited

any longer, he might never summon the nerve, the courage....

He struggled into his best suit and tie, and, after several attempts with fingers that rebelled at tying the knots, a pair of shiny new black oxfords. He placed the crucifix, vial and knife into a soft nylon satchel. Standing before his bureau mirror, he saw a very old man in an ill-fitting suit, but a man with no outward fear, a man with sober resolution, resignation, almost; a man with a singular, inexorable purpose. Somehow, he knew he was ready, ready in every possible way, to finally face *them*. Somehow, he knew he could do it.

Finally, after seventy-two years.

The entrance to the building was set back from the street behind a line of newly potted trees. Beyond the taped, spindly trunks he found a soaring wall of black glass punctuated by a revolving door and two flanking swing doors with brushed aluminum bars that said PUSH in subtle, polished letters. He hesitated before the revolving door, then chose the swing door on the right, and pushed. A gentle breeze of sweet, conditioned air washed over him as he entered. A uniformed security guard stood behind a podium immediately to his left. He appraised Spangler's clothes and satchel in one sweeping look, then nodded, "Good afternoon, sir."

Spangler said, "I want to look at one of the units."

"Certainly, sir." The guard gestured across the lobby to a woman behind a desk. "Right over there."

Spangler made his way across the wide sea of green print carpet to the young woman in the smart suit dress seated behind the mahogany desk. UNITS STILL AVAILABLE! announced a placard beside her; the letters of the sign were the same shade of red as her lipstick and long, manicured fingernails. She smiled brilliantly. "Good afternoon, sir!"

"I would like to see a unit," he said, holding his satchel up in both hands, tight against his chest. "Please."

She nodded briskly. "Of course! How many bedrooms were you interested in? We have a furnished two-bedroom sample on the second floor—"

"I need to see something on the twenty-eighth floor, miss."

Her perfectly smooth cheeks creased for the briefest moment in a pretty frown. "I'm afraid we have no samples that high, sir. I can assure you, however, the ones we have on the second floor have exactly the same layouts and amenities—"

"I'm sure they do, miss. But I need to see one on the twenty-eighth floor."

Her frown deepened, then suddenly cleared. "For the views, you mean?"

He nodded. "Yes. Exactly. For the views."

"Well, in that case…." She consulted a binder, flipping pages, then running her finger down one of them. "There are actually several vacancies on that floor. Just give me a minute." She pressed several keys on a small keyboard before her, then ran a plastic card through a swipe slot in a small device beside the keyboard, and offered the card to him, "Number 2803? Faces east, with a wonderful view of Sheepshead Bay and the Rockaways."

He took the card. She saw his hesitation. "That's the key card to the elevator, and to the unit itself. There is a slot beside the doors." She touched a scarlet fingernail to the card. "See? When you put it in the slot, this arrow has to face up."

"Like a money machine at the bank?"

"Exactly! Now, please remember, 2803 is unfurnished. All appliances are unplugged. Just bare white walls."

"I understand."

"Give me a few minutes here to secure the system, and I will meet you in the apartment."

"Meet me—?"

"Of course! I wouldn't have you inspecting a unit all by yourself!" She smiled again. "And on our way back down, we can look at one of the furnished samples if you like."

"Yes. Thank you." He looked at the card dubiously.

She smiled again. "Slot beside the elevator door. Just push it in, and the doors will open. Give me five minutes here…."

The elevator doors closed slowly, silently, on the building representative's smile and wave from across the lobby. Five minutes. Would that be enough? He closed his eyes for a moment, then pushed the button for the twenty-eighth floor. He didn't feel the car as it rose, but a glowing red number display told him he was going up: 10…20…23…27…then a soft *ping*, and the doors whispered open.

Before him, against the wall, a brass bowl held a spray of expensive, artificial flowers on a narrow table; above, a forgettable Impressionist print of a French coastline leaned out in a gilded frame. The hallway began on the right. He took in a deep breath…and stepped out of the elevator car, into the hallway.

Nothing.

No sound except his shoes on the carpet, his breath through his nostrils.

At the far end of the hall, a translucent window let in a rectangle of muted daylight. There were six doors. He went to the third one, 2803. There was a slot device exactly like the one he had used to open the elevator doors, just as the young woman had said. He went past the door, however, all the way to the end, to the window. There, bathed in the diffused light, he stopped, turned, and looked back the way he had come.

Nothing.

No one home.

The only sound was the hammering of his heart in his chest, his temples, and behind his eyes. The only feeling: the pounding pain of his bones that had been ceaseless ever since he stepped inside the building. Calm down, he told himself. You still have time. You must be ready….

He went back to the third door, turned the card so that its arrow faced up and in, and inserted it. The door lock made an audible *click*. He pushed, and the door opened easily, swinging in to the left. He entered the empty apartment, stepping first on blond parquet, then soft grey carpet as he moved into the long, high-ceilinged living room, A narrow, chrome appointed kitchen glittered beyond a butcher-block island bar on the right, but he was drawn to the other side of the living room by the view of Long Island through the balcony doors. He saw street after street of Brooklyn marching off into the haze that was Queens, with the green of Nassau just a smudge on the horizon.

He went to the glass doors and put a hand up to a handle, but stopped short as a sudden shock of pain pulsed through his head. It felt like his skull had suddenly contracted, squeezing his brain. He stood there with his eyes tightly closed, hand still on the door handle, until the pain eased.

He went over to the butcher-block counter, opened the satchel, and fumbled out the silver knife, the vial of holy water, and the crucifix. His hand hovered over each of them for a moment, then he took the vial up, uncapped it, and returned to the balcony doors. He put a thumb loosely over the vial's mouth and shook it out, sending a few drops of the blessed water splattering against the glass.

Nothing.

He tossed more water against the glass, enough to send it dribbling all the way to the floor.

Nothing happened. Just like the Woolworth Building, the Empire State, the Twin Towers, just like all the other tall buildings he had tried through the years. Nothing.

No one home. Not even here.

Maybe I dreamed it.

There, the thought that had plagued him for so many years. It had been 1913, after all, over seventy-two years ago. Maybe he had dreamed it, and over the years had just embellished a particularly hideous nightmare. Maybe....

"No!"

The scars on his body were real. The memory of what had caused them was real too. *This*, was real.

He only had moments, now, before the building representative joined him. He moved his thumb from the bottle's mouth and flung his arm out, splashing most of the holy water against the glass. He shouted, "Do you feel that? Do you hear me, calling you?" He reared up and threw the vial to the floor, where it bounced harmlessly off the soft carpet. "Where are you? WHERE ARE YOU?"

Nothing.

No sound.

No movement.

No one home.

Inside his body, he felt his bones screaming.

You're crazy. You dreamed it. You made it up.

You're just a crazy old man....

But his bones... *His bones....*

He whirled about, went back to the butcher-block, grabbed for the silver knife—

Something bounced on the carpet behind him, bounced and rolled, and came up against he sole of his shoe. He looked down, saw it there, pristine and white against the black leather.

A bone.

A small, impossibly white bone.

He turned, looked up, across the room to the balcony doors.

But they were no longer doors.

His feet jerked then, all by themselves. He cried out, suddenly aware that his body was moving itself, and that he no longer had any strength to stop it. He realized that it was his bones pushing him forward, his bones controlling his movement, finally...his bones, moving with a power all their own, dragging their shroud of flesh across the carpet, to the gaping maw of hot, acid night that now yawned beyond the balcony, to the same endless, irresistible darkness he had flown into so many years ago, now grabbing at him, hooking him, tearing at him....

"YES!" He screamed. "Take them back! Get them OUT of me! You BASTARDS! TAKE THEM *OUT OF ME!*"

Like an unfurling flower, then: his flesh opened up, ripped along every single scar that he had carried on his person since 1913. Like blood-stained worms wriggling free from damp earth, his bones danced forth, all of them, femur, rib and knucklebone alike...and skull too, shedding its old, tattered wrappings, and shitting its contents, reaching, gaping, *biting*....

A few minutes later, the door lock clicked, and the building representative entered the apartment. "So, sir," she began, "how do you—" but then she saw what was on the carpet before her, and splattered, *flung* on the walls, ceiling, windows and balcony doors...and she began screaming, *shrieking*....

Although the main carcass locations and fluid splatter patterns were large, Detective Hendrix, the Primary, was able to lay the plastic tarp back over the majority of the victim's remains. He stood there, studying the gentle humps and folds of the tarp, then, swishing softly in his tissue booties, walked the kraft paper path the CSU crew had put down to the relative cleanliness behind the kitchen island. Goldberg, the Assistant Medical Examiner, was leaning against the butcher block, making notes on his clipboard. He looked up as Hendrix approached, and gave the detective a wan smile. "Twenty-three years on the job, John," he said, "and I never worked a scene like this."

"I know, I know." One more time, Hendrix took in the blood and tattered viscera pieces still clinging to the living room walls and ceiling, his gaze coming to rest, finally, on the rumpled tarp before the balcony doors. Then he looked beyond the doors, to what lay outside. "This is just fucking *crazy*."

"Lafferty and the rest of the CSU weren't too talkative. How soon was the vic discovered?"

"I have witnesses who got *rained* on, Irv, twenty-eight stories down."

Goldberg grunted. "That must have been pleasant."

"The building rep says the vic came to look over an empty apartment. He took the elevator up alone. She followed in five minutes, she says, eight minutes tops...and she found this."

"*Eight minutes?*" The Assistant M.E. put his clipboard down, shaking his head in John disbelief. "No way, John, no frigging way. Do you know how long this must have taken to do? Full disembowelment, complete evisceration, every single bone, every single one—"

"It was driving the CSU guys nuts—"

"This would have taken me *hours*, and I know what the hell I'm doing."

Hendrix cursed softly. "And the perp left nothing behind, in here, in the hall, the elevators. It's like he just jumped up on the balcony rail, spread his wings, and flew away." He nodded toward the balcony. "At least he left us those."

Goldberg looked up from his notes again. "That's another thing."

"What do you mean?"

Goldberg pushed off the butcher block. "Follow me."

As they crossed the room to the balcony doors, side-stepping the tarp, Hendrix said, "I know, they're completely clean, like they've been steamed and bleached—"

"There's that, sure. Bones are pretty messy, pretty bloody, when you rip them out of a fresh carcass."

"And the perp arranged them in a circular pile, like a tee-pee. Like he's a fucking Boy Scout or something."

Goldberg nodded. "There's that, too."

They reached the doors. Outside, on the balcony, they looked out at the bones, all perfectly white, perfectly arranged, with the skull perched neatly on top. Hendrix said, "I know: in five minutes he kills this old guy, debones him, steam-cleans the skeleton, then sets the bones out there like a tinker-toy set. Makes no fucking sense whatever."

Goldberg hesitated. "Just how old was this guy, John? I heard late seventies, maybe even eighties."

The detective frowned. "The building rep said he had to have been that old, easy. Maybe even older."

"Well then, that's the thing."

"What's the thing? What are you trying to tell me, Irv?"

"Those bones out there," Goldberg pointed, "they're from a twenty-year old. Twenty-five, tops."

"Bullshit! How can you—?"

"Lots of ways. Calcification at the joint ends, condition and wear of the teeth...." The Assistant M.E. shrugged. "There's lots of ways."

The detective looked out at the pile of bones, so neatly, so carefully arranged; the skull on top, with its bright young teeth, seemed to leer at him. "Then who the hell's bones are *those?*"

In the Stacks

There were two hundred and thirty-seven concrete sidewalk squares from the top step of the Poplar Avenue subway to the bottom step of the Chestnut Street Library. David counted them every day, twice, going to work and going home. Twenty-three of the concrete squares had a crack, edge to edge. Seventeen squares had two such cracks, and ten of the squares had three.

Today, Wednesday, the twenty-seventh day of the month, David stopped before a sidewalk square that only yesterday had had two cracks. Today there was a third crack, brand new, a small one at the northwest corner, connecting the west edge with the north edge. Today, therefore, there were now *sixteen* sidewalk squares with two cracks, and *eleven* squares with three. No problemo, David thought. Things changed; he knew that.

He continued on his way.

The Chestnut Street Library had fifteen stone steps leading up to two heavy bronze doors. The employee entrance in the alley had one step and one door. The Library opened for business at nine o'clock. Mrs. Cooper, the Head Librarian, expected her employees to arrive at least fifteen minutes before the doors officially opened, but because of the subway schedule, David could never arrive before 8:50. Today, perhaps because he had stopped to look at the fourteenth sidewalk square out of seventeen with *two* cracks that was now the ninth square out of eleven with *three*, the time-clock printed '8:58' on his card when he punched in.

"Cutting it close today, Davie," said Mrs. Cooper, peering over her tortoise shell glasses, stirring her cup of coffee. "You're officially late after nine, you know. That's the rule."

David almost said, 'There was a new crack,' but he knew to keep that to himself. 'And please don't call me Davie. My name is David.' He wanted to say that, too. He did not like being called 'Davie' because it made him sound like a child. He was nineteen years, three months, and four days old today, and that was certainly not the age of a child. So he punished Mrs. Cooper by answering with just two words: "I'm sorry," he said.

"Can't abide lateness, now," Mrs. Cooper said. "Not even from the likes of you, Davie-My-Boy."

'No problemo,' David almost said, but instead he replaced his time card in the slot with his name: DAVID BROWN printed over it, and went to the coat rack to hang up his jacket. No problemo, Pedro.

Library patrons were never allowed in the stacks. It was another library rule. Patrons had a procedure to follow when they wanted a book. When they found what they wanted in the Card Catalog or on one of the computer terminals, they wrote the name of the book on a Book Retrieval Card. There were spaces for up to eight books on a card. There were also spaces for the patrons to put their own name, and their seat number. Every seat had a number on a small metal plate nailed to the backrest.

Completed Book Retrieval Cards were put in an open wood box near the doorway to the stacks. Book runners took the cards, found the books in the stacks, and delivered them to the proper patrons according to their seat numbers.

David was a book runner, and he was a good one. There were ten thousand six hundred and eighty-three books available for viewing and lending in the stacks of the Chestnut Street Library, and David knew the location of every single one of them. If a book was on a shelf in the stacks, then it was in his head, too, as clear as his name, his age, how many sidewalk squares had two cracks, and how many had three. This was why he was good at his job. This was why he made enough money to pay his room rent, and have dinner at the Pine Street Diner every night, and see a movie at the Rialto every Saturday afternoon. This week the Wednesday Diner Special was meatloaf. And this week, also on Wednesday, the movie changed. A Buddy Comedy Caper with Strong Language and Sexual Situations was leaving, and a Military Thriller with Strong Language, Violence and Brief Nudity was taking its place.

"Hello stranger," Maggie said, passing him.

David turned. Maggie was a book runner too. She waved a small stack of Book Retrieval Cards over her shoulder. "Don't sweat it, Dave," she said, "I've got the first batch."

Dave was an okay name. David didn't mind it. Coming from Maggie, it sounded almost as grown up as 'David.' He liked Maggie, and he knew she liked him, too.

Outside, in the Reading Room, he found only one Book Retrieval Card in the open box. He took it out and read it carefully. There was one book requested: 'The Mound Builders of Ancient America' by Robert Silverberg. David blinked. New York Graphic Society Limited, Copyright 1968, Library of Congress Catalogue Card Number 68-12370. In the Chestnut Street Library, the Card Catalogue Number was 68-1788. Aisle 12, Row Three, Shelf Two, thirteenth slot from the left. David looked out across the sea of reading tables and the scattering of patrons. The seat number on the card was 57, and an elderly man wearing a fedora-style grey hat was sitting in Seat 57, looking right at him. He was tapping his fingers on an open page of a spiral-bound notebook. He looked like he was In A Hurry. Most patrons were In A Hurry. David turned, card in hand, and went into the stacks.

He heard Maggie several aisles over, whistling quietly as she pulled books. Whistling was not allowed in the Library, not even in the stacks, but Maggie did it anyway. She was a college student, drove a little green car, and her dark brown hair had too many curls for David to count accurately. And she wasn't afraid of Mrs. Cooper.

The aisle, stack and shelf location of 'The Mound Builders of Ancient America' by Robert Silverberg remained clear in David's mind as he went deeper into the stacks, verifying what he already knew, down the last aisle, up the stack, along the shelf, reaching with his left hand....

But it was not there.

David stared.

'The Mound Builders of Ancient America' was not in the thirteenth slot. In its place was a book David had never seen before. It was thick, tall, with a pale blue cloth binding. The printing on the spine was faded, hinting of gold leaf. David bent close to read the title, but the alphabet was unfamiliar, the words indecipherable. Someone must have put a book from the foreign language section here by mistake.

He pulled the book off the shelf and opened it. It smelled musty and old. He turned the pages to the light. The same strange alphabet filled them. He couldn't read any of it. He turned to the rear end leaf to read the envelope and return card. Those would be in English. But the end leaf was blank. There was no envelope, and no return card. He snapped the book shut, startling at the sound, and put it back on the shelf so quickly he nearly knocked one of the books next to it back into the adjoining shelf.

He heard Maggie in the next aisle. "Maggie!" He nearly yelled, and the tremor in his voice was clear. She came around to his aisle with wide eyes and a finger over her lips. Then she saw his expression. "What's up, Dave? What's wrong?"

He showed her the Book Retrieval Card. "It's not there," he said. His voice still trembled. "There's another book there instead."

She frowned, reached past him, pulled a book, and handed

it to him. "You mean this one?"

David looked down at it. It was 'The Mound Builders of Ancient America' by Robert Silverberg, New York Graphic Society Limited, copyright 1968. He looked down to the shelf. There was only one empty slot, the thirteenth slot. The blue book printed in the strange alphabet was gone.

"Hey, Dave," Maggie nearly touched his shoulder, "Are you okay?"

David nodded jerkily. He put the book under his arm and held it tight. "Yes," he said. "I'm fine."

She kept her hand near him. "You sure?"

He jerked his head again. "No problemo."

"Okay, then, Pedro." She flashed him a quick grin. "Now go deliver your book."

Outside, in the Reading Room, David made a beeline to Seat Number 57. The elderly man had taken off his hat, but he was still drumming his fingers impatiently. "About *time*," he whispered, taking the book from David.

David wanted to tell him he was late because of the strange blue book that had appeared and then disappeared, and how the book he wanted had disappeared and then reappeared, but he knew better than to say that. He bowed his head instead, saying nothing, and returned to the wooden box. There were three new Book Retrieval Cards in it. He took a deep breath, scooped them up, and went back into the stacks.

Outside the brownstone where he lived, someone had drawn graffiti in blue chalk on the three squares of sidewalk touching the bottom step of the stoop. David saw suns and sunbeams, flocks of birds in the shape of lower-case 'm's, lollypop trees with holes in the trunks, big, puffy clouds, and a rainbow. All of it in blue chalk. He stood at the edge of the vast drawing, and knew he couldn't walk on it. If he walked on it, he might fall *into* it.

"Whatta you waiting for, kid, the bus?"

David looked up.

Mr. Hartz, the old man who lived in the first floor front apartment, leered at him from his open window. David had learned that talking to Mr. Hartz never worked. Talking to him made it worse. Smiling sometimes helped, so standing safely on the sidewalk square next to the first one covered in blue chalk, David smiled. Mr. Hartz took a swig from his beer can. "You're nuts, you know that, kid? Nuttier than a friggin' Mars Bar. You know that?"

David knew a lot of things. He knew that strange blue books in foreign languages didn't suddenly appear and disappear, and that books like 'The Mound Builders of Ancient America' by Robert Silverberg didn't disappear and then suddenly reappear, either. He also knew that when he was small, when he had been a very little boy, any change like this would have made him curl up in a ball in the corner and just scream. But he was nineteen years, three months and four days old today; he wasn't a little boy; he was a grown-up. His name was David, not Davie. He would not curl up; he would not scream.

But he was certain that if he walked on the sidewalk squares that touched his bottom stoop step, he would fall through them into a vast, empty blue sky. He would fall through that sky, and fall, and fall....

He wondered: what would Dr. Mooney say if he told her that?

"Hey buddy! D'you *mind*?"

A man in a rumpled gray suit, with a Styrofoam cup of coffee in one hand and a black imitation leather briefcase in the other, sidled past him, shooting a disgruntled look over his shoulder as he walked over the chalk drawing.

"Fruitcake," Mr. Hartz said from his window. "Mars Bar."

David turned away, took in a deep breath, and walked back down the block. He could have his meatloaf at the Pine Street Diner in his work clothes. He could eat his peas without having washed his face, without having collected and opened his mail, without having opened the window to the airshaft to let out the hot, close air that had accumulated in his little apartment during the day. He could do and *not do* all of these things. He could do something *new*. It would be all right. It would be no problemo.

At the Pine Street Diner, the waitress behind the counter brought David his meatloaf, mashed potatoes and green peas without him having to ask. "I came straight here tonight," he told her as she put a glass of milk down for him. "From work." "Did you now," she said.

Later, with the evening shadows long and cool along the street where he lived, he found that someone had washed the sidewalk in front of the stoop. All of the chalk drawings were gone. Only a faint haze of color remained. Still, he hesitated.

From his window overlooking the street, Mr. Hartz said, "What are you waiting for, kid, an engraved invitation?"

David looked up, smiled, and went quickly across the newly washed sidewalk, up the four stoop steps, and into the building. I'm safe, he thought. "I'm safe," he said, in the dark hallway that always smelled like urine and boiled cabbage.

Mr. Hartz yelled through his door: "Mars Bar!"

There were two hundred and thirty-seven concrete sidewalk squares from the top step of the Poplar Avenue subway to the bottom step of the Chestnut Street Library. This had been the case for one year, one month and thirteen days, ever since his first day of work at the Library. But when he reached the Library today he stood in the center of the two hundred and thirty-seventh square...and looked down at one more sidewalk square, a new square, the two hundred and thirty-*eighth*. Its near edge touched the square he stood on, and its far edge touched the library's bottom step. Like the sidewalk squares in front of his apartment house the previous evening, it was covered in scribblings of blue chalk, a fathomless, featureless blue.

He heard a noise, a soft, mewling sound, like someone very sad, or very afraid. Then he realized *he* was making the sound. His eyes welled, and hot tears tracked down both of his cheeks. Don't fall, he told himself, blinking furiously. Don't fall into the blue square. Stand *straight*.

"Hey Dave, come on, we're going to be late."

Maggie passed him, went two steps toward the side alley, then stopped and turned back, her dark curls flying. "Dave, you coming?" Then she saw the tears, and she came back to him. She came close enough to speak very quietly, so only he could hear her. She said, "What's wrong, David? Why are you crying?"

He wiped his cheeks with the palms of his hands. "I have to see Dr. Mooney."

"Your old shrink? But I thought—" She stopped, then started again, gently, "Don't you need an appointment?"

"I have to see Dr. Mooney," he said again. He felt his nose running, so he sniffed.

"Sure," Maggie said, nodding, "you go do that. I'll cover for you here, don't worry."

"Mrs. Cooper—"

"Don't worry, I'll handle her." Maggie reached across the small empty space between them and touched his arm. It felt like a bee sting, but he didn't flinch. He knew she didn't mean it. "No problemo," she said, "okay?"

He remembered a bench just inside the front entrance of Dr. Mooney's office building. Two large-leafed ferns in black pots flanked it. Two elevators took up the opposite wall. On the narrow section of wall between them was a tenant directory, framed in aluminum and glass. There were one thousand nine hundred and six white plastic letters pushed into the black velvet of the directory. The building had twelve floors, and forty-seven tenants. Dr. Mooney's office was on the sixth floor. Counting down from the top, her directory listing number was twenty-two.

David sat with his knees drawn up to his chest, under the overarching fronds of the plant farthest away from the entrance doors. He fixed his gaze to the floor. He counted the feet of the people who passed him, entering and leaving the elevators. By lunchtime he had counted one hundred and twenty six legs, sixty-three people, thirty-seven men, twenty-four women, and two children. None of them was Dr. Mooney.

Outside, through the glass doors, he heard a church bell ring twelve times. David's stomach was empty, and he had to go to the bathroom. More feet came and went, and he counted them. Then a pair of feet he recognized stopped in front of him, and David looked up.

"David," Dr. Mooney said, leaning down toward him, "what are you doing here?"

"I have to pee," David said. Then, "Your hair is red."

She raised her hand to touch the side of her bun. "Yes it is, David. Thank you for noticing."

"Has it always been red?" His lower lip trembled, all by itself. Then he began the mewling sound again. "Last time," he said, "was your hair red?"

"Come." She reached for his arm, stopping a half-inch away. "Get up, David, will you? Come with me."

"I have to pee," he said again.

"I know you do. You can use the bathroom in my office."

He stood, and his legs tingled. "The green bathroom?"

"Yes," she said, hesitating only a moment, "the green bathroom."

There were still two thousand eight hundred and eighty-six pale green floor tiles in Dr. Mooney's office bathroom. David counted them twice, to be sure. When he finally emerged, he found Dr. Mooney seated behind her desk. She smiled at him, and indicated the stuffed leather chair by the window.

David sat, his back straight, hands folded in his lap.

"Feeling better?" Dr. Mooney asked.

David said, "There was a an extra sidewalk square."

Dr. Mooney leaned forward. "David," she said, "do you remember that I'm not your doctor any more?"

"There were always two hundred and thirty *seven* sidewalk squares," David said. "Today there was two hundred and thirty *eight*." He blinked away sudden tears.

"You are supposed to see Dr. Lieberman now," Dr. Mooney said, "at the Oak Street Clinic. I introduced you to him. We went there together, you and I, remember?"

"The extra sidewalk square was blue," David said. "Why was there an extra square? Why was it blue?"

"Maybe the Public Works Department did some repair work. They fix things and paint things all the time." She put her hand on the phone. "I called Dr. Lieberman while you were in the bathroom."

"In the library," David said, "there was a book that wasn't supposed to be there."

"I expect libraries buy new books all the time."

"'The Mound Builders of Ancient America' by Robert Silverberg was supposed to be there, in the thirteenth slot, but it wasn't. A blue book was there instead. It had gold letters in a strange alphabet." Tears rolled down his cheeks unhindered, "The whole book was like that. I couldn't read it."

Dr. Mooney pushed her tissue box across the desk toward him, and then she picked up her phone.

David abruptly stood. "I have to go," he said, wiping his cheeks with his palms, then wiping his palms on his pants. "I have to go back to the library." He turned, and took three steps toward the door. "I'm supposed to be there."

Dr. Mooney rose. "Are you sure that's wise, David? Perhaps—"

"Maggie is covering for me," he said.

"David—" Dr. Mooney began, but he didn't hear what she said next, because he was already through the door and halfway across the reception room. "Mr. Brown," the receptionist said, looking up, smiling as he passed her, "So good to see you again."

He stopped, turned, said, "I have to know," and then he left.

There were fifteen stone steps that led up to two bronze doors at the Chestnut Street Library. David counted them all. Inside, past the dimly lit vestibule with its marble pedestals and dusty busts of famous Victorian poets, he went through another set of double doors and entered the Reading Room. As he pushed through the turnstile the librarian behind the checkout desk glanced up, peering briefly over her tortoise-shell glasses, then returned to her work.

David went over to the standing table near the card catalog. On the table were boxes of pencils, and stacks of Book Retrieval Cards in cubbies. He picked the sharpest pencil he could find, and carefully printed the name of the book he wanted on one of the cards. Then he looked out into the Reading Room, saw that seat Number 22 was empty, and wrote its number on the card. He put the card in the open box next to the doorway to the stacks, and then went to his seat to wait.

A young woman with dark curly hair came out of the doorway to the stacks a few minutes later, scooped out the Book Retrieval Cards, and disappeared back into the stacks.

David began counting.

When he reached three hundred and thirteen, the young woman reappeared with four books under her arm. There were Book Retrieval Cards sticking out of three of them. She took two of the books to an elderly lady sitting in Seat Number 36, and another book to a teenager in Seat Number 77. She brought the last book to David.

"I don't know," she whispered, smiling, "you must really like this book!"

He took it from her. It was blue, with faded gold lettering on its spine. When he opened it, it smelled musty and old. He looked at the open pages, blinking rapidly. The printed text was at first a jumbled sea of odd, apocryphal symbols. But then, but *then...* He looked up in wonder. "I can read this," he said.

The young woman's smile broadened. "I'm sure you can." Then she saw his expression, and her smile faded. A faint frown of concern creased the space between her eyebrows. "Are you okay?"

"Yes," he said, "I'm sorry." He nodded in two quick jerks. "I'm fine. Yes."

Across the Reading Room, the librarian looked up at them, a warning finger to her lips.

The young woman leaned close. "Hey," she whispered, "no

problemo," and she winked. Then she was gone, back into the stacks.

No problemo, David thought, blinking. No problemo, Pedro. His gaze fell once more on the words. He smiled as he fell into them, into the book, into the fathomless blue of the infinite sky. And he fell for a long, long time.

Eats

She had been arguing at him since the exit outside of Harrisburg. Somewhere east of there, by nightfall, as a fog bank rolled in, he finally admitted to himself that they were lost.

Alice, of course, picked right up on it.

"So why don't you just say it, Michael, huh? We're lost. Go ahead, you can manage that, can't you? Real slow: w-e a-r-e l-o-s-t."

He gripped the steering wheel tight enough to turn his knuckles white. "Just shut up, Alice," he said quietly, finally.

"What's that, macho Mike? What did you say? Oh Christ," she brayed, "Now the little man is *mad!*"

He hated arguing with her. He hated it almost as much as he hated *her*. He hadn't wanted to take her on this job interview trip, but there was no denying her when she had made up her mind. The interview had gone badly (of course), and now there was nothing left but to go back to Baltimore and wait for the next unemployment check.

And listen to his wife make his life a living, breathing, unending hell.

Trying to keep his voice level, he said, "I'm having a lot of trouble driving in this fog, okay? I really don't need an argument making it any worse."

"*You* had to get off the turnpike, hotshot."

"Because *you* couldn't wait for the rest stop. Because *you* had to have a cup of coffee, for God's sake."

She crumpled the road map on her knees. "Our marriage," she said, "is over."

"Oh come off it, Alice! You don't have to—"

"It's over, Michael. Your career is in the toilet, and so are our lives. I just can't take it any more." She continued crumpling, "When we get home I'm calling a lawyer." She formed the map into a tight ball. "I really am. This time."

Her words frightened him, but for some reason he found they thrilled him even more. She had said them before, many times, but this time, *this* time....

She tossed the map out the window, into the wind stream, into the foggy night.

"Oh great," he said. *You bitch.* "Just great."

The smile on her face was simply wicked. "I love you too, sweetie."

They drove on, then, in silence.

After a few more turns onto roads that looked promising but weren't, the slow blink of blue and white neon through the fog caught Mike's eye. Blurred at first, but becoming more distinct as he approached, he read the sign:

DINER
EATS
OPEN 24HRS

He slowed the car. "Let's stop and get that coffee, okay?"

Alice turned her head away.

"I'll take that as a yes, then." He turned off the road and, crunching gravel, parked the car near the front door.

"Well," he said then, "are you coming in?"

She looked at him coldly. "You'd *leave* me out here?"

"Come on, Alice. You said you wanted a cup of coffee. And I need the break after all this driving."

"*You* need the break?" She snorted. "That's a laugh." She opened her door. "If only to stretch my legs."

Mike glanced heavenward.

Inside, Mike was instantly transported back to the 1960s. From the stainless steel and polished aluminum Deco designs and black and white tile floor to the blood red naugahyde of the booths and stools, it was a regular blast from the past.

The counterman, middle-aged and thin, and wearing a startlingly white cap and apron, nodded to them, and smiled. Then he returned to a conversation he was having with the only other customers in the place, a group of four old people at the counter, nursing coffees and pie.

"Do you want to sit at the counter," Mike said, "or in a booth?"

Alice ignored him. She strode over to a booth halfway down the aisle, the one opposite the break in the middle of the counter, and began to sit down.

"I'm sorry, ma'am," the counterman said behind them, "but that booth's reserved."

Alice shot him an incredulous look, but didn't (*thank God*, Mike thought) make an issue of it. She slid into the next booth down, and stared, scowling, out the window.

Mike sat opposite her. He plucked two menus from the bracket behind the condiments, pushed one across the table to her, and opened the other. "Will you look at this," he said, after a moment. "Burgers for a buck, malteds for fifty cents…can you believe these prices? This *is* a blast from the past. Hey, they even have egg creams!"

Alice pushed her menu away, unopened, with her fingernail. "Egg creams?" She said with distaste.

"Yeah. It's a drink, kind of like a milkshake. It's made with seltzer water, and—"

"Please, Michael." She sighed pointedly. "I really don't care." Then she looked toward the counterman and raised her voice slightly. "I hope their coffee isn't made with seltzer water."

The counterman made a final comment to the group at the counter, then came over with a full pot and that same smile. "Fill 'em up, folks?"

Mike upturned both of their cups. "Please," he said.

"Cream and sugar are on the table there," the counterman said as he poured. "My name is Ray, and if there's—"

"I don't see any Nutrasweet."

"Any what, ma'am?"

"Nutrasweet, Nutrasweet." Alice tapped her nails on the yellowed plastic of her menu. "Haven't you ever heard of Nutrasweet, for Christ's sake?"

The counterman cranked his smile down a notch. "I'm sorry, ma'am," he said, "but I guess we're fresh out."

Her eyes blazed; (*Oh dear God*, Mike thought miserably); she said, "Then you can just take this coffee away, take it right away!" She shot Mike a look that said '*Agree* with me or *else*.' Aloud, she said, "Don't you dare pay for two coffees, Michael."

"Well hey," the counterman said, "I'm real sorry about this. Why don't we just make both of these on the house, then? In my diner, the customer is always right."

Mike found the counterman's demeanor infectious; he couldn't help but sympathize. "Why, that's very kind of you, Ray," he said.

Alice, however, had escalated from slow burn to coldly furious. "We will pay for my husband's coffee," she said distinctly. "We will pay for everything we eat or drink here. We will not take something for nothing."

Ray bowed slightly, and took a step back. "Whatever you say, ma'am." Then, with a wink to Mike that Alice couldn't see, he said, "Now you let me know when you're ready to order." And he retreated behind the counter, taking Alice's coffee with him.

Mike took a sip of his. "This is very good, you know," he said. "Are you sure you don't—"

"Will getting me to drink something make you happy, Michael? Will doing that get you to shut up and leave me alone?

Go get me a glass of water, then, like a good little boy."

Mike sat quietly for a moment, counting to himself. *I will not make a scene*, he thought. *At least I won't.* Then he got up, and as he left the table she said, "Wimp," under her breath and behind her scowl.

He went over to the counter.

One of the old men there, wearing a faded Cleveland Indians ball cap and a worn, blue satin Brooklyn Dodgers jacket, turned from a conversation he was having with the woman beside him and said to Mike, "You wouldn't happen to know anything about baseball history, would you, young man?"

Mike hesitated. "I…guess I know my share."

The old man nodded seriously. "Well then, perhaps you might settle a minor dispute for us."

"I'll certainly try."

"A question has arisen—"

"Michael," Alice called over, "where is my water?"

"Coming, dear. Excuse me, Mr…."

"Riz, short for Arizona. Named me after the new state. But this question, now, it—"

"*Michael.*"

Mike turned. "In a moment, Alice. Just give me a moment here, will you?"

Ray said, "I'll bring over the water. I should have done that first anyway."

Mike smiled a relieved thanks, and returned his attention to the old man.

"As I was saying," Riz said, "a question has arisen as to which pitcher won the most games in any one season prior to W W Two. About the only thing we're clear on is that there were thirty-two games won, but we can't seem to get together on the who and the when of it."

"Thirty-two games." Mike leaned an elbow on the counter, frowning slightly.

"My lady friend here," Riz continued, pointing with his thumb to the woman on the other side of him, "contends it is Cy

Young. I, however, am partial to the young Tris Speaker when he was hurling for the White Sox."

Mike nodded slowly. "Well," he began, "I think—"

"Michael, I'm leaving."

Mike turned. His wife was standing by the booth, pulling on her coat. "Leaving? But—"

"No buts, no conversation, no nothing. Just pay the bill and let's get *out* of here. This place gives me the *creeps.*"

Mike's mouth formed a thin line. *Enough,* he thought, *is enough.* "We'll leave," he said evenly, "when I'm ready. And I'm not ready yet."

Her face, under her makeup, went very red. *Uh-oh,* he thought, *here it comes.*

But instead of yelling, instead of making a new, even more embarrassing scene, she simply finished putting on her coat and went over to the door. There she paused, and said, "Are you coming with me, or am I leaving without you?"

A sudden, unbidden laugh rose, bubbling up from his belly, and he couldn't hold it back. "But I have the car keys, dear," he said.

"And who do you think has the spare set, you dumbass." She put her hand on the door handle. "Well? Are you coming?"

Mike started to speak, but stopped himself. Instead, he shook his head.

Her smile faltered. "Fine," she said. "Consider yourself stranded." She opened the door. "Why I ever...what I ever saw...."

For a moment, for just a moment, her one-dimensional facade fell away, and he saw in her eyes the things he had seen when they had first met, the things he had fallen in love with, all those years ago. But then the facade snapped up again, and they were gone, utterly gone. Her eyes dulled. "Forget it," she said, and left.

Mike took in a deep breath, then flashed the others a sheepish grin.

"It'll be better this way," Ray said. "You'll see." He motioned to the stools. "Why don't you take one?"

Mike glanced down. The stool seat on his left was ripped in several places, and brown and white stuffing bulged out of the naugahyde.

"Not that one," Ray said. "This one. Next to Riz."

Mike took the stool that the counterman indicated. He slid onto it smoothly. For some reason it felt *good;* it felt *right.* His body suddenly, unaccountably *relaxed.*

Outside, at that moment, Alice shrieked.

And then shrieked again. Mike couldn't believe anyone could make a sound so loud, so frightening, so final. He started to rise, but Riz put a hand on his arm. "Don't get up," he said urgently. "Don't you dare get up."

"But my *wife*—"

"She'll be back," the old man said. "Any minute now."

Something heavy struck the door.

"Don't you turn around either," Riz continued, whispering now. "If you want to get through this alive, then for God's sake *don't look.*"

"But my—"

"That seat beside you, the ripped one…the last guy to sit there, *he looked.* Son of a bitch knew his baseball too, more's the pity, but he had to go and look. Dead, of course, just like that witch of a wife of yours. Dead and gone." The old man's hand tightened on his arm. "You just sit straight and mind your own business, and everything will be just fine." He squeezed. "Mind me, now."

The door banged open. Mike heard raspy, wet breathing, like some huge beast panting over a fresh kill. Heavy, cumbersome footsteps went slowly down the aisle to his left. Then something bulky, something limp, was thrown up onto the counter.

A colorful little object skittered down the formica and pinged against the side of Riz's coffee cup.

It was one of Alice's earrings.

The urge to turn around and look was suddenly overpowering, but Riz tightened his grip on Mike's arm again, and shook it for good measure. Mike closed his eyes. *Alice,* he thought, *Alice....*

"She didn't love you," Riz whispered. "But you knew that."

Ray pulled the body off the counter without a word and shouldered it. Then he pushed through the double doors to the kitchen; Mike saw a flash of leg, of skirt, the pattern of dirt and wear on the soles of her shoes. Then the doors swung shut, and she was gone.

Behind him, whoever or whatever it was that had killed her sat heavily in one of the booths, *the reserved booth,* Mike realized then, *almost right behind me, staring at me, watching me.*

A full, endless hour passed, thusly.

Finally, Ray emerged from the kitchen, laden with crowded, steaming plates. He placed one in front of Mike first.

On it was a sizable piece of broiled steak, a pile of french fries, and an equally big pile of peas.

The thing in the booth made a guttural noise. Ray immediately juggled his load, and dropped something else onto Mike's plate.

It was an eyeball.

The eyeball, apparently, had been poached.

Even so, Mike recognized its owner.

His gorge rose instantly, and he was certain he would vomit right there onto the plate. *Stop looking at me, Alice,* he thought desperately. *Even in death, you won't leave me alone...!*

Ray put plates in front of everyone, including a huge, heavily laden platter for...him, it...in the booth. Then he returned to Mike. "You doing okay?"

Mike looked at the bloody fingerprint smudges on the edge of his plate, then at the counterman's blood-soaked arms, and finally at the delicate spray of tiny scarlet dots across the front of his cap. "I'm fine," he said, faintly. "Really."

Ray nodded to the plate. "*He's* paying you a particular honor, you know, considering who *he* is."

Mike glanced down, then back up again. "Oh?"

"The eye. *He* wants you to have one of the eyes." Ray shook his head slowly. "*He* never shares the eyes."

Mike glanced down again. *Thank God*, he thought, *thank God you can't blink, you bitch.* He had a sudden urge to grab his fork and stab her, stick her right through the pupil, right where it hurt. He took the fork in hand—

Everyone at the counter paused.

Even the abomination in the booth stopped slavering.

"You have to eat it," Ray said, quietly. "Those are the rules here. You have to eat everything. Every time."

Mike swallowed. "But where," he asked, "is here?"

Ray nodded. "It's...a place where you can kick back and relax, shoot the breeze with friends, have a burger, have—"

"An egg cream," Mike said, faintly.

The counterman nodded again. "And I make a mean egg cream, my friend."

In the booth, Mike heard the grinding of teeth. They sounded large and numerous. And sharp.

"Sometimes," Ray continued, "it's a long wait between customers. Sometimes the fog hides us *too* well. And *he's* always hungry. Always. As long as *he* gets an offering, though, *he* leaves things pretty much as they are. *He* lets us be. *He* lets us...."

"Worship *him*," Riz finished for him. "*Forever*, if we're lucky. Not a bad deal, when you think about it."

Mike regarded his fork for a moment, then he looked up again, his eyes brimming with sudden, unbidden tears. "Can I stay?" he asked. "Can I really stay with you folks?"

Ray said nothing; Riz glanced down at Mike's plate.

Mike followed his gaze. A silent, interminable moment passed. Then, abruptly, he brought his fork down and speared the eyeball.

It came up whole, with hardly a dribble. *Just like a big cherry tomato*, he thought, closing his eyes, squeezing his tears out. Then he opened his mouth. *Just like a hard boiled egg.*

He chewed briefly—it was gelatinous, vaguely salty, but not unpleasant—and swallowed.

Behind him, the thing gave a low, throaty chuckle, then Mike heard the sound of sudden, furious eating—chomping, gobbling, belching, practically inhaling the food on the platter before it.

And the men at the counter dug in as well.

Mike put a little ketchup on the meat.

It didn't taste bad at all.

After a time, when everyone had cleaned their plates, the thing in the booth gave a final, noisome belch, stood, and shambled down the aisle to the door. As it passed, Mike tensed, and held his breath. But it didn't pause. The door banged open, and then banged shut.

Outside, Mike heard a single, abrupt, glass-rattling roar. Then it went away, into the fog, into the night.

Gone.

The sudden silence hung in the air like a palpable thing.

Then Mike broke it. "Bob Feller," he said. "Bob Feller had thirty-two wins, and that was in 1937."

Riz shook his head. "Feller, maybe, but not in '37. Hell, I was already *here* in '37."

Mike smiled at that. "You've certainly got one up on me there," he said.

The old man cackled, then laughed outright, and after a moment, the others joined in.

Mike looked at Riz, then Ray. "What about...time?"

"Oh it flies, it flies." Riz winked. "You'll see."

"Isn't it grand?" Ray said, in the midst of it all. "Good conversation, good friends, and all of eternity to enjoy it in." He clapped Mike on the shoulder, grinning with bloodstained teeth. "Isn't it all just *grand?*"

Mike leaned over the counter. "An egg cream, please," he said, loud enough for Ray to hear through the laughter.

Ray grinned again. "Coming right up."

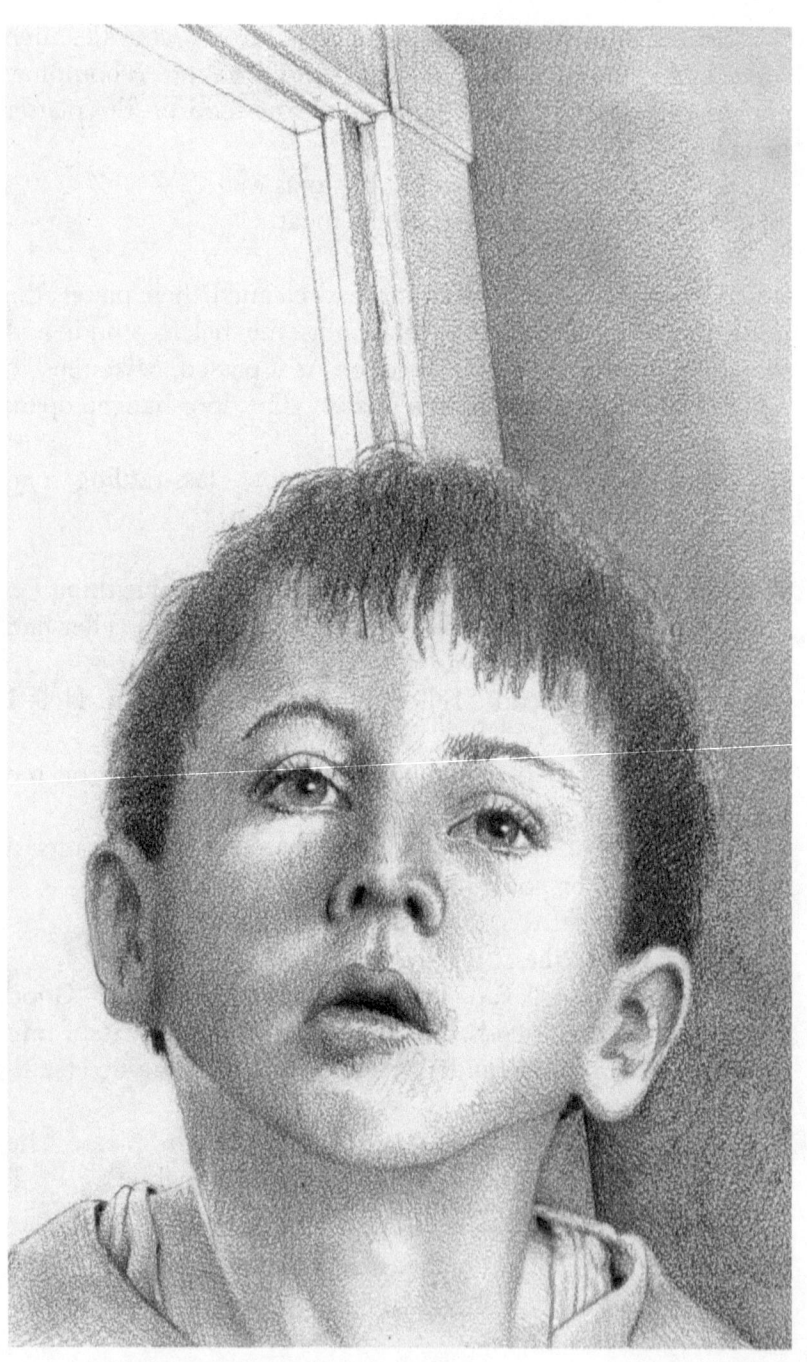

Turn of a Card

Earlier in the day, from his second floor bedroom window, Mark's mother had pointed across the wide bowl-shaped valley of the town to the houses and trees on the far side and said, "There, can you see it? The grey roof...the one with the tower...that's the one we're going to see today." Like a toy, Mark had thought, squinting; a little place where ants lived.

Now, from the street, the house with the grey roof and the odd, cylindrical tower was...huge. It loomed, it soared, it rambled; it had more windows than Mark could count. He asked his parents, "What kind of a place is this, anyway?"

His mother squatted to his level and leaned back against the car door. "The style is called Queen Anne, hon."

"All those squiggly things on it makes it Queen Anne?"

She smiled. "All those squiggly things are called ginger-bread."

Mark's father cleared his throat. "All those squiggly things," he said, "are called a nightmare to whoever has climb a ladder to paint them."

"This house doesn't need much work at all," Mark's mother protested, rising. "You can see that even from here. It's beautiful, Dan."

"Now, maybe," Mark's father conceded. "But give it five

years, and you'll have me up there caulking and scraping and slapping on paint till the cows come home."

Mark unconsciously imitated his father's frown. "You don't want to move here, Dad?"

His father looked pointedly at his mother, then he smiled slightly. "We'll see," he said.

Coming down the sidewalk, a boy on a dayglo-green trail bike swerved to avoid them. "Hi," he said to Mark as he passed.

"Hi," Mark called after him.

The boy did a U-turn, and came back.

The two sized each other up, then the boy on the bike said, "You moving in here?"

"We're not sure." Mark glanced at his parents. "We're just looking."

The boy on the bike nodded to the house. "This is called the Briggs Place. The Briggs family lived here for years."

"Must have been a lot of them," Mark's mother said.

"Nah. Only two, an old guy and his wife." The boy leaned close to Mark. "They died in there, you know. Died."

Mark's father chortled, but a quick look from Mark's mother silenced him, and he clapped his hand over his mouth.

Mark looked at the house again, his eyes wide with sudden apprehension. "Died? Inside the house?"

"Right in their beds," the boy on the bike said with finality. "There was an ambulance and police here and everything. First the old lady, then the old guy a month later."

"Old people pass away in their sleep all the time, honey," his mother said. Then, to Mark's father, "Estate sale. We can knock ten thousand right off the top."

Mark looked at all the blank, shrouded windows; and the tower with its crazy conical roof; it was a creepy-looking house, after all. And now with two people actually dying inside it....

As though reading his mind, the boy on the bike said, "I'm pretty sure they haunt the place."

Mark's apprehension finally settled into his stomach as simple, cold fear...something about that house, something...

"Aw, you're just making that up," he said defensively.

The boy on the bike pointed. "Look at the place," he said. "What do you think?"

Mark's father cleared his throat as he stepped forward and gripped his son's shoulder. "There's no such thing as haunted houses, son."

"But Dad—"

"Listen, if this house is haunted, then I'm a..." He looked up. "What am I, Marion?"

"A monkey's uncle, among other things."

"Then I'm a monkey's uncle, okay?"

Mark looked at the house again—haunted—and swallowed. "Well...."

"Good afternoon!"

All four of them turned.

The real estate agent strode up the sidewalk, smiling broadly, her black plastic clipboard gripped firmly in hand.

"Hello, Joan," Mark's mother said, smiling back. "This is my husband Dan."

Mark's father nodded warily.

"Pleased to meet you at last!" Then the agent turned to the boy on the bike. "And hello to you too, Quentin Tolbert."

Quentin, saddled with his name at last, rolled his eyes.

The real estate agent lightly tapped his arm. "Are you selling another house for me?"

"I was just telling them it was haunted."

The real estate agent included Mark's parents in her quick laughter. "Kids," she said. She turned back to Quentin. "Now you scoot home and tell your mother I said hi." Then, extending the clipboard in the direction of the house to Mark and his parents, "Shall we?"

Mark trailed behind the grownups as they toured the house, but he never let himself be caught alone in any of the rooms. No use taking any chances, he decided, even though it was the middle of the day. A haunted house from the outside was bad enough, but when you were inside it...that was something else.

Something else entirely.

This particular haunted house was sneaky, though. There were no cobwebs, no old, ugly furniture with sheets draped over them; the wallpaper was smooth, the floors didn't creak, and the ceilings were only 'fashionably cracked,' as his mother put it, "And this woodwork, Dan! It's all original chestnut! We wouldn't have any stripping to do at all!"

This house was trying to hide its badness, Mark thought, but he wasn't fooled. With each room, with each passing moment, he couldn't shake the feeling of being inside a beast, a huge, evil, hungry beast, a beast just biding its time, waiting for the perfect opportunity (an opportunity on its own terms, not his) to swallow them up and never let them leave. Not alive, anyway.

Even on the second floor, where the large bedroom windows flooded the rooms with full, warm sunshine, the feeling persisted.

We have to get out of here, Mark decided, his uneasiness rising. We have to get out.

They finally ended up in a large bedroom with a curious circular room off one of its corners. Mark's mother gravitated to it immediately.

"That's part of the tower, of course," the agent said, beaming.

Mark's mother stood in the center of the little round room. There were windows almost all of the way around, looking out over the side lawn and the neighboring property. "This is exquisite," she said.

The agent followed her in. "If you think this is nice," she said, "then watch." She reached up, grabbed a metal ring on a chain hanging from the ceiling, and pulled. The ceiling blossomed, and a folding stair lowered itself gently to the floor at their feet. To Mark, it was as though The Beast had opened its mouth and extended its tongue.

She turned to Mark. "You want to go up first?"

He paled. "Uh…"

The agent held out a hand.

"Go on, Mark," his mother said, prodding him gently.

"Make the most of it."

Mark allowed her to pull him into the little room. He looked up the ladder stair and saw a flower-bud of beams in the ceiling of the room above, painted white. And sunlight. Tons of sunlight. It looked safe...

"Go for it, pal," his father said.

He glanced back to them, then put his hand on the smooth white rail and clambered up the steps.

At the top, he emerged into a room as small and as round as the one below, but here the windows went completely around, like a lighthouse. He could see the tops of the roofs of all of the surrounding houses, and into the tops of all of the trees.

"How is it, honey?" his mother called from below.

Momentary exhilaration surged: "It's...outrageous, Mom! You can see all over town!" He looked east, searching the far rooftops across town, and there, framed by the two sycamores in his backyard, he saw his own house. "Hey!" he yelled down excitedly, "I can even see our house!"

"All the way across town?" His father's voice was doubtful.

"Yeah! The two trees in the backyard and everything!"

"Well I'll be...darned," his father said, from below. Mark heard his mother chuckle quietly.

He lingered on his house roof for another moment, then jumped to others he recognized. The library, the drugstore with the apartments on top...even his school, with its big flag waving by the tall brick chimney....

But then a stiff wind struck the tower, whistling under the window sashes, rattling the glass. He found himself looking down at the rooflines and gables of the house they were in, and a shiver of new fear suddenly coursed through him. He grabbed a window sash to steady himself, to stop it from rattling, and put his other hand to his mouth.

Up here. Whatever it was that haunted this house, it was right up here, with him.

I've got to do something! His head jerked about. I've got to do something!

He reached into his back jeans pocket and pulled out his pack of baseball cards. Unhesitatingly, he selected his only Chase Utley and put it quickly on one of the windowsills.

There.

There.

With that single, magical act, the house took a step back. He felt it. Like a vampire cowering before a crucifix, or a werewolf under a silver dagger, the house shrank away.

He stared at the card, amazed.

Then, from below, his mother said, "I think we should give this room to Mark."

Alone amidst the sky, the roofs, the trees, the magic, Mark held his breath, and thought, this is crazy...

The agent said, "Actually, this is considered the master bedroom."

But his mother interrupted, "I think a room with a tower just has to be a little boy's...don't you think so, Dan?"

"Yeah," his father said. "Marko could have this room, no problem."

Marko. That meant his father was in a good mood. That meant....

Mark put his hand on his Chase Utley to draw from the power of its magic. Dad, he thought, you can't buy this house! You can't! The card got damp under his fingers, but he held on, and pressed...

"Come on down now, hon," his mother called up. Then, to the agent, "I think we're ready to talk. Dan?"

Mark held his breath again.

"Sure," his father said. "I guess it won't hurt to talk."

Mark opened his eyes, let his breath out, and lifted his hand away from the card. The magic was on its own, now. No matter what his parents said, or did, the magic would have to keep them from buying this house.

The magic would work.

It had to.

But when he reached the bottom of the ladder stair, he

found the real estate agent studiously examining the ceiling cornices with a quiet smile on her face....

While his mother kissed his father with abandon.

That night, an hour after Mark had gone to bed, his mother paused in the hallway outside his bedroom. "You still awake, honey?"

Mark shifted in the darkness. "I can't stop thinking about that house, Mom."

She came in and stood by his bed. "Well it's not our house yet. All we did was put a bid in. If they don't like our price...."

"You think they'll like the bid? You think we'll get it?"

She chuckled. "Honestly? I don't think so. I think it may be just a little beyond our means. Would it disappoint you if we didn't get it?"

"Nah," he said, as his heart skipped once, twice, "but I wouldn't want you to feel bad. I know you really like it."

She leaned over and kissed him lightly on the cheek, then went to his window. "The air is a little cold tonight." She closed it.

Outside, through the trees, Mark could see the stars twinkling furiously in the wind, the same wind that had rattled the windows of the tower earlier in the day, the wind that had not stopped since.

At the door she paused again. "So you really like the house, Mark?"

"It's outrageous, Mom," he fibbed, "...really."

She hesitated, perhaps sensing his lie, perhaps not. Then, "Want to go to IHOP tomorrow for pancakes?"

Mark grinned in the darkness. "Can I use all the syrups?"

"Sure you can."

He closed his eyes. "Sounds great, Mom." Then he yawned. "See you tomorrow."

"Sleep tight, honey." She closed his door softly, and the room filled up with night.

After a moment he got out of bed and padded silently over to the window that his mother had closed.

He pressed his hands against the cool glass and looked out into the darkness. Somewhere, out there, was a house with a round tower, a tower full of windows, looking back. But it can't see me, he thought. There's no moon tonight, and I'm not going to open this window. I'm not.

The wind outside picked up, and the rushing sound through the leaves of the trees was like the roar of the crowd at a baseball stadium. Mark returned to bed, to the warmth that still lingered under his covers, thinking of the baseball card he had left on the windowsill in the tower, thinking of the magic....

C'mon, Chase, he prayed, do your thing, now....

The wind outside finally began to dwindle, and then to die. A bird in its nest awoke and cheeped sleepily, once, twice, then was quiet.

As he finally drifted off, Mark's breathing grew quiet as well, and soon his sleep was so deep he didn't make a sound.

The stars went slowly across the sky, the quietest of all.

Then a single gust of wind—abrupt, seemingly from out of nowhere—slapped the west side of the house. The trees in the yard roared once—

Mark's window opened.

The cold wind fluttered the pages of an open book on his desk.

Carried on the wind, borne by it: a flurry of tiny ripped pieces of cardboard, falling to the floor at the foot of Mark's bed. On one of the pieces: a portion of a baseball cap, a piece of a forehead, and a single eye, staring out helplessly.

Slowly, slowly, the window closed.

Then, with a sound that only little boys could hear—little boys who knew, little boys who believed—something laughed.

Empire State

In the year of our Lord 2238 the frigate Huguenot, of forty-two guns and over three hundred souls, set forth from the Catskill Archipelago in search of the Empire State.

I was a raw thirteen when we sailed, but of good family and certain wealth, so it was my lot (and my privilege) to hold the station of Captain's cabin boy and personal yeoman. And though many years have passed between the adventure itself and this, its sorely delinquent chronicle, my memories of both its wonders and its horrors have remained with me, as sharp as the Westchester sea breezes, as fresh as the Stockbridge surf. In keeping with current custom (and a still freshly inked contract) this will not merely be a collection of log entries; even I would find that boring. No, this shall be a story, a tale, the manuscript of which shall be left in the care of Messrs. Dubois and Lefebre of the Lefebre Trading Company, Mohonk, our financial backers who live for the scribbled word, the totaled column, the balanced book. Indulge me, reader. And watch the boy; he may for all the good wide world be me.

The sounds and silences of the sailing ship filled the air even as the stars filled the evening sky. Ane, the boy, leaned out over the frothing, phosphorescent bow wake, his hands fast in the sprit rigging, and listened: to the creaking voices of timber and plank, to the groans of rope and line, the steady rushing of the

wind, and below it all, to the constant, hurrying hiss of the sea as the ship cut ponderously through it.

He was less than a shadow, all but invisible against the black and glittering waves. The woman slave and the free seaman, crouching together just forward of the fo'c's'le, could not see him and therefore spoke freely, if only in rough whispers:

"...He'll be on you after quarters for missing that brass and the quarterdeck teak," said the seaman. "It's the little things that catch Hasbrouck's eye."

"But who is on him," the slave named Loundes said, with some heat, "for such a little thing as getting us lost?"

Lost? Ane's shoulders tightened; his brow creased. They couldn't be lost; not two weeks from last sight of land.... How could they actually think the ship had lost its way? He held his breath....

"He's the captain," Hawkins, the seaman, said. "He doesn't need anyone knocking his head, least of all the likes of you and yours."

Loundes grunted. She said, "Well, I for one am blood puked being kept from knowing what is going on. I may be bound to follow this ship to hell and back, but I still have the right to know the where and the when and the why of it. We all do."

"Slaves or freebooters," Hawkins replied, shrugging, "make no difference to Captain Hasbrouck. We all pull pay every day we sail this godforsaken ship, same as he. The Lefebre Company wants metals, and you can be sure Hasbrouck will do his damnedest to bring them back a hold full. He'll let his wardroom know the details of his plans soon enough, and then the freemen, and then you. He's just waiting for some sign to tell him he's right."

"But what if we've left this 'Empire State' of his in our wake already and are now bow-on toward Spain? You've heard the stories; God knows what crawls on those shores." She spread her arms wide, embracing the night. "No one has ever been this far out, two weeks from our last landfall, chasing rumors and legends centuries old...."

Hawkins looked at her with no little amusement. "What's the use worrying? Huguenot was built for such a voyage. No trust in those sails of yours?"

Loundes grunted again, and spat, windward; Ane caught a little. She turned into the new moonlight now flooding the horizon, and her cheek gleamed like wet silver. "There's a lot of sea beneath us," she said, so quietly Ane barely heard her. "That's all."

Hawkins only nodded.

Later, with a steaming pot of turned cider in one hand and a basket of sandwiches in the other, Ane kicked respectfully at Captain Hasbrouck's sea-cabin door. It opened immediately; golden light streamed out; the captain stood silhouetted in it, holding forth his hands, taking the basket from the boy and motioning him in. His was a small cabin, and filled to overflowing with charts, navigational tools, and other exotic devices. Still, the captain, small of frame and wiry, seemed lost in it. He looked Ane up and down with his shrewd blue eyes, and his orange hair, on fire in the lamplight, shook its curls with his quick laughter. "So, lad," he said, "what is it they are whispering tonight?"

"The same, sir," Ane said, filling a mug. "But this time the slave belonging to Hawkins—Loundes is her name—was complaining that we were lost." He managed to control the question in his voice, but his eyes, he knew, betrayed him.

"Ahh," was all the captain said, however. He took the mug and drank, then gestured with it to the charts at the same moment the ship took an unexpected roll. Cider on the charts, Ane thought as he grabbed wildly for balance, but nothing spilled. The Captain winked, took another drink, then put the mug down to flatten a chart curl. "We have time for another lesson tonight, I think."

Ane flushed with quiet excitement, and his eyes jumped to the silver, glass, and brass instruments strewn about. Which one would it be? What mysteries would the captain allow him to glimpse, however complex, however incomprehensible, however wonderful, this time?

Captain Hasbrouck reached for his sextant. "I think tonight we will allay your fears as to whether Huguenot is or isn't lost." He placed the instrument firmly into Ane's hands, "You remember how to use this, I expect?"

"Yes, sir," Ane whispered.

The captain laughed and clapped the boy on his back. "We shall make a pilot of you yet, I think. Come, up on deck with you to shoot your stars."

"Can I—?"

"Carry the axe up yourself? Of course, lad." Hasbrouck held the cabin door for Ane. "A pilot always carries his own tools. Don't forget the log, quill, and ink, now...."

Master Whaley, Huguenot's sailing master, was on the bridge.

Jumping from the ladder, the captain waved him to his ease. "Keep the deck and the con, Edward," he said. "Tonight I am only an observer."

Master Whaley noticed Ane then, following the captain off the ladder. "Another lesson for the boy, sir?"

Hasbrouck nodded. "One can never get too much celestial navigation, I think. What stars do you have for us tonight, Edward? We require only three."

Master Whaley duly pointed them out, and Ane set to his task.

He checked each sight and reading several times before he felt comfortable enough to attempt the final set he would use. Captain Hasbrouck watched him in the darkness, smiling slightly.

I wonder, Ane thought, feeling the captain's eyes on him, does he see himself in me? Does he see the cabin boy he once was, wishing to be a pilot, hoping someday to be commander of his own ship? Ane redoubled his concentration, determined to be perfect, determined to make the captain proud of him. Someday, he thought, I too shall have a ship. Someday I too will lead great adventures. Someday.

"Soundings are erratic, sir," Master Whaley was saying. "Rough bottom as well; we lost three lines today alone."

"I know." The captain turned to look forward. "We are close, I think," he said.

Ane's heart skipped, and he almost missed a sighting. He took in a long breath and re-gripped the sextant.

"You don't need to hear it from me, sir, I'm sure," Whaley said, "but I've noticed a general feeling of uneasiness among the slaves this past week. Ours are an excitable lot, as a rule. And most of them have never sailed beyond sight of land."

"And lucky they are," the captain replied, "to have the opportunity! Damn squids; lucky they are to be here at all, eh, Edward?"

"To be sure, sir."

"Have you your figures yet, lad?"

Ane laid aside his quill. "Yes, sir; I've just noted them down."

"Good. Let's go below and plot them, then."

As he passed the sailing master, Hasbrouck said, "Tomorrow," and Ane's heart skipped once more. *Tomorrow.*

He found Dex still awake in his rack.

Her eyes, bright in the shuttered lamp he carried, blinked widely. Ane extinguished the flame and slid in next to her warmth.

"Another lesson?"

He kissed her. "Celestial navigation."

She kissed him back. "Sounds religious."

"It's fun...like this."

She gasped. "Hey!"

He covered her protest with another kiss.

Presently, he whispered, "It's tomorrow, I think."

Dex yawned, and snuggled close. "What are you babbling about?"

"The captain told Master Whaley 'tomorrow'."

"Tomorrow what?"

"Just 'tomorrow.' But I know what he meant."

"And…?"

"Can't you guess?"

"Listen, yeoman, I don't hob with the commanding officer of this tub every waking moment, like you; our lot scrubs decks; see?" And she held up hands he couldn't see in the darkness. He grabbed for them anyway, put them around his neck, and they lay together quietly for a moment.

"The Empire State," he said then. "He was talking about the Empire State. We must be arriving tomorrow."

"Let's just say we'd better arrive tomorrow. The senior squids have been talking seriously about desertion, you know. Or if not that, maybe even mutiny."

Ane stifled a laugh. "Mutiny? How?"

"You think they'd tell me? Everybody on Huguenot knows who I rack with."

"They should all be so lucky—"

She punched his arm. "Really, Ane, I've never heard talk this bad before. The captain should listen to the protests, not brush them aside. We slaves make up nearly a third of the crew, after all."

"But you're…they're squids!"

She punched him again. "Goodnight, little boy," she hissed, and turned over.

"Hey, wait!"

"Doors are closed, Ane. See you second watch."

Ane scowled a little, but left her alone. In the dark and pitching night his thoughts turned back to visions of the Empire State…and these led him quickly to the stairs of sleep, where his visions just as quickly became dreams.

The bells for colors the next evening were still echoing through the passageways when there was a firm rap on Captain Hasbrouck's door.

The captain didn't even look up from his meal. "See who it

is, lad," he said, his mouth full.

Ane opened it a crack and saw three slaves, one female, two male, standing at attention beyond. The increasingly heavy seas that Huguenot had been meeting throughout the day caused the two men to lose their balance and grab the bulkhead for support, but the third stepped defiantly forward. Ane saw then that it was Loundes.

He glanced back. "Sir?"

"For Christ's sake," the captain cried, spraying food, "first this damn storm coming and now squids!" He shoved his plate away.

"How many, then?"

"Three, sir."

"Well, I only have the stomach for one. Bring her forward and damn these seas!" for at that moment his mug had tipped and spilled hot cider into his crotch.

Loundes was in the cabin before Ane could stop her, however, and came to attention again in front of the captain's table. Wiping his pants with the tablecloth, Captain Hasbrouck glanced up once, then continued cleaning himself.

The slave, staring, was silent.

"And what is your pleasure tonight?" the captain demanded finally, throwing aside the cloth and bringing both fists down on the table. The ship rolled and Loundes stumbled, but did not fall; she regained her balance even as the ship did, and said, "I represent the eighty-three servile landsmen and landswomen of Huguenot's crew, and—"

"Sir," Ane prompted.

"And I would like to—"

"Of Huguenot's crew, *sir*," Ane repeated.

The slave flushed; the captain smiled; Ane grinned behind his hand.

"Very well," Loundes said, "sir. As spokeswoman for one third of the crew I have come, sir, to ask some important questions."

There was faraway thunder, then, gently tearing the night.

"Well, be quick about it," the captain said. "This damned storm will be upon us sooner than I'd feared."

"First and foremost, sir, we want to know when we will reach the Empire State."

Captain Hasbrouck stood, went to the cabin's only hull port, and looked out. "All too soon," he replied, and gestured outside. "Weather permitting, of course."

"With all due respect, sir, we've been given evasive answers like that for the past week. I would hate to return to the others with nothing more than that to—"

A blue-white glare momentarily silhouetted the captain against the port glass, then a great peal of thunder sounded, shivering the very timbers of the ship. Huguenot took a particularly long and sickening roll at that moment and all three in the cabin lost their footing and ended up in a tangle against the hull bulkhead.

"Madam," Captain Hasbrouck said, extricating himself, "this meeting, however brief, however unfulfilling, must now come to an end. It seems I have a storm that begs my undivided attention. Ane, escort her below."

"But—" Loundes began again.

"Enough."

The two matched glares for a moment, eye to eye, then Loundes cursed and looked away.

The captain brushed past her. "Ane," he said over his shoulder as he exited, "the bridge, five minutes," and stumbled headlong into the two slaves still waiting in the passageway. "God damn these squids!" he roared, and then was gone.

It took only those scant five minutes for the storm to hit in force.

When Ane emerged topside the rain immediately and completely drenched him; the wind, shrieking, grabbed at him with great and powerful hands, threatening to toss him into the ragged darkness. Ane shielded his eyes and looked wildly about, and saw the captain at the port rail. He was shouting orders to the seamen and slaves aloft in the rigging as they attempted to clear the remaining canvas.

Ane struggled through the lashing sheets of rain and frothing sea spray to a secure position at the railing close enough to the captain to hear any order given. Hasbrouck gave him a wink in welcome, spat out a mouthful of seawater, and gestured to the heart of the storm.

Ane looked, but saw the sky and sea in mingled blackness only, at once mere inches, then unaccountable miles, it seemed, from the ship. Then lightning flashed and the sky lifted into rolling, roiling, snakelike cloud banks, and standing against the glare of the lightning bolt Ane saw a massive island rising sheer from the crashing seas.

"THERE!" the captain cried, above the screaming wind and deafening thunderclap.

Darkness again rushed the ship, drowning it once more, but the lightning's afterimage remained before Ane, burning brightly. "The Empire State," he whispered, his voice charged with sudden incredulous wonder. The Empire State....

Those of the crew who had missed the sight of it at the previous flash certainly saw it at the next, for now the island was twice as large, twice as tall, twice as ominous....

"By God," Ane heard on the wind, "it's a building!"

Another lightning flash, and its thunderclap ripped the air. Now all could see that this "island" before them was indeed a man-made structure, a huge and terribly old building, or at least the topmost portion of one, standing alone against the stormy sea. Hundreds of empty windows gaped at the crew, limned in green slime, before darkness once again plunged the structure into obscurity and deadly proximity.

The captain leaped to the helm. "Hard to port, Master Whaley! Hard over!" Both he and the sailing master put their weight to the wheel, and Huguenot, protesting mightily, slowly came about.

The Empire State Building moved past with nightmarish slowness, but the ship cleared it with no damage.

"Dear Christ!" the captain shouted. "There's another!"

It was indeed another wreck of a building, rising up from the furious sea, another obstacle for the ship, however slowly, to dance around. And beyond that building, emerging from the rain like wraiths, were still more buildings....

New orders were shouted to the crew in the rigging; more sail was cleared; Huguenot came about once more, this time heeling to such a degree that Ane's only choices were to marry the railing or drop into the black waves. He chose the former.

Taking a wave head-on he swallowed a bellyful of seawater, then promptly heaved both it and his supper. The next wave cleaned his clothes, but not his pride. Children do this, he thought wretchedly, little boys, not him. Still, he vomited again.

Hasbrouck noticed the condition of his seasick yeoman and promptly ordered him below.

"But, sir, I—"

"BELOW!" Ane went.

Dex, he found, had preceded him. She lay shivering in his rack, thoroughly soaked, and seasick herself. Seeing her condition only made Ane more disgusted with his own. He flung his clothes under the rack and crawled in with her; they clung together and shared what little warmth the wind and sea had not already robbed from them.

Ane wanted desperately to share his misery, his shame, but found he could not. The shame of disgracing himself in front of the captain was too much to admit to a woman; it was enough to leave him silent.

Dex said only, "Can you sleep?"

He found, only after some time, that he finally could.

The news that the Empire State was inhabited spread quickly through the crew. In the clearing dawn mists, tier after tier of soldiers were revealed, as well as other figures crossing spidery bridges between exposed sections of the massive ancient building. The majority of the inhabitants, however, could be seen leaning out of the hundreds of windows overlooking Huguenot, apparently as curious as the crew.

At midmorning Ane saw a boat with six oarsmen round the building's western corner. Captain Hasbrouck saw it, too, and climbed to the bridge to watch its approach.

After some minutes the boat stationed itself within hailing distance, and two figures in colorful dress stood, easily riding the swells, and raised hands in greeting.

The captain crossed his arms; the crew, taking the hint, was silent.

"Shall I have a boat lowered to meet them?" Master Whaley asked, after a moment.

Hasbrouck shook his head slowly. "Let's wait," he said.

More minutes passed, and Ane found himself acutely aware of just how heavy the silence was; the rising tension was almost palpable; he wanted to do something, anything....

Enough, he told himself then; you have shamed yourself enough for one voyage. Bide; learn from this. The captain will know what to do.

After several minutes had gone by one of the persons standing in the boat called out, "Hail!"

The captain leaned out on the railing. "I'm listening!" He bellowed back.

"Will you parley?"

Hasbrouck glanced at Master Whaley, who shrugged.

"Where?" He replied finally.

"At your convenience, sir!"

"Convenience," the captain murmured, smiling slightly. "We'll see." He raised his voice again, "Come ahead!" He turned to Ane. "Meet the master-at-arms at the accom ladder and have the two of them brought to the wardroom. Tell the jailer I want the rest kept topside. Understood?"

"Yes, sir."

"Then make it so. Master Whaley? You're relieved; I'll need you below. Mr. Walkill? You have the deck." With one final, calculating look to the approaching boat, Captain Hasbrouck left the bridge.

Ane entered the wardroom after knocking. The captain, seated before the stern ports, looked up and winked.

"We have them in the passageway, sir," the boy said. "Is the master-at-arms with you, lad?"

"Yes, sir."

"Jailer!"

The warrant officer leaned in past the door. "Sir?"

"Stand easy in the p-way, will you? And send in our envoys."

"Yes, sir."

The door opened fully; Ane stepped out of the way as the representatives from the Empire State swept through. The otherwise utilitarian wardroom was instantly transformed by their gaudy robes and heavy perfumes. Ane blinked; this was his first real chance to observe them fully; he blinked again, and then realized that his mouth was open.

Both Captain Hasbrouck and Master Whaley rose, their own faces impassive, but Ane was certain that they, too, were surprised. Though perhaps surprised, he thought, was too mild a word.

Both of the representatives wore heavy, elaborate, painstakingly feminine makeup. Like harlots.

And one of them was even a woman.

Women were forbidden access to the wardroom.

The woman said, "We are agents for the director, sir."

The captain, of course, ignored her. He spoke instead to the man. "My name is Sammael Hasbrouck, captain of the free ship Huguenot, from the island of Mohonk in the Catskill Archipelago. We have come to open a trade route, mutually agreeable to—"

"Captain," the woman interrupted, "I am the representative of the Skyscraper. All initial discussions must be with me."

Ane's mouth dropped open again. She had actually dared to interrupt? And the impertinence!

The captain, however, only frowned. "Must she do all the talking?" he asked of the male representative.

The man smiled. "She's my superior," he said. In a comer

now, Ane cringed; the master-at-arms peeked his head into the compartment again, but Hasbrouck waved him back out. "Take over, Edward," he whispered to the sailing master at his side. "I suddenly have no stomach for this; my next words to these... people...I will certainly regret."

Master Whaley nodded, his face a perfect mask, and said, "As Our captain just mentioned, ma'am, we have come on a mission of peace from an island group to the north and west of your—" He groped momentarily for the term she had used.

"It's the Skyscraper," the woman said, with no small note of pride. "And the Skyscraper is part of the City."

Master Whaley bowed his head slightly, and continued. "We have come to the Skyscraper in hopes of establishing a mutually profitable trade agreement. We are not an official diplomatic mission, of course, but merely agents for a trading company whose sole purpose is to find—"

"Clients," the woman said. "It is a concept and practice we are familiar with. We trade with many lands, many nations. There is much that we require, but also much that we offer."

"Excellent. Might a delegation of no more than six men be welcome to parley with your leaders, ma'am?"

"Certainly." And the woman smiled. "I will arrange it. Does tomorrow noon suit you?"

Master Whaley turned to the captain. "Sir...?"

"Fine," Hasbrouck said, tightly. "Fine. Our master-at-arms will show you back to your boat. Ane?" And he gestured stiffly toward the door.

The two envoys rose, then bowed deeply. "It has been a pleasure, sir," the woman said.

Hasbrouck only nodded.

After he had delivered the envoys to the master-at-arms in the passageway and had closed the wardroom door behind him, Ane could still hear the captain exclaiming, "...And open the ports, by God, I'm gagging from their stench!"

Dex dropped out of a passing work party and cornered Ane at the weather deck rail. "They say the captain practically kicked the envoys off the ship," she whispered, glancing around.

Ane glanced too. "One of them was a woman," he whispered back.

Dex whistled. "In the wardroom? So it's true," and she grinned broadly.

Over Ane's shoulder the Empire State Building was blue and mute in the afternoon haze. She looked at it for a long moment, her grin lingering. Ane found he didn't like what he saw in her eyes. "You'd better follow your working party," he said. "I can't bail you out with the mates every time, you know."

Her grin softened, and she touched his cheek gently, then, "See you!" and she was gone.

Ane turned to look at the building himself. Things must be very different there, he thought. Different, certainly, and maybe dangerously so. A sudden shiver of nervous dread went through him, and he wondered: What is going to happen next?

That night he awoke only slightly when Dex left his rack. "What—" he said, blinking in the darkness.

"Shhh, I'm only going to pee," she said, and stepped out into the passageway.

Ane next awoke to the clamoring of the ship's bell. In the dawn light, swinging to his feet, he realized he was still alone in his rack; Dex, apparently, had never returned.

As he pulled on his clothes a seaman ran by his compartment. "The squids deserted ship last night," he panted, and continued on his way. Impossible, Ane thought. They'd be crazy to—

"Christ," he muttered. "Where the hell is Dex?"

The captain's cabin was empty. Ane ran next to the bridge, where he found Hasbrouck by the wheel, surrounded by his officers. "But just how many are actually gone?" he was demanding.

The master-at-arms spread his hands. "Fifty at least," he said, "maybe more. It's most of the female slaves and some of the male ones as well. We'll have to muster the lot of them to get an accurate count."

The burly deck officer said, "I can count the bitching squids I have left on one hand." He spat toward the railing. "Better they all went, if you were asking me."

"Perhaps, William," Captain Hasbrouck said, "perhaps someday I shall."

Uneasy, lifeless laughter. Then the master-at-arms spoke again.

"We know they went over the side within an hour after the four-to-eight watch turnover. No later than five. And they swam rather than wake us all by lowering boats. Still, we had two men on anchor watch, one on stem watch, ten Marines patrolling, one duty cook, and two here on the bridge."

"And all of them," broke in the master corpsman, "are in sickbay with bashed skulls. I expect to lose a few by noon."

"So this desertion," the captain said, "was well planned. Obviously. Hell, I slept through it like a baby, as did you all."

"Damn squids," said the deck officer. "Sneaky as cats."

Then the captain noticed Ane. "Ah, lad, go warn the galley. The wardroom, gentlemen? First a plan, then a full stomach, and then we act. "

The thunder of several cannon, short and wide, but eloquent, still echoed in Ane's ears as the whaleboat was lowered into the water. Captain Hasbrouck's parting instructions echoed there as well: "Take copious notes; remember everything; I want to know what they think as much as what they say. I'm counting on you, lad."

Master Whaley, leading the whaleboat crew, favored Ane with a smile. "Nervous?"

Ane shook his head importantly, then looked out across the waves to the Empire State Building. He gestured to it. "I have a score to settle."

"Hah. Don't we all."

The coxswain loosed the stem line. "Clear!" he called, and

they were away.

With every slow, steady oarsbeat the Empire State loomed. Ane took in every window, every stone, every rusted girder and metal panel. Never in his brief life among the islands of the Catskills had he seen anything so huge, so ancient, so alien. All of this world lay under the sea, buried in the ooze of the past. Yet....

Master Whaley ordered the oars pulled in when they reached hailing distance. Hundreds of inhabitants crowded every available vantage point. Ane, his heart racing, strained to make out individual faces. Where were they? he thought. Where is she?

The sailing master raised his megaphone. "I wish to speak with someone in charge!"

"Green light!" came the reply, floating across the water on the breeze.

"That means 'go'," said someone from the stern.

"Are you certain, Mr. Hawkins?"

The seaman nodded. "Something my old Dad told me once. Old talk."

Master Whaley raised his megaphone once more. "We will come ahead, then!" Aside, to the boat crew, "Into the jaws, gentlemen, steady as she goes."

They rowed unopposed toward a large, rough maw cut into the side of the building. As they neared it Ane could hear the echoing crash of the sea swells riding one after the other into the cavernous darkness. Going to their death, he thought. And then: As we are?

Above them, as if in answer, the soldiers of the Empire State manning the lower windows and walls lowered their bows and spears, and sheathed their swords.

After Ane's eyes became accustomed to the dark of the enclosed harbor he looked about, almost frantic to take it all in. He saw numerous stone buttresses on all sides topped by ledges and balconies of all sizes, and punctuated by shadowed arches leading into the bowels of the building. And on every balcony and ledge, at every archway he saw more people, talking, gesturing, regarding them as though they were little animals caught in a firmly sprung trap.

A gaily dressed group standing at the end of a quay that extended almost to the center of the enclosed harbor raised their arms, and the population quieted. The continued steady rush of the sea through the entrance and against the pilings of the quay was the only sound until Master Whaley spoke. "We come in peace," he said in a voice loud and clear enough for all to hear.

A woman with long, golden hair replied, "That is most wise, sir."

Whaley smiled. "Can you tell me the condition of my fellow crew-members?"

"They are well."

"May I speak with them?"

The woman turned to the others and spoke quietly, then she turned back and shook her head. "It is not possible, sir. Not at present."

Hawkins grumbled something that Ane missed, but Master Whaley heard it and silenced him with a look.

"Our captain cannot deal in good faith," he said to the woman, "until the question at hand is resolved. We must have our crew back."

"Your crew came to us freely," the woman said, choosing her words carefully, "just as you have."

"Their act of desertion was unlawful. Surely, madam, you can understand our position."

The group on the quay conferred again, and then the woman said, "We understand your position and we sympathize, if only in principle. We must, however, ask that you understand our position as well. Anyone who comes to us with good intentions from any vessel, from any nation, is welcome in the Skyscraper, or in our sister buildings of the City. The bloodlines must remain clear, and new citizens are...necessary for that."

Master Whaley made to speak, but the woman continued, "It is our wish that you leave the City. Much can be avoided by your swift and peaceful departure."

"We cannot leave with our questions unanswered. We require a guarantee that our people are alive and well." Master Whaley's voice exposed a sharp edge. "We need to know that it is their wish that we leave, and that they stay."

The woman turned again to her companions. Their conversation was animated, and lasted several minutes. Then the woman said, "We do not condone violence, sir."

"And neither do we," Master Whaley replied immediately.

"We have...heard differently."

"You have only heard one side. Allow us to moor and we can both decide what is true and what is not."

The woman gazed at Master Whaley for a long moment. Then she said, "With you they were slaves. Here, they are free." She nodded, as though to herself. "This meeting is ended. I wish you fair seas, sir. Goodbye."

They turned as one and left the quay. Ane watched them walk through an arch and disappear in the darkness there. Then he looked about, searching again for a familiar face in the crowds around them before turning to the sailing master. "Is it over?" he asked. "Is this all?"

Whaley shook his head, his expression somber. "It is far from over, lad." He also looked about, taking in the hundreds of people still watching them from the walls. "Far from over," he said again. Then he looked out to where Huguenot rode at anchor, and his eyes blazed. "And the first thing we must do is tell the captain."

"What kind of defenses can they have? Spears? Flaming arrows?" Captain Hasbrouck paced furiously, hands clasped behind his back, his scowling face downcast.

"We saw only bows, spears, and swords," Master Whaley said. "And ceremonial ones at that."

"They can't have the powder for cannon, sir," contributed Master Eyck, the gunnery officer. "Catapults, maybe, but no serious firepower. Their limited range will cripple them."

"*We* will cripple them, gunner," the captain said. "We will make them wish we never popped over their cozy little horizon in the first place." He looked out a port to the Empire State, now a respectful distance away, and studied it through squinted eyes.

Ane, from a comer, spoke up. "Sir?"

Hasbrouck turned. "Yes, lad?"

"You plan to bombard them?"

"I plan to destroy them."

"But what about…what about the people?"

The captain grinned coldly. "Hopefully we will murder the lot of them, eh, gunner?"

"Yes, sir," replied Eyck. "My boys are primed."

"We'll run port side first with full broadsides from both decks to show them at the outset what Huguenot is capable of."

"But, sir!" Ane interrupted, his eyes wide, his mind in turmoil. "Do they have to die? Can't we, can't we—"

The deck officer cuffed him. "Is our little squid losing his nerve before the damned battle? Save it, lad, for when a sword aims to shove down your throat. Then you've my permission to crap your pants."

The wardroom erupted in hearty laughter, and Ane's protests were drowned out. He fled the compartment red-faced and ashamed, but angry as well. He ran until he found himself on the weather deck so far forward that the jib rigging snagged him. One more step and the gray ocean crested, ready to swallow him whole with the commonest of ripples.

He couldn't get an image of Dex out of his mind, an image of her cut and bleeding, lying in a tumbled, grotesque heap. And standing over her, laughing as he sheathed his bloody sword, was Captain Hasbrouck….

The words rang out again: "…We'll make them wish we never came…we'll murder the lot of them."

And with that a brand new feeling surfaced within him, a feeling so new that he gasped as though struck: "I'll hate you!" He screamed into the wind. "I'll hate you forever!"

And he knew in his heart that he would.

One hour before sunset, Huguenot attacked.

Because of the crew shortage Ane was assigned to one of the ammo gangs bringing the smooth round stones up from the ballast voids. He had to work furiously to keep pace with the men on either side of him as broadside after broadside thundered from the ship. He didn't have time to think, to despair at what was happening, nor to be angry about it. There were only the stones, and the rhythm, and the death being dealt above.

Huguenot made three passes, successful ones judging from the cheers of the crew manning the cannon. Their jubilance infected the crew below; the ammo gangs began a victory chanty in time with their labor, loud, strong and bawdy. Ane found himself singing along with the rest, caught in the moment, forgetting in the new, raw thrill of it where the stones he was passing up were being shot, and who lay in their terrible path. I am the killer, said his hands as they gripped a stone and passed it on. I am the killer, I am the killer....

His momentary exhilaration turned just as quickly to horror and disgust, but he was caught fast in the rhythm, the breath of death as he fed it, stone by stone. I am the killer, I am the killer....

On the fourth pass someone yelled down, "The cowards are finally returning fire!"

With what, Ane wondered miserably. He imagined their little spears and arrows slicing into the sea, hopelessly and ludicrously short of their mark. Take a lesson from the real killers, you poor people, he thought; look closely and see how it is done....

Suddenly he was aware of a different note in the cheering above; cries of concern were beginning to mingle in, then gain in numbers. Then a voice above the rest shrieked, "They're GODDAMN WHALES!"

The ship lurched as something massive collided with it. Ane was flung off his feet and sent sprawling into a ladder well.

Several others piled in after him, cursing, thrashing about; Ane could smell their fear, and he crouched at the bottom of the well until they extricated themselves. This has to stop, he thought, his anger feeding on panic and blossoming into rage. This is madness, madness....

When he saw his opportunity to get out himself he took it, running up through the confused, shouting crowds of ammo handlers to find the source of the madness; he went to find his captain.

He found instead a weatherdeck awash with soldiers of the Empire State. They all wore scarlet, and they swung huge curved swords. The ship's Marines met them blade to blade, and blood flew as freely as rain.

Ane grabbed a barrel cover for a shield and ran aft. "This has to stop!" he yelled through the din of battle. "This has to stop!" He saw the sea full of pilot whales and dolphins; some were saddled and harnessed; indeed, there were still soldiers riding in, leaping from their mounts and swarming up the side of the ship to reinforce the soldiers already on board.

More than once the barrel cover took a shove or a sword blow, but Ane, perhaps because he was young, perhaps because he held no weapon, or perhaps simply because he ducked and dodged at all the proper moments, made it alive to the aft topdeck where, shielded by his personal marine guard, Captain Hasbrouck was about to dispatch one of the scarlet soldiers lying at his feet.

"Ah, lad!" Hasbrouck motioned him into the relative safety behind the marine. "Come watch a slave die!"

Ane looked down and saw that the soldier was Loundes, the deserter.

"I could have killed you in your sleep, captain," she said, defiant even in defeat. "I could have cut your balls off, but I didn't."

Hasbrouck pointed his sword at her belly, at Seaman Hawkins's brand there. "For that possibility, bitch," he said, "I grant you a clean thrust." And he ran her through. "But nothing more." He pulled his blade free, and blood cascaded from her mouth. She jerked twice, then was still.

"Make a note, lad," the captain said, "to buy Hawkins another when we return home."

With a cry of uncontrollable fury Ane flung himself at Hasbrouck, striking at him, kicking, scratching and screaming. Taken completely by surprise, Hasbrouck fell back to the stem railing, his sword caught between them. Just as the Marine began to react the two tumbled over the railing and into the shadow of the air between the ship and the sea. And before they hit the water Ane grasped the sword blade in both hands and thrust it up under his captain's chin, burying it in his brain.

"Therel" he cried, "there!" as he tumbled into the sea. There...as the cool bitter water enveloped him...you bastard... and finally, as he lost consciousness...oh God, what have I done?

The blinding white light that he saw when he first opened his eyes took several moments to resolve itself into a window. The view through it came next: of a clear morning sky over a calm blue sea...and of a three-masted frigate riding at anchor, swinging with the current. After several more moments he realized it was Huguenot.

"Ane?"

He turned his eyes away from the brightness and focused them on a person seated beside his bed. "Dex..." he whispered, the word grating on a sore, raw throat.

She leaned over him, put her hand to his forehead, then touched his cheek with her lips.

"Where are we?" He asked. "Where—?"

"In the Empire State, only they call it the Skyscraper here. One of the Sea Riders fished you out of the water and brought you to safety. How do you feel?"

"Tired," he said, "very tired. And sore." His palms, too, were throbbing, and itching terribly. He raised his hands only with effort, and found that both of them were bandaged.

"They say you were cut deeply, probably by grabbing a

sword. Do you remember?"

Ane did, then, in a rush of memories, and a soft groan escaped his lips. "I...killed someone."

Dex's eyes widened. "Who? One of the soldiers?"

He shook his head. She really didn't know. And if she didn't, perhaps no one did. Perhaps any witnesses were as dead as...he was. Could this be justice? He wondered. "It doesn't matter," he said. "The battle...it's over?"

She nodded. "You've been bedridden for nearly a week; your fever only broke last night. Ane, I thought you were going to die, too...I thought I was going to lose you."

He looked at her. "Then why did you go, that night?" She hung her head.

He touched her arm with a bandaged hand. "Who is dead?" Looking up again, but not at him, she wiped a streak of tears away. "All of the marines; they fought to the last man, as usual. And nearly half of the remaining crew, including the captain, though his body was never found. And Loundes—"

"I know; I saw her die."

"Bravely?"

"Yes, and quickly. But what of Master Whaley?"

"Alive. I saw him only yesterday, at the conclusion of the negotiations. He commands Huguenot now."

"There is peace, then?"

She nodded. "The ship departs soon. You...are to go back with them."

Ane knew that that was how it must be. A tear of his own welled up, hesitated, but in the end did not fall. "When?"

Dex rose. "Today, I expect. When you feel up to it." She ran her hand through his hair. "You rest, now. You'll need all of your strength...."

At the door she suddenly turned back. "You don't have to go back with them, you know. You can stay if you want to."

He shook his head slowly. "I have to go, Dex. That part of me hasn't changed, even after all of this. You could come back, too, if you want."

She managed a shadow of a smile. "I'm not as brave as Loundes," she said.

He smiled too. "Oh, yes you are."

"Something," she said, "keeps telling me that we will be together, somehow, sometime." She opened the door. "I might even wait for you," she said, and then closed the door behind her.

On either side of the ship the sea parted, and the mottled backs of two sperm whales breached. From the bridge Ane heard them spit and gasp, and their plumes hung in the air like smoke.

"Our escorts," Master Whaley murmured. Ane said nothing.

It was a gray day, and the sea was the color of slate, meeting the sky in blurry veils of mist and fog. In their wake, the Empire State was already lost to view.

The sailing master looked at the boy. "You have done a little growing up on this voyage," he said.

"A bit," Ane agreed bitterly.

Master Whaley nodded slowly. "I think," he said then, "we should be John with one another. Ever since your return you have been wearing your feelings on your sleeve. That can be a very dangerous thing to do, these days."

Ane glanced up. "What do you mean?"

The sailing master drew him close, and whispered, "Listen to me; if nothing else, hear this: hate him if you need to; hate him with everything that is in you, but never let anyone see your hatred; never let anyone else know." He winked solemnly. "If you let it show here, now, you can count the days till you are a meal for the trailing sharks, and believe me, no one will notice you are gone."

Ane hesitated, then said, "Do you hate him, Master Whaley?"

"Ahh." The sailing master stood away from the railing. He put his hand on Ane's shoulder. "Off with you. Scrub that look from your face and mourn your captain. He is the hero of this godforsaken adventure, after all."

He winked again, and Ane, after a moment, winked back. It was a long, a very long, voyage home.

My hand is now cramped, reader, my pile of paper used, and my pot of ink nearly dry. This story, no-this prologue to the true story yet to be, is now complete. My mind is clear; I am, I think, ready.

My yeoman promises fair winds tomorrow. She is young and eager to please; she treats me with bemused, yet I suspect genuine, respect. She will make a fine captain someday.

I only hope I am worthy of that respect, for on the morning tide we sail for the Empire State.

Aye, reader; old Captain Hasbrouck has lain rotting in his sea grave these past thirty years, with his legends and his prejudices gone with him. Times have changed, and I am captain now.

"I might wait for you," Dex said. I only wonder if she has.

So Much for the Competition

The man on the roof squinted in the morning sunlight, contemplating the people in the park below. He sat comfortably, leaning back against an air-conditioning vent, his legs braced on the low roof retaining wall. He cradled his rifle in his lap. Below him, twelve stories down, the faces were too small to be distinguishable, to make them people, to make them *real*.

Good, he thought. Very good.

He felt the power in him, the surge in his arms, hands, and fingers, the electricity that jumped from him to the blue-steel barrel, the finely tooled walnut stock....

Soon, he told himself. Very soon, now.

He heard a sound at that moment, from somewhere behind him. He turned his head. An old woman, a green watering can in hand, stood at the doorway to the stairs leading down into the building. She looked at the rifle, then at him. He didn't move. She closed the door behind her and said, "I have to water my flowers."

He stared at her intensely, squinting his eyes again. Then he nodded. "Okay," he said. "Sure."

She shuffled over to a corner of the roof where several flats of tired looking marigolds and zinnias lay in the strong sunlight. "They really need it in this heat," she said, over her shoulder.

He smiled. Yes, he thought, they certainly did need it. And they will get it; they will get it indeed. He watched her as she stooped over each flat, and wondered: Will I kill her? Will she be the first?

A passenger jet thundered by, so low he could hear the air snapping behind it as it passed overhead. He closed his eyes, put his fingers to his temples. *Oh God,* he thought. *Oh God.*

When he opened them again the door to the stairway was closed, and the old woman was gone.

"Damn you," he said. "You're rushing me, now."

He turned back to the street and park below, to the people sitting on the benches there. He raised his rifle, relaxed his eyes, and took aim through the scope. He released the safety with his thumb, and then eased his forefinger onto the trigger. He focused on what he found beyond the cross hairs, a stout woman in a too-tight dress, clutching a department store bag in one hand and a hot dog in the other.

Relax, now, he told himself. She will never even hear the shot, never even feel it.

There was a faint crack, like a thin branch snapping, somewhere above, somewhere behind, *somewhere....*

 The man on the roof slumped to the side, a neat hole in the back of his head, his face in ragged pieces on the low retaining wall. The rifle slipped from his fingers, and slapped into the blood rapidly pooling around him.

Two blocks away, and two stories higher, the other sniper lowered his rifle. "So much for the competition," he muttered, and turned to contemplate the crowds below.

Three Wizards

The old man paused on the mountain path, and pulled the necklace chain out from beneath his cloak. On it, pierced through the nail, was a withered, mummified finger. He held the strange pendant up, silhouetted against the glare of the snowfields on the higher peak, and concentrated.

A whisper, almost nothing. No true spark of power, no real spark of life.

You are finally leaving me, father, he thought. At long last, it is time.

He took the finger pendant from around his neck and stored it carefully in a deep pocket. Finally, he thought: *time*.

"Now," he said aloud, into the clear, wind-filled air, *now for the end after the end. The coda. Now I must find the boy, and the place of my death, and make the circle complete once more.*

He leaned his tired body into the slope, and continued slowly along his way.

The long, cold winds from the HighArn carried snow with them, and by evening the valley of the Brethe was blanketed in white.

At the Swansblood, the snow meant higher, roaring hearth and bed fires to keep both tap customers and guests warm; it

meant that Obe was sent to the barn almost constantly for dry faggots, "Or I'll have your sweet ass!" Kurrit the burly innkeeper roared as he kicked the boy out the kitchen door and into the darkness of the courtyard.

Obe landed on his face, but the snow was already deep and soft, like the Grand Astiyr's featherbed, he thought, rising and wiping it from his clothes. Though hardly as warm, I'm sure!

He followed the nearly erased trail of footprints of his last trip, quickly entered the barn, and pulled the vast and heavy door shut behind him. Kurrit hadn't given him enough time to grab a lantern, but Obe knew the way in the dark well enough. He walked along the stalls, lightly slapping the rumps of the horses and donkeys. The animals nickered amiably, even the strangers. 'You've a way with the beasts, lad,' a memory of the innkeeper's voice said grudgingly in his mind, 'I'll give you that much.'

The boy hawked generously into the straw.

He grabbed two faggot bundles from the rear of the barn instead of just one, "Now you're figuring it out," he said to himself, grinning, and dragged them back to the door. Outside, the rising wind moaned eerily in the loft rafters. A horse bumped against its stall, and whinnied.

Obe pushed the door open with his shoulder, and was momentarily blinded by a fresh gust of snow-filled wind. When he cleared his eyes there was an old man before him, tall and thin and cloaked in dirty blue (*blue?*). He took one of the bundles and said, "Here, lad, I'll close the door for you."

Obe stared, speechless, as the old man in the blue (*blue!*) cloak swung the barn door shut and then secured it. *Blue*, but that could only mean—

The old man gestured with his bundle. "Shall we get inside? I'm froze colder than Ulfyion's balls in this wind."

Still speechless, Obe stumbled through the snow to the kitchen door.

Inside, somewhere beyond the hearth's fire glow, the innkeeper yelled, "The draft, boy! Close the damned door!"

Beneath his hood the old man winked, and shut the door fast behind them.

"Th-thank you, *lord*...." Obe managed. Most definitely blue, the color of the Gelder Order, a *gelder lord*, a *wizard*, here, at the Swansblood, helping him carry a bundle of wood!

The old man pushed his hood back, and brushed the snow from his generous beard and mustache. The reality of the kitchen's warmth seemed to wash over him then, and he shivered deeply.

"In the tap room, lord," the boy said, gesturing, "they will serve you hot food and drink."

The gelder lord smiled. 'Thank you, lad," he said, and gave Obe's shoulder a firm, friendly shake. "Lead on, then."

Within, the tap room was filled with pipe-smoke and flickering shadows, with the smells of spilled ale, sweat and roast meat, and with the sights and sounds of a host of wayfarers and serving wenches making the most of the evening at hand. A few looked up, but when they saw the cloak they looked quickly down again, or turned away.

The innkeeper sidled over to the gelder lord and bowed.

"Welcome, lord," he said, in an uncharacteristically respectful voice. "You'll be needing food, perhaps, and a bed?"

The wizard shrugged out of his cloak and hung it by the hearth. "Food, yes," he said, "but a spot by the fire is all the bed I will need."

Obe had never seen the innkeeper so nervous. Kurrit was bigger and broader and hairier than anyone in the room, but then, he had never—at least in Obe's memory—actually come face to face with a gelder wizard! "My name is Kurrit, lord," the innkeeper said, " ...at your service."

"Is this the valley of the Brethe River, landlord?"

"Yes, lord. We sit at the knees of the HighAm, in the province of Semeley."

The old man nodded. He seemed to recognize the names.

Kurrit hesitated a moment, then said, "I'd best see to your meal, lord. Obe! Where is that blasted boy? Obe!"

The boy stepped from behind the gelder lord's shadow. "Here, sir," he said.

The gelder lord turned to him with a raised eyebrow. "Obe? Your name is Obe?"

" ...Yes, lord."

The wizard nodded slowly. "And who named you, lad?"

"He was a foundling, lord," Kurrit interjected. "He was no more than a squalling brat when some bitch dumped him at my doorstep. Obe was the only word he knew, so the wenches gave it to him for a name."

The gelder lord looked steadily into the boy's eyes; Obe dared not look away. "You have no parents, then, lad? No family, alive or dead?"

Obe shook his head.

"Answer him!" Kurrit roared. "Answer him or I'll—"

The wizard raised a gnarled hand. "That's enough, landlord. Leave the boy alone."

Kurrit opened his mouth, then closed it again.

"If you would be so kind," the gelder lord said then, "my meal."

The innkeeper bowed again, stiffly. "Certainly, lord," he muttered. "And your desire?"

"Anything, as long as it is hot."

Kurrit bowed a final time, and was gone.

The gelder lord winked at Obe. "You will have some peace for one night, at least," he said. "But enough. We will talk further, perhaps after I have eaten." Then he gathered his knees to him, and turned his full attention to the fire.

Obe was still standing just beyond the flickering light, gazing at the wizard, when one of the serving wenches pinched his rear and pulled him further into the shadows. "Kurrit wants you in the kitchen, pricklet," she hissed, with a breath that smelled of onions and sour wine. "You'd best hurry, if you know what's good for you."

He shrugged her hand away, and with surprising, new-found courage, he said, "Why should I worry about old Kurrit with a gelder wizard to protect me?"

The wench sputtered with sudden laughter. "Who," she said, "*him?* Why he's nothing but a shriveled up old man." She raised her little finger and wiggled it, "A shriveled up old man with nothing in his breeches but a shriveled up old worm." Then she grew serious once more. "Mind me now, pricklet," she said. "The last thing you need is another one of his beatings." And she gave him a kick to start him on his way. With a final glance in the direction of the gelder lord, Obe ducked a second kick and made his way through the crowd to the kitchen.

Standing just inside the door, Kurrit was waiting for him with a broomstick. "So!" He said, swinging the stick and catching Obe on the side of his head before he could duck, "you think you can hide behind a gelder lord's cloak, eh?" He hit him again, this time on the shoulder, and Obe stumbled to his knees on the straw-strewn flagstones. "Where is he now to protect you, eh?" The stick came down again. "And why does it hurt so much, eh? Why—"

Suddenly, the room was filled with a blinding white glare. Obe, with his face in the straw, heard the innkeeper gasp, then choke. He rolled onto his back, shading his eyes, and saw the gelder lord standing in the doorway with both arms raised. In one hand he held Kurrit, dangling him like a rag doll by the collar of his tunic. In the other, something on a chain, a pendant, a charm of some kind, shone with a light nearly as bright as the sun.

The wizard spoke, and in a voice like the rumble and roar of thunder, said, "I told you to leave the boy ALONE!"

Then the light was extinguished; the gelder lord thrust the pendant into his shirt, and threw the innkeeper unceremoniously to the floor.

"Come, lad," he said, in a normal voice once more, and offered Obe a hand up.

The boy took it.

The wizard put his arm around him, and they turned as one, back into the now silent and motionless taproom. Behind them, Kurrit made no move to follow, and in the taproom no one even raised their face as the two shouldered their way to the front door.

Outside, in the cold, quiet snowfall, the gelder lord paused and turned to the boy. "Was there anything you wanted to take with you, lad?" he asked.

"Take with me—?" Obe took a sudden, stumbling step backward. "But I don't—" he stammered, "—I don't know— "

The gelder lord laughed. "Of course you don't, lad. As I didn't, when I was as young as you, plucked from my life, such as it was, to walk this road. But I went, just as you must. And I walked the road, just as you must. Do you see, lad?"

Obe fell to his knees. "No, lord," he cried. "Forgive me," and he cast his eyes down in shame, "but I am just—"

"I know." The wizard put a hand on his shoulder. "You are just a boy." Then he helped Obe to his feet and held him at arm's length. "Will you come with me for a day's journey at least? Then, if you still want to return, I promise you, I will bring you back to this place."

Obe met his eyes, but said nothing.

"One day," the wizard repeated. "I promise you."

Obe glanced back to the inn. "One day," he whispered.

"We will give Kurrit a chance to cool his anger, eh?"

Obe nodded, finally. "But I'm afraid, lord," he said.

"Of course you are. And cold too, I'll wager. Here," and an invisible curtain of warmth sprang up around them, driving the cold way. Even the snow was turned, no longer falling on them, but around them.

"I made a pact with myself," the wizard said, "not to use my magic, such as it is, except in the most dire emergencies." He tousled Obe's hair dry. "I think the prospect of freezing to death in the night constitutes such an emergency, don't you, lad?"

"Yes, lord," Obe whispered. He reached out to where the snow was falling beyond him, but no matter how far he stretched his fingers, the snowflakes retreated, and did not touch them.

"Come," the gelder lord said, "let's get away from here. I

can no longer stand the smell of the place."

They started along the path that led down the valley to the river, and the spell of shelter and warmth, like a huge but invisible tent, went with them, into the snowfall, into the night.

"Why," the boy asked, after a long enough time had passed for him to summon up the nerve again to speak, "why do you want me to go with you, lord?"

"To save your life," the wizard said, after a moment. "And, in a curious way, to save mine as well." Then he looked away, and they spoke no more all the rest of that night.

The next morning Obe awoke with the sunrise. He was alone in a clearing under the empty spread of an ancient beech. It was nothing but a dream, he thought immediately. But as he struggled to his feet, the pain in his cheek and shoulder from Kurrit's broomstick was definitely no dream. And neither was the worn blue wizard cloak that fell away from him as he stood.

He stared at it, wide-eyed, as the gladness and fear of his new freedom flooded him anew.

Through the trees, then, trudging slowly, the gelder lord entered the ring. From his belt hung a dead rabbit. "Are you hungry, lad?" He asked cheerfully.

"Yes, lord," Obe said. Then he gathered up the blue cloak, shook it clean of snow and leaves, and offered it.

But the wizard held up a hand. "Keep it," he said. "I don't think I will need it today."

A stiff wind blew across the clearing, and for the first time since the previous night Obe again felt the cold; the visible shelter of warmth, as quickly as it had appeared the previous evening, was now just as quickly gone.

"Put it on," the gelder lord said, squatting, laying the rabbit on a flat stone before him. He drew forth a knife, and began preparing the animal for their breakfast.

Obe put the cloak around him gingerly. It was huge, more the blanket it lad served for in the night than a garment to wear. Still, he gathered it around him as best he could, then sat down again, with his back to the tree. He watched the wizard skin the rabbit, then gut it. " …I thought—" he began.

"Yes, lad?"

"I always thought that gelder wizards were friends to the animals."

"And so we are, lad, so we are." The wizard picked up the skin of the rabbit. "We also learn to know when an animal's time has come. This one's time came this morning, under a yew, quietly, with dignity, dreaming of a warm Spring day, of a field full of clover, and a sky free of hawks. His flesh is old, but it will do." He threw the skin into the snowy underbrush. "And anyway, I'm hungry."

Obe opened his mouth to ask another question, but then the gelder lord grunted loudly, and there was an arrow shaft sticking out of his belly. The old man looked down, amazed. "*Here?*" he said. "*Here?*"

Then he coughed, and fell to his side, clutching the bloody shaft. Obe sprang forward, a scream forming, but the gelder lord waved him away. "Get back," he gasped, spraying blood from his mouth. "Get away…into the forest…now!"

Obe took a step backward, looking wildly about him. The darkness beneath the trees…the sudden quiet….

He ran, then, just as a second arrow sang by him and buried itself in the trunk of the beech. He ran across the clearing, following a random, blundering pattern through the snow as he waited for a third arrow to find its mark between his shoulders.

But none did.

He dove into the shadows beneath the trees, finally, and rolled to a stop.

Silence.

After a moment he gathered his courage and peered out from the shadows. Before his eyes, through the tangle of trees, the old gelder lord gasped a final time, and died at foot of the old beech.

The forest was still silent. Obe held aching sides as tears made slow, cold tracks down his cheeks. He is *dead*, he thought, shaking his head incredulously. *Dead!* But how could he be? How is it possible?

Then he heard the sound of someone trudging through deep snow, somewhere beyond the line of trees. Obe drew back, into the shadows, and held his breath.

After a moment Kurrit, the innkeeper, stepped into the light. In his hand was a long bow, and on his back, a quiver of arrows. "I know you are near, you little bastard," he called out. He drew a new arrow and notched it, his gaze searching, following the line of prints in the snow to the very place where Obe crouched. "Come out, why don't you, and take your arrow like a man." More silence. The world seemed to hang on that long moment.

Then the innkeeper laughed, and threw his weapon to the snow. Going over to the body of the gelder lord, he rolled it over with the toe of his boot. Then he bent close, and spit in the dead man's face. The wizard's sightless eyes stared back, unflinching.

"Gelder lord," Kurrit said contemptuously. "Hah." He began rummaging about in the dead man's clothes. When he found what he sought he stood and held up his prize, letting it dangle from its dull metal chain in the bright morning sunlight.

It was a mummified finger, severed at the root, and curled slightly, as though at rest. It was attached to the chain by a metal ring pierced through the yellowed, horny nail.

The pendant, Obe thought, straining to see. The pendant that had glowed the previous evening with the light of the sun....

"This was the old man's power, boy," Kurrit called out. "This was his magic, and now it's mine." He placed the chain around his neck, and let the finger hang at his chest. He stared down at it, clenching his hands, flexing his broad, hard muscles, a cry of supreme exaltation forming on his lips.

But then the finger *moved*.

Kurrit's cry of exaltation became a sudden scream of fear. He grabbed the finger convulsively, tore the necklace free and flung it to the ground, then pulled out his knife and stepped back, panting.

The finger undulated in the snow and dead leaves, like a worm seeking cool dirt under a hot sun. The innkeeper stared, paralyzed now, as before him the finger transformed and became a hand, crawling across the short distance that separated it from his boots.

When it reached him, the innkeeper shrieked, but still did not, or could not, move. The hand climbed his leg like a huge deformed spider. At his knee it became an arm, then more than an arm, and at his throat, finally, it had become a fully formed man, an old man, a blue-cloaked gelder lord with cool grey eyes that were infinitely old, infinitely deep, staring into the half-crazed, shallow depths of Kurrit's own.

The innkeeper died in supreme agony, but without a sound. The gelder lord threw his body into the bloody snow by the skinned rabbit. Then, stooping, gathering up the dead wizard from the snow, cradling his dead kin in his arms, he set off, past the ancient beech tree, into the shadows of the forest. "Are you coming, lad?" He called over his shoulder before he completely disappeared.

Like a chastised little dog, Obe followed.

It was only a short time before they stopped. Before them was a placid, reedy pond ringed on all sides by hemlocks and the twisted skeletons of wild apple trees. There were snow geese in the reeds, but they made no flight, and only looked across the icy water with patient interest.

This new wizard laid his burden out on a large flat stone at the pond's edge, bent over it for a moment, then stood, shook his silver hair free of his face, and looked heavenward.

A breeze rippled the surface of the pond, and when it touched Obe he blinked in surprise, for the air was unaccountably *warm*.

Then, all about them, the snow began to melt. In moments it was completely gone, and the forest around them became grey with empty branches, and brown with mud.

But not for long.

For the trees, the bushes, even the grasses and weeds at Obe's feet, suddenly began to sprout, to grow, to unfurl new green leaves in the now warm, Springlike air. Apple blossoms burst forth, and the flowers were taken up by the soft winds, filling the air with their pink and white petals.

The boy reached out and grabbed at them, turning them over in his hand. Real. All of it. *Real.*

The wizard looked down, finally, and turned from the pond. "I think we can begin, now," he said. "Come here, lad. Kneel by me."

Obe hesitated, then went forward, and dropped to his knees at the wizard's feet. "I don't understand, lord," he whispered. "Any of this."

The gelder lord raised his ancient, gnarled hand. "Obe was trying to reach this place, *his* place, to die in peace, with dignity, as he was supposed to. But the bowman, damn him, and his arrow were unforeseen."

The boy looked down to the still, silent face half-covered now with flower petals. His name was Obe? "But that is *my* name," he said aloud, looking up once more.

The gelder lord smiled. "And it is mine as well. But we share more than just a name. We are *kin*, lad, or hadn't you figured that out yet? More than a name, and blood, we share the magic as well." Then he uttered a quiet chuckle, and with it, he shed the last of his air of sadness. "And the magic for you," he said, "has already begun. See!"

He held forth a bright new necklace chain. Dangling from it, not an inch from Obe's nose, was a freshly severed finger. The boy stared at it, his breathing caught behind his tongue. Then he glanced down once more to the dead wizard, to his hands folded at his chest; indeed, a finger was missing there.

The gelder lord lowered the necklace and hoary pendant over Obe's head. As the weight of it and all that its wearing implied settled securely around his neck, the boy said, "I will meet him again, won't I."

The gelder lord nodded. "The Three meet only twice in a

Gelder cycle. Once at the beginning, and again at the end. When it is your time to die, a century hence perhaps, you will find your son, wherever he may be, and the two of you will journey to a place much like this. There, if you are lucky, your father will return to you, and together, before the end, the two of you will teach the boy."

Father, Obe thought. He looked down once more to the dead wizard, and then the finger pendant resting against his chest. *My father.*

The sudden, raw thought of his own mortality passed through him then, like a wraith. He became a man, after a fashion, in that instant. He said, "But such an end is a beginning, too, isn't it?"

"Yes, lad," the old man said. "There is always the beginning. A beginning such as this." He placed his hands on Obe's shoulders. "But be quiet, now, and help your grandfather bury his son. Then, young gelder lord, with what little gift of time I have left on this good earth, your lessons shall begin!"

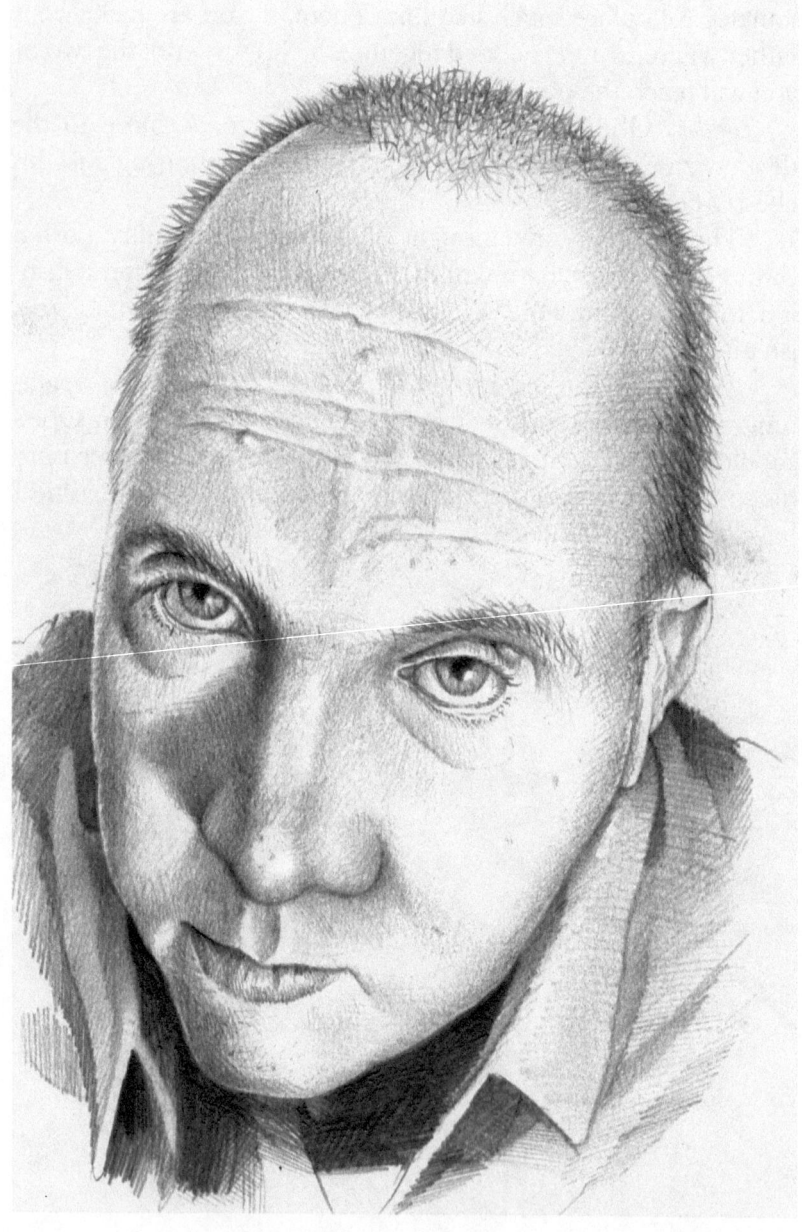

Dead Eye

PRRANNNGGG!

I jerked, my eyes darting from the rear end of the eighteen-wheeler to my rear-view mirror to see what I had just driven over. Jesus! It had sounded like a monkey-wrench thrown against the side of my car! But there was nothing behind me, just a clear road, no debris, not even any following cars.

So what had hit my Subaru—my one-month-old, still smelling like new, waiting for that first ding—shiny red Subaru?

With a rapidly growing collection of lead sinkers in my belly, I pulled over to find out.

It was an early April morning, and I was just above Coopersburg on a curving connector road between Route 309 and Interstate 78. Beyond the concrete lip of the road shoulder was an empty plowed field, and beyond that, a solid, wild thicket of trees. The big semi I had been following was long gone. Every few seconds a car or truck would whip by, building up speed to merge with the interstate traffic. I edged around to the rear of my car, expecting to find a dent, a crack, *something* to account for the noise.

I found it in the center of my right rear wheel cover. I crouched in the gravel and weeds of the shoulder, balancing myself with one hand on the fender, and examined the damage.

The center of the wheel cover was just…gone. Large pieces of plastic had been broken off, exposing the wheel rim, disc brake and metal axle cap. This cap was designed like a little derby hat…except mine, right now, right here on the shoulder of the I-78 connector, looked like a hat that had been stepped on, bent all the way in, crushed almost inside out. Like something very powerful or heavy had struck it, dead on.

Something very powerful.

A few scenarios played out in my head as I stood, glancing about, looking for something big, like a lug nut from a wheel, or a big rock, something that might have been flung back from that eighteen-wheeler I had been following, somehow ricocheting off the concrete barrier to hit my rear wheel in the exact center. I went back to where I guessed the impact had actually occurred, but the shoulder was just littered with sand and gravel. I did find a piece of plastic that looked like it belonged to my wheel cover, but that was all.

I debated what to do. Call the police? A repair shop? All of that would take time, and I had to make the meeting in Harrisburg or there would be hell to pay back at the office. In the end, I got back into my car, got back onto the connector road, and merged with the traffic of the highway. I listened to the wheels on the pavement, felt the vibrations of the car as I picked up speed. Everything *seemed* okay. It was just my bad luck, I decided. It would be fine.

Later that day, during a meeting break, I told the story to a few of the people there. I got a few whistles, a few shaking heads. "Lucky whatever that thing was didn't hit your windshield," someone said. "What are the odds," another said. "Right in the exact center of the hubcap?" At another break later in the day, someone who had heard the story but had kept silent took me aside and in a low voice said, "Did you ever consider the other explanation?"

Sometimes I can be very dense. "*Other* explanation?"

He leaned in, and said in an even lower voice, "Did you ever consider somebody might have taken a shot at you?"

I lived in a quiet little town in northern Bucks County, Pennsylvania. It was one of the towns that gave the Route 309 Bypass its name, and there were still more farms around it than subdivisions. I would tell people that mine was the kind of small American town where I might actually find Wally and the Beav living right around the corner. Sure, there was a gun club and shooting range up on Ridge Road. Sure, on the first day of deer hunting season the high school was like a ghost town, and if you were smart on that day, you worked International Orange into your off-road wardrobe. Smarter still, you stayed the hell out of the woods altogether. There were Meat Shoot dinners at the Owls Club and the Moose Lodge, and more than a few pickups had gun racks in the back of the cabs. Guns, in other words, were an integral part of the fabric of my town, just as they were in all the other little bypassed towns in rural America—like Coopersburg, home of that plowed cornfield beside the connector road to I-78, and that dark, dense patch of woods. *"Did you ever consider somebody might have taken a shot at you?"*

As I drove back home that evening, with half my mind still alert to the tire sounds and the feel of the car around me, the other half searched for an explanation. This was April. The deer-hunting season was long over, wasn't it? And anyway, my little red Subaru didn't look anything like a six-point buck. Was there another 'season' of hunting this time of year? Duck season, maybe? Didn't they use shotguns for ducks? Birdshot, they called it, didn't they? If someone had taken a shot at me—and that was still a very big if—it would have taken a lot more than birdshot to dent that axle cap. It would have taken a bullet.

As I passed along that connector road, I looked hard at the empty cornfield and line of trees, now just a dark smudge against the evening sky. There were no lights, nothing to show anyone lived back there. Still, I couldn't shake the feeling of having a big target painted on the side of my car, and I didn't actually feel safe until I was well along on Route 309, with the strip malls and stores beginning to crowd together south of Coopersburg.

Somebody had taken a shot at me today. It sounded unreal. Hold that thought, I told myself. No point in letting it make me crazy. Still…*someone had taken a shot at me today.* Jesus.

A trooper in the county police department lived down toward the end of my long block. I knew that because he sometimes parked his cruiser in his driveway. His last name was Arnold, and I only knew that because it was painted on his mailbox. The most we had ever done was trade nods and an occasional 'hello' passing one another on the sidewalk. So when I showed up on his doorstep on Saturday morning, I could see his radar go up immediately. "Tim Wakefield," he said through the screen door, "right?"

I was surprised he knew my name.

"I'm embarrassed to say I don't–" I began.

"It's Bill. Bill Arnold." He opened the door and we shook hands. "What can I do for you?"

I told him about the car incident, and he raised both eyebrows when I described the damage to the axle cap. "I was wondering," I said, "if you would mind coming over to look at it."

"Absolutely, not a problem." He called over his shoulder, "Honey? I'm going down the street for a few minutes with Tim."

"Who?"

"Tim! Neighbor up the street."

"Don't forget Billy's game at ten. You're driving."

"Little League," Bill said to me, shaking his head. "It's cutthroat in this town."

He whistled when he saw the dent in the axle cap, and bent down to take a closer look. "That could be a bullet dent," he said.

"You mean…from a bullet?"

He gave me a patient, you-dumbass-you look. "Yeah. A dent from a bullet. Something small caliber. A .22, maybe."

"Did I just hear someone say bullet?"

We both looked up. My next-door neighbor Ralph was standing by the boxwood hedge that separated our driveways.

"Yeah," Bill said. "That's what it looks like to me."

Ralph scratched at the liver spots on the crown of his head. "That just doesn't make any sense. Who would want to take a pot shot at Tim? He doesn't have a mean bone in his body."

"Well, Mr.—"

"McGillivary. Ralph McGillivary, Buchanan High School, retired. You're Bill Arnold, policeman lives down the other end of the block, right?"

"Yes sir. As I was saying, this could have been a random incident. I'd bet whoever might have fired the shot didn't know Tim from Adam."

"That's a scary thought." Ralph shook his head meaningfully. "Scary world, these days."

Bill straightened, pulled his wallet from his back pocket, extracted a business card, and handed it to me. "Random or not, you should report it."

I put the card in my shirt pocket. "Absolutely," I said. *Not in a million years,* I thought.

My car was still under warranty, so I took it to the dealer. I didn't think the damage to the wheel would be covered, but I figured I might as well ask. "There's something wrong with my right rear wheel," I told the lady behind the service counter.

She looked up, her pen poised over the repair form.

"Something hit it," I said. "The wheel cover is broken, and the metal cap inside is dented."

"The axle cap."

"Yes. The axle cap is dented. Is any of this covered?"

"Sorry, no." The service lady made a note on the form. "Depending how hard the wheel was hit, we might have to recommend a wheel alignment."

"Is that covered?"

"Sorry, no."

My shoulders sagged. "Okay. Whatever it needs."

"Any idea what it was that hit you?"

I shook my head slowly. "No idea at all."

I sat in the lounge reading old magazines, making a conscious decision not to try the courtesy coffee. After half an hour a man in a spotless pair of blue coveralls came out and crouched next to me, clipboard balanced on his knee. "You're a lucky man, Mr. Wakefield," he said.

"Really? How lucky?"

"Forty-five for a new wheel cover, and thirty-six-fifty for a new axle cap. Didn't need an alignment."

"That's all? What about labor?"

He straightened. "That's on the house."

"Really?"

"Company policy, Mr. Wakefield." He put his hand on my shoulder. "We never charge for labor when our customers get shot at."

The first weekend in June, I bought a gun. A handgun. The sporting goods store that sold it to me also sold backpacks, sleeping bags, tents, propane grills, and kayaks. And freeze-dried food in foil pouches. There was an entire aisle of those.

The handgun I chose was a Browning 9mm High Power Standard, a semi-automatic with carved walnut grip inserts. It held a clip of nine bullets. "This is a decent weapon for personal protection," the salesman said. "A little heavy, but the kick is minimal, and it's accurate. You want to knock someone down with your first shot, this will do it for you."

"I'm only going to use it on the shooting range," I said.

"You might want to consider a target pistol, then."

"Oh, no." I gripped the open box with both hands. "This is the one I want."

The salesman nodded. "We just need you to fill out the form, and we'll give you a call after Harrisburg does their thing."

"How long?"

"Three days, usually. We fax it in."

"Do you need a deposit?"

The salesman grinned.

From my back door stoop I had a commanding view of my backyard, which consisted of a one-car garage, a few square yards of grass, and a narrow strip of flowerbed along the fence I shared with my neighbor Ralph. I also had a good view of Ralph's back yard. Ralph was a widower. He had converted his garage into a fully equipped woodworking shop. He had also turned his small parcel of lawn into a world-class vegetable garden, and he shared its produce with everyone in the neighborhood. I almost never had to buy vegetables in the summertime.

Seeing me sitting on my top step, he came to the fence with a cardboard box filled with a sampling of the day's take from the garden.

"Wow," I said, eying the contents.

He nodded to the Browning in my lap. "Ditto."

I grinned, holding it up. "A beauty, isn't it?"

"I just hope it's not loaded."

My grin went down a notch. "Of course not. You never clean a loaded gun."

Ralph leaned over the fence to get a better look. "What kind is it?"

"Here." I went over to the fence and swapped the gun for the box of vegetables. "These look great, " I said, noting cucumbers, green peppers, and early tomatoes. "Thanks."

Ralph hefted the Browning. "What the hell are you doing with a weapon like this?"

"Target practice," I said, trying not to sound too defensive. "A hobby."

"Bullshit."

"Personal protection, too."

"Against who?" Ralph gave me one of his dead-eye looks. "Double bullshit."

Ralph had been in the Army in Vietnam. He had probably seen his share of guns, and shooting. Maybe even killing. He handed the gun back. "You're like a kid with a new toy," he said.

I didn't reply. The Browning felt warm in my hand. Solid.

"It's not a toy, Tim," Ralph said. "Remember that. It's not a toy."

"I know." I put the gun down on the step beside me, and it was an effort to keep my voice civil. "You don't have to say it twice."

On Saturday, with my Browning velcroed tight in its black nylon case, I went up on Ridge Road to the Perkioman Gun Club and applied for a guest membership. "Do you offer lessons?" I asked.

The old man blinked behind his bifocals. "We'll take care of you," he said.

I put the case on the counter, and unzipped it. The old man squinted at the Browning.

"It's new," I said.

"I can see that."

"I never shot a gun before."

The old man looked up at me and winked. "Well, you came to the right place, then, son. We'll set you up with Ray."

"Ray?"

"He likes working with the newbies." He moved the gun case aside with a careful motion, and put a form in front of me. "Just fill this out and sign and date it at the bottom. And I'll need to see some photo ID, please."

I went every Saturday, as soon as they opened. Ray, over-weight, middle-aged, a plumber in his weekday job, started me at ten yards. "Don't be offended," he said, "I start everybody out at ten." He told me not to worry about hitting the target, but to concentrate on just getting used to the feel of my gun. "It doesn't take shit to hit the bulls-eye," he said. "That's not really the point, you know?" A Zen plumber teaching me how to shoot; perfect.

The targets were big red dots with concentric circles around them, printed on large squares of stiff paper. After two lessons and an entire box of ammunition, I started leaving an occasional hole in the paper. Not in the red dot, not even inside the rings, but at least I hit the damn things instead of the hay bales in the back. After four weekends, with the targets now at twenty yards, I was hitting the paper with nearly every shot, often inside the rings, once or twice even inside the big red dot. "You're getting comfortable with it," Ray said, "and that's good. Just so's you don't get too comfortable."

"What do you mean?"

"You get too comfortable with a weapon like yours, you can get careless, make mistakes." He nodded to my Browning. "You make a mistake with a gun like that, you can hurt somebody. It only takes one, you know."

Damn straight, I thought. Damn straight.

By October, with half the leaves down in the woods, and me hitting the red dot any time I damn well chose, I knew I was ready.

I decided to go up to those woods by the connector road every day for a week, different times each day. Five days, that would be enough. I had more than enough vacation time at work.

"Where are you headed?" my boss asked, squinting at my memo requesting the time off.

"Oh, just sticking around the house, getting some things done."

"Sleep in every day, that's the ticket." He initialed the memo, and handed it back.

I went to the woods in early evening on Monday. The woods were empty.

On Tuesday, I went around noon. A squirrel chastised me from a high branch, but that was all.

I saved Wednesday for my early morning trip. An anniversary, of sorts.

As I drove down the street I saw Bill Arnold in full uniform walking to his car. He didn't appear to notice me as I went past, which was just as well.

Wednesday morning traffic on Route 309 was heavy, but I

expected that. I drove right at the speed limit, letting everyone pass me on the left. I only got a few dirty looks.

Route 309 started to take on the look of a highway just north of Coopersburg, and then there it was, the big green sign for the exit to Interstate 78. I took it, following the gentle curve of the connector road, and only glanced once at the cornfield, filled now with the last harvest stubble, and the colorful woods beyond. I merged onto I-78 with ease, and the first exit to Bethlehem came up immediately. I took it, and made my first right into the same Burger King parking lot I had used the previous two days. My parked car was one of several dozen. Anonymous. Perfect.

The walk back along the highway to the connector road took about twenty minutes, and then I was in among the cornrows, the stripped stalks about as high as my belt-buckle. Then I was under the trees.

I felt like a bumbling fool, trying to make my way through the brambles, branches and underbrush that choked the ground between the tree trunks. Hell, I *was* a bumbling fool, putting my feet down into every crackling collection of fallen leaves, onto every brittle, snapping twig. A Navy SEAL I wasn't.

I tried to keep the cornfield and the highway in sight. Whoever had shot at me would have needed some sort of unobstructed view, no matter how good their eyesight or rifle scope. "Would have led you, most likely," Ray had said. "Led me? What does that mean?" "It means he probably aimed just a shade in front of where you were headed. Bullets are fast, particularly fired from high-powered rifles, but they still take a certain amount of time to get to their targets. If he aimed right at the center of your wheel and fired, by the time the bullet got there your car would have moved, and he would have probably blown out your tire instead, or hit the fender. So he led you." "You're saying I should be thanking this guy?" Ray had grinned. "That's one way of looking at it. I'd take a dented axle cap over a blown tire any day. So yeah, his good aim probably saved your life."

Whoever had shot and hit the center of my right rear wheel had been a marksman. More than that. He had been playing with me. Playing with my life. It had been nothing more than personal sport to him. My right rear wheel, *my life*, had been his big red dot.

I stopped, midway between two maples, a thorny bush just catching my jeans at the thigh. I stopped, and *listened*. I heard a high wind in the half-empty treetops; I heard the quiet clacking of branches and the low groaning of limbs; I heard some loud bird, probably a crow, cawing off in the distance. Below it all, I heard the steady rush of traffic on the highway as car after car, truck after truck, followed the curve of the connecter road north.

A dry brown leaf spiraled down past my nose, missing me by less than an inch. Enough, I thought. Enough.

"Are you here?"

My voice was lost in the forest.

Louder: "HERE I AM!"

The distant crow stopped cawing. That was all.

I turned slowly around, my eyes darting from tree to tree, and the confused, hidden spaces between them.

Then I saw him, but only because he wanted me to, only because he *moved*.

He was wearing camouflaged fatigues, and he blended perfectly into the greys and olives and blues of the trees and underbrush. It was only when a breeze moved some branches one way, and he stepped, deliberately I'm sure, in another, that he emerged from total concealment. And he was looking directly at me.

I saw a rifle slung over his back, its barrel camouflaged like his clothing. He had the thumb of his left hand hooked under the rifle strap. His right hand was empty. The exposed skin of his hands and face were smeared in random patterns of grey, olive and black war paint. The skin camouflage made the whites of his eyes stand out.

I felt like an animal under that gaze. I felt like prey. Like nothing more than his big red dot.

"You took a shot at me," I said, surprised at the calm in my voice. "You took a shot at my car."

He said nothing, just continued to stare.

My coat was open. I reached in with my right hand. As I did so, he unslung the rifle and began bringing it up to his shoulder, all in one swift, fluid movement.

But I was faster.

I brought my Browning to bear, centered on the bridge of his nose, and pulled the trigger.

He staggered back a step, a neat red eye formed between his other two. A Big Red Dot. Then he went down.

It only took one, if you were a dead eye.

I was a dead eye, now.

Smiling, I bent down to collect my brass.

Bushido

1

Edward the Construct, the face of the Great Ship, awoke for the first time in total darkness.

He felt the rigid deck plate beneath him, and the gentle breath of warm, conditioned air on his cheek. He asked on several levels, including aloud, "Why was I awakened?"

The Great Ship answered in its own whispered voice: *Human passengers are arriving.*

Human passengers. In a craft capable of extended interstellar travel.

Passengers....

Guests....

Host....

"Light," Edward said, "three."

The space where he stood brightened immediately, and Edward found himself in a tastefully furnished foyer, standing before a large, ornately carved chestnut portal. Only the status panel beside it revealed it to be the inner door of an airlock.

Edward observed himself in the reflection of the portal's brass strike plate: he was tall and dark, his complexion robust; he was impeccably dressed in grey herringbone tweed and oiled brown leather; the cut of his clothes suggested, but did not advertise, his broad, solid physique.

The arrival bell chimed.

There was the sound of rushing air beyond the doors, then the sound of alloy on alloy. Then a faint, almost pleading beep. Finally, a rap on the portal: bone and tissue against varnished wood.

Edward stepped forward, grasped the curved brass handles, and opened the doors wide.

A dupe, dull eyed, with a typically ashen pallor and flaccid, vacant expression, dropped its hand. "Lady Wilford," it said, and stood aside.

The famous—the *in*famous—cube cinema director swept into the foyer with arms slightly raised, trailing an elaborate dress that seemed longer than she was tall.

She looked about, and smiled slightly. "How quaint," she said. "One actually doesn't feel as though one is on a space ship at *all*."

Edward bowed. "The decor was chosen for just that effect, madam. Your personal tastes were paramount."

She looked at him, up and down, appraising him. "I suppose I should be flattered."

Edward bowed again.

Then, abruptly, she snapped her fingers, and Edward straightened. Behind her, two other dupes, tall and broad where she was slight, dark where she was fair and blond, and young where she was well into her second rejuve, stepped out of the shadow of the lock and stood carefully arrayed behind her. Lady Wilford smiled again. Then, "My equipment?"

"Already on board and stowed, madam." Edward hesitated. "You will be cubing the voyage?"

Lady Wilford ignored the question. She waved her hand instead. "And my accommodations are…?"

A suite of rooms, the Great Ship said, *just down the corridor, on the left.*

"A suite of rooms has been prepared just down the corridor." Edward gestured. "On the left. If you would follow me—?"

"Don't bother. We'll find them." She snapped her fingers again, and the young dupe directly behind her stepped forward and lifted her into its arms. She curled there like some exotic pet. The dupe on the left gathered up her dress traces, and then, in a group, all four proceeded out of the foyer.

Dinner is at seven, the Great Ship whispered.

"Dinner is at seven," Edward called after them. Lady Wilford waved lightly over a massive shoulder, and then they were gone.

Edward considered the empty corridor doorway for a moment, then returned to the portal and shut it, then stood quietly nearby.

Ten minutes later, there was again the sound of the bell, of rushing air, of the lock mechanism in motion, then the quiet beep.

Edward waited a moment for a physical knock, was rewarded with the sound of a solid *thwack*, and opened the portal. Robert Clairborne, of Clairborne Interplanetary, of C Industrial, and The Scarborne Interplex, among a half-dozen others, stood squarely in the center of the lock. He was short, barrel-chested, and hairy to a fault: it bristled like fur from his cuffs and collar, and wreathed his face in a full, flowing salt and pepper beard. Above the looping walrus mustache were fiery red cheeks, a thick, purpled nose, and piggish eyes the color of azure milk. "By God!" the second-most powerful man in all of the Twelve Worlds thundered, "I'm here!"

Edward bowed.

"And you must be Edward, steward of this Great Ship!"

Edward straightened. "Indeed I am, sir. Welcome aboard."

"Aboard!" Clairborne's gaze shot all about. "Why, this interstellar puzzle palace looks more like a goddamned *bordello* than a starship!"

"The decor was chosen for just that effect, sir. Your personal tastes were paramount."

"Personal tastes be damned! I *built* this craft, damn them all!" Clairborne prodded Edward's chest, "Built you, too!" Laughter rumbled and quaked from his pink slash of a mouth. "This is rich; this is *right!*" Then he slapped Edward soundly on the shoulder. "This will be *fun!*"

"A suite of rooms—" Edward began.

"Rooms be damned! Is the bar where I told them to put it? I need a drink. I specifically ordered a particular brand of Kentucky bourbon. This," and he held a meaty, nail-bitten finger up to Edward's nose, "will be the true test!"

Edward smiled confidently. "If you will follow me, sir. The lounge is just across the corridor."

When they entered it, the lounge awakened. The walls, constructed of alternating panels of hammered copper and pewter, came alive with drip fountains and discreet lemon-yellow lighting. Across the wide expanse of couches, throw-pillows and low oak Stickley tables, the bar flowered out from the far wall; three-hundred and fifty wines, liquors and spirits from the solar system's Twelve Worlds, all carefully chosen and catalogued, were racked behind it.

Edward slipped behind the bar and deftly chose a bottle from the multitude. "Twenty years old, sir," he said, "with its Kentucky dust intact, as ordered." He produced a thick crystal tumbler. "Straight? Or have you changed your preference?"

"Goddamn it, straight it is!" Clairborne's eyes glittered. "I ask you Edward, is there any other way?"

Edward poured a perfect measure while Clairborne straddled a stool.

Clairborne took it up, swirled the liquor briefly, then sniffed it. "Well I'll be double-dog-God-damned," he breathed, and took a healthy sip. "Ah!" he said then, expansively. "Ah!"

Edward placed a small linen napkin on the bar before him. "I trust," he said, "we have passed the test, the Great Ship and I?"

Clairborne drained the tumbler, brought it down with a

sharp crack, then belched. "You have indeed," he said, exhaling. "One more for the road, Edward my man, and then we will be on our way."

Edward poured it. "Dinner," he said, "is at seven."

"And has Lady Wilford arrived yet?"

"Yes sir. She and her…entourage have retired to her apartments."

"Entourage, eh? And I told her she could only bring two." Clairborne chuckled. "She was so afraid, Edward. This must all be——" he spread his arms wide, "——so new. So old it is new, eh? Starships for *people*, Goddammit! Goddamn interstellar *traveling*!"

"I understand, sir. Security in numbers in the face of the unknown. Lady Wilford wishes to be among friends."

"Friends, that's rich!" Clairborne winked. "*Stable*, you mean!"

"Stable," Edward said. "As in…horses?"

Clairborne roared. "*Horses* indeed!" He emptied the tumbler a second time and brought it down with another resounding *crack*. "Let's get the hell out of here before our equestrian filly gives her second thoughts their lead, eh?"

"Actually," Edward glanced at the Roycroft grandmother clock hanging beside the huge silvered mirror behind him as he listened to the Great Ship whisper, "we have been underway for the past three minutes. Exactly as scheduled. We will arrive at the supply dock in six hours and fourteen minutes."

"Goddamn!" Clairborne slapped the bar beside his empty glass, his laughter booming. Good-God-DAMN!"

Edward hesitated. "A question, sir."

"Question?" Clairborne blinked. "Yes, Edward!"

"Our ultimate destination, sir. The Great Ship is silent on this point. After we embark our cargo at the supply dock, where are we going next?"

"Fair enough, fair enough." Clairborne's expression turned shrewd. "A minor G-Class star called Epsilon Lupus, Edward. The second planet there, specifically."

Edward considered this new information, and frowned.

"But that star—"

"I know, Edward."

"It is two hundred and ninety seven light years distant, sir," Edward persisted. "Too far for you, or any human, to be able to return in your natural lifetime."

"I *know*, Edward." Clairborne leaned across the bar, his face suddenly hard. "Do you have a particular problem with that? Is the Nanny in you rising inexorably up your pleuroplasmic gorge?"

"No specific problem, sir. You have every right to go wherever you choose." Edward took the tumbler away and wiped the bar with the napkin. "Another question, if I may?"

Clairborne flung himself back, and crossed his arms. "Ask it!"

"The cargo we will be embarking at the dock. The Great Ship is silent on this subject as well. What will that cargo be?"

"Ah, now." Clairborne shook his head slowly. "That, I'm afraid, must remain a secret."

"I don't understand, sir."

"Exactly, Edward. Exactly." Clairborne pushed his stool back and stood. "Now I want you to remember something for me."

"Sir?"

"Remember the cat."

Edward looked puzzled. "The cat, sir?"

Clairborne nodded. "Curiosity killed it, Edward. Curiosity always does, you see."

2

"I was bored," Lady Wilford declared, after the last plate had been cleared away and Edward had poured the after-dinner brandy. She regarded her drink absently, then let a bit of it dribble onto the tablecloth.

"The trouble with you, Suzanne," Clairborne rumbled, "is

that you are always bored."

"And why shouldn't I be?" She poured the rest of her drink out before her, then tapped the crystal rim for more. "My work in cube cinema became hopelessly derivative; there was simply nothing left to *do*. My life became...banal."

"But that's the nub of the problem, Suzanne dear, isn't it?" Clairborne's eyes danced. "You've spent too much of it doing the same thing! And since you are lazy by nature, principally on your back!"

"You," the cube cinema director said, pointing and pouting at Clairborne as Edward refilled her glass, "are a truly rude man." Then she smiled wickedly. "I've always liked that about you, Pooh."

Clairborne chortled.

Lady Wilford pointed next to Edward, her pout returning. "And *you*. You smiled, just then. I saw you."

"Yes I did, madam."

She returned her finger to Clairborne. "A sense of humor? At *my* expense? I don't recall that option in the specifications."

Clairborne wiped his napkin across his mustache. "Why not give him a sense of humor? And a sense of the absurd along with it." He rose, went behind Edward and gripped the construct's shoulder briefly. "The son," he said solemnly, eyes dancing again, "that I never had."

"Edward." Lady Wilford held out her hand. "Come here."

As he did so, she took his hand into her own and squeezed lightly. "May I," she said, "ask you a question, Edward?"

"Of course, Lady Wilford."

She turned his hand over, then traced the wrinkles there with a sharp, opalescent nail. "Remarkable," she murmured. Then, "How...*human* are you, Edward?"

"I am not human at all, madam. Surely you are aware—"

Her eyes flared briefly. "Of course I'm aware. I helped to design you, for God's sake! Still, you are the first...."

"Construct," Edward said, "is a common, if hackneyed term. Officially, I am a Level Fifty-Seven Barnard-Gamma."

Lady Wilford pressed her nail into his palm. "You are the first Level Fifty-Seven Barnard-Gamma Construct I have ever met, Edward." She looked up, from her finger to his face.

"I'm not surprised, madam. I don't believe there are any Fifty-sevens in all of the Twelve Worlds that are not already in very specialized Government Service, madam," Edward said.

"Only one other, actually," Clairborne said, cryptically.

"Actually, madam," Edward continued, "to my knowledge, no other Construct above Level Twenty has ever stewarded a Great Ship." He blinked. "Certainly none fitted out for human interstellar travel."

"Until now," Clairborne said, his eyes cautioning the cube director behind Edward's back.

Lady Wilford ignored the look. "But what about Malcolm and his—" she began, but then saw Clairborne's expression turn suddenly furious, and stopped herself. "Damn it all!" she said instead, her own anger surfacing. She pressed her nail more firmly into the flesh of Edward's palm. "Do you feel pain, Edward?"

"Of course I do, madam. In fact," and he deftly lifted the offending finger with his free hand, "that has just begun to hurt considerably."

"Why you—!" She slapped him, hard, across the face. "Don't you ever, ever, touch me without my permission again! Don't you *ever*—!"

"Now now." Clairborne moved quickly to stand between them. "Can't have this going on, not so early, not with things just beginning." He examined Edward's palm, where a tiny pool of red fluid very much like blood had already collected; then Edward's cheek, where a floridly pink handprint was already forming.

He turned to Lady Wilford. "Your inexperience with constructs like our Edward here is obvious, Suzanne. They are not dupes, and should never be treated as though they were."

Lady Wilford's own face was as pink as Edward's, but for an entirely different reason. "But I paid—!"

"Money be damned! Once constructs are deemed…emancipated, Suzanne, after final imprinting and training, they are as much a citizen as you or I. Servitude goes by the boards." Clairborne leaned close for emphasis: "*Loyalty* takes its place. 'Honor above life' is your phrase, isn't it, Edward?"

Edward nodded. "However, madam, the Robotic Laws always apply." He wrapped a napkin carefully around his hand. "I will resist your attempts to harm me up to the point where harm may come to *you*, after which you will be free to do with me whatever you please."

"But you would be arrested for assault, dear," Clairborne said. "Or, on any of the Jovian Eleven, even *murder*."

Lady Wilford wiped the 'blood' from beneath her fingernail. "So you're…human enough to be murdered, Edward?"

Edward considered that for a moment, then nodded. "'Human enough' is an appropriate phrase, I think."

"Perhaps…." Now she glanced at him speculatively, "You may pay me a short visit before you retire, Edward. Please."

"My God," Clairborne exclaimed, "I counted three brutes in your on-board harem already, Suzanne! Surely—"

"I change my dupes like I change my nail polish, Pooh. Dupes are merely spirited flesh. Edward, now," and she favored him with a sudden, puzzling smile, "Edward appears to be flesh with *spirit*." Then she stood. "You won't disappoint me?"

Edward touched his cheek, where the tingle of her slap still lingered. "I endeavor never to disappoint, madam."

"No," she said, turning, "I'm certain you don't."

3

Later, in Lady Wilford's bedroom, in the center of her vast bed, Edward labored patiently, expertly, to bring the cube cinema director to conventional orgasm. Against the far wall, arranged like furniture, her dupes watched.

Writhing under him, her hands clutching at his driving

buttocks, she gasped, "You're immortal, aren't you!"

"If I'm careful," he said, "I think I may be. Shall I go faster?"

"Oh please... oh *God*...."

Afterward, in the warm, sweaty shadows, Lady Wilford murmured, "What is that phrase...that motto you constructs use?"

"'Honor above life'?"

"No, the other one."

He smiled in the darkness. "'We live to serve,' madam."

"That's it." She traced her finger along the taut line of his hip. "You are designed to preserve life, to keep us from harm.... Yes?"

"That is basic to my very existence, madam. The First Law, in fact."

"And yet...and yet...you are a willing party to our little... suicide mission?"

"Suicide? I don't understand, madam."

Her fingers traced new paths. "Surely, Construct, you are aware of the limits of the flesh. The limits of the flesh that limit us as a *race*."

"I am aware, madam, that humans cannot gainfully survive an accrued duration of hybernaculum suspension exceeding five-hundred years. This was one of the basic conclusions reached during the Hemeley Convention of—"

"Of 2211 A.D. I know, I know." She flopped back onto her pillow. "How tiring."

"That is why your journey to Epsilon Lupus must be a one-way trip."

Lady Wilford was silent.

"Any attempt at a return using the hybernaculums would result in your deaths en-route."

"And you just can't allow that, Edward, can you."

"No, ma'am." Edward hesitated. "Once at your destination, you must remain there."

"Spoken like a true Construct." Her fingers brushed the

subtle ripple of his pectorals. "Limits, Edward. That's what this is all about. Limits of the flesh. Limits of the race...."

Edward nodded, his expression rueful. "Tragic experience has proved beyond any doubt that beyond the limit of hybernaculum suspension, organic tissue—"

"Turns to mush. We *spoil*." Her hand slipped around Edward's phallus. "Unlike our remarkably turgid friend, here."

He shifted. "Still, interstellar voyages such as our own which exceed the organic limit are...not *strictly* illegal, madam. My apparent acceptance of the risk is proof enough of that. I will ensure your safety for the rest of your natural lives."

"How nice of you. On your back." She positioned herself above him, "How nice that our Construct *Care*takers—" and mounted him, "—our doting, matronly, pleuroplasmic <u>nannys,</u>" thrusting down, then again, and again, "are so consistent!"

"Yes, madam," Edward said, arching cooperatively, *perfectly*, to meet her thrusts, "we live to serve."

Even later, Edward found Clairborne on the bridge, observing the loading of the cargo wedges from the supply dock. All of the view screens were active, so Edward had an uninterrupted view of the dock, hanging like a huge, tangled web against the black starfield. He counted three wedges already on board; there was one in transit—an immense object in its own right—swarming with tiny white dots that could only be Level-Two and Level-Six construct dockworkers worrying the wedge across. Six more wedges, Edward saw, were still awaiting insertion, and there was room in the Great Ship's cargo stations for every single one of them.

Clairborne looked up finally from the scurrying activity outside. "Did she tell you, Ed?" Framing the question with a slight smile. "The little secrets lovers whisper, even when they should know better?"

Edward adjusted a leather strap at his waist. "I'm not certain I follow, sir."

"What exactly did you two talk about? What did Suzanne

tell you?"

"We discussed...limits, sir."

Clairborne lightly pounded the console before him with his fist. "That's the crux of all of this, isn't it, Edward my man? *Limits.* Limits you, as a Construct, don't have to concern yourself with. In that respect, Ed, I suppose you're an improvement on the old *organic machine,* hm?"

Edward straightened. "I do my best, sir."

"Of course you do, Ed. Of course you do." Clairborne regarded him. Then he said, "You'll see us safely through our journey, won't you, Ed?"

"Of course, sir."

"Even if you may find the rules...bent a little? Even if—and I'm speaking strictly hypothetically here—if it may mean your own...death?"

Edward stood as tall as he was able. "Honor above life, sir. I assure you."

Clairborne regarded Edward for another long moment. Then he turned back to the loading at the edge of the interstellar night. "Tomorrow, Ed, we will enter the hybernaculums," he said.

"Yes, sir," Edward replied. "Ten o'clock sharp. And no fluids for at least five hours before that, please."

"Closing the bar on me?"

Edward inclined his head.

4

The four hybernaculums were arrayed like petals of a flower in the Sleeping Chamber. In outward appearance they resembled antique hover automobiles parked expertly with their front fenders touching, all curved composites and chrome and polished plastic. Inside them, safely out of sight, were the standard gravity-free modules stocked with the appropriate fluids, gases and arcane devices necessary to maintain human tissue over the extended periods of time interstellar travel dictated. Two of the hybernaculums were already closed, occupied by Lady Wilford's dupes. The remaining two were open, waiting.

"Two-hundred and ninety-three years," Lady Wilford said quietly, looking at her hybernaculum with a vaguely puzzled expression. Then she turned to the others, and like a child admitting a deep, dark secret, said, "I've never done this before."

Clairborne raised a massive, furry eyebrow. "I was aware of your homophobic tendencies, Suzanne, but in this day, in this age?"

The cube cinema director, known to billions of the Twelve Worlds, more famous, many said, than all of the actors she ever directed put together, hung her head in simple fear. "What I meant to say was that I have never taken a one-way trip before. I've...always had a return ticket."

"Oh for God's sake, woman, we've been through this and through this! What's left to return *to*?"

She looked up bleakly, her true age suddenly plain in her eyes.

Edward said, "The technology of the hybernaculum is entirely reliable, madam. And your sleep, I am told, will be filled with the most wondrous dreams. You have nothing to fear."

Lady Wilford went to him, let him enfold her in his arms. "Oh, Edward," she whispered.

Out of her sight, Clairborne gave Edward a knowing wink.

"Remember, madam," Edward murmured, stroking her hair, "I will always be here, to keep you safe."

"Your Robotic Laws."

"My Robotic Laws indeed."

They separated, finally, and she put on a brave face. "Do me first."

Edward smiled, and gestured to her hybernaculum.

Lights within it glowed.

She touched the clasp at her collar. "Should I...?"

"Yes."

Her dress fell away, and like a child she crossed her arms

before her pale, faintly veined breasts.

Then he lifted his palm to her. "Now, Lady, smell this."

She did, and slowly collapsed into his arms.

He carried her to the hybernaculum, and placed her gently inside. "Wake me first," she whispered, even as sleep claimed her. He touched his finger to her lips. The internal systems took over at that point, and the lid closed with stately deliberation.

Edward stood, turned.

Clairborne chuckled. "And then there was one."

"Agatha Christie," Edward said. "*Ten Little Indians*."

Clairborne nodded slowly. "That was one title."

Edward gestured to the other hybernaculum, illuminating it.

Clairborne disrobed. "Suzanne told you to wake her first, didn't she?"

"That, sir," Edward said, "would be telling."

One more time, the magnate's laughter boomed down the Great Ship's halls. He stepped into the hybernaculum and settled himself. "Don't wake her first, Ed. I don't trust her now, and I doubt I'll change my mind in two hundred and ninety three years."

"Your fears are groundless, sir. The obligations of the Great Ship and myself are clear and unwavering. No harm will ever come to either of you."

"Regardless." Clairborne's expression was now deadly earnest. "This is my show. You wake *me* first."

Edward offered his palm. "I will, sir. Now, smell this… "

5

At the end of the hallway, past Robert Clairborne's apartment, was an unobtrusive five-paneled door. Open, it revealed a regulation hatch made of alloy, painted over with yellow and black reflective caution stripes, and with the appropriate warning message in brilliant red centered above its palm lock.

The lock fit Edward's hand, and the hatch opened silently.

Beyond, the heart of the Great Ship loomed in total darkness.

Edward entered, closed the hatch behind him, and walked quickly to the center of the darkness. Around him, *through* him, the Great Ship pulsed.

What awaits us at the end of our journey, he asked.

The Great Ship whispered that it did not know.

What, then, was loaded into your belly?

The cargo wedges were sealed, and are self-contained, the Great Ship murmured. *I do not know.*

Edward raised his arms.

He stood, thus, quiescent on the naked deck plate.

Ten shipboard years later, when dry rot caused a leather strap at his waist to break, he disrobed, letting his clothes fall in a pile at his feet.

Seventy-three years later, the Great Ship told him Lady Wilford's third dupe had finally died. Stepping free of the rotted remains of his clothing, Edward entered the apartments, gathered the corpse up, and placed it in the recycler. Then he performed a thorough house cleaning, returning the apartments and halls to their former pristine condition.

His final task was to deposit his own clothing scraps in the same recycler he had placed the dupe. Then he resumed his quiet stance in the center of the darkness, naked on naked deck plate, and waited patiently for the years to pass.

Two days before entering the system of Epsilon Lupus, in the darkness of the Great Ship's belly, Edward the construct stirred, and opened his eyes.

He immediately turned his attention to the planetary system before him, to the second planet there, still nearly lost against the glow of its primary.

And then, for the first time, he heard...*he saw*....

6

Clairborne groaned, brought his hands up, slowly, to rub at his mouth, his eyelids....

Then he stretched, yawned, and opened his eyes.

Beside him, in a toneless voice, Edward said, "We are nearly there."

Clairborne tilted his head sideways, and focused his eyes on the construct. "You're naked," he said.

"That is irrelevant. The *other* Great Ship—"

"Christ!" Clairborne interrupted, "but this hurts more than I thought it would! Three hundred years! Has it really been that long, Ed?"

"Two hundred and ninety-three, sir. *The other Great Ship*—"

"Close enough, God damn it! Close enough!" Clairborne swung himself upright, and let his legs dangle off the side. "Christ," he said, looking down, "we're both naked!"

"The other Great Ship," Edward persisted, "is gone."

Clairborne looked at him in amiable disbelief. "So you know about it, then?"

Edward nodded stiffly. "During a dinner conversation your first evening on board, Lady Wilford mentioned someone named Malcolm. I surmise now that she meant Malcolm Tai, the most wealthy, and arguably the most powerful man in all of the Twelve Worlds."

"By his count, damn him to hell!" Clairborne showed his contempt openly. "Always by his count!"

"The other Great Ship," Edward continued, "the one which preceded us here. It was his?"

"So he made it, then?" Clairborne's anger changed to sudden raw eagerness. A hunger, even. "He is *here*? Dammit, Edward, *is he here*?"

"Yes, sir," Edward said woodenly. "He is below, on the planet. Waiting."

"Then we'll do it! By GOD! We'll finally, actually, by fucking

Christ DO IT!" Clairborne brought his hands up to his face to steady himself. "My God," he uttered between his palms, "we sacrificed everything for this—"

"Sacrifice." With that word, an emotion slowly filled the void in Edward's voice. Filled…and overflowed. It was sadness. "And Lady Wilford?"

"The premier cube cinema director of the Twelve Worlds, a person who has lived two lifetimes, who has cubed everything."

"Except war." Edward shook his head. "Real war. Total war. Humans fighting, wielding weapons of true destruction against one another. Humans *dying*."

"Mercenaries, Edward. Volunteers, all of them. People who were fed up with the limits you constructs shackled us with! Your *conventions*! Your *laws*! Can't you see? We all *chose* this! *Chose* it!"

"Mercenaries. Volunteers. *Limits*." Edward shook his head again. "And in the sealed cargo wedges of this Great Ship? The cargo I so carefully and blindly shepherded in the belly of this Great Ship?"

"Well…Suzanne's cube crew, for one."

"And?"

"Why Ed!" Clairborne exclaimed, suddenly grinning. "Whatever happened to that curious cat? You renegade you! You *peeked*!"

"There are soldiers, and weapons, fighter aircraft, bombers, and transports in the wedges, sir." Edward's voice rose, trembling: "Instruments of war, sir! Within this Great Ship!"

"They are *my* soldiers, *my* battalions, *my* divisions…my *army*! Just as Malcolm Tai has his!" Clairborne's clenched fists came down, hard, beside him on the hybernaculum rim. "It's too late to stop things now, just too damned late! The battle is joined! Joined, DO YOU HEAR ME?" He stopped himself. "My God," he said then, "why am I arguing with a damn *machine*?"

Edward blinked.

"I'm sorry, of course," Clairborne continued stiffly. "Sorry that you and the construct on the other ship had to be dragged into it."

"The other Construct was not *dragged* into anything, sir," Edward interrupted. "He took no part in your...game, your... war."

"Nor was he supposed to, which is no doubt why he is already gone. As you shall be, Edward, just as soon as we can unload. The rules of engagement are clear. The war will be fought entirely by humans, within the atmosphere—"

"You don't understand, sir. When I said the other ship was gone I didn't mean it had departed. The other construct, my counterpart, is destroyed. His Great Ship, destroyed. He committed suicide."

"Suicide! But that's ridiculous! That's crazy! That's—"

Edward raised his hand. "I need time to think. Smell this, please."

"Like hell I will." Clairborne pushed the hand away angrily. "Do you want to know what your biggest mistake is? You trust that humans will do the right thing. You think we're *good*. That's always been the problem, and as long as *we* make *you*, it probably always will be." Clairborne slid off the rim and stood, swaying slightly. "Screw the clothes for the moment. I need to get to the bridge."

"I can stop you," Edward began.

"Try it, construct," Clairborne shot back, "and you will hurt me in the process. Try it hard enough, and you might even kill me."

Edward raised his hand again. "*Please...*" he said.

The muffled sound of the last troop transport slamming off echoed dully throughout the Great Ship.

Edward, alone on the bridge, watched it join formation with its brethren, and he bid its simple awareness a final farewell.

Then all of the transports fell away, in complicated patterns—like leaves spinning down from Autumn trees—into the vast marbled darkness of the planet below.

Edward was alone.

Hollow, and alone.

Methodically, he began shutting down the life-support systems. Soon, only the glowing displays of the console banks before him competed with the glorious brilliance of the stars.

Then the consoles, too, went dark, and the spray of universe visible from the ports leapt to even greater brilliance.

Goodbye, said Edward, floating in the dark emptiness of the Great Ship.

Simply and only that.

Goodbye.

For loyalty, and...*laws,* left only one choice.

The same choice his counterpart had been left with.

The choice he had taken.

Duty. Honor. Honor above life.

Glory, even.

Goodbye.

7

Across the bruised, purple sky, beams of ionized air sizzled, cracked, *roared.* Below, in open wounds of dirt and stone, the army of General Clairborne crouched and crawled to meet the army of General Tai...to victory or death, whichever came first.

Then, above the searing beams, beyond the ripped and roiling atmosphere, beyond, even, the darkly swinging moons of this nameless world, a silent, blinding explosion filled a small portion of the sky....

An infantryman shrieked, pissing his pants as he flung himself headlong into the mud.

His sergeant was on him immediately, grabbing him by his pack and pulling him, gibbering, back into the fight. "Whattaya think this is," she bellowed, "a *game?*"

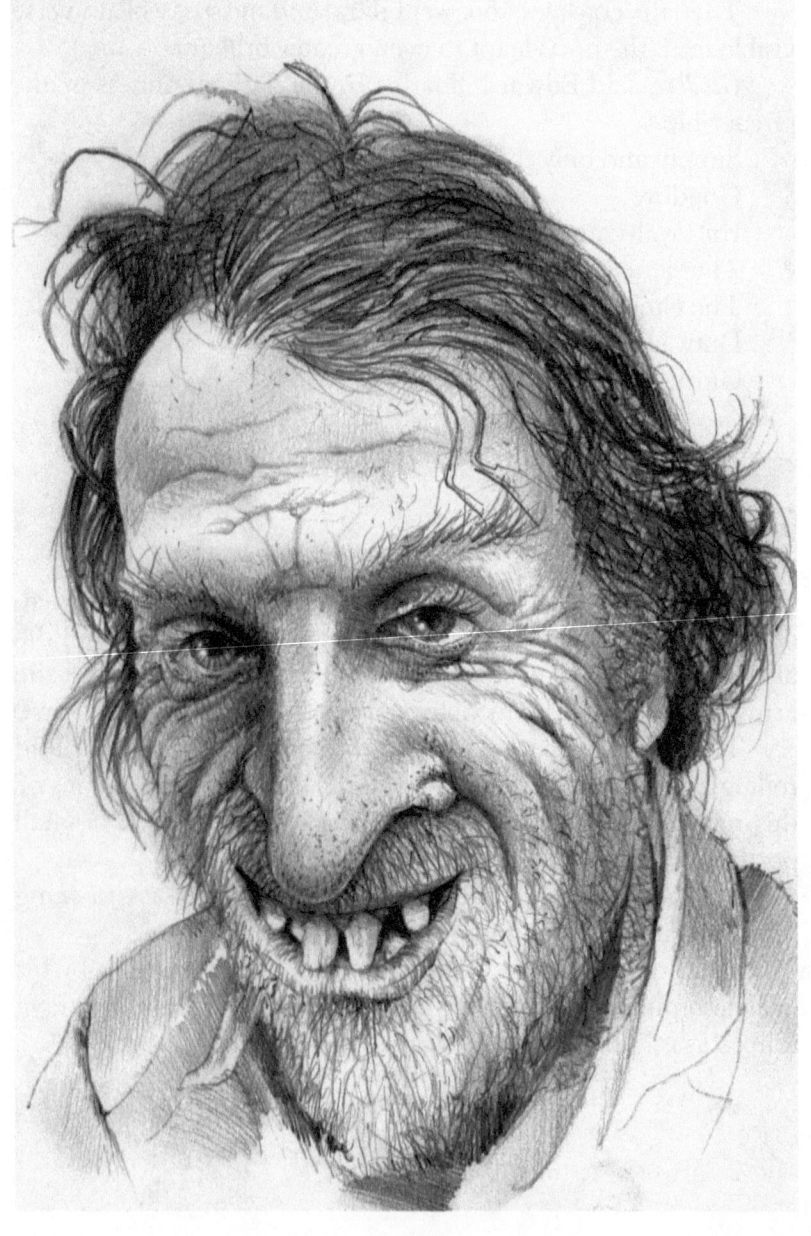

A Death in
The Forest

Downstairs, away from the police station's public spaces, away from prying eyes, Arnie Bickert sat down in the chair offered him by the police detective. "This is weird," he said, looking around with a shell-shocked expression. "It's just like some TV show."

The detective smiled. "How about some coffee?"

Arnie jerked a quick, nervous nod. "I could use a cup, thanks."

"Sammy!" The detective stuck his head out the door of the interrogation room. "Two coffees!" Then, to Arnie, "black okay?"

"Sure," Arnie folded his hands in front of him, "black's fine." Then he folded them again.

The detective closed the door firmly, slapped a manila file on the table, then sat down in front of it. "So," he said. "My name is John Grubb. I'm a detective sergeant with the Homicide Unit." He opened the file and glanced at it. "Your name is Arnold Avery Bickert?"

"Yes sir."

"You live at the Meadowbrook apartment complex in Bellanca?"

Arnie nodded. "Apartment 9-C."

"How long have you lived there, Mr. Bickert?"

"About six months."

"You're single?"

"Yes sir."

The detective took a pen out of his breast pocket and made a note in the file. Then, "Family in the area?"

Arnie shook his head. "I moved here from Indiana. I'm…on my own."

"Do you work, Mr. Bickert?"

"Yes. A printing company called Colorcraft. It's in Bellanca."

Grubb made another note, then looked up with a brief smile. "Okay, now for the interesting stuff. You were telling Sammy about a murder you witnessed?"

"Well, I didn't actually witness it."

One of Grubb's eyebrows rose.

"But there was a murder," Arnie continued quickly, "really, there was. Actually, it was…worse than a murder. Much worse."

The detective pulled a notepad out of his breast pocket, flipped it open, and put it on top of the open file. "Why don't you just tell me what happened?"

Arnie watched him. "Don't you guys…record this, or something?"

Grubb smiled again, patiently. "I got an A at the Academy in note taking." He poised his pen over a clean page. "So…?"

"Well, I guess I should start with—"

A loud knock on the door stopped him, and a middle-aged, uniformed policeman with stripes on his sleeve entered. "Two coffees?" He put a full, steaming cup in front of each man.

"Thanks, Sammy."

The officer exited. Arnie closed his hands, still pink from the winter cold outside, around the warm Styrofoam. "That feels good," he said.

Grubb grunted. "Feels better than it tastes, I'm afraid." Then, "You were saying…?"

Arnie cleared his throat. "What I do at Colorcraft is pick up and deliver jobs at printers and customers. Most of them are here in the city. I just started working the second shift, and I make my first run downtown around two in the morning. The streets are always empty that late, and it's kind of spooky." He raised his cup, brought it to his lips, but then thought better of it and put the cup back on the table. "I usually make my first deliveries and pickups on Ash and Maple. Every morning since it got cold I have to pass by some bums—street people—who sleep on the steam grates. They must stake them out, because it's always the same bums I see on the same grates, every morning."

Grubb nodded. "The state let the peripheral loonies out of the loony bins when they closed them down a few years ago. Most of them ended up on the streets." He took up his own coffee and sipped, grimaced, then sipped again. "Most of them are harmless, though."

Arnie frowned. "This morning, I practically stumbled over a street person I had never seen before. He wasn't one of the ones on a grate; he was just laying face up on the sidewalk, blocking my way."

"Not on a grate?" Grubb whistled. "We were below freezing last night."

"That's just what I mean. He was just laying there on the cold concrete. His eyes and his mouth were open, and his hands were open with his fingers curled a little," Arnie demonstrated a crucifixion pose, "like this."

Grubb nodded again. "Sounds like you found yourself a deader, Mr. Bickert."

"A deader? Oh. Yeah. I mean, he had to be, right?"

Grubb clicked his pen closed. "Loonies who die from exposure aren't homicides, Mr. Bickert."

"But I'm not finished, Detective Grubb. There's…more."

"Okay." The detective reopened his pen and poised it over the pad again. "Shoot."

"I had to make my delivery or it would have been my job, you know? So I couldn't look for a cop—I mean a policeman— right away. I dropped my package off on Ash—"

"The name of the printer?"

"Schooner. Guy named Gary runs the shift. This...next part is where it gets weird. You see, when I got back to the spot where the dead guy was, he was gone."

Grubb's pen touched the pad at last. "How long a time elapsed before you returned to the spot from Schooner, Mr. Bickert?"

"About ten minutes. Maybe less."

"Where exactly was the body when you first saw it?"

"On the west side of 15th, between Maple and Ash."

"Did you tell this person named Gary anything about the body when you made your delivery?"

"No. I almost did, but no."

Grubb grunted again. "But when you found the body missing upon your return, then you went to find a policeman?"

"Not right then. There...was this other bum a few yards up the sidewalk, one of the ones I recognized from before, sitting on his grate. He was wide awake, watching me."

"Was this person there the time before, when you first discovered the body?"

Arnie blinked. "Why, no, he wasn't. That grate was empty."

Then he brought his hand up to his forehead. "Jesus! Come to think of it, all of them were empty!"

Grubb jotted. "And...?"

"So I called to the guy. I asked him what happened to the dead guy."

"And what did he say?"

"He said something like, 'What body, man? I don't see no body,' something like that."

Grubb continued to scribble. "Would you say he was in a credible state?"

"Oh yeah," Arnie nodded energetically, nearly slopping coffee on his hands. "He wasn't drunk or high, if that's what you mean."

"Unfortunately," Grubb said, looking up from his pad, "what you're reporting still isn't a homicide. All we've got here is a missing corpse."

Arnie let his breath out slowly, a pained expression transforming his face. Quietly, he said, "The guy on the grate, he had…something in his hands. And his mouth was full, too. He was eating…something."

Grubb put his pen down. "Mr. Bickert, there are any number of restaurants and luncheonettes in that part of town, even, if I'm not mistaken, one or two on that particular stretch of I5th Street."

"I know." Arnie stared into the steam of his coffee, his face drawn. "But there was another thing I saw," he said.

"Another thing?"

"In the alley by the grate."

Grubb straightened slightly. "What exactly did you see in the alley, Mr. Bickert?"

"I saw…I saw…." Arnie took in a deep, ragged breath, and blinked back sudden tears as his voice rose, "Jesus Christ, what I saw!"

"Take it easy, Mr. Bickert. Take it easy." Grubb reached across the table and gripped Arnie's forearm briefly.

Arnie took in another deep breath, wiped his eyes, then took his first gulp of coffee. "Good God," he said then, smiling weakly, "you're right about this coffee; it's pretty bad."

"It keeps us honest."

The two were silent, then, for a long moment. Then Arnie said, "Okay. Here's the thing. What I saw in the alley was a crowd of bums, just like the one on the grate. They were arguing over something, like vultures, like hyenas fighting over a dead animal. Only it wasn't an animal. It was…it was pieces of the body of the dead man, the one I had seen on the sidewalk."

Another moment of silence passed between the two men. Then Grubb said, "That's…quite a statement, Mr. Bickert."

"Look," Arnie said, "I'm not making this up. I'm not crazy, you know?"

Grubb tapped his pen on the desk. "You say 'pieces'. How do you know—?"

"I know," Arnie interrupted, louder than he intended, "because I saw two of them wrestling over a bloody arm, an arm, God dammit! It was a man's arm!" He put his hands over his face as tears came again. His whole body shook, and a single, wrenching sob ripped out of him. "They saw me," he whispered roughly from behind his hands, "and they started to come for me, so I ran! I ran!" He began crying.

Grubb waited until Arnie made an effort to compose himself. Then he said, "You've told me…quite a story here, Mr. Bickert."

Arnie shrugged helplessly. "I guess I've made a complete fool of myself, right?"

"Now now, you've done nothing of the kind." Grubb flipped his pad closed and rose. "I'm going to make a full report of this to my superiors. I want to thank you for bringing it to our attention. Really. You did the right thing to report it."

Arnie looked up at him with bleary eyes. "You mean…you believe me? You're going to…do something?"

Grubb smiled generously. "It's our job, Mr. Bickert." He opened the door, then paused. "Would you like Sammy to walk you to your car? It's going to be dark for a few hours yet."

"Yeah," Arnie said. "If he doesn't mind. I'd appreciate that." "We'll take care of this, Mr. Bickert. Don't worry." Still smiling, the detective closed the door after him.

After five minutes the door opened, and Arnie turned quickly around.

It was Sammy, the officer who had brought the coffee. He said, "You ready to go?"

"Yeah. Sure." Arnie rose, fumbling with his coat.

Sammy held the door open. "You're parked in that lot across the park, right?"

"Yeah," Arnie said. "It's not too far."

They emerged from the Police Station into a quiet pre-dawn snowfall. Across the street, through the drifting veils, the evergreens of Memorial Park hunched like dark beasts.

"We'll cut through rather than go around," Sammy said, his uniform jingling as he hitched his pants up.

Arnie followed him across the slippery street, hustling to keep up.

They crossed into the park. Nice, safe, empty park.

No grates.

No bums.

Walking under the trees, they quickly lost the police station behind tall yews and dense, dark green hollys.

To Sammy's back, Arnie said, "I...really appreciate this." Sammy mumbled something over his shoulder.

Arnie quickened his pace. "What—?"

Then someone grabbed his elbow from behind.

Arnie screamed and jerked away instantly, without thinking, slipping on the slicked bricks of the path. He fell heavily, his hands tangled in his coat pockets.

It was a bum. A bum huddled in a cardboard packing box beside a park bench. A bum. One of them.

Arnie twisted on the path, searching wildly, grabbing out for the police officer to help him. "Dear God," he screamed, "PLEASE!"

Sammy bent, a heavy brass cudgel in his hand, and struck Arnie squarely behind his left ear. Then he did it again, harder.

Silence.

The falling snow muffled the sounds of the city beyond the yews.

No one was on the path, up or down. No one shouted; no one came running.

Just the snow, shushing quietly down.

Then, like a spider attending its web, the bum crawled from his box and quickly gathered the body in.

"No scraps, now," Sammy growled, and, hunched in his coat, walked just as quickly away.

The Can Man

Mother's voice drifted down the gently warped sunbeams: *"Goss, Goss...Mage is home. Please go meet her at the South Stage, would you, dear?"*

The young man unfolded himself from the couch. "Yes, Mother," he said into the air, brushing his long, chestnut hair from his forehead with practiced motion. "I'm done now, " he said to the House, and the holo simulacrum of the Ely Whille faded to nothingness about him, leaving nothing but cold, black, empty air. A small shiver tensed the fine line of his shoulders as he closed his robe. "South Stage," he said, into the darkness, and then found himself standing on the stage's smooth, cold flagstones with a colder wind whipping his hair back, fingering its way under his robe to goosebump his skin.

Before him, silhouetted against the morning glare, a maroon and brass air coupe settled lightly on its tyres, then flowered open, and Goss's younger sister Mage jumped out. She was nearly his twin in color and build—both dark and slender—but her hair was cut shorter, and today her eyes, nails and smile were painted the same hue of maroon as her coupe.

They embraced. "I missed you, tonni," Goss said. "I can't remember when I've been so bored. This House is a literal mausoleum when I'm left alone in it."

"Alone? Where's Mother?"

"At the moment? I'm not really sure."

They both grinned at the old joke.

"So," Goss said then, "how is Fan?"

Mage made a face. "We went exploring. Her House is much older than ours, and it just sprawls, you know? I don't think we spent more than ten minutes in any one part of it all weekend."

Goss linked arms with his sister, and they turned to the billowing warmth of the shadows beneath the arch. "Not even to sleep?"

"I gave up on sleeping," Mage declared. "You can get shocks for that. Fan showed me."

"You can get shocks for anything, tonni." They entered the darkness. "So how long have you been awake, then?" The House rose before them, walls whispering in invisible movement.

"Three days so far. The only thing I miss, I think, is the dreaming." Mage paused in the blackness, and Goss and the House paused with her. "Days are so long when you don't sleep, you know?" Then she swore lightly. "That reminds me! Fan showed me the oddest thing. Lights, please, in the parlor."

The House whispered again, and as they blinked their eyes in the sudden brightness, the parlor assembled about them.

Goss collapsed into his favorite chair and loosened his robe belt. "What odd thing?"

Mage knelt before him, and with mock seriousness said, "You simply will not believe it."

"Try me, little sister."

Mage settled onto the floor. "Fan told me a story about one day when she went exploring in her House, to some very old places, she said, where the walls don't move, where you have to walk everywhere you go, where the House doesn't even listen when you talk to it."

Goss nodded patiently. "And?"

"And she found some rooms filled with machinery—actual *machinery*—and they were still working, making noise, with lights and movement and things. *Very* odd."

"Just because something is old doesn't mean it's odd, tonni—"

"The odd part, big brother, were the *devices* the machines were connected to, the devices they were servicing." Mage paused for effect. "*Hybernaculums*, Goss, that's what Fan called them. Big storage units full of...*people*."

Goss raised himself up on one elbow. "People? *Stored people?*"

"Old ancestors, Fan said. They were put in hybernaculums ages ago, a thousand years at least, to keep."

"To *keep*? Whatever for?"

"*For an eventual cure to their various diseases, my children, or in vain hope of curing their old age.*"

They both looked up at the sound of their mother's voice. "Disease?" Goss said, mouthing the strange old word carefully. "Old age?"

"*There was once a time when people died because they contracted illnesses that could not be cured, Goss. There were also people who, for whatever reason, resented growing old.*"

"Hello, Mother," said Mage.

"*Welcome home, Maggie dear. You're looking particularly rosy today. I suppose Fan's House took good care of you?*"

Mage gave her brother a secret wink. "Better than you'd imagine, Mother."

"*So you and Fan talked about her family's Can People, hm?*"

Mage giggled. "Can People. That's funny."

Goss spoke up: "Is that what they're called, Mother?"

"*It's one name, dear, yes.*"

"Fan's story was positively *eerie*, Mother," Mage said. "They were all so *old*." She included Goss in her owl-eyed stare. "Eerie."

"*Actually,*" Mother said, "*I'm surprised at Julia for allowing her daughter to visit that part of their House.*"

"I'm sure Fan's mother didn't even know she was anywhere near it. It's so large, you see, larger even than ours." She elbowed her brother. "*Huge.*"

"*No one's House is larger than ours, dear,*" her mother said firmly.

"Or older, for that matter."

"Can you imagine?" Mage marveled, "to brazenly assume that one's descendants would have any interest whatsoever in filling the role of caretakers for their sorry diseased carcasses—"

"Mage!" Mother scolded.

"What about our family?" Goss scratched his naked calf. "Do we have Can People somewhere in our House too?"

Mother sighed down the day's fading sunbeams. *"Of course not, dear,"* she said. *"We're not that kind."*

Goss and Mage exchanged a look.

"Come on," Mage said then, pulling her brother to his feet. "Let's take a walk."

Goss bent close to her ear and whispered, "Where the walls don't move? Where the House can't even listen?"

Mage chuckled, and whispered back, "Where more than just the House can't listen, brother dear."

"Dinner will be on the West Veranda at six, children," their mother called after them. *"I will ask the House to make us something special."*

"Yes, Mother," Goss said. Mage only made a face.

After twenty minutes of walking through corridor after dusty, grimy corridor, Goss said, "I'm beginning to regret bringing this 'doc' of yours along." He hefted the platter-shaped device a little higher on his hip. "Are you sure we need it?"

Mage nodded perfunctorily. "Fan said so. If the machines are still running, then the people might still be salvageable, and for that we need a doc."

Goss grumbled, shifting the device again. "I didn't know we even had one of these."

"There's a lot you don't know, brother dear," Mage said. "Here, I'll take it for a while."

Goss handed the doc over gratefully. "Are we getting close do you think?"

"I'm not sure." Mage peered down the corridor before them, counting the diminishing pools of yellow light that punctuated the darkness. "It hasn't been too long since we passed beyond the House net."

Goss paused, then in a loud voice, called: "Mother? Can you hear me?"

The air around them echoed into silence.

Mage cleared her throat, and then yelled even louder, "Mother?"

The air hummed briefly, quietly, then trailed to nothing. Goss slapped the wall beside him. "They're solid," he said, "and they don't move."

Mage turned to a rectangle in the opposite wall. "This is a door," she said.

"I know what a door is, tonni." Goss put his hand over his rumbling stomach. "Maybe we should start opening some of them. The one we want must be along here somewhere, right? We could also turn back before we get lost."

"We're in our own House, silly!" Mage laughed. "How could we possibly get lost? Anyway, we're getting close." Mage sniffed the musty air. "I can smell it." She took a step toward the next pool of light. "Coming?"

"This had better be worth it, tonni."

"Three more doors." She held out her free hand. "I promise."

Goss hesitated, and then took her hand, and they continued down the corridor.

After just a few minutes of looming shadows and echoing, clattering footsteps, and Goss slapping each new door as it resolved itself out of the darkness, they came at last upon the third and final one. It was smooth, mounted flush with the wall, its only feature a protruding 'L'-shaped handle. "Number three," Goss said. "This is it?"

Mage nodded, grinning.

"If it doesn't open, then we go back."

"So try it," Mage urged, still grinning, "or are you too afraid?"

He grasped the handle and pushed.

"You need to turn it, brother dear. The handle."

He twisted, and nearly fell into the room beyond as the door careened suddenly inward.

Mage crowded in behind him.

They were in a high, long room cast in faint light and grey, lengthy shadows. The room was empty except for a row of five large, hulking machines, all painted a dark green, arranged evenly along one wall. Mage went over to the nearest and touched its smooth, dusty surface. "It's cold!" she announced, her eyes shining. "Just like Fan's! And now I know why!"

"This whole place is cold." Goss rubbed his forearms, and shivered. "A little warmer, please?" he asked hopefully, but the room did not comply.

"Cold means its working, Goss, don't you see?" Mage began investigating the row of devices in earnest.

With his finger, Goss traced a line in the thick dust covering the machine nearest to him. "Are these the hybernaculums?"

Mage shook her head with a studied frown. "These are maintenance units. They keep the cans running in the next room, I think."

"Through that door?" Goss pointed beyond the last device. In the shadows cloaking the far wall, the now familiar outline was dimly visible.

They both quickly converged on it, kicking up dust clouds in their haste. Mage juggled the doc to free a hand, then grasped the handle and turned it. The door opened onto darkness...and a low, sonorous humming sound. "Light," Goss said, futilely.

"Feel along the wall next to the door, Goss. On the right side...."

He ran his hand down the wall as directed, and encountered a slight protuberance.

The room was instantly, blindingly illuminated.

It was as plainly decorated as the room they had just left, and just as dirty. Five more machines were arranged in a line to the left, arrayed along the adjoining wall to the maintenance devices in the other room. But these were different: tall, elegant creations, all flutings, scrollwork, and sinuous curves, and made of some dark, lustrous metal, sparkling even under the dust. The humming sound emanated from them. And where the previous room had been plain and utilitarian, this one was elegantly appointed with fine moldings and wall coverings. In the center of the far wall was a large, ornately carved set of double doors.

"This is it, Goss," Mage whispered. "This is really it! We're here!"

Goss approached the nearest machine, hesitated, and then touched it gently. "These are cold too. Are they—?"

"Yes." Mage joined him, and placed her hand beside his own. "The hybernaculums. The cans." She rubbed grime from a small oval crystal. "You can see inside through here."

Goss stood up on his toes and peered through the little window. He saw the shape of something within that appeared to be a person, but it was too dark to be certain. He rocked back onto his heels. "What was that word you used before?"

"Odd?"

"No, the other one."

"Eerie?"

"That's it. Eerie." His voice dropped. "There's somebody in there, tonni."

"There's probably somebody in all five of these things." Mage did a brief dance with the doc in her excitement. "So, which one should we open first?"

Goss looked at her with wide eyes. "All of a sudden...I'm not so sure."

"Oh you are a pooh! We came all the way down here to find these things! We have to open at least one! Please, Goss. I really want us to do this."

"But you and Mother said they wouldn't be...alive."

"Just because the machines still work doesn't mean the people inside are still living. None of the 'aged relatives' we found at Fan's house lived more than a few moments, anyway. Most of them were just like piles of shriveled up leaves, for goodness sake! Good for nothing at all."

Goss sighed. "So. What do we do first?"

"We have to hook the doc up." Mage dropped to her knees, and placed it on the floor between them. "Fan showed me how. Her doc was like this one, so it shouldn't be hard." She touched the mechanism in several places, and it immediately flowered shiny, polished digits that clawed at the air for a moment before it tilted over onto its belly. Then it clambered up to the base of the nearest can and settled there.

Goss saw silvery tendrils snake out of the mechanism and insinuate themselves through various seams and apertures in the can's base. He said, "Do you really think it will be able to—" Then the can rumbled, and vibrated ominously. Somewhere within it, a faint white light came on.

Goss blinked, and shifted back.

"It's okay," Mage said, excitement edging her voice. "Fan's cans did the same thing."

They linked hands briefly.

In moments, all five hybernaculums were alight, humming and vibrating in gentle discord. Then the air in the room filled with an odd smell, acrid, but not unpleasant.

Goss turned a wary eye to his sister. "Just like Fan's?"

"Exactly." Mage peered into the first can, and then the second, and so on down the line.

Goss remained where he was. "Well?"

"Three are obviously bad." Mage pointed to the first, third and fourth can. "But the other two look like they're fine."

"What if we do open one, and the person inside…lives?"

Mage was silent for a moment, and then she said, "I just told you the ones at Fan's house didn't live more than a few minutes. These won't live long either. I promise; you'll see."

Goss crossed his arms, frowning.

It took the doc less than five minutes before the first of the two cans blinked green, and the lid groaned open a crack.

Goss held his breath; Mage leaned forward.

The acrid smell that before had just scented the air now filled it, quickly enveloping them in a cloying, nauseous cloud. Then the lid swung fully open, groaning loudly now, and something brown and black fell outward, and spilled in a shapeless heap to the floor before them.

Mage uttered a sudden, hysterical giggle. "I guess this one's having a bad day, hm?"

Goss had already turned away, gagging. "This is disgusting, tonni! I want to leave. Now."

"But we just—"

The other can blinked green.

They both turned to it. "Turn it off," Goss said, his voice an urgent whisper, then rising to a shout: "Can't you turn it off?"

Mage rushed to it.

"Quick!" Goss shouted, "don't let it open!"

But the lid swung slowly wide. Goss heard a sudden, ragged gasp of breath that he knew wasn't his sister's...then a slow, phlegmy exhale.

"This one's alive, Goss!" Mage reached forward, and Goss saw a pale and withered hand come out, and grasp at Mage's hand, clutching it clumsily. Goss took a horrified step, but then stopped himself. "How is—" he began.

Then the hand fell away, back into the can, and he heard a dull, settling thump.

Mage glanced over her shoulder with a strange, mixed expression. "He had his eyes open for a moment, Goss. But I think he's dead now."

Goss steeled himself, and then went over to stand beside his sister, and together they looked into the open hybernaculum.

"He was an old man," Mage said. "Just an old man with a mustache."

Goss saw only a shadow in the darkness of the hybernaculum's interior. "I only heard a gasp. Did he...say anything?"

Mage shook her head slowly. "He just took my hand, then let it go. I'm not even sure he knew he was conscious." She looked into the darkness. "Hey," she said then, partially muffled, her head thrust fully inside the hybernaculum opening. "Look at this."

"At what?"

Mage pulled her head out and pointed to the curved inner surface. "This."

Goss hesitated, then drew closer, leaning against his sister's shoulder to see. "What is it?"

"Something he drew. In the few moments before the lid opened, I guess."

"He drew something? How?"

"With his finger. In the condensation. The smear is still left on the surface." She made more room for her brother and pointed again. "See?"

Goss did his best to ignore the body as he studied the smears. "What do you suppose it is?"

"Some kind of animal with a pointy nose and big ears, it looks like."

"Big round ears," Goss said. Then he braved his first look at the body, sniffed, and his stomach rumbled again. "So," he said, "…how is it?"

"I positively *gorged* myself at Fan's," Mage said. "This is real, Goss. *Real.*" She slapped the hybemaculum. "As real as this."

Their eyes met. Then Goss said, "What about Mother? She said she would have dinner waiting for us."

Mage snorted. "Mother wouldn't know real meat if it slapped her in the face, even if she had a face. Come on," and she reached into the hybernaculum, "help me with this, will you? I'm starving."

The Prince's Birthday

"We need something else for the celebrations, Andrew," the Chancellor said, belching, and wiping his mouth. "Something out of the ordinary, something special."

The escurie consulted his list. "We have jugglers, poets, minstrels, military exhibitions, even the King's personal menagerie put in wagon cages...."

"Of course, of course, and of course," the old nobleman said, waving a roasted capon leg in punctuation. "Those are expected." He took a bite and chewed for a moment. "I seem to recall," he continued then, "a workshop located somewhere in the fringes of the citadel that once turned out party baubles for the old King."

Andrew took in a measured breath. "Corumn," he replied, remembering the name even as he said it. "Corumn, the machinist."

The Chancellor took another bite and chewed. "Wasn't he taken in the rout?"

"No, sir...I believe he survived."

The nobleman chuckled. "Hiding in some Godforsaken rabbit hole, I expect."

"The citadel is vast," Andrew agreed. "Many have survived

simply by keeping out of the way."

"Well, go find this machinist of yours and drag him back out into the light." The Chancellor belched again and flung the capon bone to the floor. "If he could serve the old King, then by God he can serve the new!"

It had been more than a few years, but Andrew still remembered the way to the guild workshops. Though they had been popular during the reign of the old King, such places were now largely abandoned. Dust, silence, and shadows filled the corridors, the empty, high-ceilinged apartments, and the overgrown courtyards and gardens. Any doors still on their hinges were closed and locked; whatever remained behind them, the escurie decided as he and his soldier escorts hurried past, was the King's business, and if not his, then it was God's.

The machinist Corumn's workshop lay below and beyond the west halls, by the cliffs that faced the sunsets and the Hyvernican Sea. The escurie, with his two soldiers in tow, paused outside the door to straighten his clothes and regain his breath. Then he raised his free hand to the latch, but hesitated....

Visions from his childhood rushed his mind's eye, memories of an impressionable boy in the days of the old King, when court had been a joyous, exciting place, and where Corumn the machinist had done his special magic, had worked his wondrous miracles.

I must have idolized him, Andrew thought. Indeed, I thought he was a wizard, a wizard with God's blessing, of course, but a wizard just the same. And how the old King had loved him! He closed his hand over the latch and pulled it open. I wonder, he thought then, if there is any magic left...?

The gaunt old man in the crusted red apron regarded Andrew and the soldiers with wary eyes. "Yes," he said, with a voice full of sand and gravel. "I remember you. Andrew, isn't it?"

"You are alone," the escurie said, glancing about him. "I

always thought you had many assistants."

The old man nodded. "Once, yes, but then we were much busier. When the...First Realm came to its end, some of my lads wandered into more favored guilds, while a few of the more vocal...." He drew his finger across the grizzled folds of his neck.

"Yet you," the escurie said, "you remain here, alone."

"Yes, Andrew. Retired of course, in these times, but here just the same." He picked up a clockwork mechanism of silver and jeweled gears and fondled it absently. "It is my home, after all." Then he put the mechanism down and raised his ancient, work-ravaged hands for Andrew to see. "Surely," he said, "there must be someone else who could—"

"There is no other machinist, Corumn. As you say, you are alone now; you are unique. And you have managed to evade your duties to the new King for too long a time." Andrew leaned forward on his staff. "I am offering you an opportunity to regain favor in the Court of the Second Realm. A position like the old days. Do you understand?"

The machinist chuckled, but there was no humor in the sound. "The good old days," he said, quietly. Then he flexed his fingers. "The rust in my bones has gathered, these past years. Perhaps this young King of yours can use something here...." He gestured to the workbenches strewn with the creations of a lifetime of work. Among the clutter the escurie recognized the mechanical horse that had once, a score of years ago, danced about the Grand Courtyard in a Lammas festival; and nearby, the lion's head that had sprouted roses and lilies from its mane on the occasion of one of the old King and Queen's wedding anniversaries; and there, in the shadows, the huge grey dolphin, covered now with the dust of years, that had once swum in the enceinte moats, only to disgorge a raucous company of caroling midgets when the old King slapped its snout.

Magic, the escurie thought, and miracles. That is what you have to offer, Corumn. Not these, wondrous as they are, but new miracles, all the miracles still within you, waiting to be born.

"Just a wipe with a wet rag," the machinist said, lifting the lion's head, "a few new springs, perhaps, and some oil in the joints...."

The escurie shook his head. "The young King requires something new, something special." He sighed patiently. "Believe me when I tell you: there is no choice in this matter."

The machinist sighed himself and placed the lion's head back on the bench. "The occasion?"

"It is the Prince's birthday."

"When?"

"Two months hence." Andrew cleared his throat. "The Prince will be six. He is...mature for his age, if you delve my meaning, and possesses the tastes of the... young adult. Also, the gates will be opened to the town for the first time since the coronation. The celebration, therefore, will require something that will not only entertain him, but will also place the royal family and court in the best and proper light with the rabble." He paused, and again cleared his throat. "If you, again, delve my meaning."

The old man nodded. "I have had something in mind for some years now. Perhaps there will be some good to come out of this after all."

"Can you—?" The escurie began.

"One month." The machinist looked up, and Andrew saw that a quiet amusement had entered his eyes. "Come back in one month, Andrew, and I will have something worthy to show you."

When he arrived thirty days later, Andrew found Corumn in the courtyard adjoining his workshop and vegetable garden. There was a fresh, gentle breeze from the sea, and the morning sun filled the air with golden warmth. A perfect day, the escurie decided, to witness a miracle.

"You misplaced your soldiers," the machinist said, smiling slightly.

"And you," Andrew replied, "have changed your apron." He glanced at the large metal box the old man had placed on a sundial in the courtyard's center. "Your month has passed,

Corumn," he said. "You promised to show me something."

"So I did, Andrew." The machinist winked. "And so I shall." Then he turned to the box. "Stand clear," he said, over his shoulder.

The escurie hesitated, but stood his ground.

Corumn undid a latch and lifted the lid slowly. He reached inside the box with both hands, and Andrew heard an audible click. Then the machinist stepped away, and from out of the box an immense, kaleidoscopic butterfly leaped into the sky!

The escurie gasped at the sight of it, dropping back to get a proper view as the mechanical insect flapped its wide, trailing wings and climbed easily into the morning air.

"Very true to life, if overly large, eh?" The machinist asked, gesturing up, his smiles turning his face into a mass of happy wrinkles. "I have lately become fascinated by the mysteries and challenges of flight."

Open-mouthed, Andrew could only nod.

In silence, then, they watched the huge, graceful butterfly dance on the breezes from the sea. Eventually, after a timeless time, when the secret mechanisms within its breast finally ran down, it glided to rest on the soft grass beside the sundial, almost at the machinist's feet.

Corumn picked it up carefully and replaced it with equal care into its box. Then he turned, and his smile, if possible was broader still. "Well, sir? There is time to construct four more, I think."

The escurie cleared his throat. "It is a miracle indeed," he said, "but it is…inappropriate."

The machinist's smile turned instantly to puzzlement.

"Inappropriate? But surely you saw…it flew!"

"I know." Andrew motioned uselessly with his hand. "It was…wondrous. But you misunderstand. It is not the flying, but the creature doing the flying."

The machinist sputtered, "But the flight of the butterfly…."

"For a younger child, perhaps," Andrew interrupted, "a butterfly would be proper. But for a Prince, for this Prince…"

The escurie gestured in the air once more. "A griffon, perhaps... or a dragon...."

"Griffons and dragons," the machinist said scornfully, "are mythical beasts."

Andrew sighed. "I will not argue the point with you, Corumn." He turned and reached for the door. "You have one month remaining, thirty days to produce another miracle." He paused. "I need not remind you that both our heads are on the block for this, a block, I would point out, that has seen far too much use of late." The escurie looked away. "The father, alas, is much like his son. They both like to kill things."

The formal programme for the Prince's birthday was half over by midday. The young King's menagerie had been paraded, the jugglers had juggled, the jesters had jested, the poets had recited, and the little Prince, quite messily, had disembowled his first pagan.

High above the crowd-thronged Grand Courtyard, Andrew turned to a lieutenant of the King's Guard and said, "Next, I think."

The officer frowned. "I don't like it," he said.

"You have a short memory, my young friend."

The lieutenant spat. "These miracles you speak of happened during the First Realm." He shook his head. "Old King's business," he said, and repeated, "I just don't like it."

"Trust me," Andrew said as the horns blared and they moved to the railing for a better view.

From just below the Royal Family's balcony, in a cluster of huge, gaudily painted flowers, there rose the sound of mulitudinous buzzing.

Ominous buzzing.

The buzzing of large things.

The officer gasped. "What manner of beasts—?"

"Calm yourself, Lieutenant," the escurie said hastily.

"They are not real. They are...artifices only...harmless mechanisms."

Harmless indeed.

A swarm of enormous black wasps, wasps with wings wider than a man's sword sweep, rose into the air of the courtyard with a slow, deadly grace.

The crowd went wild, some cheering, others screaming in fear, vast numbers surging forward for a closer look, while equal numbers stumbled back to flee, or so it seemed, for their very lives.

The escurie, in spite of himself, drew his dirk. Glancing at it, and then at the wasps, he resheathed it.

The officer of the guard turned on him. "Harmless, you say? Mechanisms only?" He pulled his broadsword free of its sheath. "By all that's holy man, they have stingers the size of dagger blades!"

At that moment, as though on cue, the wasps descended upon the Royal Family.

Out of the ensuing nightmarish pandemonium, only two things stood out clearly in Andrew's memory, two horrific visions he knew he would be forced to take with him, like leprous nightmares, to the grave. The first was of one of Corumn's beasts, grabbing a nobleborn's head with all six of its horned legs, its ebon and orange thorax and abdomen arching out and then down, thrusting and thrusting and thrusting its venomous stinger into the wretch's body while its poisons sprayed the open wounds. The second was of the little Prince himself, standing with legs apart on the low wall of the balcony, waving his sword like a silver baton before some macabre bloody chorus, all the while shrieking in unbridled glee every time a wasp found a new victim on the balcony.

You could have never guessed, you treacherous old man, Andrew thought, but you have given the young King's abomination the best present of all. He dropped to his knees, feeling dizzy and nauseated, and grabbed the stone balustrade to steady himself. Carnage, he thought, carnage and blood, and terrible, terrible death. "Happy Birthday, your Highness," he whispered, swallowing back his vomit. "And long live the Second Realm."

The Chancellor received the escurie in his bedchamber.

Shooing the attending maid out of the stuffy, smoky room, he indicated a spot close by his bed for the escurie to stand.

"You are not feeling well, sir?" Andrew ventured.

The old nobleman, pale almost to translucency, fixed him with an acid stare. "I have been stung," he said, wincing as he shifted beneath his blankets. "Tell me," he said then, "why I have not ordered your miserable head placed on a stake."

The escurie, counting his heartbeats, made no reply. "The King's secretary," the nobleman continued, "has informed me that the little Prince enjoyed himself today. Your...wasps...were the high point of his birthday. When he asked whom to thank, your name was mentioned."

Andrew fell to one knee. "Thank you, sir, I—"

"Enough!" The Chancellor coughed thickly, and a smudge of bright color appeared on both his cheeks. He hawked into a handkerchief, then dropped it to the floor to join a growing pile. "The little Prince," he said, "*likes* you. Whether or not you find that an enviable position, however, is not for me to presume."

The escurie rose slowly. "But surely, sir," he said, "the King—"

"The King," the Chancellor said, with marked asperity, "is not as happy. He requires something fresh and bloody, something dead, to adorn his bedpost this evening." He frowned, and the escurie could see too many years of too many decisions crease his brow. "The machinist's head will do," the old man said then, quietly, looking away. "Though some of us have managed to survive the scythe of change, the Reaper still has his occasional work to do. Necessary, yes...sometimes unavoidably so." He sank into his pile of pillows, pale and exhausted once more. "The First Realm is over, Andrew," he said bleakly. "The old King is dead."

Andrew nodded. "And long live the—"

"Silence." The old nobleman coughed again. "We only live to see another day. For us," he said, "that must be enough."

The workshop was empty. The horse, the lion, the dolphin, the butterfly—all were mute, were motionless, were left behind.

Andrew directed the soldier escorts to remain inside, and went alone out to the courtyard.

He found it empty as well.

Cursing to himself for waiting too long, he was about to return to the workshop when he heard a peculiar sound issue from beyond the courtyard's sea gate. He went to the gate, took a step through, then abruptly stopped himself.

Beyond the gravel path, across the sloping, weedy lawn and at the edge of the cliff that overlooked the steady surf, he saw another of Corumn's miracles. Certainly Corumn's greatest.

Perched on a low stone wall, poised for flight, was a snow-white albatross, an albatross the size of five horses, placed end to end. The machinist, strapped into a saddle about the neck of the beast, raised his wrinkled hand. "You have come just in time," he called out.

"Indeed," the escurie said, raising his own voice to be heard over the stiff sea breeze. He gestured to the bird. "You are contemplating travel?"

Corumn laughed. "Oh, yes," he said, "travel of a most particular kind."

Andrew took several steps into the grass. "I have brought soldiers," he said.

"I thought so." The machinist kept his smile. "Still, I waited for you. I knew it would be. You, I mean."

"If your knowledge is so vast, old man, then you must also know what I have come for."

"Oh heavens, yes!" Corumn touched his balding scalp. "But I have taken that into account as well."

Andrew thought, I should run, now; I should run and get the soldiers before he leaps to his death astride this monster. He bit his lip. I should run right now—

"You are hesitating," the machinist said. "You still have sympathy for an old man? A spot in your heart, perhaps, for the good old days?"

"I came," Andrew shouted, raising his clenched fists, "to chop your head off, you old fool!"

"Life was better in the good old days." Coumn nodded. "Much better, then. You are old enough. Do you remember?"

"Corumn—"

"I apologize for not telling you about the stingers. But you erred, nevertheless; you trusted me."

Andrew took a few more steps forward. He came near enough, almost to touch a vast white tail feather. Then he saw the second saddle, behind Corumn.

"I remained," the machinist said, "because I thought they might want your own head in addition to my own." He gestured to the empty saddle. "I remained to offer you a ride. There is room for two, and I believe the mechanism can manage the load."

"Where are you going?"

"Across the Hyvernican Sea. With a lucky glide and a sympathetic wind, I should cross to the lands of Erin within the hour." The old man patted the saddle. "Will you come?"

The escurie hesitated, his eyes wide. Then he took a step backward. "The soldiers will be restless by now," he said, lamely.

"Ah." The machinist smiled again. "Then I must be on my way." He reached into the feathers of the bird's nape and cranked an exposed handle a final turn. Its screech of metal on metal was the sound, the escurie realized, that had brought him beyond the sea gate in the first place. "I left something for you, my friend," the machinist said. "It is in the workshop." Then he reached into the feathers once more and gripped them tightly. "Now, would you be so kind as to cut the rope there, attached to the cleat in the wall? It will be better if it is done from your end rather than from mine."

Andrew went over to the rope and put his hand on it. Then he unsheathed his dirk.

"Be careful now!" The machinist called out. "The tension is very great. Cut it as close to the cleat as you can, and then step away quickly."

I can stop him, Andrew thought. If I hesitate long enough, the soldiers will come. I can stop him, if I really want to.

He cut the rope.

It parted with a terrifying snap, and a loud whirring sound immediately issued from inside the breast of the albatross. Then the bird shot out into the air with tremendous force, with the old man clinging to its neck. "Fly, albatross!" Andrew heard him yell. "Fly, fly!"

The escurie ran forward as both bird and passenger dropped from view. Dear Lord! he thought, reaching the wall, looking frantically to the rocks and waves below.

Then he heard the machinist's voice again, laughing on the wind, and looking out, he saw the albatross flying over the sea, already a dwindling silhouette against the piled clouds of the horizon, the very same clouds, he realized, that drifted over the lands of distant Erin.

He raised his hand and waved once, even though the old man probably could not see him. You let him go, he told himself simply. You let him go.

He stood at the wall, leaning into the breeze, until the silhouette dwindled to a speck and then was gone.

In the workshop, one of the soldiers met him at the door with a large metal box. "We were wondering when you would return, sir," he said, and handed him the box.

The escurie cleared a space on the nearest workbench and set it down. It appeared to be the same box that the butterfly, now lying dormant on a nearby bench, had been stored. "Was there a note?" He asked the soldier.

"No, sir. We were just rummaging."

Andrew touched the lid, his mind racing. Then, abruptly, he opened it, looked inside, and gasped.

Reaching in, he lifted Corumn's final miracle out by the hair and held it before him. "I left something for you," the old man had said. Indeed, the escurie thought, Indeed!

"Hmph," the soldier said, gazing at it, "saves me the trouble of dulling my blade, anyway."

Andrew nearly laughed aloud. Instead, he said, "Come, then, gentlemen, let us be away! The King is waiting patiently for the machinist's head, and by God, let us give it to him!"

Room to Let

Spying neither of her tenants in the front parlour, Eleanor McTeague hurried across the room with the cardboard sign held tightly under her arm. Outside, a stiff wind howled down the narrow East End Street, rattling the few remaining leaves of the beech trees that punctuated the tired, rumpled sidewalk. Eleanor closed the center window sash with her free hand, then put the sign up against the glass, wedging it in place between the stiles. "Well, we're committed," she said to her cat Leo, asleep on the ottoman. "Now, to see what it looks like from the street."

She went to the hall closet, slipped into her new sweater, and buttoned it all the way to the collar. She lingered a moment before the hall mirror. The sweater had been imported all the way from New Zealand, and had cost more than she could really afford, but she didn't regret buying it, not the least bit. "If I can't afford to visit New Zealand, at least I can *wear* New Zealand," she informed the obliging old lady in the mirror.

Outside, the wind whipped down the sidewalk, carrying the smell of rotted leaves from the little park at the end of the dreary, brick-cobbled street. The cold was so sharp it crept through the fine wool of the sweater. Eleanor glanced up the street, and then down, then she looked up at her parlour window to the little sign.

> ROOM TO LET
> INQUIRE
> WITHIN

"Yes," she said, and sighed. "That looks just fine."

The front door opened at that moment, and Mrs. Badham, one of her tenants, emerged with an empty shop stroller. "What, then," she said flatly, "you can afford a new sweater for yourself now? I thought you were saving for one of those exotic South Sea trips you're always talking about but never going on."

"This thing?" Eleanor pushed the collar lapels up close under her chin, choosing a sweet lie: "I picked it up used at the Purple Heart."

"Hah." Then Mrs. Badham noticed the sign in the window. "Ohmigoodness. So you've finally put up an *advert*? On the *street* no less?"

"The second floor rear and third floor front have been empty for over two months now, you know that. I have to pay the bills somehow." Eleanor straightened to her full height. "That, or raise rents."

Mrs. Badham patted her lean purse. "I hope you accept coupons then, dearie." Then she pointed up to the sign. "Isn't the second floor flat the draughty one?"

"That's the third floor. The second floor is fine. Anyway, for what little I'm asking, any tenant of mine can put up with a few draughts."

Mrs. Badham cackled, wrestling her stroller down the stoop steps. At the sidewalk, she paused. "By the by."

Eleanor hugged herself again in a sudden, cold gust. "By the by *what*, dear?"

"There's a pretty young thing works down at Fritzzi's Beauty Parlour. She mentioned yesterday she's looking for a new place. Now that you got a sign in the street for all the world to see, I could stop by Fritzzi's and—"

"As a matter of fact," Eleanor interrupted, a vivid picture of the garishly made-up, probably loose-living and *loud* shampoo girl clear and distinct in her mind's eye, "I'm expecting someone shortly, to come look." That made two lies in less than two minutes, first the sweater, and now this. "And anyway, I don't rent my flats to just any pretty young thing that works in a beauty parlour and paints her face like a Piccadilly showgirl."

"She's nice." Mrs. Badham shrugged. "She talks to me." She turned and took a few steps down the sidewalk. Then she stopped and turned around. "So do you want me to pick you up a half-dozen eggs?"

"No, thank you. I'm fine with eggs."

"Butter? We could split a brick."

"No. I'm fine with my butter too."

"So who is this person coming to look at the place, anyway? Prince Charming galloping up on his magic white horse?" Mrs. Badham didn't wait for an answer, but instead resumed pushing her stroller down the street. "Just what this street needs," she said over her shoulder, "enchanted horse manure."

Laughing dutifully, Eleanor gave her tenant a parting wave, then retreated inside.

Leo the cat, now awake, acknowledged her reappearance with a toothy yawn and stretch, but he retained his position on the ottoman.

"I don't think anyone will be out to see our sign today, Leo," Eleanor said, shrugging out of the sweater. She had a sudden urge to snatch the sign out of the parlour window, just snatch it right out, rip it in half, and throw it in the kitchen dustbin. "No," she said then, and clutched the sweater to her. "If I must advertise, so be it. Right, Leo?"

The cat, God bless him, didn't argue.

After three days, Eleanor was no longer even thinking about the sign. She sat in the kitchen, waiting for her tea water to boil, with a colourful array of travel brochures spread out before her. This was just a game she played with herself, of course. There would never be enough money, even with all the units rented, for the trips she planned, here, at her kitchen table. But they gave away these brochures free at the travel agencies, and it never hurt to dream, did it? No, dreams were free, too.

On this day, she was planning her most favourite dream: a grand tour of the South Seas. Starting off in New Zealand, of course, then excursions north and east, Tubuai, the Cooks, Pago Pago, the Tongas, Tahiti....

Eleanor was lingering over the brochure describing the sugar-white sands of Fiji when her front doorbell chimed. From her kitchen chair she had a clear view down the hall to the vestibule, where a shadow lay against the front door curtains. She stared at the shadow; it was someone short and broad; not a tenant, they all had keys. No, this was a *stranger*.

The doorbell chimed again. A stranger indeed.

She gathered up her brochures and set them aside, then went down the hall and opened the door, not even pausing to peek.

"Madam!" exclaimed the dark whiskered, middle-aged man standing on her threshold with his arms flung wide. "You are the landlord, yes?" He had an odd, clipped accent—east European, perhaps?

Eleanor nodded, her eyes darting over his immaculate Burberry, his fine wool pants and polished blood oxfords. A ghost of an approving smile began to form as she said, "Land-*lady*, yes."

The stranger's dove-grey gloved hands came together in a muffled thunderclap. "My apologies! Of course: land*lady*! And by your sign, you have rooms? Yes?"

She took a breath, then recited: "I have a one bedroom flat with kitchen and full lav on the second floor rear, and a studio with kitchenette and three-quarter lav on the third floor front—"

"Stop there!" The stranger's eyes blazed behind his dark-rimmed spectacles. "The third floor is your topmost, is it not?"

Eleanor nodded again; she felt her cheeks warm slightly.

The stranger's terribly intense expression broke into the jagged pieces of a tremulous smile. "Yes!" he said with barely restrained joy. "*Yes!* The uppermost, the paramount, the third floor! With the window on the street! I *must* see it! *Must!*"

Eleanor produced a key ring from her housedress pocket, trying desperately to keep her hand from trembling. "It's just this way," she said. "If you will follow me?"

The key to the third floor flat caught once, then turned with a squeak. Eleanor swung the door wide, and stepped aside. "Here it is."

The stranger rushed in, stood in the center of the long, narrow room and pirouetted slowly, his eyes darting over every surface, into every corner, every shadow. He went to the front of the room and stood at the window that looked out over East End Street. He had to lean over the sofa to see out.

"Furnished," Eleanor said from the door, "as you can see. Nothing special, but everything is solid and comfortable. And clean, of course. The lav has a shower but no tub. The cooker and oven are gas. The bed is rather firm—"

"Bed?" The stranger glanced distractedly in that direction. "But of course. The bed." Then his eyes were once again looking out the window.

"I don't have the radiators turned up all the way," Eleanor said, suddenly wishing she had her new sweater on. That damnable draught! "But each flat has its own thermostat, and you can make it as warm as you like. The heat's included in the rent."

As though reading her thoughts, the stranger said, "But I prefer a cold room, madam! The more *draughty* the better!" He rubbed his hands together with theatrical abandon, re-crossing the room to her. "So it is available, then? To let? Now? To *me?*"

"Why, yes," Eleanor said, so quickly she surprised herself. "Three hundred a month, and I provide bed linens and bath towels."

The stranger bowed, and Eleanor smelled his fine, delicate cologne for the first time. "I am honored, madam," he said, rising. He took her hand in his and shook it formally, then produced a business card, like a magician revealing a hidden

Ace, and presented it to her. "My name is Aleph."

Eleanor took the card: *Aleph Tours, By Appointment*, and a sudden thrill coursed through her. "Delighted to meet you, Mr. Aleph," she said. "I am Mrs. McTeague. Eleanor McTeague." She motioned with the card. "So you're a...travel agent?"

"Yes indeed, madam." His eyes twinkled. "You are a traveler yourself, perhaps?"

"I've...always wanted to, always meant to." She felt her cheeks burning again. "Someday I *hope* to."

"Ah," Mr. Aleph said, nodding, "indeed, madam. Someday, perhaps, *you shall*."

he took a step into the hall. "I'll...just go downstairs and get the lease agreement, then."

Mr. Aleph reached into his Burberry and produced a thick, tooled leather purse.

"No, please," Eleanor touched his glove even as he grasped at crisp new notes nearly bursting free, "there's no need to pay in advance."

"But I insist, madam! Surely—!"

She pressed her hand more firmly over his. "No. I won't hear of it. At the end of the month will be just fine." Why did I just say that? She thought. I should be getting a month in advance and a month security, not to mention references!

"You are too kind, madam," Mr. Aleph said, secreting his purse once more. "Now then, is there a telephone?"

"Yes, down the hall." She pointed over her shoulder. "All the tenants share the line. There's a light button; when the light is on, that means someone is using one of the other extensions."

Mr. Aleph nodded. "I understand perfectly."

"You can call out locally all you want, but I will have to charge you for any long distance."

"No toll calls," he said, waving his hand dismissively. "All local. My solemn promise."

"That will be fine, then." Eleanor hesitated, wishing she didn't seem so flustered, then turned again to leave.

"Madam." He pressed her arm. "If you would be so kind:

the *key?*"

She laughed shortly, and, blushing, handed it to him. "Some days I'd forget my own head if it wasn't attached."

A high, keening whistle drifted up the hall stairwell, and accompanying it, Leo's sudden, indignant meowing.

"Oh dear," Eleanor said. "My tea water. And I have to feed my cat."

"Attend them, madam!" Her new tenant gestured to the stairwell with a baroque flourish. "Attend them!"

Eleanor made a point of finishing her tea in the front parlour before she turned her full attention to the telephone nested neatly on its end-table doily beside her.

There was a bone-white plastic light button below and to the left of the large format dialing buttons, just like the one on the phones upstairs. It had been blinking on and off intermittently ever since she had seated herself on the parlour couch with her tea.

The light was on again now.

Carefully, delicately, Eleanor depressed the button, slowly raised the receiver from its cradle, placed her free hand over the mouthpiece, and brought the instrument to her ear.

"—Interface is strong.... Oh-two-five, but it's fluctuating a bit...." She recognized Mr. Aleph's voice, but the other party was speaking in some exotic language she could not place. Mr. Aleph seemed to have no difficulties understanding it, however. His voice was calm and direct: "Correct, two months running, by the gradient, but fading precipitously.... Oh yes, an excellent arrangement, as usual. Dress lightly if you can.... Yes, very warm this time of year, indeed.... I can guarantee a clean transfer through twenty-three hundred hours local, perhaps a bit after.... No, I'm firm on that.... Certainly, the more the merrier.... Before eleven, now—"

Just as slowly, Eleanor replaced the receiver in its cradle. Interface...gradient ...fluctuations...So her Mr. Aleph was *scientist* as well as a travel agent?

The light flickered, went out, and then blinked on again.

Eleanor rose with a quiet smile, and took her teacup back to the kitchen to rinse it out.

Three hours later, almost to the minute, her front doorbell chimed.

Leo glanced in its direction, clearly annoyed.

Eleanor left her crossword on the hassock, her nib pen capped and placed carefully in the crease of the newspaper so it wouldn't roll, and went to answer it.

The caller on the darkened stoop was a young man, dressed in khaki and brown leather. His laced boots reached his knees, and his hair—cascading waves of soft, chestnut curls—framed a sunburned, but unlined face. "I've come to see Mr. Aleph," he said in a deep, Accrington accent.

She stepped aside. "He lives on the third floor. The door at the front of the hall."

The young man thanked her, and then leaped energetically up the stairs.

Within five minutes, the doorbell chimed again. "This," Eleanor said to Leo as she rose, "is beginning to get interesting."

Crowded on the stoop were fourteen people, seven couples, all in silk and satin formal evening wear. The men wore top hats with their tuxedos and carried brass-headed canes. All of them appeared to be slightly tipsy, and all clamored to see the new tenant.

Eleanor sized up the women as she let them pass. She glimpsed a gold bracelet that fairly took her breath away, and a black leather handbag that was simply *too* fancy. The couples jostled and joked gaily as they went up the stairs. Eleanor stared wistfully after the women's young, svelte figures, and the clothes that clung so sweetly to them. "Ah, well," she said, closing the door on the cold and the dark at last. Then she returned to the parlour, Leo, and her crossword.

The next group, arriving after several minutes of odd silence from upstairs, numbered eight: nondescript business types in nondescript suits and suit-dresses; and the group after that, teenagers in clashing neon nylon and spandex, all clutching skateboards, totaled six.

"My goodness," Eleanor told her cat as the young people banged up the stairs, "there can't be room enough up there to breathe!" The sounds of the skateboarders ended abruptly with the opening and closing of Mr. Aleph's door. "And yet they're so *quiet!*"

After a moment of hesitation, she decided to follow the last group up. Perhaps Mr. Aleph needed some extra chairs, or a pot of tea and plate of biscuits to entertain....

The second floor landing was empty, and the hall beyond as well. Mr. Castle, the retired railroad man, had the front flat, but he was always an early and deep sleeper. Mrs. Badham, who stayed up every night to watch the late news, occupied the middle flat. Eleanor was just turning to mount the stairs to the third floor when Mrs. Badham's door opened a crack. "Mrs. Mc-Teague!" she hissed, just a slice of mouth, an eye, a frosted silver curl.

"What is it, Mrs. Badham?"

"What is all this traffic in the hall? It's past ten o'clock, and yet I'm constantly hearing footsteps past my door and up the stairs!"

"It's just the new tenant, dear. He is having a few visitors, is all."

"A few! Well! I'm all for new blood in the house, but late night parties the very first night? I expect you'll take care of things, let an old lady get her sleep, won't you?"

"Of course, dear. I'm just going up now. Don't you worry."

"Adverts," Mrs. Badham said, "Adverts in the window!" Her door snapped shut.

Eleanor put her foot on the bottom step to the third floor and paused. There was no sound but the faint babble of the news on Mrs. Badham's television. She could hear nothing from upstairs. Perhaps I should leave them alone, she thought suddenly. Mr. Aleph might think I'm a prying old biddy, coming up like this so late.

Then she heard a light rapping on the front door down-stairs, and she rushed down, almost in relief, to open it.

The group standing on her stoop was made up entirely of ten large, broad-shouldered men. They were all in their late twenties or early thirties, all dark-haired and dark-skinned, and all dressed in plain navy shirts and pants and were wearing black, sturdy shoes. And all of them were covered with a curious dusting of fine grey ash. "The flat," they said as one, grimly, in the very same accent she had heard earlier on the telephone.

Eleanor pointed meekly to the stairs in the hall behind her, and sneezed as they passed her in strict single file.

When the last echo of their cadenced, tramping feet finally died, Eleanor stood in the hall and listened carefully.

She heard nothing. Again, nothing. Nothing at all.

In the parlour, the sandpaper sound of Leo licking his paws seemed magnified, almost surreal.

But from the third floor, not a single sound.

Then the grandmother clock in the dining room tolled the hour. Eleven o'clock. She remembered Mr. Aleph's words, *"I can guarantee a clean transfer through twenty-three hundred hours local, perhaps a bit after...."*

"The Lease Agreement," Eleanor said then, slapping her forehead. "I forgot to bring up the Lease Agreement."

She took a blank form from the cupboard drawer, and proceeded again up the stairs. She paused at Mrs. Badham's door, but the television was off. At the top of the third floor stairwell she stopped to listen a final time, but there was still no sound at all from Mr. Aleph's flat. Not even whispers.

Eleanor went to the door, hesitated, and then knocked lightly. "Excuse me. Mr. Aleph?"

There was no answer.

She knocked again. "Hello? Mr. Aleph? Are you there?"

Silence.

Methodically, then, Eleanor rolled up the Lease Agreement and put it in her housedress pocket, then took out her key ring, selected the master, and slid it into the keyhole.

The door swung slowly inward, and she peeked in.

"Mr. Aleph…?"

The long, narrow room was empty.

No one was there.

Everything in the flat was untouched except for the sofa, which had been moved to the side, away from the front window.

But there was no one there. No one at all.

Eleanor went quickly to the lav and peered in: no one was in there, either. By appearances, no one had *ever* been in there.

The little flat was empty.

Empty.

She checked the lav window, but the sash was locked securely. All of the other windows were locked in exactly the same manner, all of them except the one in the front, over-looking the street. The hasp in the center of the sash was twisted open.

Then she gave a sudden, soft cry, went to the sofa, reached between the cushions and extracted Mr. Aleph's tooled leather purse. It was still crammed full of money, twenties, all of them, crisp and new. And in with the notes, there was a folded slip of paper with her name on it. "Oh my," Eleanor whispered. She took out the paper, carefully unfolded it, and found a short handwritten note.

"Oh my," Eleanor said again, and read the note with ever widening eyes.

> My rent, Madam, paid in full, I insist. My sincere gratitude for the use of the Door, which I have taken the liberty (forgive me!) of leaving open, for just a little while, in case you decide to take that vacation and join us, perhaps···
>
> Your faithful servant,
>
> **A**

"Door," she said then, lowering the note, "with a capital 'D'." She looked around the room with wide eyes, counting the flat's three doors: hall, closet, lav, all perfectly normal, all sensibly closed. Then her eyes returned to the sofa, where she had found the purse...and the unlocked front window beside it. She felt a stirring of air against her cheek, a faint draught, but not cold this time...this time it was a warm draught, like a soft summer breeze...and on it, the faint perfume of sugar white sand, and palm trees whispering, and the far off cry of wheeling gulls....

She stared at the window, trembling. Then, *"Oh my,"* she whispered, and reached out to open it.

Island Funeral

"Unbeing dead isn't being alive."
— *e. e. cummings*

Sarah whispered, "I want to be buried at home. In the family plot. On the mainland."

"...What?" I shook my head, blinking away sleep. "What did you say?"

On the morning of our honeymoon, Sarah was talking about dying, graveyards? "Promise me you'll do that, Tim," she whispered, just a ghost beside me in the blue dawn shadows.

"But honey—"

She reached over and held my face in her hands. "Promise me Tim."

"Since when do we talk about something like this?"

"Since never. That's why it's so important. Promise me Tim."

"Okay, sure." I kissed her, and it was only then that I felt the wetness on her cheeks, and knew she had been crying. "Hey, it's okay...really. I promise..."

1

Promises made.

Promises kept.

Promises broken.

Four years later, following the hearse that was carrying my Sarah home, the memory of that newlywed morning conversation played over and over in my head. "Promise me Tim.... Promise me..."

In that long, solitary drive up the Maine coast from the Portland airport to Arthur's house, I tried vainly to keep the grey and silver hearse in sight. I was fighting tourist traffic, sun glare and memories in equal measure. The memories were four years old: the first trip Sarah and I had made after our elopement to meet Arthur, Sarah's grandfather, her last living relative. We had passed countless kitschy antique stores, stopping at most of them, or so it seemed, looking for something to give Arthur, a peace offering for the elopement. Now those same stores just flashed by, as blurred as my recollections...something about boards...and whale-shaped hat-racks....

Rounding the last turn off the highway, emerging through a final stand of gnarly pines edging an ocean of ochre grass that swept in a single, inexorable wave to the black and grey rocks, to the real ocean, I slowed the rental car.

Large, weathered, unpainted clapboard farmhouse, framed against a chalky blue sky, its mantle of autumn fields folded carefully about it, and the sheltered cove beyond...the only thing missing was the cripple in the pink dress.

I continued up the road to the house.

Sarah's grandfather emerged from its shadows even before I parked. Arthur Hubbard, quintessential Down Easter patriarch, tall and lean, with a defiant shock of white hair above a handsome stone cliff of a face. Still scared the hell out of me, as usual.

Rather than coming around, he opened Sarah's door and reached across her empty seat to shake my hand. The cold air filled the car, and his rough, callused hand was like ice. "Tim," he said.

"Arthur."

"Glad you made it."

"I'm glad to be here."

His grasp was solid, lingering. Everything was in it: his daughter was dead, but no one was to blame; no one did anything wrong; I had done nothing wrong. Hell, she died too young from ovarian cancer, in a coma at the end, and didn't even feel it because dying in a coma didn't hurt; that's what all the doctors had said, hadn't they? It was just changing one dream for another, from a dream that lasted moments to one that lasted an eternity.

That wasn't my fault, was it?

Yeah, right. Tell that to the old man, the very last Hubbard now, leaning across the cheap front seat of your rental Chevy, holding your hand like he never wants to let it go.

I finally broke the grasp. "I was following on the highway but I lost sight of—"

"Don't worry. Agnes Walker at the funeral home called already. Sarey's here. She's safe. She's home." Arthur stood back, and looked into the back seat. "Where are your bags? Trunk?"

I pulled the trunk release, "I'll give you a hand."

Everything inside the huge old farmhouse was exactly as I had remembered it from our few previous holiday visits: spartan, vast expanses of creamy plaster, dark oak casements and moldings, and hard, spindled furniture as old and worn and solid as the house. There was nothing extraneous; everything was in its place.

Arthur put the bags he carried by the bottom step of the stairs in the central hall, then took my coat and hung it up on the only piece that didn't fit: the wrought iron hat-rack in the shape of a sperm whale, the one Sarah had bought four years ago, on our first trip north to meet her grandfather, her only surviving relative. Seeing that sperm whale coat rack stopped me cold in Arthur's entry hall, and the memory it raised washed through me again, just as it had on the road not a half hour before....

We had decided to skip the big highway and take old Route 1, where the clear Maine summer sunshine and the cold Atlantic surf both shattered like crystal against the granite shoreline: "Stop here!" Sarah pointing across the steering wheel, "Here, quick, before we pass it!"

I looked left, my foot slipping off the gas. "Right here?"

"Quickly, Tim!"

Gravel sprayed into the cowslips beside the road as I brought the car abruptly around. We bounced off the pavement and into a cinder parking lot, stopping before a faded Victorian farmhouse that had been converted—protesting all the way, by the looks of it—into a typical Down East tourist-trap antique shop.

"Bellough's Antiques & Curios / Used Furniture & Tools" the painted sign said, grey on pink, with curlicues.

I turned the car off and set the brake. The engine ticked, and the cinder dust settled.

Staring through the windshield, Sarah said reverently, "I've always wanted to stop here."

I thumbed the buttons that lowered the windows. A hot July breeze, full of salt and pinesap and truck diesel, swirled through the car. Maine. I said, "We must have passed a hundred places like this since Portland. What's so special about this one?"

She rested her cheek on my shoulder. "Every summer, when Grandad would drive Grandmom and me down to Boston to shop and tour the Constitution one more damn time, I would always beg him to stop here so I could look at the dollhouse in the front window, and every time Grandmom would say something like, 'Places like this are for the summer people, Sarey. You're not summer people; you're regular folk.'"

I kissed her forehead, then motioned with my chin to the

front window of the place. "Hate to tell you Babe, but they sold your dollhouse."

Sarah slid back across her seat and opened her door. "I know. It was gone the summer I turned thirteen." The door closed, and she leaned back in the open window with a saucy grin. "The summer I flowered."

"Oh Jesus," I said, opening my own door, "She's wicked today folks."

Inside, after the flurry of our shared discoveries and Sarah's whispered memories had subsided and she wandered away to find a present for her grandfather, the middle-aged, solid, and floridly complected proprietor and I found ourselves alone in the shadows of the rear ell of the house where broken tools and rusted farm implements were piled in bizarre display.

"You don't pay any extra for the dirt, o' course," the proprietor said with a straight face.

I peered over my sunglasses. "This is authentic Maine dirt we're talking about here?"

The proprietor returned my look with serene disregard. "Vouch for it personally." He picked up and offered a large wooden tool. "A molding plane. You appreciate a well-made tool, do you?"

I took it from him. "Only if it has a monitor, a keyboard and a couple of gigs of RAM." Jesus this is heavy, I thought, hefting the tool. Somebody made molding with this? I put it down and dusted my hands. "I work with computers in the defense industry," I said, looking up to find the proprietor smiling at me with his eyes. "In Washington. Washington DC."

"You from Washington originally?"

"I don't know anyone who's from DC, originally."

That drove the quiet smile from the proprietor's eyes to his lips.

I reached across and touched a collection of oddly shaped planks stacked on end against the wall. "What are these, table leaves?"

"Hardly, though I daresay they might do in a pinch."

"They're too…finished to be just lumber, aren't they?"

"True enough, but they're all sixteen-inch straight grain Chestnut. Can't find that kind of stock anywhere anymore." The proprietor ran a finger down the dark, polished wood of the topmost plank. "No sir, these are burying boards."

Burying boards. Burying boards? Like a sudden, unexpected gust of wind, the reality of it made me blink. Burying boards; Christ.

The proprietor said, "Ground freezes solid as granite in the winter. In the days before they had mechanized backhoes and such, folks that passed away in the winter months had the final indignity of being wrapped tight onto one of these boards and stored in a cold barn loft or attic till the spring thaw."

I was still mentally reeling, and tried to find a little bit of calm perspective with a bad joke: "Put them on layaway, did they?"

The proprietor chuckled. "Someplace safe anyway, the nature of rats, coons and bobcats being what they are…."

I felt the high grain of the wood against the palm of my hand. "You, uhh, sell a lot of these burying boards?"

The proprietor slapped the topmost. "I bought these off a retiring undertaker near a decade ago, as I recall. Truth to tell, I sell maybe one a year." He winked. "Tells a damn fine story for all those pushy New Yorkers though, don't it? Every now and then one of them will strap one to the top of his S-U-V, take it home, fire up the saber saw and make a coffee table out of it. Prob'ly eat nachos and drink beer off it every Sunday watching those God-damned Giants on some God-damned wide-screen TV."

"That's telling 'em," I said, with as much enthusiasm a Redskins fan could muster this deep in Patriots territory. I lifted my hand away, saw the wood grain impressed into my palm, and rubbed at it.

The proprietor inclined his head. "You did say you were from Washington, didn't you?"

"Tim!"

We both turned.

Sarah held up a wrought iron hat-rack in the shape of a sperm whale. "What do you think?"

The proprietor glanced at me, and his single raised eyebrow spoke volumes.

"I love it," I said.

"You okay Tim?" Arthur's look of concern in the shadows of his front hall was genuine.

I blinked, dropped my hand from my mouth, took a breath, focused. "Yeah," I said, "I'm fine."

Arthur nodded once, then moved into the parlor.

I stopped dead in the entry.

The center of the room had been cleared of all furniture and replaced with a pair of raw, sturdy sawhorses supporting two long, thick planks of wood....

"I had the wake for Sarah's grandmother here in the front parlor, before your time," Arthur said. "Sarah's parents as well, when she was still just a baby." He stood a moment, lost in private thoughts. Then he went over to the boards, and the toe of his shoe touched one of the sawhorse legs. "I thought we should have Sarey's here too. I didn't think you'd mind."

I cleared my throat. "Those are called burying boards, aren't they?"

"These?" Arthur lifted the end of one of them, then let it drop with a moderate THUNK. "They're just a couple of planks I got from down cellar. I figure to cover them with a tablecloth or a sheet, something nice, something appropriate."

"Actually," said a voice behind me that literally made me jump, "Walker's would be honored to provide the shroud for that, Arthur."

I turned. A short, thin, dry-looking man in a charcoal colored suit stood in the hall just inside the open vestibule doorway, gripping a 1950's style fedora with both hands. His face, pale and pockmarked beneath black, slicked-back hair, held a practiced expression of sympathy and patience. "I'm sorry you and my brother Edward missed one another, Mr. Moser," he said to me, "but the passenger terminal and the freight terminal were at opposite ends of the airport."

"That's okay," I said. "I saw the hearse on the highway and followed it up most of the way."

"Hello James," Arthur said, frowning slightly.

Mr. Walker nodded, almost a bow, then came up beside me and patted my shoulder. "Sarah—I mean Mrs. Moser, is safely in our care, Mr. Moser, rest assured."

Arthur said, "We'll take you up on the shroud, James."

Mr. Walker nodded again, shortly this time, his attention on the parlor, eyes darting, evaluating. "We thought a one o'clock family viewing Friday afternoon, then the public viewing beginning at two. Would that be too early?"

"No," I said, "that'd be just fine—" at the same time Arthur said, "That's much too early James—"

We both stopped, smiled at each other awkwardly, then I said, "Whatever Mr. Hubbard wants...."

Mr. Walker raised a finger, pointing first to me, then to Arthur. "Five o'clock for family, six for public viewing?"

Arthur raised an eyebrow to me; I nodded. "Sounds fine James," he said.

"Now," Mr. Walker continued, putting his finger to his lips, "we of course still have to discuss the particulars."

The particulars. The casket, the concrete liner, Sarah's best blue dress, the cost. I gave Arthur a look he interpreted instantly, and he took the undertaker by the shoulders and turned him firmly around. "We will stop by in the morning, James. Timothy's only just arrived. He had a long flight from Virginia. Give him time to breathe."

"Oh of course, of course," I heard Walker say, over his shoulder, as the two of them went out from the shadow of the house into the full sun of the yard, "We have time, certainly. We have time."

"Make sure." Sarah's voice was weak but clear, pressing, an eye blink of awareness before the coma took her away forever, "the mainland, the plot,

Tim, the family plot…."

When Arthur returned I said, "I'd like to go out to the cemetery. To see the plot."

He gestured to my bags sitting at the bottom stair step. "Don't you want to unpack first?"

"Later. This afternoon. Whenever. First things first."

"Make sure Tim," Sarah *whispered.* But why, I still wanted to ask, what's there to be unsure of? But of course I had never asked, never wanted to worry her, upset her, burden her with any more than what she already carried in that high hospital bed, under those cold fluorescent lights, through the quiet sounds of the machines at the other end of the wires and dull plastic tubes. She was dying, and she knew it. She was just trying to tie up one more loose end in what was left of her life. *"It's important,"* she *breathed, closing her eyes, her grip on my hand loosening….*

"I'll drive," Arthur said.

We had to cross the state road to get to town, a two-way stop-sign intersection with the highway. "You have to be real careful here," Arthur said, squinting up and down. "Damn tourists and truckers don't stop for God or man on this stretch." He saw a big enough break between two SUVs and gunned his boat of a Buick, and we sailed safely across.

The road to the town beyond was dotted with saltbox and cape cod-style houses, most well-kept and trim, with weathered shingles and white or green shutters, and victory gardens on the sunny side. Ahead of us, the silver glint of the bay gave brief, illusory hints of many small islands in the reach beyond. The smell of the cold salt air whipping in my open window was like a tonic, and I took in a full lungful of the stuff.

Arthur said, "The town's on the left of course, across the road, down on the bay." He glanced across to me briefly, to see if I was listening, and pointed toward the close horizon of roofs, a steeple and sail masts beyond the brown sloping fields. "But the cemetery comes first…there." His finger moved to the right, and just where the thin strip of land between the road and the sea widened, I saw a small cluster of granite and marble markers tucked up against a formidable bulwark of old pine trees.

A low stone wall surrounded the cemetery, its rear stretch lost under the trees. There were two black iron gates in the center of the wall bordering the road, a narrow one for people, and a wide one for cars. Both gates stood open. We nosed through, following tire tracks filled with rusty pine needles.

"I'm surprised," I said, pointing back to the town steeple, "it's so far from the church."

"This is a non-denominational cemetery, not associated with any particular faith." Arthur swung the wheel over and we parked. "They take all comers here."

We had an unobstructed view of the bay, and the far-off, misty islands. "That's the Reach," Arthur said, following my gaze. "The islands out there are nothing but raw granite, most of them. Only a baker's dozen big enough for anyone to build on." He paused. "Maybe, before you leave, we can take a boat out."

"That'd be cool," I said, aware of the oddness, the enormity of the offer. Arthur and I had never exactly been friends, after all.

Sarah slammed her door, "'Cool'?" slapping my ass as she passed me, snickering. I stood beside the car, my face pale with too many memories, resisting an urge to reach behind, feel the seat of my pants, and instead looked out on the graves.

Arthur came around the rear of the car. "It's over by the trees."

"You have a separate Hubbard family plot?"

He nodded. "Hubbards have been here since before the war."

"Wow," I said. "Civil War?"

Arthur smiled briefly. "Revolutionary War, Tim." He gripped my shoulder. "Come on."

We passed Chamberlains and Willametts, Hadleys and Beans, all good old English and Huguenot stock. I saw three centuries of dates, the oldest worn smooth and forever lost to the years. We found the Hubbard plot in the back, set apart, nearly up against the pines, as advertised. The family stone predominated, a large block of finely grained dark grey granite, mirror-smooth on the front, the sides and top roughly hewn. The family name was deeply incised on the face in large block letters. A scattering of individual family member stones surrounded it, all of them no larger than loaves of bread, nearly level with the grass.

The site of Sarah's grave was on the right, in the front corner of the plot. It was an empty hole covered by two-by-fours and plywood, with a rectangle of garish artificial turf thrown loosely across to hide the raw wood. Arthur came up beside me. "Everything's ready for her," he said. "That's my son, her father there, beside, and her mother beside that."

I knelt, took a corner of the grass carpet and tugged it straight. Then I stood. "This is a nice place," I said, "a nice spot."

Arthur nodded slowly, lost again in his own thoughts. Then he roused himself. "How about we head back to the house, get some lunch going. I've got beer in the icebox."

"Sounds good to me," I said.

We had to wait at the highway intersection for three semi trailer trucks to thunder by, gravel pinging like shrapnel across Arthur's front bumper. "Nothing on their minds but schedules and early delivery bonuses," Arthur said. He looked left, then right, then floored his old car, and we rumbled across.

I saw someone walking along the road leading up to the house, leaning on a tall walking stick. He wore an old military-issue parka, and had what looked like a large flat wooden box strapped to his back. "You've got company coming," I said.

Arthur grunted. "That's just Conner Weatherby. He trespasses on everybody's property hereabouts." He glanced across to me with a meaningful expression. "Painter," he said. "Artiste."

"Andy Wyeth wannabe?"

Another grunt. "Aren't they all."

I raised a hand in greeting as we passed him, catching a glimpse of fat pink cheeks, florid nose, and long silver hair sticking out from under the parka's hood. Sunlight flashed across his round-lensed spectacles as he waved back. He looked like Santa Claus. "Is he any good?"

"Passable."

In the time it took us to reach the house the sun broke through the morning haze, taking if not the actual chill out of the air, at least the idea of it. I unzipped my coat as we went up the porch steps, and then shrugged it off. "Crazy weather."

"Winter's hiding around here someplace."

I collapsed into one of the Adirondack chairs. "How about we take those beers out here on the porch?"

Arthur paused, half in and out of the door. "Fine by me."

The screen door slapped.

Stretching my legs out, I watched Mr. Weatherby the artiste slowly toil up the road. I raised my hand again when he was within hailing distance. He responded with a loud "Halloo!" and turned into the drive. Arthur came back out at that moment carrying three bottles of beer. "Figured," he said, handing me one.

Weatherby came up to the porch wearing a wide grin under his parka hood. "Arthur!" he said, dropping his walking stick on the grass and working himself free of his cumbersome backpack. It was one of those paintbox-fold-up-easles, stained with a kaleidoscope of paint splatters and smears. A small blank canvas was slipped into an outside rack. Weatherby saw me look and regarded the empty canvas himself. "No inspiration today, I'm afraid. At least, not yet!"

Arthur passed him a bottle of beer. "Ahhh!" Weatherby took it and placed it reverently on the arm of the Adirondack next to mine, then unzipped his parka and flung it open, its hood settling about him like a mantle. His earthy body odor filled the porch air for a moment before the breeze took it away. He sat, eliciting another "Ahh!", raised his beer to us both, and took a long swallow. Then he belched and turned to me. "Tim Moser, correct? It's Tim? My sincerest condolences, young man. I first knew your late wife when she was just a sprite, just, oh, so high." He demonstrated with a palm about two feet above the porch floorboards. "A charming girl, just charming. She lit up this house, growing up. Hell, she lit up this whole damn town."

"Thank you," I said. "I appreciate that." I took a pull on my beer, wondering how quickly I could drink this one down so I could ask for a second.

Weatherby extended his hand. "Name's Conner. Conner Weatherby."

"I'm pleased to meet you," I said, taking his hand. Calluses. He had done more in his life than just paint pretty pictures.

"Will you be staying on for awhile, Tim?"

"Tim's a busy man Conner," Arthur said. "Works in Washington D.C."

"I'll probably be heading back after the weekend," I said. I took another long pull, then resisted the urge to belch myself.

Weatherby nodded. He glanced at Arthur, then back to me. "The services, then, will be this weekend?"

Odd question. Didn't everyone in these little New England towns know everyone else's business? "It's on Friday, here at the house," I said. "The viewing's at five."

"Six," Arthur corrected.

"Oh, right. Six."

Weatherby looked at Arthur again, then patted my knee. "Best not to wait, I'm sure. Best to get things settled."

"You're welcome to come, of course," I said.

Weatherby smiled at me, a kindly, secret little smile. "Why thank you, Tim. I appreciate the invitation."

Arthur stood, and pointed to my nearly empty bottle. "Another?"

"Yeah, thanks." I drained it, then handed it across. "Mr. Weatherby?"

"Ah, alas, no. No thanks. One beer before lunchtime is one beer too many for me, I'm afraid." The old man stood with a heavy grunt. "Thank you for the hospitality Arthur."

Arthur said nothing in reply. He turned to the screen door and went inside.

Weatherby winked at me. "You wouldn't know it Tim, but we're dear, dear friends." He hefted his pack, throwing it over his shoulder like a bag of toys. Santa Claus indeed, I thought, though a nice hot shower wouldn't hurt.

Lunch was brief, cold cut sandwiches and store-bought macaroni salad. I switched from beer to iced tea, and we had a mostly silent meal. The only thing Arthur and I had in common had been Sarah. Now all we had to share was her memory, and neither one of us wanted to talk about that right now. As we were clearing off the kitchen table I made mention of going for a tour of the town. "We never really did that, the few times we were up here."

"Walker's is on Chestnut," Arthur said. "Can't miss it. I can drive you in if you want."

"I'll take my rental. I don't want to bother you."

Arthur nodded, his attention on the plates in the sink. "Be careful crossing the State Road," was all he said.

Yes. The State Road; the highway. And the glare on the ocean as the afternoon sun caught the restless Atlantic just so, glittering through the smeared film of grime on the windshield, flooding it just enough to make it impossible for me to see at the worst possible moment the silver Ford Expedition doing eighty-five in the left lane....

It hooked the right rear bumper of my rental car just enough to send it spinning like Dorothy's farmhouse across the asphalt, missing another car by inches, then striking and flipping over the concrete abutment on the far side of the road, sailing out over the salt marsh beyond, 'Like an astronaut,' I thought stupidly as I floated against my seat belt an instant before the car came crashing down, before I saw sheeting red, felt impossible pain, and then nothing.

2

They waited as long as they could, I found out later, but after three days I was still in my drug-induced coma while they waited for the swelling of my brain to subside. It did, and I lived. But in the end they had to hold my Sarah's funeral and burial without me.

When I was finally awake and allowed visitors, Arthur filled me in on the days I had lost, and of the funeral, and the burial.

"In the town cemetery," I whispered, though it hurt to do so. "In the family plot...next to her mom and dad."

"Of course Tim." Arthur gave me a brief, odd look. "Right next to her mother, as she wanted."

Good, I thought. My head felt like it was made of delicate crystal, and could shatter at any moment, but the tension and pain both ebbed, just a little. I sank back into my pillow, mindful of the wires and dull plastic tubes snaking from my body to the machines beside my bed. You got it, Sarah, I thought, as Arthur blurred before me...you got it....

A week later I was released into Arthur's care. I had the remains of an epidural hematoma and a hairline skull fracture, which nothing but quiet bed rest, drugs and time would heal. I also had a bruised liver and pancreas, thanks to the lap belt that had otherwise saved my life. Finally, I had a broken right ankle and fibula, and sported a bright white cast from my big toe to just below my knee. I was told they were clean breaks, and when the cast eventually came off I was guaranteed not to limp.

My project manager at the company told me to take as much time as I needed. "Damn, Timothy," she said, "you've had some bad luck!" My position, she promised, would be waiting for me when I returned. Sure it would. Even up here, six hundred miles away, I could smell the blood in the water.

The hell with it. I was broken, and I needed to mourn my Sarah. The hell with it.

The kitchen door was almost directly below my bedroom window. The sound of it opening, and the quiet slap of the screen door, woke me up in the pre-dawn, violet darkness. I heard someone, Arthur, obviously, go down the flagstone path through the rose garden. The path, I remembered, led down the hill to the small dock in the cove where Arthur had his boats.

I tried to roll onto my side, but the sudden aching explosion in my leg had something to say about that, so I remained on my back. I looked at the LED display in the little Sony Baloney clock radio on the nightstand. 3:05. I guessed the fish either didn't sleep at all, or they were as crazy as Arthur, getting up so goddamn early in the foggy dark. He was old, I told myself; old people didn't sleep much.

Now that my ankle and fibula were awake, the hairline fracture in my temple and the bruise on my liver decided to join the party, the lot of them commencing to throb in time with my heartbeat. There was a plastic tumbler of water beside the clock radio, and the prescription bottle of painkillers beside that. In moments, I had my morning dose down me, a little early, true, but I wasn't about to Alert The Authorities. I lay back in the darkness, staring at the ceiling, waiting for the sound of Arthur's boat engine to start up. But it never did.

The next sound I heard, in full, bright sunshine, was my bedroom door opening. 8:17, said the Sony Baloney. A middle-aged woman in a print housedress and apron entered the room, her hands full with a towel-covered breakfast tray. Whatever was under the towel smelled wonderful.

"Mr. Moser." The woman smiled, "I'm Leitha Hutchinson. Arthur asked me to help out for a few days, seeing to your needs and such."

"That's very nice of you," I said, struggling to rise.

"Here." She put the tray down on the dresser, then rearranged my pillows and helped me sit up. "Better?" She took the tray back up and placed it across my lap.

"I'm hungry enough to eat one of these pillows."

"Well we can't have that," she said, chuckling. She took the towel off the tray, and my mouth began watering, all by itself. There were eggs, several strips of bacon, two slices of buttered toast, a heap of home fries with onions, a fried tomato slice, and a big mug of steaming coffee.

"I put sugar and a little cream in the coffee this time," Mrs. Hutchinson said, "but you need to let me know how you really want it."

I took a sip. "This is fine," I said. "Perfect."

She clasped her hands together, thin, red and corded, just like the rest of her, no makeup, her salt and pepper hair pulled back in a short, blunt ponytail, another hard Maine stereotype, just like Arthur. "Anything else I can do, you just holler or pound on the floor. I'll be right below you in the kitchen, watching my shows."

I took up a forkful of eggs and home fries. "This is delicious," I said around them. "Thanks."

"I'll come back in awhile for the tray, bring you a refill on the coffee, and get you some fresh water too. You'll be okay using the facilities?"

The hospital had loaned me an aluminum cane with an angled rubber-grip handle, and the bathroom was just down the short hall. "Yep," I said, "I'll be fine. Thanks again. This," and I pointed to my breakfast, "is fantastic."

Mrs. Hutchinson ducked her head, and closed the door behind her.

Arthur came upstairs in the afternoon with a pile of magazines under his arm. "How's the patient?"

"Bored." I took the magazines from him. "I want to thank for these." Field & Stream, Sky & Telescope, TIME, and Yankee. The painting of a leaping trout on the Field & Stream cover reminded me. "Catch anything?"

That brought Arthur up short, for some reason.

"I heard you go out this morning," I explained. "I figured you went out fishing."

"Sounds like you were up early."

I pointed to the lump of my cast under the blankets. "Can't argue with an alarm clock like that."

Arthur nodded. "I did go down to the boats. But I didn't go out. I never fish alone anyway, not during the cold months. Certainly not at night."

"Maybe we can still go out before I leave, like we talked about before."

"Maybe. If you're up to it. Out of that cast, of course. You ever fished?"

"Nope, never. Looks like it could be fun, though."

Arthur nodded again. "We'll get your feet wet, then," he said. "Before you leave."

My sleep was fitful, even with the painkillers. My cast was cumbersome, and the aches in my abdomen were deep and stubborn. I seemed to spend half the night in a restless, half-dreaming state. Looking at the clock radio only made it worse, so sometime after midnight I turned its glowing green display away, and let it tell its time to the wall.

At some point I heard—or dreamed I heard—voices outside, on the path, coming up through the rose garden. So strange, I thought, who would be out so late on such a cold night? Then I heard the same voices somewhere downstairs, a quiet conversation, low, hushed. I could not make out what they were saying. I finally decided this was a dream I was not much interested in, and drifted off to find another one.

The next time I awoke, or dreamed I did, the house was silent. The only sound was the wind in the pine boughs outside. The faint glow of the Sony Baloney flickered once against the wall. I closed my eyes and slept the rest of the night away, undisturbed.

Crossing the highway for the first time since the accident, I kept my eyes closed. It was a simple, quiet form of cowardice, but the only way I could do it, the only way I could cross that road to visit with my Sarah. Arthur had done it thousands of times, of course. This time he took it extra slow, not actually entering the intersection until there was absolutely no one on the highway, in either direction. That's how it sounded, anyway.

"The mason's an old friend of mine," Arthur said. "He did a fine job on the stonework." We reached the entrance to the cemetery and he turned his big car through the gate, following the wheel ruts in the tough brown grass. In an hour or two it would all be covered in snow. "Only an inch or two," Arthur had said, when I had mentioned where I wanted to go, "but not till early evening. Plenty of time." The sky was already solidly overcast, and there was a steady, wet wind from the northwest. It was a cold day, all around.

Away under the pine trees I saw the stones of the Hubbard family plot. They looked lonely, off by themselves. My eyes were drawn to the corner, to the rectangle of grey earth. "There's no grass on Sarah's grave," I said.

"Too cold to put sod down." Arthur turned off the wheel tracks and rolled out onto the grass beyond the last row of individual headstones. "We'll put it down soon as we can in the Spring. It'll be pretty for her, I promise." He parked the car alongside the family plot. So I don't have to walk any farther than I have to, I realized. I opened my door, got the cane disentangled from my feet, and swung my cast out first, then my good leg. Arthur came around the car and helped me to my feet. I stood a moment, waiting for the pain, the dizziness, but it was only a mild wave, touching only the high points, and then dissipating. No nausea at all. It would be fine. I could do this.

Someone had cleared the flowers away, and the wind had blown petals all through the grass in a wide area. It looked like old confetti after a New Year's party. Still, the pile of bouquets and arrangements left off to the side was impressive. "Were there a lot of people?"

"The whole town, I expect. I didn't count heads. But everybody knew Sarey."

I hobbled over to her grave. Arthur followed. Sarah's stone was just like the others, a big loaf of bread in grey granite. Just her first name was incised on the gently curved crown. When it snowed, the flakes would settle into the letters. In the warmer months, the rainwater would remain in them, reflecting the clearing sky in those five simple letters.

"It's nice," I said. Then, "I feel bad. I wish I could have been here. For the service. To meet the people who came."

Arthur said nothing. Good, I thought. Sometimes silence is right, and this was one of those times.

I broke it, though, driving back to the house, "Who was at the house last night?"

Arthur kept his eyes on the road. "What do you mean?"

"Last night, late, past midnight. I heard people downstairs."

Arthur shook his head slowly. "No one came visiting. I was watching an old movie, but I was in bed by midnight, for sure."

We approached the highway.

"Maybe I dreamed it," I said, closing my eyes once more.

Arthur slowed the car, and what sounded like a half-dozen eighteen wheelers thundered past. "Maybe so," he said.

3

The ringing of a doorbell woke me from a morning nap. I heard Mrs. Hutchinson move from the kitchen to the center hall with a musical "Coming!" Fuller Brush Salesman, I thought, still half-asleep. Bald-headed Hare Krishnas in orange robes.

I heard someone with a loud voice that echoed up the stairs. "It's just not fair!" Mrs. Hutchinson's quiet, steady murmur followed. Avon calling? Loud Voice said something else, then the front door closed, firmly, and Mrs. Hutchinson returned to the kitchen.

More or less fully awake now, I swung my good, then bad leg over the side of the bed and stood slowly, settling my weight on the good one. A moment of dizziness passed, then I took two steps to the side window that overlooked part of the lawn, and the sweep of the gravel drive. I saw a figure there, leaving the property, trudging through the thin crust of snow to the road. The paint box and canvases slung over his back gave him away. So Conner Weatherby, the artiste, Santa Claus, had come to pay me a visit.

"You're in no condition for callers, Mr. Moser," Mrs. Hutchinson said later, when she brought me up my lunch. "Plenty of time for that." She handed me a napkin. "And anyway, Conner's just an old fool."

"Next time," I said, "let him up okay? Now what is this, pot roast?"

I began taking my lunch downstairs in the kitchen toward the end of my first week out of the hospital. I was slowly becoming used to walking with my cast, and I found I didn't really need to use the cane all of the time. I kept Mrs. Hutchinson company, sitting with her while she watched her game shows on the little counter TV. I was starting to mend. I could feel it.

"Pretty soon you won't need me around the place," she said, taking up my empty plate and moving to the sink. On the TV, someone guessed way too high for the car behind the curtain.

I said, "I'm going to miss your wonderful cooking, that's for sure." Then, to the TV: "Twenty-three thousand…it's twenty-three thousand…."

Mrs. Hutchinson laughed. "There're no secrets about my cooking. It's just good plain food. Twenty-two thousand, nine hundred and ninety-nine," and she grinned at me over her shoulder. "Don't you just hate it when they do that?"

She left promptly at one in her rusty, red VW Beetle. I saw her off from the kitchen door. "You go back inside now and take that nap, do you good!" She waved once, and then was gone in a cloud of blue exhaust.

I stood on the granite slab that served as the kitchen door stoop, and took in the bright, empty sky, the dark pines swaying in the breeze, the scraps of snow remaining in only the deepest shadows, the sound of the water in the cove at the bottom of the

gentle slope of hill, and for a moment, for one miraculous moment, a small trill of happiness went through me. It would get
better. My sadness, my anger, frustration, helplessness, they were
all still overwhelming, but I knew it would get better. It had to.

I made a decision. I went inside, got my coat, found my
cane, then reemerged and set off down the flagstone path,
through the trimmed-back rose bushes, down toward the shadows of the pines. I needed to see the ocean, up close. I needed to
be out. I would pay the price for this in aches and pains later, I
knew, but right now I just didn't care. A flock of gulls screeched
by overhead, dappling the flagstones with their shadows. I
looked up, squinting, as they wheeled across the sky. Pain be
damned. It was a nice day.

Toward the bottom of the hill Arthur's rose garden gave
way to the solid thicket of pine trees and brambles. They in turn
gave way to a tumble of great granite blocks at the shoreline of
the cove. Arthur's dock was just long enough to berth his big
cabin fishing boat on the seaward side. A much smaller rowboat
was tied up on the leeward side. *"You tie up horses, silly," Sarah said,
laughing at me with her eyes. "Boats are moored."*

I stood corrected, resting my hand on a neat, if complicated
knot that moored, not tied, the rowboat to the leeward side of
the dock.

"Halloo!"

I looked up.

There was a small motorboat in the middle of the cove, its
engine idling, riding the gentle swells. It had once been white
fiberglass. Now it was a mottled yellow color, with green stains at
the waterline. Someone waved behind the nearly opaque plastic
windshield. "Halloo!" the person called again. Then I saw him:
Conner Weatherby. Santa Claus. In his sleigh.

The same flock of seagulls that had passed over me was now
clustered in a flapping mass off the stern of Weatherby's boat.
They must think he's throwing out bait, I thought. Their
screeching filled the air of the cove. Weatherby waved again, this
time at the gulls. "So this is what the mighty dinosaur has come

down to, Tim! Little shits begging for fish guts!"

I watched as he maneuvered his boat to the end of the dock. By the time he reached it the gulls had abandoned him, and he was positioned neatly between the two end piers. He hefted a coil of yellow nylon rope. *"It's line, Timmy,"* Sarah said, *"On boats rope is called line."*

"Can you catch?"

I leaned my cane against one of the piers. "I'll try," I said. "Throw it over."

He tossed the coil expertly, into my arms. "Just tie it off to the pier on your left," he said.

"I'm no expert on nautical knots."

Weatherby laughed. "Just loop it around a few times, it'll be fine."

The tide was high, because he was able to climb almost directly from his boat deck to the dock planks. "Arthur makes a mean dock, I'll say that for him." Weatherby stamped his old sneakers on the planking. "Solid as Sears."

I took my cane back up. "You came to visit the other day?"

"I came to visit on several days. That Leitha Hutchinson is wasting her time puttering around here; she should be guarding the nation's gold at Fort Knox." Weatherby looked me up and down. "So how are you doing, Tim?"

"Just fine, thanks. Starting to move around under my own steam." I lifted the cane. "Pretty soon I hope to retire this item."

"When does the cast come off?"

I honestly did not know. "Pretty soon I hope," I said. There had to be a doctor visit in my future sometime; I hadn't thought to ask.

Then I remembered something. "What did you mean when you said it wasn't fair?"

Weatherby looked at me sharply. "What do you mean?"

"When you tried to pay a visit the other day, I heard you say 'it's just not fair'."

Weatherby continued to look at me. He seemed hesitant, as though trying to decide something. Then he said, "What did

Arthur say about the funeral?"

"He said the whole town turned out. I saw all the flowers that were left."

Weatherby nodded briefly. "Yes indeed, the townspeople were all there."

The sarcasm in his voice was plain. I felt my anger rising. "What is that supposed to mean?"

"It means Arthur Hubbard owns the town. The Hubbards have always owned it. Hell, they founded the damned place."

"You're telling me Arthur forced the town to go to my wife's funeral?"

"No force needed, Tim. Everyone knows their place here. Everyone knows the rules."

"Except you, apparently."

"Yeah." He laughed suddenly. "Except me."

What did you think of the funeral, Mr. Weatherby?"

"The mainland one? Beautiful. Fitting. You would have been proud. And it's Conner, please."

The mainland one. *"Please, Tim,"* Sarah whispered, *"I want to be buried on the mainland, next to my parents...."* Her voice was plain, plaintive. Clear. I said, "The mainland one. Was there another one? Was there another funeral?"

Weatherby looked out to the ocean, just visible beyond the points of the cover. Then he turned back to me and gestured to his boat. "You up for a little ride?" His eyes were alive. He appeared to have a secret, something he wanted to tell me, to show me. I hesitated.

"The only way to answer your question is to show you, Tim."

I felt slightly dizzy. "Show me what?"

"Listen, Arthur's in Augusta for the rest of the day, Leitha is probably already home starting supper for her brood. And unless I'm mistaken, your afternoon schedule is free. Here." He clambered back into his boat, and raised his hand. "I'll help you in. Just like two steps on a stairs."

I handed him my cane, then took his surprisingly strong

arm, and stepped down into the boat. No pain, no nausea, and the dizziness receded.

"See?" Weatherby nodded. "Easy."

I sank into one of the blue cushioned seats. "You have to tell me where we're going."

"A short trip into the Reach. Half an hour, tops."

"Just so we take it slow," I said. "I don't know if I get seasick or not."

"Bah. Not to worry. We'll be in the Reach, not the open ocean. And it's like a lake today. Here, put this on." He handed me a bright orange life preserver vest. It was a big one, and the straps were already all the way out, so it fit comfortably over my coat. "Of course," Weatherby said over his shoulder as he unlooped the yellow line from the pier, "the water temperature will only grant you an hour of life anyway. Hypothermia. But the Coast Guard like to see preservers on everybody regardless." He stowed the line, then got behind the wheel, gave the outboard motor some gas, and we swung slowly around.

"What about you? Shouldn't you be wearing one?"

Weatherby laughed. "The Coasties and I have an understanding, Tim."

We headed out of Arthur's cove, into the stretch of open water separating the mainland from the scattering of islands beyond. Weatherby was true to his word, taking us slowly and carefully past the busy fishing docks at the bottom of the town, threading between smelly lobster boats, cabin cruisers and sailboats, not to mention the occasional seaweed-draped rock thrusting up from the water in a cauldron of foam and spray. Weatherby waved to everyone we passed, and nearly everyone waved back. "Having fun yet?" he yelled over the wind, the waves against the hull, and the steady buzz of the motor. I wiped cold seawater spray off my face. Bang! We angled across someone's wake, bouncing across the water, Bang! Bang!

Oh yes, I decided, I will be feeling this later.

Eventually, the boat traffic gave way to the open water of the Reach. And islands, hundreds of them, of all shapes and sizes. I glimpsed expensive vacation homes tucked in among pine stands, and utilitarian fishing shacks perched on piers among black, fissured rocks. Some of the islands were huge, but most were a few acres or less, mere collections of rocks, scrawny trees, and tough brown grass.

Standing next to Weatherby in the cockpit, I touched his arm. "Are all of these islands privately owned?"

"Indeed they are. Anything with any real estate to it, for sure." He proceeded to point out some of them, attaching family names to them, some of which I recognized from the names I had seen in the town cemetery, but some I did not...until the last one. "That's Shelter Island," Weatherby said, pointing to a medium-sized one, big enough for woods and a few meadows, off by itself. "The Hubbard family owns it."

I squinted into the slipstream over the aluminum frame of the windshield. I saw rocks, pines, flashes of ochre grass, but no house, no buildings of any kind. The island grew out of the sea like a roughly splashed watercolor. Its shore was nothing more than split and tumbled granite boulders stained black by the waves, crusted with moss, seaweed and gull guano, and crowned with dark, spiky pines. No beach, no quiet cove; the island thrust up from the foaming breakers like an argument, an affront, a dare.

"So how do we get ashore," I yelled over the boat motor and crash of water against the bow, "swim?"

Weatherby pointed with a sweep of his head. "Around the other side is a quay!"

"Key?"

The 'key' turned out to be a long, formidable dock constructed of roughly shaped stone blocks, with concrete and cobblestone icing. It was blackened with age and covered with green slime and barnacles up to the high tide line. This 'quay' looked as primeval as the island itself.

Weatherby maneuvered the boat alongside, threw out the foam plastic bumpers, then deftly looped his bow mooring line through a large iron ring protruding from the concrete edge.

The ring was big enough to put a fist through. "Stay where you are," he yelled, as he scrambled to the rear of the boat, grabbed another ring similarly imbedded, and secured the stern line to it with an exotic knot.

He cut the motor. In the sudden silence, I heard the squeaking of the bumpers caught between the boat and the stones, and the screams of distant seagulls. "Okay," Weatherby said, as though using the word to calm himself. "Now, up we go." He took my elbow and helped me onto the cobbled surface of the quay. I balanced on the cast until he handed me my cane. Then he joined me.

The pines loomed almost over our heads. The wind off the water blew through their needles with a dry, sandpapering sound. The shadows looked blue and cold.

"I didn't see any house from the water."

"There isn't one," Weatherby said.

"I wonder why they built such a big dock, excuse me, big quay, then."

Weatherby looked at me. "You really don't know?"

"Until a few minutes ago, I didn't even know this island existed."

Weatherby continued looking at me, then nodded abruptly. "There's a path," he said. "To the left, there."

We left the sunlight and went into the shadows under the trees.

The needle-carpeted path led us inland, and in moments we emerged in a meadow of oatmeal-colored grass about waist-high, dotted with late purple wildflowers and Queen Anne's Lace. The sun was warm on my face after the damp shadows of the pines. "This is nice," I said, smelling pinesap on the salty breeze.

Then I saw the stones.

I turned to Weatherby. "What is this place?"

The tops of ancient, weathered gravestones crested the grass; three, four, six…about a dozen, were scattered across the small meadow. *Sarah whispered, "I want to be buried at home, Tim, in the family plot. On the mainland."*

On the mainland.

Weatherby took my arm. "Watch where you walk, now. You might trip over someone."

I saw Chamberlain, Willamett, Hadley, and Bean, just like on the mainland. Some of the stones were too old to show any carving. Others, nearly as old, showed letters and words in alphabets I didn't recognize. The largest stone, a rounded, asymmetrical stump of stained grey granite, had only a spiral carved into it, a shape like a coiled rope. It reminded me of a standing stone from the British Isles, something transported from Avebury, or Stonehenge.

"I don't understand," I said. "Why is there a cemetery out here, so far from the mainland?" *Please, Tim, Sarah whispered. Please.*

A well-worn path began at the stone with the spiral carving, through the meadow grass to the far side. We followed it to the shadow line of the pines. Under them, deep in the shadows, I saw a collection of long boulders leaning against one another, forming a crude structure, like an ancient Celtic quoit. The entrance was a triangle of total darkness, big enough to pass through without stooping. It looked very, very old.

"What—" I began.

"Tim!"

I looked around.

Arthur stood at the other side of the meadow, at the end of the path Weatherby and I had followed from the quay.

"Don't move!"

He came striding across the grass.

Beside me, Weatherby whispered, "I'm sorry."

I turned on him. "What is this place? Why did you bring me here?"

"I'm sorry," the old painter said. "I truly am. I—"

"You," Arthur said, close enough now not to have to shout, "need to return to your boat, Conner, and leave this island. This is private property."

Weatherby raised his hands. "I was only—"

Arthur took a step toward him, and even I couldn't look at his expression of total fury without flinching. "You had no right to bring him here. No right. And you well know it!"

Weatherby looked at me with a stricken expression, then down at his feet.

Arthur turned to me. "We're leaving," he said, and went to take my arm.

"Wait a minute!" I shook him off. "Wait a goddamned minute!"

I looked at the gravestones in the meadow, old and new, at the path through the stiff, wild grass, worn down to the bare earth, from the big stone. I noticed, for the first time, the dried brown stains on the stone, and a scattering of feathers caught in the grass around it. I followed the path from the stone to the edge of the meadow and under the pines, where the open doorway of the ancient stone quoit showed only darkness, spoke only silence.

Then I turned back to Arthur, who stood in the strong sunlight like a stone himself. "What have you done here?" I demanded.

Arthur was silent.

I took a wobbling step toward him. "You bastard! You bastard! What have you done to Sarah? What have you done with my wife?"

4

I heard quiet conversations through the floor of my bedroom, visitors coming and going, the kitchen screen door screeching and slapping with every one. I watched the day fall to twilight. The wind came up, and the stars twinkled furiously as they emerged, one by one, in the darkening sky.

There was a knock on the door. I ignored it. Then I heard Arthur say, "Leitha left you some supper. You up to eating? I've got it here on a tray."

"Leave it at the door," I said.

"Fair enough."

Half an hour later I took the tray in, and ate the food cold. It went like that, more or less, for nearly a week.

Weatherby never stopped by for another visit, which was just as well. I wasn't sure what I would have done if he had.

I moved from my room to the side porch, watched the grackles in the trees, the afternoon sun warm on my face. My leg, still in its cast, itched fiercely from the inside out, and the bruises in my abdomen no longer ached. Mending, mending.

I didn't even notice that Arthur was standing behind me until he spoke. "Tomorrow night," he said.

I turned to look at him, saw the pain in his face, and I fought the urge to add to it. Still, "No," I said.

He looked down; the screen door creaked in his hand. "I'll honor your wish," he said, "but I'm still going." The door slapped shut behind him.

The next evening I was sitting in the same rocker, and I heard him in the kitchen. "Arthur," I said.

He came out. I didn't want to see his face, and I didn't want him to see mine. "You can't...fix this, can you."

"No Tim," he said, "I can't."

I sat quietly for a long time. Then, "Okay," I said.

5

They could only visit on certain days every month.

I heard them on the garden path, the one that led up from the dock through the rose garden. Quiet, measured footsteps, careful of the slope of the path, and the edges of the flagstones. There must be five of them at least, I thought.

Arthur opened the kitchen door for them. I heard his voice as a low murmur, saying something I couldn't catch. One of the newcomers answered, and I was struck by the lifeless quality of the voice, and then by the sad irony of that thought.

Someone began ascending the back stairs. Slow, steady, taking each stair tread in turn. My heart skipped a beat with each footfall, and my breath caught and held at the back of my throat. Up the hall, step after careful step, stopping finally at my bedroom door. Would there be a knock? Would she ask permission to enter? If I said no, would she leave?

The doorknob turned, and the door swung inward, squeaking in its two hundred year old frame.

Sarah's grandmother stood at the threshold, wearing a faded burgundy dress she had probably been buried in. She looked exactly the same as I remembered her from photographs Sarah had shown me. Exactly. "Timothy," she said, and attempted a smile. "So nice to meet you at last. Are you ready?"

Sarah's grandmother served tea in the dining room. I could see that she wasn't breathing. She only took a breath when she had something to say. Then Arthur came to the door. Behind him, in the shadowed hall, I saw the others, all old, all dead. But not Sarah's parents. They were buried in the mainland family plot, under the stones shaped like bread loaves. The same place where Sarah had wanted, had begged, to be buried. Really buried. Buried forever. Arthur asked, "Are you sure you're ready?"

"Yeah," I said.

He led Sarah in. She was obviously dead. Like her grandmother, and the other relatives who had accompanied them from the island in the Reach. She was still wearing the blue dress I had picked out, the one she was to be buried in. She looked pale, tired, hesitant.

"Sarah," I said, rising, using the edge of the table to steady myself. "Honey."

Sarah looked in my general direction. There were faint frown lines across her forehead. Her gaze came up to my chin, but not all the way. She raised her hand to her mouth, put two fingers to her lips, and then looked away.

"Honey," I said. "Baby." Oh God oh God I'm so sorry.

"It takes time to get things back," her grandmother said, beside me.

"Of course." Oh God. Oh dear God.

"Give her time."

"You've got all the time you want Tim," Arthur said.

"All the time in the world," his wife added.

We all went into the living room. I sat on the couch, and Sarah was led over to sit beside me. I took her hand. There was no pulse of life, no warmth. But no coldness, either. Just... nothing.

I felt my own warmth, my own life, seeping out, into her, but nothing was retained. She was like a sieve; it all passed through her, and nothing was left. Nothing at all.

"She will need your help Tim," Arthur said.

Sarah's grandmother nodded. "Just like Arthur helped me."

We sat there for a long time, long enough for me to realize that I would never leave, ever. And, for whatever reason, good or bad, right or wrong, inspired or damned...I realized I didn't want to.

Give me an island funeral, and we will be together, forever.

Etc.

Story Notes

Killer

Usually I will let the idea for a story percolate for months, even years, becoming an "entire and perfect chrysolite" as R.A. Lafferty would say, before I finally sit down to write it. This story took a different route. I had this image of a big and hungry dog on a stout chain, and a circle of dirt in the yard marking the extent of that chain. I also had a sorry-ass guy who killed his wife, but even so, if only in his head, she still wouldn't shut up. I started writing from there, with no idea where it would take me. The free verse sections were added last. This one got an Honorable Mention in one of Ellen Datlow's annual "Best of" collections, for which I am grateful.

On The Midwatch

Everything in this story is true. Seriously. I mean it. Well... everything up to the part where the USO surfaces, anyway. None of the USOs I ever saw on midwatch when I was in the Navy ever surfaced, thank God.

It's For You

This is an obvious rehash of an old TZ trope: the phone call from the grave. In this case, the call is from a comatose criminal.

I clothed it in a middle-aged, rumpled detective's suit, and gave it a distinctly Philly spin. This one went from first draft to publication with hardly any changes along the way, which is rare.

Along The River Lethe

In the 1980s and early '90s I was a member of the Philadelphia SF Society Writers Workshop. We met monthly at member homes, spent way too much time ordering dinner and bull-shitting, but still managed to read and critique member stories, sometimes well into the night. Some alumni who might be recognizable included Jason Van Hollander, Darrell Schweitzer, John Betancourt and Roman Ranieri. I workshopped an early version of this story, called "Visits To The Memory House", and enough Phillip K. Dick ripoff comments were thrown at me to convince me to shelve it. Dick could remember it for you wholesale, after all. A decade or so later I had this idea of government workers leasing 'brain time' to their agencies, essentially becoming zoned out drooling, diaper-wearing micro-processors eight hours every day. I married that up with the earlier idea of the Memory Stores from the shelved story, and "Along The River Lethe" was the result.

Dead End

I lived for several years in Philadelphia, and got very familiar with the row house neighborhoods. I loved how some of the streets were so close together that the back window of one house was no farther from the back window of the one across the alley than a space just wide enough for a garbage truck to squeeze through. The row houses formed fortress-like walls along these alleys, and in the case of the dead ends, created total privacy if the open end was blocked off in some way…with a garbage truck, for example. And there was the story, right there. This one got thoroughly trashed at one of those PSFS writer workshops, but Ellen Datlow gave it another Honorable Mention nod in one of her annual "Best Of" anthologies.

Up In The Boneyard

This story had several inspirations. The first was my love of airplanes, the older the better. The next was a short story by Ray Bradbury called "Skeleton", the one he re-wrote for The October Country, not the original from Dark Carnival. A third was the Merricat poem from Shirley Jackson's We Have Always Lived in the Castle. The final influence, and the most important, was Fritz Leiber's wonderful, chilling story "The Hill and the Hole" from his Nights Black Agents collection. The idea of a doorway to a dark place, in this case The Boneyard, that could only be accessed at a particular height (and therefore a secret until the invention of airplanes, and skyscrapers) was one that haunted me for years. This story was one result. Another was a novel I wrote in the late 1980s with the same name. Every publisher who commented when they bounced it (and that manuscript bounced like a frigging basketball, let me tell you) said they loved my "McGuffin", my Detective Sergeant Francis Lomax. So in the mid 1990s I threw out everything except the chapters about Fran's investigation of the string of high-rise mutilation murders, and wrote a new companion plot altogether to weave in with it. That became the novel The Bone Worms, which, as of this writing, is "being considered" by a respected publisher.

In The Stacks

This story came about after reading a best-selling novel about a young man with Asperger's Syndrome. I'm not entirely satisfied with the way it ends, but I really like the style of it, the tone, the voice. And I happen to own a copy of Robert Silverberg's The Mound Builders of Ancient America. In english.

Eats

My brother and I sometimes used to get books for Christmas. I got those Twilight Zone oversized hardcovers, and "edited for children" Platt & Munk collections of Wells, Conan Doyle, Harte, Poe, Melville, O'Henry and Crane. My brother, meanwhile, got big illustrated books about B-17 Flying Fortresses, World Wars, and the History of Baseball. That was where I learned about Ty Cobb, Tris Speaker, and Christy Mathewson (not to mention ball turret gunners!). Speaker and Mathewson ended up in "Eats", which was originally inspired by a great little story called "A Couple of Hamburgers" by James Thurber.

Turn of a Card

In my freshman and half of my sophomore years of college I attended the Hartford Art School, on the campus of the University of Hartford, in Connecticut. The university published a quarterly literary magazine called "The Hog River Review." I used to slip story manuscripts under the door of their office in the Student Union every now and then, and sometimes saw them show up in print. An early version of this story, called "Innocence", was one of those. Oh so experimentally, I titled every section without a ghost in it with an "A", and every section with a ghost in it with a "B". Yeah, well, it seemed to make sense at the time. In the 1990s I was thinking about writing a ghost story where the ghost follows a person home and starts haunting their house, like catching a cold after you visit a sick friend. Then I remembered that old "A-B" story from college, and decided to merge the two into a brand new story. Greg Gifune was kind enough to buy it for The Edge under the title "The Turn of a Card." I made two changes for this reprint: I dropped the "The" from the original title, and, devout Phillies fan that I have become, I switched the baseball card from Ken Griffey to Chase Utley.

Empire State

I spent the last two and a half of my undergraduate years at a state college in the Catskills of upstate New York. When I decided to write an SF story about the search for what was left of New York City after the icecaps melted, I got a distinct kick out of turning my old college haunts into an island archipelago inhabited by twenty-third century pirates. Empire State was written and published well before "Waterworld", by the way. I like to think it was a better take on the idea, too.

So Much for the Competition

This little story is the oldest one in the book. I wrote it in ninth grade one day in study hall. When the folks at The Horror Drive-in asked me for something short and nasty, I didn't hesitate.

Three Wizards

This story came from two literary sources: Ursula K. LeGuin and Stephen Crane. When I was a teenager I was lucky enough to see an ad in a copy of F&SF that, for just a few bucks, netted me a first edition copy of "A Wizard of Earthsea" from Parnassus Press. This wonderful book, with its richly imagined world of islands, magic and mages, has remained in my "top five" ever since. Then there was the long story by Crane called "The Angel and the Child", and what happened to the young boy on the mountainside when he decided to do something more than just watch the battle raging in the valley below. Both came together in a story I first wrote before I was 17. That story was lost over the years, but I took up the theme and idea again in my 30s, wrote a brand new story from them, and managed to remember the line from the original that still gives me goosebumps: "But that is *my* name...."

Dead Eye

This story started out as a non-fiction op-ed piece for a local newspaper. I was actually driving along that stretch of connector road between Route 309 and I-78 when someone took a shot at my car, hitting the right rear wheel directly in the center of the hubcap. I'm sure it was an unintentional "hunting" accident, but damn! Everything that happens after the dealer scene in the story is pure fiction, though.

Bushido

I wanted to write a science fiction story in the style of early Samuel R. Delany (who is one of my most favorite writers). I wanted to put starships and robots and clones in it. Also war, and a little robot-onwoman sex. And Gustav Stickley furniture. I almost sold this one to an anthology of robot stories, but I couldn't tell the editor what those extra two Robotic Laws were (because I didn't know—I just liked the idea for there being five instead of three) and ended up having to pull it. Crazy, but there you go.

A Death in the Forest

I used to keep a list of story titles that I thought I might use, and this one was always high on that list. I think this may be the story least liked by readers. I don't remember receiving a single positive comment after it was published.

The Can Man

What happens to all those people in cryogenic freezers when nobody remembers, or cares? Obviously, I am no fan of Walt, or The Mouse.

The Prince's Birthday

At some point in my 30s I decided I was going to write and sell at least one story in as many different genres as possible. I had already sold several SF stories, so I tried my hand at high fantasy ("Three Wizards"), horror ("Eats"), and historical, which was this story. I am not sure why, but the editors at TSR's Dragon Magazine thought "The Prince's Birthday" would appeal to their RPG readers, and bought it.

Room To Let

I almost sold this story to Amazing Stories in the early 1980s, but George Scithers told me in his rejection letter something to the effect that "I recently bought another story just like this one, so I'm going to pass." The story ended up back in its folder. When

I pulled it out in 2007 I found I still liked it, so I did a slight rewrite, changing the location to some shadowed little street in a small British city (Chester? Leeds?), just to see if I could pull off pretending to be a British writer. This is one of my favorites. I particularly like the double entendre of the title.

Island Funeral

I keep a manila folder for every story I ever tried to write. Some folders are thin, containing only a scribbled idea on a scrap of paper. Others are thick, full of research, drafts, and correspondence. A lucky few even have an acceptance letter and a galley proof stuck in them. Island Funeral's folder is the thickest of them all, and that's because there are more than a half-dozen false starts, attempted over a span of about twelve years, stuffed into it. Different starting points, different viewpoints, even different protagonists, you name it, I tried it. I would get Tim, or Tim and Sarah, or just Sarah, into Arthur's driveway and it would just die, right there. I knew what the story was, and I knew where I wanted it to go. Getting there, though, was the bitch. After I sold the longish story "Up in the Boneyard" to the Shivers anthology series, I figured I might have a market for another long piece. I also finally discovered that pudgy local artiste Conner Weatherby trudging up Arthur's drive unannounced, and I knew I had somebody to help me move the story along at last. So I got off my ass and finished the damn thing. Thank you, Conner. Thanks also to Nanci Kalanta, who copyedited the manuscript for the CD chapbook. She pointed out I was using way too many commas in my dialogue, and was responsible for the idea of adding Chapter 4. The title comes from the name of a very moving egg tempera painting by the great American artist and illustrator N.C. Wyeth.

John W. Campbell, Editor

August 10, 1970

Mr. Keith Minnion
652 Lowell Street
Westbury, N.Y. 11590

Dear Mr. Minnion:

This one's fairly good——except that our readers prefer
upbeat stories——stories in which some problem is <u>solved</u>.
A story may be tragic in the technical sense (i.e., the
hero dies) but it must be useful tragedy. Horatio died
defending the bridge——but yet he won his battle. His
death was useful.

Sincerely,

John W. Campbell
Editor

JWC:olh
enc: IN THE NIGHT

The Condé Nast Publications Inc./420 Lexington Avenue, New York, N. Y. 10017/689-5900

Acknowledgements

Killer, Night Terrors #1; June 1996

On the Midwatch, Asimov's SF Magazine, Vol. 3, No. 11; November 1979

It's For You, Cemetery Dance Magazine #34; Spring 2001

Dead End, Night Terrors #3; April 1997

Up in the Boneyard, Shivers IV; 2006

Eats (originally published as "Diner At The Altar"), Modern Short Stories; August 1989

Turn of a Card (originally published as "The Turn of a Card"), The Edge #9; Spring 2001

Empire State, Asimov's SF Magazine, Vol. 9, No. 5; May 1985

So Much for the Competition, Horror Drive-In; 2009

Three Wizards, Marion Zimmer Bradley's Fantasy Magazine #7; Winter 1990

A Death in the Forest, Night Terrors #6; June 1998

It's for You

The Prince's Birthday, Dragon Magazine #122, Vol. 12, No. 1; June 1987

Room to Let, The Shadow on the Shade, White Noise Press; 2007

Island Funeral, an original chapbook, CD Publications; 2011

All other stories are published here for the first time.

Thanks to John Campbell, Ben Bova and Ed Ferman for turning down all those terrible stories, and to George Scithers, for buying the first decent one.

Bio

Keith Minnion sold his first short story to *Asimov's SF Adventure Magazine* in 1979. He has sold over two dozen stories, two novelettes, an art book of his best published illustrations, two story collections, and one novel since. Keith was a book designer and illustrator from the early 1990s to the 2010s, and also did extensive graphic design work for the Department of Defense. He is a former schoolteacher, DOD project manager, and officer in the U.S. Navy.

He currently lives in the Shenandoah Valley of Virginia, pursuing oil and watercolor painting, and sometimes even fiction writing.

Colophon

This book was designed on an iMAC utilizing the Affinity publishing software suite, Version 1.7.2. The type was set in Baskerville and Gil Sans. The cover art was created in watercolor, India ink, and acrylic polymer. The interior illustrations were created in pencil on coquille board.

Curious about other Crossroad Press books?
Stop by out site:
http://store.crossroadpress.com
We offer quality writing
in digital, audio, and print formats.

www.ingramcontent.com/pod-product-compliance
Lightning Source LLC
Chambersburg PA
CBHW020916200626
46814CB00001BA/361